Torc Of M

...The historical detail is immaculate, as is the authentic detail of modern student-life, the whole suffused with a rich pagan sexuality... Superbly gripping...

... full of vivid imagery and rich descriptions...

Praise for

The Bull At The Gate : Book 2

...a crafted blend of Crime, Thriller and Myth makes the reader question their grasp of reality...

...uses the history and landscape of York superbly, making the city itself a mystery and a character...

Praise for

Pilgrims Of The Pool : Book 3

...the moral ambiguity of modern life is reflected in a wonderfully evocative portrayal of the faith-tests of a mediaeval monk...

...shot through with a delicate sense of landscape so vital to this spiritual story...

For further information visit
www.lindaacaster.com

Torc of Moonlight: Book 3

Pilgrims

Of The Pool

For Michael
...for keeping the faith.
Toss a coin for me

Linda Acaster

Linda Acaster

Torc of Moonlight: Book 3
Pilgrims Of The Pool

This book is a work of fiction. Names, characters, places and incidents are either the product of the author's imagination or are used fictitiously.

First Edition
This edition copyright © 2017 Linda Acaster
ISBN: 978-1974202492

Also available as an ebook in Kindle and ePub formats
© 2017 Linda Acaster

All rights reserved.
No part of this publication may be reproduced or transmitted in any form without the express written permission of the author. This book is protected under the copyright laws of the United States of America. Linda Acaster also asserts the moral right to be identified as the author of this work under the UK Copyright, Designs and Patents Act 1988.

Acknowledgements

Fiction is nothing if not based on fact. Special thanks are due to:

The City of Durham, Durham Cathedral, and the University of Durham, for their individual instructive online presences and their welcome of on-foot visitors;

The North York Moors National Park for its instructive online presence and the maintenance of its physical domain;

Forgotten Books for republishing in 2012, and the Surtees Society for publishing in 1844, *A Description or Breife Declaration of All the Ancient Monuments, Rites, and Customes Belonginge or Beinge Within the Monastical Church of Durham Before the Suppression - Written in 1593.*

Hornsea Writers, for members' input and support during the many months of bringing this novel to fruition.

Prologue

Ernald had been at the heel of Brother Maugre since the bell for Prime, yet the sub-prior had said barely a word, certainly not spoken of the reason for Ernald's summonsed return to the priory. *In the confidence of Christ* the messenger had mewled: he was to discuss his summoning with no one.

Ernald's initial shock had turned to panic as he had searched his memory for an office neglected, a misdemeanour unintended. He had lingered in the comfort of the manors, true, but the possession-relics of Saint Cuthbert needed to be guarded through the long hours of the night, as well as being carried in joyful procession between hamlet and village through the hours of the day. Inked with care, his reports had been as full as the coffers he had returned to the monastic house at Durham. There should be no reason for displeasure.

Still, he had journeyed prepared, exchanging his soft linen undershirt for the rough woollen issued by the priory's chamberlain, renouncing his warm hose and replacing his comfortable riding boots with the sandals worn when his small procession had left the priory's gates. More than that, he had taken only rough bread and small ale during the return. A little hollowness in cheeks and stomach would bide him well when confronted in the Chapter House.

Yet there had been no confrontation, and here he was in the refectory, sitting close below the sub-prior on the dais, listening to the droning of the scripture from the lectern while eating bread and drinking small ale. At least the bean pottage had been spiced.

When the standing brother's voice drifted to silence, Ernald willed the bell to ring, and with relief joined those at the tables in the post-graces closing of the meal. Once beyond the refectory door he again fell into step with Brother Maugre.

'Stay close,' he was told. 'Watch closer.'

It sounded as if part of a riddle. Out in the world riddles were sport to be bandied over ale jugs and strong cheese. Here they were for the lay-brethren, not for those who held a seat.

The sub-prior led along the east cloister as the masters drew close their novices for study. The building work restarted before they were halfway to the south door, the mason's calling booming over the heavy chink and faster tapping of chisel on stone from the yard. Ernald told himself he'd become used to it again, but he would miss the relative quiet of the world beyond the wall. He was, he knew, growing to like it too much and needed to make confession and receive penance.

As they entered the church the noise became thunderous, the towering stone building resonating as if a bell. Despite the chill that bit his ankles, he fought to acclimatise himself to the true glory of God, to hear only the cantor's interrupted singing practise in the nave, and the low chanting of the brothers fulfilling holy offices in the part-constructed Chapel of the Nine Altars. Despite the draughts from the empty window spaces, the incense heavy in the air splayed his nostrils and caught at his throat. He breathed it as if it was the elixir of God's life eternal banishing worry and illness and strife.

A line of pilgrims extended along the northern aisle, some whispering in low tones, others on their knees appealing to the Holy Trinity and for the indulgence of Saint Cuthbert. Ernald followed the sub-prior as he turned down the decorated nave and crossed behind the great chevroned pillars. There Sub-Prior Maugre paused, gazed into Ernald's face, and raised his cowl. With a bent head, he eased his gait and started towards the altars. Swallowing his bewilderment, Ernald did the same. Whatever it was he had to note had missed his wits, and he reached for his chaplet, fingering the beads in an effort to better concentrate.

As they began to pass the pilgrims, Ernald heard a caught

breath, a whispered prayer, a rattle of the native tongue, and felt palms smooth at the base of his habit, even touch his bare heel. He took a side-step to escape them.

To his surprise the sub-prior did not. Unless Ernald's eyes deceived him, the sub-prior moved closer to the reaching hands. The pilgrims' sighs and intonations were audible and Ernald was grateful to be hiding within his hood. He was used to this on the hollow-ways when carrying the possession-relics of Saint Cuthbert, but was it not unseemly in Our Lord's house? From the sub-prior's example, perhaps it was not. He moved back, offering surreptitious succour to the crippled and to those determined to ease their way through Purgatory.

The novices attending the line withdrew as they neared, bowing their heads in deference and warming the pilgrims' fervour. Sight of the monks was not usual; mere glimpses through the rood screen into the quire during Mass. Touching those who touched the reliquary within the shrine gifted blessings from the Saint.

As they passed into the part-completed Chapel of the Nine Altars, and within sight of Saint Cuthbert's Shrine, the sub-prior left the line to stand at the wall and look back.

'Do you see?' he hissed as Ernald joined him.

See what? His gaze raked the pilgrims, some with staff and satchels, others in whatever clothing they owned, each with bright eyes and a trembling hand offering what they could to the waiting plate. He inclined his cowled head in acknowledgement, though in truth he could not follow the sub-prior's path. It seemed to be response enough, for Sub-Prior Maugre did not press.

Together they stood watching proceedings – the infirm being carried to the alcoves beneath the shrine, holy water touching dirt-ingrained brows, the chanting of prayers, the tinkling of bells and wafting of incense – it all calming Ernald as it lifted the penitents to joy.

Different sounds reached his ears. Ernald peered down the quire aisle into the gloom of the nave. A body of men were processing slowly to the altars. One was shrieking.

The pilgrims in the line turned to look as a priest in full raiment, flanked by two brothers swinging incense holders, passed through a shaft of window-light. The man, a merchant's clothing torn to rags about his starved limbs, was in turn prostrating himself on the tiles and rising to beat at his chest and cry for mercy. Bleak-faced servants followed, the first carrying a small effigy on a wooden board, the second an open box on a child's pillow. Ernald knew then, and his heart went out to the man for his loss, for his guilt, and for his fear.

The aisle novices began pushing back the line of pilgrims, drawing penitents from beneath the shrine and easing them back into the line. The priest rounded the screen behind the high altar giving the man his first sight of the Blessed House of Reliquary. With a heart-rending cry he stood transfixed, then pushed aside the brothers to throw himself at its base as if seeing Saint Cuthbert made flesh before him.

Ernald felt a tap on his arm and drew his gaze away. The sub-prior was already retracing his steps along the aisle. Ernald knew he had to follow even though it was difficult to command his feet. As he passed the waiting retinue, he glanced at the effigy on its plain board. A girl, he thought, taken without warning, without prayer to cleanse her soul. The box on her pillow gleamed beneath the candlelight with coins and jewels and ribboned parchment scrolls.

Ahead, the sub-prior re-crossed the nave. Pulling aside his hood, he waited by the door to the cloisters.

'Did you see?'

Ernald drew a breath and nodded. 'To the glory of the Illustrious Saint and the Holy Mother and the—'

With a dismissive wave of his hand, the sub-prior snapped, 'Of course, of course.' He looked at Ernald afresh. 'I meant the people. Those who know nothing of the Holy tongue, those who know not our own tongue, cannot even speak the English tongue as we were taught it. *They*, with their clasped coin and wide eyes. The pilgrims.'

Ernald blinked at him. 'They are here every day.'

'Yes,' breathed Maugre. 'Duty-bound by faith to visit Rome but can travel only to Winchester... York... *Durham*... Walk with me, Brother Ernald.'

In the cloister the sub-prior kept his silence until they were clear of the novices at study, then he leaned in, his voice low.

'Do you know of the talk of the Cistercians intent on the greater glory of our Lord in the wildwoods?'

'It is not my place to hear—'

'Make it your place! There are those who wish them among the boar and bear.' He stopped and looked steadily at Ernald. 'And there are those who believe they seek a divine treasure among the boar and the bear.'

Ernald schooled his expression. 'Wild talk from wild men.'

'So thought I until the praises of a village priest came to my attention.'

The sub-prior stepped on. More wary now, Ernald followed him through the door into the confinement chamber. He had been inside but once, as a novice instructed to take food for a brother incarcerated there. He had not seen the man, or even beyond the outer room, merely looked into the cold eyes of the brother-keeper and left the alms dish on the table.

It was, he saw, the same table, the same crucifix upon the wall, doubtless the same stool – except it was not a brother guarding the inner door, but a layman wearing hose and a beaten leather coat. On the table sat a blanketed bundle Ernald's travels had taught him hid a cudgel. No words were exchanged. The man merely opened the inner door, they stepped into the gloom, and the door closed behind them.

The floor was planked, Ernald could tell by its spring even before his sight adjusted to the meagre light of the two tallow candles. Another man in a leather coat, more robust and fully bearded, stood by a bench. Between it and an open trapdoor, mithering as if a child, a thin man knelt on the planks, his hands clasped tight in supplication. Ernald wrinkled his nose at the smell of the man's faeces, of the man's fear. From his sleeve, the sub-prior flourished a small scroll, waving it at Ernald who stepped into the guttering light as he unrolled it.

'A testament from the serf's priest stating that he knows the man as one carrying pestilence, poxes, suppurating sores...'

Ernald stepped back as the man, in pitiful entreaty, reached out to grasp the bottom of his habit.

'Show his arms.'

Ernald had no need to start at the command for it was the bearded man who moved to roll back the serf's clothing. Of pox and sores there were signs enough, but they were faded scars. Ernald bent to the light, trying to decipher the crooked lettering more scratched into the parchment than inked. *Cleansing water. A... pond.* No, *a spring.*

Maugre demanded that the man's shirt be removed, and the kneeling man set up a fearful wailing, something about saints, but his tongue was twisted beyond any dialect Ernald could understand. The sub-prior called for a candle to be taken close to the man's skin, and again he set up a crying as if expecting to be set alight. A few gruff words and he calmed. The gaoler, it seemed, knew his tongue.

'Look closely,' the sub-prior instructed, and Ernald held his breath against the stink as he complied. Again, scars aplenty but no sign of living pestilence or sores.

'He's speaks of a saint,' Ernald ventured, 'but the rest is—'

'My man tells me he speaks of Cynibil, a brother in God from a family of brothers in God who took the word of Our Lord to the heathen Saxon and had them destroy their idolatrous images.' He gestured with his hand. 'Long before the blessed Conqueror William crossed the narrow sea.'

'The brothers of a religious house, Lastingham?'

Maugre nodded. 'There were those seeking it even then. They'd heard. They knew of its existence. The power to heal, the power to cure.'

'A place of foul men who husband travellers as others might husband stock.'

The sub-prior was not listening. 'Whosoever brings these

waters beneath the Light of God, who builds a House of Our Lord to protect it from the ravages of man and beast, will have pilgrims lining the hollow-ways from here to Winchester clutching their tiny coins.'

He raised an eyebrow and turned to Ernald. 'And now my brother questor, we not only know of it, we know where it lies.'

Ernald watched the sub-prior smile as he opened his hand towards the kneeling man. Both looked at him, setting off another fearful clamour as he clutched his tunic to his bony chest. The guard cuffed the crown of his head, sending him sprawling forwards.

'Did he say *angel*?' Maugre asked.

'I— I believe so,' Ernald replied, unsure of what he had heard.

He turned to the gaoler for confirmation only to see the man's gaze slide away. Ernald had not been mistaken. What he'd heard was not *angel*, but *angel-woman*.

Except... except that could not be right.

Chapter 1

Timothy Glossmer finally found the farm, though in truth it would have been hard to miss due to the small signs running at intervals along the puddled verges. He'd wondered whether they were legal, and that thought came again as the car drew level with the large sign by the entrance. *World Famous*. That was spinning it a bit, considering he'd had to hunt the internet for it, but then again he'd had to hunt for all the springs.

Once over the cattle grid, the gravelled drive led onto a concrete parking area which looked as if it had once been a fold yard. He pulled up next to the two other vehicles, not wanting to make a statement by leaving the Freelander on its own. Fingerposts pointed to the house for *Bed & Breakfast*, to an outbuilding with picnic tables and potted plants for *Tea & Cake – Closes 4pm*, down the yard for *Petting Enclosure* and *Toilets*, and out the way he'd driven in for *The Pool*, which seemed a bland title considering it was supposed to be *World Famous*.

A board informed him the parking fee was £1 and he wouldn't begrudge the farmer the coin. It had to be pretty bleak up here in winter, bleak, in fact, when it was raining. He glanced at the louring sky hoping there'd be no more showers. His waterproofs had had enough of a trial.

Clothed and booted, he shouldered his rucksack, picked up the Ordnance Survey map, and checked for his compass. He'd need to add this one to the map. Artesian springs were usually marked. On the North York Moors they seemed to be mostly named, though this one was too new for that.

The stile opposite the entrance had been pinned with a hand-drawn route and a warning for suitable footwear and inclement weather. Two miles, it stated. Tim hadn't expected it to be so far, but there was still plenty of time to be there and back before dusk gathered.

He gazed along the narrow route of mud and puddles, fenced to keep walkers from spreading onto the pastures either side. He wondered how many it deterred in favour of the picnic tables and *Tea & Cake*, and whether it had been fenced with that purpose in mind. Not often enough by the imprint of boot treads, and he stepped down from the stile to add his weight to the quagmire.

To his surprise the slippery conditions lasted only to the ridge. There the wire fencing made an abrupt turn and the moorland grass and heather began. As he strode on to the open ridge a black-faced sheep looked up then returned to its nibbling. A wooden stake carrying an arrow showed the direction, but at nearly two metres wide the beaten path was unmistakable. The Pool had a lot of visitors.

The path followed the downward slope of the land before snaking between hillocks and sparse outcrops of eroded rock. After twenty minutes Tim paused on a rise to check the terrain through binoculars, one eye-piece catching at his swollen eyebrow and making him flinch. Away to his right leaned a row of decaying shooting butts; away to his left stood the edge of the conifer plantation he'd passed in the car. Shouldn't that be behind him? Twisting his heel into the ground's crumbling surface, he brought the path into focus. Meandering, yes, but he could trace the rises back in a line. Again he looked at the dark edge of the plantation, pulling out the map to check its position. Perhaps those were not the trees he'd driven by, yet there were no others marked.

As he reached for his compass, a large raindrop exploded across the paper. Grunting with annoyance, he wiped at the map and pushed it inside its plastic folder. He wasn't going to get away with the weather after all. Better to make it to the Pool and take bearings with his phone. The coordinates could be added to the map later.

Pulling tight his hood, he set off again, wondering if the two miles mentioned at the stile had been calculated as the crow flies or via footfall. Some of the calculations marked on the traffic signs left a lot to be desired.

Heavy raindrops splattered around him, bending the flowering heather and making an odd chittering sound. The meandering path was wide enough for a quad bike to negotiate, though the only tracks to be seen were boot imprints and dogs' paw prints. Up and over and round, the dark tan earth led him on, the sea of quivering vegetation either side no higher than his knee.

A pheasant called. Another responded. Some tiny animal long and slim scurried across the path in front of him. A pair of partridges took flight, crying in alarm. The squall grew heavier. Tim lowered his head to protect his face and strode along the sunken path as it began to run with rivulets.

The rain eased a little and he checked his watch. Another ten minutes had passed. He had to be close, yet when he scanned the horizon there was little to catch his eye. There were supposed to be trees planted round the Pool but he could see no sign of them. As he looked about there was, he realised, little sign of anything. Certainly the conifer plantation had disappeared below the skyline, and when had he last passed a pointer stake? He felt a sudden panic of being adrift in a wilderness, but the notion was ridiculous and he swallowed it down. A blind man couldn't get lost on such a width of track. The Pool was probably just beyond the next rise.

When he reached its height and looked around, he slapped his thigh in annoyance. *Two miles*? If he saw the farmer on his return he'd give him a piece of his mind. It was clear, too, that the track was no longer straight but looping on itself, half-hidden by the heather. What was the point of that? To drive walkers back to his picnic tables for *Tea & Cake*?

Pulling free his binoculars, Tim scoured the dull undulations trying to discern a change of vegetation that might mark a water course. Clumps of bulrush and spiky marsh grass occasionally rose in a hollow, but apart from that...

His eyebrow was giving him hell, and he stopped to lick his index finger and stroke it. That made the tingling worse rather than giving respite, and he persuaded himself he could ignore it.

Adjusting the binoculars' focus, he scanned the terrain again. A rocky outcrop on a ridge was too linear, too flat to be natural. This wasn't limestone pavement country, and that was grass below it. He thought about striking out across the heather, but decided such an action would be stupid. His over-trousers would get covered in plant debris and he'd be liable to twist an ankle or a knee, so he kept to the path as it detoured back and forth.

When he arrived at the outcrop he saw that the path carried on below its ridge. A fine sheep-track led up the rise. At the top sat a man-made pond. It was so true a rectangle it had to have been quarried during the period there'd been mining in the area. The edges were silted and full of decaying plant stalks, the water at its centre a dull black. He looked at it for a few seconds, trying to work out what was drawing his attention.

It was the rain, he realised. Now it was easing he could see individual raindrops hitting the pond, but they weren't plunging through its surface tension. They were being held a moment before being... *absorbed*. Something was bound in the water making it viscid. Peat from the colour, though he wouldn't rule out agricultural waste. He'd never trusted farmers. He leaned over to sniff. A bit of decomposition, but nothing particularly gross.

The grass fanning from its stone-cut edges had been nibbled short enough to turn it to velvet. It put him in mind of somewhere to lay out a cloth on a sunny day and have a picnic – if it hadn't been for the dank water, doubtless a haven for mosquitoes. He was almost pleased it wasn't sunny.

From his vantage point he looked out, his binoculars held ready. They weren't needed. A little way off, a curve of trees stood a lighter green than the surrounding heather. Slithering down the bank he rejoined the path.

It was the camping area he came upon first, at least that's

what he took it for, flattened ground seeded to grass and scattered with sheep droppings, despite the lack of sheep. The path petered out at its lip, as if the multitude of boots which had created it had been absorbed into the landscape the same way the raindrops were being absorbed into the pond. On a flat stone at the edge of the grass sat a roll of green bin liners, a fist-sized rock acting as a securing weight. There was no *Take Your Litter Home* notice, but the message was clear enough, and as he glanced around its message seemed to have been heeded.

The arcing line of trees were a mix of native deciduous, in truth more tall shrubs than trees, set so close together he had to force his way through their wet branches, one hand pulling at his hood to protect his face so as not to make the itching worse. He was almost to the other side when his gaze locked onto a ribbon, its colour leeched by the elements, tied to a straggly frond. The information he'd read had been correct: people did leave offerings. How quaint. He'd seen the same at Stape, but there'd been the remains of a Roman Road passing that spring.

His next footfall squelched, and he placed his weight carefully as he pushed aside branch limbs to gaze across the Pool.

It was roughly circular, bigger than he'd expected, though it didn't stop him chuckling at the *World Famous* epithet given by the farmer. People expecting something special would be disappointed. Yet on a clear day, with sunshine and a bright blue sky reflecting from its surface, he could understand why people would want to come. There was a tranquillity about its setting framed by the trees – though perhaps not with dogs and raucous youngsters splashing in its shallows. He was thankful, now, for the glowering sky and fitful rain. Besides, it meant he didn't have to explain himself.

With the water reflecting the dark cloud cover and the pattering rain denting its surface, it took a while to locate the feeder spring, a group of bubbles dissipating into soft ripples almost as soon as they broke the surface. There seemed to be only a single set, which was disappointing as they were situated near the very centre. He toyed with the idea of removing his boots and wading in, but the bottom was liable to follow the contours of the moorland. In this light, there was no telling where it twisted and shelved.

From his pack Tim brought out a set of rods, fitted them together and fixed a cup in its holder. Stepping into the water until it threatened to slop over his laces, he reached as far as he was able and dipped the cup, bringing it and himself back to drier ground.

With the water poured into a bottle and the rods and cup repacked, he pulled out his phone to scroll through its apps. It took so long for the GPS to register a bearing he thought it couldn't find a signal, despite the bars showing on its screen. Eventually it locked. He made a note of the figures on the bottle's label and stowed the sample safely in his pack.

He hadn't taken much notice, dismissed it as due to the weather, but as he pushed back between the trees he realised his feet felt uncomfortably cold, his soles numb despite the thickness of his hiking socks. He hoped his boots hadn't sprung a leak, but surely that would have affected only one foot. Once through to the camping ground he stamped his feet to help restore his circulation and began the trek back to the road.

Nick dreamed of Alice that night. He knew he would.

Once the house was locked and he was alone in his room, he lifted the display case off the wall beside his bed and withdrew the Roman votive plaque from its cushioned housing. It felt fragile in his palm but he kept to the ritual, stroking it with the tip of his finger bearing the ring carrying strands of Alice's hair. He envisaged her in York where she'd given it to him; tried not to envisage the horrors of her encased in ice, in stone. Better to envisage her in Hull, after they'd become lovers, when her need of him matched his need of her.

When he grew drowsy he laid the plaque aside to concentrate on the ring alone, intent on invoking the soft caresses and searching lips that had sustained him through the dark days.

But she didn't come to him softly, she came smiling and animated, the sun shining through her auburn hair to create a corona of blinding yellow light which kept hiding her face as she moved. A part of him was there with her, feeling the sun hot on his bare arms, hearing the birds in the surrounding trees when he couldn't hear what she was saying. Part of him was marvelling at the memory his mind had reached for, wondering where it was from, how it could have been submerged so long. He tried to catch her hand, but she laughed without sound to dart beyond his reach.

They were playing tag in tall grass resplendent with meadow flowers, their scents heavy in the still air. He was running barefoot, laughing with her, catching her, letting her slip free, caught her. She clasped her hands to his shoulders, her breasts pressed against his chest. They were naked as he knew they would be. Her lips reached for his and he took possession of them, took possession of her as she took possession of him, and he gave himself to her, mind and body and soul.

Chapter 2

'Your phone's ringing.'

Nick was already walking into the dining room, drying his hands on a towel. His mother sat at the table as she had all afternoon, her coffee beside her. Nick wondered if it had been drunk or was cold.

Scooping up his mobile by the skirting, he hit accept before it cut to voicemail, and he disengaged the charger so he could stand straight. Doubtless it would be work telling him to come in later, or not at all. His allocated hours were becoming more erratic by the week.

'Hi, Nick. How's it going?'

Not work. He blinked and then his brain locked on to the unfamiliar voice. The caller, though, was quicker.

'Y'know, man,' the accent was broadening, 'Si from Durham, like. It's been a while, I know, but—'

Nick was smiling now. 'Sorry, mind on other things. I'm so used to getting text-jokes from you I'd forgotten you could speak.' And then he wished he hadn't said that because he couldn't remember when he'd last received one of Simon's texts. 'Great to hear from you.'

'How's it going?' The bolstered accent had receded, the tone flattened.

Nick walked back into the kitchen, closing the door behind him.

'Okay. Still dusting the condolences cards. It's photos at the moment, but at least she's not crying over them now. And thanks for your card. It meant a lot.'

'Mmm. I, er... I didn't say while your Dad was ill, but we lost Gran. It was sudden. Mum's gone off a cliff.'

Nick winced. 'I'm sorry to hear that. What happened?'

'The way she tells it – the way she *continually* tells it – one moment they were in a shop discussing a blouse or something and the next Gran looked at her and fell as if she'd been pole-axed. The doctor has Mum on enough tablets to knock out an elephant but they don't seem to be making a difference.'

'I'm sorry,' Nick said again. He thought of adding a platitude about it being better to go quick and painless, but he knew it wouldn't help. It hadn't him.

He angled his head hoping for an echo of Alice's touch, but they were dreams of memories, self-induced during the sleepless hours of the night. Alice couldn't reach him so far south.

'So, what are you doing?' Simon asked.

Nick dropped his shoulders and matched his friend's brighter tone. 'Oh y'know. Get yourself a degree, go work in a bar.'

'Could be worse. You could be in a restaurant.'

'Oh we do food, too. It's great. I come home reeking of cauliflower.' He heard Simon splutter and he smiled again. 'How's life with you? Seems an age since I was ferrying you all to a gig. A record company hammering at your door yet?'

'We split. I'm concentrating on the conservation. How's the book going?'

Nick leaned against the kitchen counter wondering where that one had come from. 'Fantastic. Publication to remainder bin in less than nine months. There are boxes of the things languishing beside my bed.'

'Then you'll be wanting to sell some. I've a speaking gig for you. Can even rustle you the rail fare.'

The air chilled in his lungs. Going up to Durham would mean —

'I don't think so,' he said. 'It's not a good time.'

'It's not today, you idiot. Besides, you've sisters haven't you?'

Nick laughed. 'Yeah, two, and both have a life. Natalie is teaching in Edinburgh and about to make me an uncle, and Joanne's back aboard her ship keeping us all safe in our beds.'

'It's a weekender. Your Mum will be fine for a weekend, surely? It'll be good to see you. It'll do you good to visit old haunts. 19th. Say you'll do it.'

'*19th?* That's only...' he crossed to the calendar to flip the page, his finger trailing down the dates, his gaze searching out the icons for the quarter and full moons. The dates didn't tally; this couldn't be Alice's doing.

'Yeah, near enough three weeks. Told you it wasn't today.'

'Your speaker's dropped out.'

'Would I lie to you? But you were my first thought for a replacement.'

'Your desperate thought for a replacement,' Nick countered. He couldn't draw his gaze from the lunar icons. Could she be calling him without the pull of a super-moon? Without even the pull of a full moon?

'Not at all. The committee agreed you're the perfect fit. Glad you're coming. I'll email the details. Gotta go.'

'What? I never—' but Nick was talking down a dead line.

He focused on the pumping of his heart. It had been a long time since he'd believed in coincidences. Alice never had. Was she reaching others so they could reach him? She'd done so in York. Had she managed it from...?

A sudden flutter of misgiving coursed through him and he curled his fingers to feel the patterned ring he'd had made to hold strands of her auburn hair. He'd promised her... It hadn't been his fault. His Dad... His Mum...

The lunar icons stood more prominent in his sight than the calendar's printed dates and his hand-written notes on work shifts, bin collections, doctor's appointments. How would she look? How would they communicate? Did he even want—?

His betrayal bit hard. He'd promised and he'd let her down. He let the page of the calendar drop back into place. Taking a breath, he walked into the dining room to stand by the open door.

'That was a friend. Remember Simon? He's offered me a speaking engagement in Durham next month.' He wanted to say more, but wasn't sure what.

His mother turned in her seat to look at him. 'Are you taking it?'

'I'm not certain.'

'You should, it'll do you good.'

'It's a weekender, but he, er... might want me to stay on a few days.'

She smiled. 'Your friends are thinking about you. Don't shut them out. Take the car. I won't need it.'

'You need to get back into driving.'

'Tomorrow,' and she turned back to her photos as she spoke.

'I can take the train,' he offered. He opened the door wider and then looked again at her turned back. 'I'm putting the lasagne in now. Dinner in about forty minutes.'

He dreamed of Alice again that night. He left the display case hung on the wall, hadn't even rubbed at the ring carrying strands of her hair, though he thought about her. He'd been thinking about her ever since Simon's call.

It didn't seem six years since Hull when he'd met, and loved, and lost her. It was over three years since York. How could time pass so easily?

He knew how it had happened, and there had been nothing easy about it. The desperate call to return home, his parents' need of his support, needing him to intercede, to make sense of what could never be made sense of. It had been impossible. He couldn't split himself between worlds, and Alice was locked in the water.

He must have drifted off without realising because she came with the usual caressing touch. He wanted her to hold him, to tell him she understood, but the dream morphed into the previous night's where she was smiling and animated, the sun shining through her hair to create a blinding yellow light that kept hiding her features as she moved around him. He could feel the sun on his arms, hear the birds in the trees when he couldn't hear what she was saying. He wanted to talk to her but didn't know what to say, and she was reaching for him, her naked shoulders glistening in the corona of light that suffused the dancing tendrils of her hair. And he couldn't stop himself from reaching for her.

When his father stepped out from behind her shoulder to stare at him, Nick gaped — and sat upright in the darkness to shiver as the sweat sheened cold across his skin.

Chapter 3

'I've brought your bag.'

Nick turned from stowing his walking gear beside the boxes of his books in the Nissan's boot to take his sports bag from his mother's outstretched hand. In her other she held a carrier with a flask and sandwiches he'd seen her making when he'd come down for breakfast.

'Thanks, but you didn't need to.'

'You haven't the money to waste on food and coffee at the services. Better you save it for evenings out with your friends.'

He smiled at her. 'Yes, Mum,' he said as if chastened.

She smiled at him then stepped forwards to kiss his cheek. 'Enjoy yourself. And drive safely.'

'I will, I promise.'

She stepped back to the edge of the driveway as if deliberately cutting their link, leaving him to climb into the car and start the engine. It purred into life, and she was there in the rear-view mirror, her hand held up in a wave. He should have hugged her, he realised, but he hadn't and it was too late now. Reciprocating her gesture, he depressed the clutch and pushed the car into gear, watching her grow smaller in the mirror until he lost sight of her at the corner.

He hoped she wouldn't cry, but he didn't think she would, when for so long she'd done little else. The change in her since Simon's call had been nothing short of miraculous. But also somehow unsettling.

The cards had been the first to go. He'd been stunned to find she'd taken them down while he'd been at work. He'd thought they'd take them down together, talk about the senders, how they connected to Dad. Reminisce. She'd walked to the local shop for milk and eggs, *to see people.* Talk to people, she meant, get over hiding away in case she burst into tears. And she had, she'd said, that first time, and the lady in the shop had come round the counter to give her a hug. He'd felt oddly annoyed that he hadn't been there, that it hadn't been him supporting her.

He recalled being woken by the Nissan's engine turning over, him tearing back the duvet thinking it was being stolen from the drive; staring down at it from his window, at his mother as she reversed out onto the road, shopping bags filling the passenger seat. The moment she'd returned he'd been ready with a beaming smile to help unload, telling her how well she'd done, how pleased he was she'd found the courage, making her a coffee as she'd put away the groceries on different shelves from his. Her shelves; her system.

He'd known, then, to back off, to let her cook, to let her garden, thanking her for giving him the time to write his talk, making it sound as if a two hour lecture with detailed handouts rather than a forty minute chat and reading. It had made him realise how he'd crammed his days, crammed them so as not to think of Alice. And she hadn't returned, had she, not since his father had stepped round her shoulder to stare at him.

Had he? Had it been a figment of his imagination? His own brain telling him... telling him what? To stop? To grow up? To let go?

As he neared the centre of Southampton the traffic became fraught, despite it being well beyond the morning's recognised congestion, and he concentrated on getting through it. Just over six hours with stops and he'd be in Durham, timing it right to meet Simon after work and dump his bag in the flat before they headed for a beer.

I'll treat you to a steak, mate!

He was looking forwards to that, to the laughs, to re-engaging with the energy they'd created during his year at the city's uni, except from the text he'd received the previous night the steak might have to wait. There was a problem. Not with Simon's mother, Nick had deciphered, but with the event he was joining. Sponsors or something.

Just turn up. Text when you arrive.

Beyond the city's limits he listened to the radio for a while, jumping channels when idiots started pontificating. The road reports were full of snarls and accidents on his route, and the usual gridlock on the M25 away to the east. He remembered sitting with his Dad, letting him talk, letting him reminisce about his own youth, about the building of the motorway ringing London.

Straight through the factory where I had my first job. I went back for a look while they were still marking out the road system. I couldn't even work out where the factory had been. Bulldozers had flattened everything. Even your Gran's house. It was as if it had never existed, as if we'd never existed.

He'd got his father a drink, he recalled, to sever the thread of conversation, restarted it on a more upbeat note. His Dad had been right, though. Nothing ever remained the same.

In the stark-walled meeting room of the water bottling plant no one was saying anything. Oscar stared into his laptop, as cowed as ever. Trevor's chair remained tucked beneath the table despite his folder on its top. Douglas narrowed his eyes as he watched John tap the rubber tip of his pencil on the polished mahogany. In the sunshine pouring through the windows the marks it left were clearly visible on its surface, and those marks irritated Douglas more than being kept waiting. He took a breath and focused on the muffled sounds of the bottling line cycling through its automated workflow – a golden opportunity fast turning into an albatross round their necks. Their father would turn in his grave.

Below, the outer door slammed, the noise echoing up the breeze block walls. Douglas checked his watch. That molly-coddled lab assistant in late again. How he'd ever been talked into allowing the company's resources to further a university project was beyond him, and in his annoyance his gaze flicked across to John. Too laid-back by half. He needed to have words.

Trevor powered into the room, his cheeks flushed, his white coat flapping.

'Sorry about that. Couldn't be helped.' He pulled out his chair. 'Where are we?'

'Waiting for you. What did the bank say?' Douglas watched the man shrug and wanted to give him more than just a mouthful of invective in response.

'They're not going to pull the plug—'

'Damned right they're not. They're into us for too much. It would be a disaster on their balance sheet. Which means we have leverage.'

Trevor started waving his arms, a drowning man if ever Douglas saw one. As their financial officer, their brother-in-law was proving a disaster.

'It's never that simple. They're bound by their code of—'

'They're shit scared to make a decision and stand by it.'

John slapped his pencil on the table. 'I'm not sitting here to re-sieve this; I have work to do. Let's cut to the chase: what are the figures?'

Their collective gaze turned to Oscar.

'Flat.'

John rolled his eyes. 'Is that it? Is that what we have convened this meeting for? *Flat?*'

'What would you like me to say? That my throat is hoarse from sparkling on the phone? It is. That I've cajoled past customers until I'm blue in the face?' He stared as if a rabbit in headlights and pointed to his chin.

At the head of the table, Douglas fumed. His youngest brother could be so damned childish. 'Did you feed the papers good-news items?'

'Yes.'

'I've not seen any.'

'They're not interested, Doug. Good news doesn't sell newspapers. Shock-horror stories about potash mining and hydraulic fracturing do.'

'It's a bloody National Park.'

'Don't tell me, tell the *bloody* government.'

John sat forwards patting the air in front of him. 'Calm down, everybody. It's not happened yet.'

'The potash has.'

'And it's been with us for years with hardly a complaint. This is going to be like the GM food scares. Its bubble will rise, there's a clamour, and then the bubble bursts. Nobody bats an eyelid now.'

'That's not our problem,' Oscar said. 'Our problem is the next quarterly payments, the next quarterly receipts. If they don't start matching we'll—'

'We'll what? Trim our salaries again? We've already outsourced distribution. Personnel is down to a skeleton staff. Two people go off sick together this winter and we're in shit street.'

'We can cut loose that assistant of yours,' Douglas said, pointing his finger at John. 'Moves at a snail's pace as if work is an optional extra, and I don't like him using our paid-for resources to further his degree.'

'Timothy Glossmer is our direct line into Durham University, with all the added cachet that brings to the company's name.'

'I've noticed none,' Douglas huffed.

'Most of his salary is covered via funding; he costs us less than a cleaner. But if anything goes wrong we can get samples put through the university – their equipment is a damned sight better than ours – and it means we won't be paying a fortune to DEFRA which, God forbid, if we did have even a sniff of a problem, would be the last body we'd want to run it by. *Isn't it?*'

Douglas said nothing, and neither did anyone else. The flare of irritation dissipated. He drew a breath and looked round the table.

'I suggest we all carry on doing what we're doing. If we can keep our heads we'll ride this out. There's no report needs writing until we're due for a minuted meeting, and in the meantime nothing goes in an email. There's to be no paper-trail, understand? If there's something the rest of us need to be informed of, it's spoken.'

Placing his palms flat on the polished mahogany, he sat back to look at them again.

'And *in the meantime* I suggest you look to your personal finances. If we need cash-flow another five will be trimmed off our salaries.' He gave them a wry smile. 'Think of the upside. It'll be less tax for the bloody government to waste.'

Beyond the car's windows the countryside changed from the gold of harvested fields to the industrial sprawl of the Midlands – Leicester, Nottingham, Mansfield – then left behind their grime for the rumpled landscape of the Peak District. It wasn't long before signage for the M18 and Hull loomed. Nick wasn't going east, yet the blue boards kept catching his eye, pressuring him to detour.

After the third he refused to acknowledge them. He was never going back to Hull; had made too many bad choices in Hull. In Hull life had changed irrevocably. Especially for Alice. He'd promised to go back for her, to free her from the water. All he'd done was call her from memory to enjoy her touch. When he couldn't sleep, when he didn't want to think about his father's illness.

He felt too morose to listen to his iPod. He didn't want to be here driving north, didn't want to give the talk. In truth he didn't want to face her. It had been too long. How could she ever understand?

It was a relief when the motorway veered west, its ribbon of tarmac full to capacity, traffic slowing as it cut between Sheffield and Rotherham, dawdling between Dewsbury and Wakefield. It came to an exasperating series of stop-start halts as myriad routes tumbled out of Leeds. And Nick felt tired now, itchy-eyed from the concentration, from the sun reflecting from red and white traffic cones closing off lanes, guarding chicanes, shining off paintwork and obliterating brake lights. He wished he'd taken a break at Woolley Edge. He needed a pee, to stretch his back.

Clouds gathered, giving him respite enough to flip up the sun visor, but soon the greasy windscreen was smearing with raindrops. As he crawled onto the A1M the heavens opened and he wished for the return of reflected sunshine instead of dark veils of spray from the wheels of lorries. Overhead displays warned of surface water and tried to slow the traffic's speed. When he saw the sign for Wetherby Services he edged into the inside lane to peel away from the cacophony, and braked his way into the relative calm of its puddled parking area.

Ignoring his mother's sandwiches, and her admonishments, he ate a meal there, burger and fries with a card cup of coffee. He walked to ease his back and shoulders, to get the blood pumping in his legs again. Beside him the rain pummelled the floor-to-ceiling windows, and the seating area filled with people shaking out jackets and towelling their hair with paper serviettes. He sent Simon a text telling him he was running late. He didn't receive a reply.

At the damp and draughty entrance he checked a map highlighting coming roadworks. He tried to concentrate on the icons, to see where on the motorway they were exactly, but his gaze kept being drawn to the expanse of fawn and brown contours to the east of its blue line. The North York Moors stretched to the sea, not a single road splitting its centre west to east. Was Alice waiting for him, living on the hope of past promises? Or had she faded, been absorbed by the entity that had taken her?

His betrayal appalled him. He'd denied it so long, but there was no hiding now he was so close.

Forcing back his shoulders, he took himself in hand. He wasn't betraying Alice. His boots were packed. It was planned. He'd visit the Pool on the return when he had time to sit and wait to see if she appeared. Pushing through the glass door, he strode along the covered walkway as the rain reached in to wet his jeans. Durham, that's where he was going, to keep a promise, to give a talk. He would concentrate on Alice on Monday. Whenever Simon was back at work.

Between the shadowy rain, the lifting spray, and the headlights reflecting from the wet road, regaining the motorway was less a judge of distances and more a prayer and a foot hard on the accelerator. No horns screamed in his ears, no headlights flashed anger in his mirrors. Nick let his held breath escape and forced himself to relax. Motorway driving was an art, and he was out of practice.

He tucked the Nissan behind a broad white saloon and kept a good distance, hoping no idiot would press between them. Junctions were sparse so he had no fear of being side-swiped by traffic filtering in. And then his windscreen was full of bright indicators from the outside lane, and the road ahead erupted in red brake lights. He added his own, repeatedly tapping the pedal in an effort not to skid, despite the ABS, and coming to a crawl. Too far ahead to read, signage was flashing a warning. He hit the radio and caught the end of a traffic report. The A1M was blocked. A car had aquaplaned, a lorry had braked, a pile-up had ensued. Traffic was being re-routed via Thirsk and Northallerton. He felt a sudden shudder, grateful he'd been in the services.

At the Dishforth turn-off the police were out in force, their whirling blue lights streaming across the wet road as they funnelled the three lanes of the motorway onto the two of the exit ramp. It was achingly slow.

By the time he was on the road to Thirsk the late summer downpour had eased. There was even a streak of blue sky reflected in his mirrors. Ahead, the hills marking the rise to the North York Moors were half-hidden by leaden clouds and curtaining rain. He was going to Durham, he reminded himself. How far was it to Thirsk?

He thought about switching on the sat nav but vehicles were already indicating left. *Rainton?* What was at Rainton? Surely it was too close to the motorway to lead back on to it – and then his indecision was fixed and he remained on the dual carriageway following a lorry. Thirsk was safer, he decided.

More indicators blinked yellow. A 'B' road – to where? As he peered at the sign it exploded in flaming incandescence. Narrowing his eyes against the glare, his fingers dragged down the visor. The lorry in front, the trees crowding the verge, the metal barriers alongside the roadway, every drop of held water burst into multiple prisms of refracted colour. Just as fast it subdued to sunlight shimmering silver off the pylons in the stubble fields, draping the hedges in multiple shades of green. As the sparkling road dipped, the hills across the wide valley lifted higher in the windscreen, their true colours rising from their foot as if soaking up the sudden burst of sunshine. And there it stood below the ridge, pure white against the earthy greens and browns, the great White Horse guarding the approach to the Moors.

Nick felt his heart jump. They'd never come in this way. He and Alice had driven from the south, from Hull. He'd travelled the same route when he'd come up alone, to say goodbye. There was no road crossing the Moors this way, he reminded himself.

A green sign: the turn-off for Thirsk, ahead for Northallerton and Teesside. He didn't want to go to Teesside; he was going to Durham.

He kept glancing at the White Horse as it backed slowly across the windscreen into his side window. He was an hour from Durham; fifty miles from Durham.

He took the exit, following the lorry down the ramp past caravan tops as white as the Horse, left at the junction and into the town. A flower-filled roundabout, too small to cope with the sudden congestion, held a sign pointing him back to the motorway along a road choked with lorries and cars. A traffic warden was meeting each vehicle, sending it back, sending it on to Northallerton, to connect to the motorway there.

Nick sighed in frustration and waited for the lorry's long trailer to shudder round the tight island. More signs. *Town Centre. Sutton-under-Whitestone-Cliffe.*

The cliff of the white stone horse.
No Caravans. Severe Gradient.
A free and empty route.
An hour from Durham.
He chose the Moors. And Alice.

Chapter 4

Despite surrendering to the rhythm of the priory, keeping the offices, accepting the tasks allotted to him daily in the Chapter House, Ernald felt restless.

It had been days since Brother Maugre had demanded his attendance, and seeing the sub-prior fulfilling his duties about the monastic house it seemed to Ernald that he was being shunned. To add to his discomfort, two of the brothers had asked why he had returned so early in the harvest season. What could he say? To lie was a sin. Was it a sin to remain silent when he knew something was amiss?

Angel-woman.

His chest heaved as he recalled the meeting in the shadowed confinement chamber. The crying man, all skin and bone, his scars of torment healed. Healed by what? By whom? God's grace or... or darkest devilry?

Ernald knew how easy it was to succumb, how easy it was to take the less stony path. His sleepless hours were haunted by the smiles and blessings he had bestowed upon the inhabitants of draughty hovels when declining a night's rest beneath their roofs. He'd told himself, made himself believe, had he stayed his small retinue would diminish their hosts' meagre stores and leave families hungry. Was not the truth of it that his limbs coveted the comfort of a manor's hall where it would not be a bowl of rough pottage but a plate of spiced meat and a goblet of Burgundy wine? Had he not feigned aching muscles, a cut foot, to rest another night?

What had he heard from the lips of that crying man? Why had his gaoler refused to meet Ernald's gaze?

He had broken bread twice before he'd gathered the courage

to walk the cloisters in his contemplation hour. But that had been a lie, despite the chaplet passing through his fingers, the prayers across his lips. His sight had been fixed on the door to the confinement chamber, his feet slowing as he neared it, passed it; quickening on the turn, down the aisle and turn again, until he could slow, willing, praying, for the door to open, for someone to appear.

By the third day he was decided. He walked the cloister three times saying prayers once for His Father, once for His Son, once for the gifts of the Holy Spirit that guided all men's hearts. On that third circuit, his heart pounding, Ernald stopped at the door, turned the ring-handle and pushed. He entered the confinement chamber in a shaft of bright sunlight and closed the door, the cool of the interior embracing him.

There was no candle lit against the darkness, only fine golden sunlight reaching in quill-thin lines either side of him to pick out the edge of the table and meet on the opposite wall. Ernald could hear muffled noises from the masons' yard, an occasional shout dulled by the thickness of the stone, but there was no sound from the inner chamber. He glanced to his left, seeing the shadowy outline of the Crucifix hanging there, the reflected light glinting from the polished nails holding his Blessed Lord in His pain.

Reaching for the table's edge, Ernald drew his fingertips along its wood until his leading arm touched cold stone and his exploring fingers found the inner door. As the latch lifted in his hand, as the door opened onto a blackness as thick as a damned soul's abyss, light flooded his arm and the wall beside him.

'Brother Ernald?'

He turned to the cracked voice, to the door to the cloister open wide, a bent figure silhouetted in a corona of yellow light. At his shoulder the Blessed Crucifix shone with an unearthly glow, the pale body and raised eyes of Jesus the Christ beseeching him to answer true.

Ernald looked back towards the inner chamber, the ambient light catching a ladder laid across the timbered floor, across the closed trapdoor. He took a step back along the table.

'What ails you, Brother Ernald?'

It was Brother Gregory, he saw now, infirm Brother Gregory with his tapping stick and twisted shoulder, the man's voice thin with age.

'I thought...' but Ernald's gaze was drawn to the Crucifix and his tongue felt like lead in his mouth.

'Come boy, come. Sit with me a while,' and the old man led into the daylight of the cloister, to a stone seat warmed by the sun.

Ernald could not look at him, and for long moments both listened to the drone of the Novice Master at his teaching, and the calls and hammering from the masons' yard.

'I have watched you walk the aisles,' Brother Gregory said, 'seen your step falter and quicken as if a reflection of the tumult of your thoughts. You return to us before the harvest tithes, and it seems to these dimming eyes that your heart does not rest easy.'

Ernald let his shoulders sink. What could he say? He was laid bare.

'The position of questor is an onerous burden for a brother,' Gregory continued. 'You have carried it well these years. But temptations are many, and sometimes the worst are not the most clear to our gaze. Give yourself to blessed Confession, my friend. Ask to be relieved of so onerous a duty. Seek manual labour. Offering your hands to God's soil replenishes the soul. I know this.'

Bony fingers reached out to pat Ernald's arm. Grunting with effort, Brother Gregory pushed himself to his feet, steadied his legs, and tapped his way along the cloister aisle leaving Ernald to his contemplations.

The bell for Sect could not come fast enough. Filing into the church with the convent, the comfort of God's grace wrapped about Ernald's shoulders as a balm. He sang loudly at the cantor's direction, and silently to himself when it was not his place. The Mass which followed enriched him, and he prayed for Brother Gregory, trusting to God to relieve the pain of the older man's infirmities. Brother Gregory, he realised, had not remained silent when he had seen something amiss.

After the readings during the midday meal, Ernald did as Gregory advised and sought manual labour. He helped lay-brethren carry fresh rushes to the fermery, and stayed to rake and sweep out the old. He sat with a sick brother in his delirium, listening as the man spoke as if Ernald were his father, or older brother, Ernald could not tell.

From there he went to the almonry and helped to distribute the doles, watching the bare-footed fall upon the bread and thinned pottage, gratitude standing in their wary eyes.

'Too many,' muttered the almoner. 'I shall have leave from the sub-prior to visit Saint Giles'. The brothers there have the effrontery to send the wretches here as if the tithes were already stored.'

It was, indeed, harvest-time. The hedges of the hollow-ways gave up their nourishment as goodly as the tilled fields. Ernald looked over the group, wondering how many who clustered at the gate would return during the onset of chill winds and cold rain. How many would be able to? If he journeyed with the crying man, if the crying man led to the miraculous spring that cured afflictions, might they be able to return with a cask of the blessed water to relieve those in need here? Might that be God's life-deed for him?

'Giving Penance, are you?'

Ernald stared at the almoner. The man squinted at him.

'Never back before the first tithes, you,' he said. 'Drink too much fine wine in the manors, eh?'

Ernald flushed, and the Almoner laughed.

'I did not,' Ernald returned. In truth he probably had, though he'd never disgraced the House by being in his cups.

'Aye, well, you will be giving Penance if you loiter here. That was the bell for None. Didn't you hear it?'

The wooden bowls hit the table with a clatter as Ernald opened his hands and made for the gate. He might not have heard the bell, but the almoner's laughter rang clear enough.

He did not dare cut by the Prior's lodging in case his haste was seen from a window. Instead he crossed the open work space, dodging artisan lay-brethren working with adze and chisel, and on through the frater hall arch. He was almost to the cloister, intent on taking his place in the quire for the service, when across the garth he saw two lay-brethren dragging a struggling novice by the arms. In front walked a brother Ernald did not recognise. Behind walked Sub-Prior Maugre.

Without reason, Ernald pressed himself behind the near stone embrasure. Only when he heard faint sounds of voices raised in praise did he realise that no brothers sat on the seats along the cloister aisles. The service of None had begun. He alone remained without.

The slap of sandaled feet, the distant singing, did not mask the mewling of what sounded like a child. Stealing a glimpse, Ernald saw that the door to the confinement chamber was open. Maugre stood by while the lay-brethren fought with the novice who had stayed his ingress by bracing his feet against the stonework either side. In the writhing of the men, in that quick look across the garth, Ernald noted that the novice's jaw bulged, that something had been forced into his mouth which he was trying to shake free. Then came the blow. From whom and with what Ernald did not see, but the novice sagged in the arms of his restrainers and he was dragged inside. Sub-Prior Maugre bent to pick up a loose sandal and followed, closing the door behind him.

Chapter 5

The land began to rumple as soon as urban Thirsk was left behind. The green of full-leafed trees and farming pasture shone as if items newly washed, the land holding no barrier of distance as when seen from the through-road. Nick switched off the air-con and lowered the front windows, not caring about the cold drips spitting at him from the edge of the windscreen. The organic scents of the world outside the car tantalised his nostrils, urging him to breathe deeply, to fill his lungs to a capacity he'd forgotten they owned.

The great White Horse, far flatter on the hillside than it had seemed when viewed from the dual carriageway, glowed through tree-line and hedgerow as the narrow road wound towards the ever-rising ridge.

Sutton-under-Whitestone-Cliffe arrived as a chocolate-box village of grey stone houses and red pantile roofs, trimmed verges and splurges of yellow and white flowers. As he took its last bend to return to the verdant green, the White Horse blinked at him through gaps in the trees then disappeared. A change in the engine's note made Nick check his speed, lifting his gaze to see road signs announcing *Sutton Bank – Engage Low Gear – 25% Gradient* and, more alarming, *Blocked 78 Times Last Year by HGVs*.

He scanned the route of the twisting road. Over the hedges he could see no lorries, only the gleam of a silver delivery van way ahead. The engine's note changed again, his speed slowing, and he engaged third gear to spurt forwards. The bends were coming fast now, no straight road to see at all, trees filling the verges on either side, double white lines down the centre of the narrowing carriageway. Groups of vehicles filed downhill in convoy. A blue car was looming in his rear-view mirror, but he ignored it. There would be no overtaking now.

A sharp left-hander and the snaking rise was upon him, sheets of rock lifting vertically from the roadside to his right. To his left the tops of trees pressing against flimsy fencing reminded him of his race after Alice up the precipitous path to Newtondale Spring, and he lingered over the memory of their first making love. It was nothing like in his dreams, more a naïve exploration. He thumbed the ring carrying strands of her hair, felt its wavy decoration indent his skin. It seemed an aeon ago. A different lifetime.

The rear doors of the silver van filled his windscreen, snapping Nick's mind back to the present. Down into second, the engine complaining as the van's speed was matched. A right bend, a left. As long as the van didn't stall they'd be fine. Beside him the tree-tops were thinning and he snatched glimpses of sunlit flatlands spreading far below, velvet-bottomed rain-clouds chasing north almost at eye level.

The van slowed to a crawl. Nick eased his pressure on the accelerator, his left foot hovering over the clutch, his hand on the gear-stick ready to change down into first. And after first? A prickle of concern swept through him, but the van jumped forwards and Nick's car followed, barely under his control as they were spat onto flatter land where leafy trees were replaced by brooding pines. There was signage for a visitor's centre. The van turned off leaving Nick to rise through the gears, the road ahead full of sunlight and expectation. The white stone cliff, Sutton Bank, had been tamed.

The road skirted the southern extent of the Moors, giving glimpses of purple to one side and an expanse of harvested fields to the other. Despite it being the major, the only route to the coast, traffic was both light and genial. Most of it was tourist out to visit the sights, happy to defer to the occasional milk tanker leaving the dusty tracks of stone-built farms. He didn't remember the farm he was aiming for looking so bright, but it had been late autumn on the two occasions he'd been there, and on neither had he been sight-seeing. He wasn't even sure what it was called, only that he'd know the route once he was close enough.

Helmsley's wide marketplace drew him up short, forcing him to consult the map. Thank goodness his mother insisted on one being kept in the car. Sat nav was useless when there was no named destination to input.

He'd been right to stop. Not yet was he due to turn on to the Moors proper. The ruined monasteries of Rievaulx and Byland would have led him astray.

After eating the rest of his sandwich, he opened another bottle of water and eased back on to the main road. He didn't want to drive as far as Pickering with its steam railway leading where no road dare venture. There were too many memories wrapped in its shrill whistle and huffing smokestack.

He drove through Wombleton and Sinnington, his mouth growing dry with anticipation. There was no glimpse of the Moors now, just the greens and yellows of cultivated landscapes. And then the turn-off for Lastingham arrived and he took the unclassified road.

The fields remained deceptively benign and he wondered if he'd taken the wrong route, but Cawthorne appeared with signs to the site of its Roman Camps. Nick gritted his teeth as he averted his gaze. He was on the right road.

The land rose so gradually it was at first only discernable by the change in the fields. Then round a bend, down a dip and up, and the deciduous trees gave way to pine and the hedgerows petered out to verges tall in deadman's oatmeal, hemlock and vetch. He knew there were Iron Age settlements hidden among the pines, howes and cairns and a Roman Road mere centimetres below the turf, all speared by tree-roots trying to keep the past bound in its grave. Or pinned to the present; he'd never worked out which.

The trees to his left finished with an abruptness only the

Forestry Commission could devise, the Nissan rumbling over a cattle grid to cross into a land undulating in glorious shades of purple and mauve. The smell of the heather's nectar drifting on the air was intoxicating, its colours a cushion to Nick's mind. They were interrupted only by the white wool of sheep shining in the sunshine as bright as the White Horse on its cliff.

Nick regretted leaving it so long to return. Yet, in truth, what could he have done? In a couple of months it would be six years since he'd lost Alice, three since watching her disperse in the waters at York. His fault. All of it.

He eyed the cars parked by the bridge, the picnickers, their dogs and children playing in the stream, and he rolled his shoulders to disentangle his guilt. Life was for the living and Alice wasn't dead, not in the true sense of his father's passing. He could rescue her yet. He would have returned as he'd promised, should have returned... yet an image of his mother rose up to smile at him; his father, gaunt and breathless, patting his hand in acceptance. Life was never the way it should be.

To his right, the last trees peeled away leaving the moorland to sweep wide on every side, the blue of the sky arcing from horizon to horizon, a backdrop for the changing play of light and shadow from the clouds. Nick eased his speed for the bridge, careful of loose dogs and unheeding children, and drove across the single-track road laid a handspan above the water, its white flood marker standing as high as the car. He carried on up the hill to where the Roman Road erupted from the thin soil, kept safe from sheep's hooves by a wire fence.

Slamming his foot on the brake, the car's back-end fish-tailed as its wheels locked. Only then did he check his rear-view mirror, grateful to see no vehicle behind him. He was breathing hard, but wasn't sure why. Had he seen...? No. Yet he didn't trust himself to be sure, needed to check. Something on the fencing had jumped out at him.

Pulling the offside wheels onto the verge, he cut the engine and swung open the door. There was no heather here, just rough sods of grass making it difficult to keep his footing. He jogged down the tarmac slope, his gaze locking on the metal plaque which had caught his eye. As he drew level, his jaw dropped.

An arrow. An icon of a pine tree and a picnic table. *The Pool.*

It couldn't be, though it was pointing in the right direction. Yet it couldn't be. Surely, *surely* the Pool hadn't been turned into a tourist attraction.

Alice...

Chapter 6

Nick's hand trembled as he reached to touch the sign, hot from the sun, its colours bleaching with age. It was very real and not hand-made, machine-made, fixed to the fencing by plastic snapties through corner eyelets. His ire rising, Nick grasped hold and pulled, making the wire fencing shimmy along its length. He'd no cutters, had he? Not even a penknife. He was useless. He'd always been useless. He hadn't listened; hadn't saved her; he'd not come back. What did he expect? Nothing remained the same, nothing. *Fuck!*

Jogging back to the car, he restarted its engine without strapping himself in. There was no worry about missing the turning to the farm. He saw the marker long before he saw the narrow route angling off the tarmac. The Pool was *World Famous* now. In his anger, Nick struck the heel of his palm so hard on the steering wheel he had to nurse it against the resulting pain.

He'd kill that bastard farmer. What did he think he was doing? What had he *done*? Turned the Pool into a fucking *theme park*?

Shoving open the car's door, he strode onto the verge. This sign was bigger, fixed to two wooden stakes hammered into the earth. In anger, Nick kicked it and saw it give, so he kicked it again, and again, paying no attention to the vehicles crawling past the abandoned Nissan. One stake snapped, and he kicked its face some more, stepping forwards to wrap his arms around the metal rectangle and pull. It came free of the crumbling earth and he threw it back into the heather. It didn't disappear from view; it lay floating on the brushwood stalks.

Breathing hard, he stared at it. He couldn't leave it there.

Holding his breath to ease his racing heart, he grasped the remaining stake to pull the sign towards him. Standing on its metal face, he levered free the length of wood, and gathered the debris to open the car's boot. Two boxes of books smirked at him. What the hell had he brought all those for? Who was going to buy two boxfuls of bloody books on myths and legends? The publisher had remaindered them, hadn't it? Had that told him nothing?

Curbing his anger, his sports bag and boots went into the back seat footwell and the stacked boxes were laid side by side, leaving enough room to shove the sign and its stakes on top. He slammed down the boot and stood there, his hand on the hot metal of the car. It was his fault, this; no one else's. He should have been watching; he should have been here.

There were more signs, small ones hammered into the ground, hard to see, overgrown with grass and wild flowers. Nick slowed at the first, but didn't stop. Down a slope, the narrow roadway meandering, its tarmac breaking up at its edges, tufts of green in its centre... Another sign, overgrown with vetch and tall daisies. Another bend, another dip and a rise, the beginning of fencing, a plantation of trees.

He saw the bloom of flowers ahead and eased back on the accelerator to glide to the spot. The sign nestled in their midst, difficult to see but marked by the flowers. Who had seeded them? Or were they as wild as they appeared, seeded by nature? Surely not in one spot. By Alice? Could she do that? Chewing at his lip, he carried on.

More wooden fencing showed him he was close. It wasn't new, but it was substantial and hemmed in both sides of the road. The farmhouse came into view, and then the sign, grotesquely huge, attached near the entrance. He hardly dared look at it. *World Famous*. And it came to him that he'd seen the Pool during those first months, watched it day after day. Someone had set up a webcam feed. Why had he thought nothing else would have changed?

The car clattered over a cattle grid, sounding his approach, and he crunched along gravel to enter the yard – the car park – becoming more despairing as he caught sight of the picnic tables and directions to *Toilets* and *Petting Enclosure*. He drew into a bay on the almost empty concrete and laid his forehead on the steering wheel. Did he want to do this? Did he *really* want to do this?

He'd opened the Nissan's door before he'd sat back in the seat, and once on his feet found himself facing an arrow pointing back the way he'd driven in: *The Pool*.

'You okay, there?'

Swinging round he saw a man pushing a wheelbarrow full of manure, an incongruous brimmed hat pulled low over his forehead. Was it…? God, what was his name?

The man stopped, the wheelbarrow's handles held high as he stared.

'It's Nicholas, ain't it?'

Nick pulled himself together and stepped round the back of the car.

'I'm surprised you remember me. It's been a long time.' He was going to offer his hand, but the man wasn't releasing his wheelbarrow.

'Didn't think you'd come back.'

Nick shrugged. It sounded very much as if he wasn't welcome. Or perhaps he was wondering how Nick would react to all the signage.

And then the man blinked as if coming out of his shock. Easing down the wheelbarrow, he wiped his palm on his trouser leg and stepped forwards to offer both his hand and a smile.

'Good to see you, lad. You're looking well. Come special, like?'

Nick shook the offered hand, feeling the man's calluses, ignoring the ingrained dirt.

'Sort of. I'm due in Durham tomorrow and was going to call in on the way back, but there was an accident on the motorway and we were diverted, and…' He was talking for talking's sake so shut up.

'Come on in an' see Rosemary. She'll be right glad to see you.

We'll put the kettle on. Doubtless there'll be a scone or summat on offer.'

Nick thought he was chattering, too, but let himself be guided round the front of the house. *Rosemary...* Rosemary and...? Rosemary and... *Phil*. He felt relieved to have their names, and then he was passing through the open front door and into a stone-flagged passage.

It was the map that did it. The Ordnance Survey map of that part of the Moors was still attached to the wall, still defying viewers to make out its detail in the dim light.

'Look what Providence washed up,' Phil was saying in too cheery a voice, and Nick followed him into the large kitchen to see Rosemary turn with a smile, see the smile drop away, taking the colour from her cheeks.

'Nicholas.'

He blinked at her. How could these people remember him so well?

'Cuppa tea, Rosemary. The lad's parched an' so am I.'

The smile returned, forced, and she moved back to the worktop. It was a shaking hand that reached for the kettle, Nick noted. Was it the signage? Were they worried what he'd say about the *World Famous Pool*? How bad was it across there? And then he thought of their wrecked sign hidden in the Nissan's boot, and he felt guilty, too.

'He's up in Durham tomorrow,' Phil ventured. 'Got caught in a detour. Thought he'd pay us a visit.'

'That's nice.'

It was all so stilted. Nick wished he hadn't come, wished he'd parked the car further up the road and walked across the moor, ignoring the farm.

Phil washed his hands and Rosemary placed a platter of scones on the table. Plates and jam and cups and saucers followed. No one said a word. Then Phil plugged the yawning silence.

'Fresh outta the oven,' he said, rubbing his hands together as if he were about to tuck into a Sunday roast.

Rosemary brought over the teapot and joined them at the table. She smiled at him and started with the opener he feared she might.

'Are your parents keeping well?'

He drew a breath and faced her. 'Dad died three months ago,' and he watched her expression turn from polite enquiry to renewed shock.

'It was a blessing in the end. As these things often are.' He forced a smile of his own and reached for a scone. Neither of them was going to say anything.

'Mum took it badly for a while, as you can imagine, but she's finding her feet now. It's, er... the reason I took this gig. I'm giving a talk. Helping out a friend.' He produced a chuckle for effect. 'Their speaker dropped out.'

'I'm sorry to hear about your father,' Rosemary said.

'Aye,' echoed Phil, and Nick watched the pair exchange a look. Yes, he thought, Dad was about your age.

Rosemary poured the tea. 'So you thought you'd come to pay your respects at the Pool on your way up to Durham.'

'It was my intention to come on the way back, but there was an accident—'

'You'll be stopping the night then. I'll make up a room.' It was her turn to conjure a smile. 'On us.'

'Aye,' added Phil, 'and there'll be casserole waiting for when you get back, so you won't be needing to leave it too long afore y'go.'

Nick stalled partway to biting into his scone. He'd hardly touched his cup of tea and he was being hurried out the door.

'That's very good of you both,' he said in a measured tone, 'but I'm expected in Durham tonight.'

'Nonsense,' said Rosemary. 'Night draws in faster than you think up here, and we don't want you travelling roads you don't know in the dark.' She picked up her cup. 'It's not safe.'

He was going to argue, but remembered the road which had crumbled beneath his feet in the dark; the phalanx of Roman soldiers marching towards him out of the rain. He managed to suppress the shudder, but couldn't stop the spurt of perspiration between his shoulder blades.

'That's good of you,' he said again.

Rosemary topped up his tea, even though he'd hardly touched it. 'So... you're giving a talk?'

'I wrote a short book some time ago. *Countryside Lore & Legends.*'

That killed the conversation. He tried to retrieve it as he drank too-hot tea.

'How's the farm doing?'

Again, they looked anywhere but at him.

'Aye, well,' started Phil, 'you'll have noticed a few changes as you came in.' He waved his knife in the air as he shrugged. 'Had to in the end. Townies abandoning cars all over the place. Blocking field gates, walking anywhere, frightening the sheep. Then coming to us when they needed an ambulance for their twisted knees.' He looked pointedly at Nick. 'Brought more than those trainers for your feet, have you?'

'I've brought my walking boots.'

'You'll need a torch,' Rosemary said.

Nick looked at her aghast, but she was already rising from her chair. He turned to Phil. 'It's not far, is it?' He thought of the bumpy ride in the Land Rover taken years before, of the walk across rough ground.

'A couple of mile.' Phil licked his fingers, intent on not meeting Nick's eye.

The torch appeared at his elbow, a wind-up torch, the type he'd used in York.

'They're good,' said Rosemary. 'No batteries to run flat.'

As she sat again, she glanced at him and smiled, then picked up her knife and cut a scone in half. Nick lifted the jammy remains of his own. The sooner he left for the Pool the better. This was almost a rerun of the conversations he'd had with his mother when his father had first been diagnosed, when what was being said hid a tsunami of what dared not be broached.

Chapter 7

The low level hum of the machinery in the lab was punctuated by the muted roar of percussion from the earbuds dangling round Tim's neck, and he pressed his iPod, cutting the tune mid-song. His gaze was intent on the read-outs from the ancient mass spectrometer, his hearing waiting for the wrap-up note that heralded the printed report.

He studied the page in his notebook as if expecting the figures in the columns to have changed, hoping his mistake would jump out at him: a misplaced decimal point, a transposed number sequence. He'd been tired, hadn't he? It had to be his mistake. Yet the chromatograph had registered the same. But how could it? The whole thing was bizarre.

Inert on the counter, his tablet's blank screen sprang bright at his touch, the bar graph clear. The spike above 'Unidentified' was almost off the scale.

He'd filled a pre-used vial, had to have done, though how had that occurred? He'd checked the box and the integrity of its clean-room contents hadn't been breached. Besides, if the vials had been contaminated in production all the sample results would have flagged it. Only TG15-29 had given a false reading. He rubbed at his eyebrow, hoping the reading was false, because if it wasn't he was going to have to chase down the contaminant before John found out about it.

He stared at the specks of skin on the counter. He must not rub at his psoriasis. It would start itching and— Perhaps that was the contaminant? He shook his head, dismissing the thought and saw another flake on the counter. He needed to cream his eyebrows, needed to calm himself. He was just making it worse.

With the edge of his hand he swept the scaly detritus together and deposited it in the bin. He was sure it wasn't him, but there was definitely a contaminant somewhere in the lab. Had John been sloppy with his hygiene? If this result came in suspect, he'd go over the entire room with the old UV light he'd found stored in a cupboard.

The door opened and he swung round to see John walking in.

'Tim, a word to the— What's the matter?'

'Nothing, I—' He forced a makeshift chuckle and shrugged his shoulders. 'Eyebrow itching.' He watched John's gaze refocus on his forehead and wished he'd kept his mouth shut. 'Sorry, miles away. Thinking about the weekend. Going up to Durham. Meeting friends.'

John narrowed his eyes, closing the distance between them to reach out and tap the iPod standing in the breast pocket of Tim's lab coat.

'Lose that. I've told you before, only during lunch breaks. Doug's on the warpath and is looking for any excuse. We might be paying you no more than a nominal salary but you have to abide by company protocols. Besides, it'll disrupt your research to be shunted back to the university, won't it? And I want neither to write the report to your supervisor nor lose a good man. Do I?'

'Yes. Sorry. Appreciate it.' Tim freed himself from the wires to wrap them round his hand. He bundled them and the player out of sight in his trouser pocket. They gazed at each other and Tim hoped John wasn't considering his eyebrow, prayed it wasn't swelling with inflammation.

The spectrometer sounded catching John's attention, and Tim held his breath as his supervisor looked first at that and then back at him, his expression no longer amiable.

'Are you only just—?'

'No, no. The plant's daily samples are completed.' Any moment the machine would cough up its print-out. John would look at it and the shit would truly hit the fan.

Tim reached for the appropriate ring binder from the shelf,

flicking it open and laying it across the machine to tap sharply at the current page.

'I was going to leave it another couple of days before mentioning it, but might as well bring it to your attention now. Nothing to worry about, of course, but the...er... calcium readings from the chromatograph are somewhat volatile.'

He laughed to cover the whirr of the printer mechanism. 'I'm talking hundredths of a milligram, of course, nothing to fret about, but I was wondering if there was a logical explanation, whether something had changed at the well-head. Groundwork or something.'

He was talking too much and shut up, relieved to hear nothing but the fizz from the pipes on the wall behind him and the click of their attached valves. His eyebrow was itching like hell and he curled his fingers to stop himself from rubbing at it.

'I was thinking of adding the inconsistency to my research findings,' he said, 'and wondered if that would be okay?'

John reached for the file, but Tim leaned on its edge to keep it in place, lifting the pages for John to see the differences in the readings.

'...and this one from three days ago,' he said, hoping he wasn't going to blush. It was painfully obvious there was nothing wrong with the readings.

'Natural fluctuation,' John said, standing back to look at him.

'So it'll be okay to add this data to my findings? To explain about nominal fluctuation and tolerance allowance in a control?'

'If you're just using the calcium reading, that's okay. So what are you analyzing?'

Tim balked and caught himself. 'I'm off to Durham at the weekend and was going through the current batch of off-site samples. I realised I'd missed one.' He shrugged. 'Too many late nights poring over books. I've a uni deadline in a fortnight.' He closed the file but left it on the analyzer.

'Best of luck with it,' John said. 'I'm glad all that's long behind me.' And he left.

Sighing with relief, Tim licked at his finger and drew it across his irritated eyebrow before slotting the file back into place on the shelf. Reaching down to the analyzer, he tore off the results slip.

Through the door's narrow window John watched Tim tense as he stared at the print-out, watched him snatch up his tablet and check its screen. He'd been right; something was going on.

Chapter 8

Boots on, torch pushed into his shirt pocket, Nick scrolled through his mobile's contact list as he locked the Nissan. His call to Simon went straight to voicemail again. Either he was forever on the phone or he had it switched off. Nick only hoped that the talk was still on for tomorrow. He'd be pissed if he arrived to find it cancelled.

'It's Nick. Change of plan. Won't make your place tonight. See you at the venue in the morning.'

He cut the call but carried the phone along the length of the gravel drive, hoping Simon would catch the message and ring him. Once across the cattle grid and the narrow road, he stood in front of the stile looking down the track at the impressions of boot prints dried in the mud. Lots of boots, hardly a blade of grass between them. His shoulders slumped as he thought of the tourists with their dogs and children playing in the stream by the bridge. But there were no cars at the farm, were there? Perhaps he would be on his own.

He gazed at his phone, caught between needing to hear from Simon and wanting peace and time to commune with Alice. If she was there. If she could hear him.

Damned Simon. He could leave a voicemail.

Switching off his phone, he zipped it into his trouser pocket and mounted the stile.

At the ridge the uneven track between fenced pastures opened onto purple moorland. Nick wanted to stand and drink in its vista, but the shock of seeing the wide footpath Phil had scarred into the land overrode everything. For this to have been made there must be swarms of people visiting the Pool, and he didn't want to share it with anyone.

Following the path by eye as it meandered through the landscape, he was grateful no walkers seemed to be in sight. The track led roughly in a diagonal before disappearing in the folds of the land. Two miles. Half an hour there, half an hour back. He checked his watch. That would give him a couple of hours, minimum, at the Pool. Rosemary's concern was ridiculous.

The sun felt very warm on his face, the scents of the knee-high heather cloying, overwhelming every other smell. Sheep with their bulky lambs still close raised their heads to stare at him. Pheasants called and distant responses carried on the breeze. A single skylark took to wing an arm's length from him to sing out its heart high above his head. Nick stood to stare as the sheep had, to pick out its beating wings against the vivid blue of the over-mantling sky. He was pleased he'd come here first; pleased he'd not gone straight to Durham.

He kept a steady pace along the track, bare mud and natural stone now except where ruts and wash-outs had been filled with gravel. There was no need for a compass, no need for a map. There was time to marvel at the colour and curl of bracken fronds in a damp hollow, the bright furze at the top of a woody bulrush stalk, to notice red ladybirds and black beetles, to follow the flight of a butterfly, the run of a sleek weasel scurrying across the path. When he reached the rectangular pond he climbed the sheep-track to stand on the nibbled grass at its edge. He remembered this, remembered Phil running ahead, shouting that it was a sheep drowned, not Alice. He'd still had time then, had kept calling her, his blistered and bloodied feet slowing him, slowing him too much.

Alice...

Tightening his fingers to feel the grip of the ring, he brought up his fist to press the warm metal to his lips and shuddered free of the building memory. He'd tried. He'd tried here; he'd tried in York. Too late. He'd always been too late.

A fortifying breath helped subdue his rising anguish. He couldn't change the past but he could the future. He'd promised to change her future, had believed he'd prepared himself during his time spent in Durham. Now on the brink...

Another breath and he told himself he was being stupid. In York he'd nearly had Alice in his grasp and there he hadn't been prepared at all.

A fetid odour caught at his nostrils and he refocused on the cut bedrock, stepping back a pace to escape the stench. Discoloured stems of grass and rush drooped forlorn in the corners, dank water in the centre defying the sky's reflection. With so many people taking this route he couldn't believe it had not been filled in, at least fenced off.

Turning his back on it, he gazed over the rolling landscape and breathed in the wafting heather scents. Shades of purple and mauve spread on every side, shifting in the breeze as if a sea-swell. He could understand, now, why Phil had cut the path. Twisted knees would have been the least of it, and no road ambulance could get out here for accidents. They'd not even been able to get the Land Rover this close when they'd searched for Alice. Laying out the track must have cost a fortune.

Checking his watch, he slithered down the sheep-track to rejoin the path and stepped out with determination. It was good to marvel at the scenery, to fill his lungs with clean air – he'd been buried in a city too long – but he'd been dawdling.

A line of green caught and held his attention, growing taller, thicker, as the winding pathway progressed. At first he told himself it couldn't be, that the planted saplings had been mere knee-high shrubs and couldn't have grown so fast, not in soil this thin. By degrees the line shouldered into an arc, and his heartbeat increased as he closed on it.

The grass pasture came as a surprise, the ending of the heather too abrupt for it to be natural. A ewe was sunning itself, its lamb nestled into its side. It raised its black face to shake its curl of horns as if to ensure Nick would notice them, before making itself comfortable again. Bin liners sat wedged beneath a rock. He surveyed the grass afresh. Surely camping wasn't allowed.

The path finished with no obvious lead between the trees, so he chose the closest and pressed between the leafy branches. A tiny bell on a thin ribbon appeared at eye level. He lifted a finger to touch it, but drew back. Instead, he shouldered aside the supple limbs to step around it, his movements deliberate as he looked for more. A strip of pale orange cloth hung among leaves to his right; on a frond behind he saw a red cord tied tight about something wrapped in paper.

Realisation came in a slow sweep of ease to release tight muscles. The Pool wasn't used as a playground. It was too far from the road for a family carrying a picnic basket. People came here for a purpose, for a spiritual connection. His thumb stroked the ring and he hesitated as he felt a suck at his lifting boot. Peaty water was rising over the welt. He didn't remember this, either.

Pushing through the branch fronds, the matted ground gave gently beneath each footfall, and as the variegated leaves thinned he glimpsed water. The Pool was much bigger than he recalled. It had been only as wide as the path when he'd dragged Alice from the subsiding geyser; a mere pond when he'd set adrift flowers believing he was saying goodbye. It stood a true Pool now, hiding its depth across its wide diameter, its transparency showing grass beneath its edge, green leaf-tips stretching for the air. It was increasing its size, soaking and plumping the ground beyond its visible reach.

Nick glanced at his wet boots and took a side-step, watching his footprints fill with water, clear now, not peaty. He'd need to keep moving.

Further along the shoreline something stood in the shallows, a short log. And then he noticed the flowers half hidden beneath the lower branches of the trees. Pink and yellow and white wildflowers were clinging to a damp existence among their root boles. Were they the same flowers he'd seen on the drier verges leading to the farm? He should have taken more notice.

Water lifting from his heels spattered the back of his jeans as he walked, his gaze on the log, his heart giving a thud when he realised he was looking at a shrine.

The log had been chain-sawed, perhaps dragged across the moorland to create a seat for two, perhaps brought on a quad bike by Phil when the path had been created. Water surrounded it now, its splayed ends home to tiny sprouting ferns. Pressed upright into its crumbling bark, laid among its curling moss, were a mass of silver coins. Nick licked his lips as he looked at them, then dug into his jeans. He'd carried the fifty-pence piece so long, its draped Britannia figure sitting on a lion, one hand holding an olive branch, the other clutching a spear. Touching the coin to his lips, he placed it on the log and reached over with a cupped hand to collect a drink. His fingers broke through a set of ripples which began to lap the log and wash around his boots.

There didn't seem to be any sound, just the glint of sunlight reflecting yellow from the water, shining from her t-shirt as she strode towards him, the yellow t-shirt he'd slipped from her shoulders years before at Newtondale. His breath expelled in a burst as he straightened, his fingers opening to cascade the icy liquid down his forearm and on to his shirt to chill his chest.

Her auburn hair danced in waves about her shoulders as she walked across the surface of the water. She looked the same – pale eyebrows, high cheekbones, the translucent quality of her skin – yet she seemed different, more poised than he remembered. Then he saw it, and the breath he dragged into his lungs felt full of hot coals. The sunshine wasn't glinting from her t-shirt, it was glinting from the gold torc round her neck.

Alarmed, he scanned the churning water about her ankles. Silver mist heralded the shape-changing *thing* that had taken Alice. Would mist be visible in sunshine? Which one of them was striding towards him?

Chapter 9

She was closing on the bank, her steps creating waves against the silver-laden shrine. There was no mist around her feet. His gaze jumped back to her face, to her fixed stare. Could she see him? Was she being drawn to the shrine or to him?

Her pace slowed. She wasn't wet, he realised. She was walking in the water but her black trousers weren't wet.

She was faltering, her head angled to one side as she peered at him. He recognised the gesture; remembered it from York. She was seeing him through water. Of course she was. *Alice.* His excitement soared.

Her left hand rose tentatively towards him and he shot out his right, slotting his fingers through hers – so cold, but she was whole – and he clamped his palm to hers, feeling the give of her flesh against his own.

'Alice.' He was breathing so fast he could hardly speak her name.

Her face lifted, her head tipping back as her eyes slowly closed, her expression softening into a smile.

She could feel him.

Stepping over the shrine he wrapped his free arm around her, burying his face in her hair as he drew her body into his, murmuring her name again and again into her neck. She smelled wonderful... of meadow flowers, of forest fruits... his Alice. His chest heaved to feel her arm about his shoulders. He couldn't stop hugging her, couldn't stop saying her name.

And then he couldn't feel her hand, couldn't feel his own for the cold. Yet he could feel the torc pressing into his collarbone. He opened his eyes to stare at the twisted strands of metal. He could feel that.

They were parting. He wasn't sure why. He saw her hand pushing against his shoulder, her other disentangling her fingers from his. He was shivering, shivering so much he could hardly breathe. He couldn't feel his feet. They wouldn't move and he was going to lose his balance and fall into the water. But she was supporting him, guiding him, smiling, her pale eyes roving over his face.

Sunshine on his back embraced him as if a heated blanket, and he blinked as his shivering lessened and his limbs shot through with pins and needles as the feeling began to return. She wasn't holding him, he realised. Her hand was reaching in case he staggered, but she wasn't holding him and he felt bereft.

'Hello, Nick.'

He blinked, unsure of what he'd seen and heard.

'Can you hear me, Alice?'

An off-beat pause.

'Yes, Nick. It's wonderful that you're here.'

He hadn't been wrong. There was a mismatch between her lips moving and hearing her voice.

'I saw you,' he heard, 'glimpses of you in the half-light. I called you but couldn't make you hear, and then you'd gone.'

The mismatch was disconcerting. He focused on her eyes, on the sound of her voice.

'I knew you were real,' she was saying, 'that you were trying to find me. I kept looking for you.'

A wave of guilt rose around him that he refused to acknowledge.

'I'm here now, Alice. I did find you. I'm here. I've come to free you, to take you back with me.'

That mismatch in time again, that double beat. Her expression clouded. He needed to ease their sudden awkwardness but didn't know how.

'Let's get out of this water; it's freezing.'

He reached for her hand, but she was cold, so very cold. He needed gloves, he realised. It was York all over again. He should have brought gloves.

He tried to turn, to lead her to dry ground, but he couldn't feel his feet. His legs were numb. His boots were covered in water, its sun-glinting surface halfway up his shins, and he felt a mismatch of his own. The water was lapping the top of the shrine log, dislodging the offerings.

'I need to get out of here,' he murmured. He staggered, only the shrine-log keeping him upright.

Alice was looking at him oddly. She was lip-reading, he realised, or trying to. She wasn't hearing him at all. He wasn't sure what to make of that, was too cold to reason. He needed to get out of the water.

Concentrate. Concentrate!

His hands were shaking, but he clamped them around one thigh and pulled as he lifted his leg. He could feel nothing attached to it, despite being able to see his boot through the water, and there was a moment's panic until it broke the surface.

A heaved breath; a move. One leg; the other.

Alice was beside him, not touching, shepherding, willing him on. He could do this. The shore was close. He fell onto it, dragging himself the last half metre on his stomach, his fingers digging into sodden earth that became puddled hollows beneath his weight.

'That's it,' he heard. 'You'll soon dry off.'

He twisted onto his back. She was kneeling over his legs, wringing water from the bottom of his jeans. He couldn't even feel her touch.

'Alice...'

It took a moment, but she looked up, her hair swaying in an arc to clear her face. She grinned at him, her pale eyes so wide with joy that he had to mirror it, and he hauled himself up to sit and push the wet down his trouser legs. He glanced at hers. There wasn't even a mark.

Her lips moved, the words coming after. 'It's wonderful to see you.'

She settled on one hip close to his knee, her fingers reaching out to touch his legs, but not quite making contact. Her feet, her boots, incongruous hiking boots he saw, were in the water. He drew his gaze away, sensing his smile losing its strength.

I've come to free you. How hollow was that when he couldn't even touch her?

Cursing himself, he lifted his hand to stroke her hair. He could feel it beneath his fingertips – not chilled – and he combed its length with his fingers, watching its pale auburn waves change through russet tones in the sunlight. She turned to look at him, her hand reaching for his face. Her touch would be cold, he told himself, but he leaned into it, needing her caress, ice against his cheek.

'Nicholas...'

He caught her fingers in his own, closing his eyes as he pressed them to his lips. She felt so real. Was real. How could she be so cold?

'Nick...'

He didn't care. He needed to kiss her, needed to hold her.

Their lips touching was a burst of light followed by a streak of frost that tore down his throat. He opened his eyes, gasping, to find her hand flat against his chest.

'We need to be careful, Nick. There's no sun to warm you. You need to leave.'

'No, I want to stay. You must come with me.'

He frowned at the contradiction, unable to make sense of it, sense of anything. Branches were combing his hair. She was pushing him into the trees. Was he floating?

'Come with me, Alice.'

'I can't. You have to leave. They'll come with the dusk and I want you safe.'

'Dusk?'

He looked around him, at branches dark with subdued leaves. One caught at his cheek and he reached up to fend it away, seeing not his hand but just the shadowed shape of it. Her finger pressed cold against his lips.

'Wait for me, Nick, wait for me.'

His eyes widened as he watched her retreat through the trees, the torc glowing golden about her neck, firing the colours in her bouncing hair, radiating from her skin. As he opened his mouth to call her he fell backwards, his flailing arms doing nothing to break his fall.

He was lying in the pasture, the trees in front of him a dark mass against the diminishing glow of the sky.

'*Alice!*'

He rolled over, desperate to crawl back to the trees, and felt the torch in his shirt bounce against his chest. He was shivering as if with hyperthermia, or shock, and he scrambled upright on numbed feet. His jeans were soaked to the thigh, his boots full of water. The sky was turning cobalt with the creeping dusk, the trees beside him an impenetrable wall.

He threw his arms about his chest to increase his circulation and the torch bounced again. With fingers he didn't feel he owned, he pulled it free and shone the beam on his wristwatch. 5:10.

5.10? The second hand wasn't moving; his watch had stopped. He tottered back on unsteady legs, trying to make sense of what had happened. His phone. Unzipping his pocket he pulled it free to switch it on. It felt slick with damp, and for a moment he feared— But it was working, trawling through its wake-up ready to give him the time. It opened onto 16:18 and he stared at it, not understanding, then the figures began to roll, flicking forwards at speed, slowing, jumping. When they began to reverse he gasped, jabbing at the button to switch it off.

He stared at the dark wall of trees, at the dimming sky above, at the diminishing glow from the torch in his hand. They'd known. It was all he could think as he started across the grass. Rosemary and Phil had known.

Chapter 10

Ernald did not cross the cloister to take his place in the quire, but returned to the outer garth to hide among the lay-brethren working there. Except he felt exposed, his habit marking him against the shirt and hose of the labouring men.

He considered walking to the fields, or better the orchards, but that would mean leaving the confines of the walls, perhaps being seen by the almoner and laying himself open for more ridicule, more questions. A brother was at work or he was at prayer or contemplation. He was not, should not, be free to witness what he had. And Ernald felt sure, seeing the novice with his mouth stuffed with cloth, that the youth's incarceration had been timed so no one would see.

First the crying man and now this. It seemed to Ernald that he was seeing far more than he should.

Was that, in itself, meant for his eyes, his ears, alone? Had he been chosen to bear witness? He was a questor, not a true quire monk, not a steady-handed scribe whose lettering could imbue God's word with the faith to dazzle men's eyes. If he had been chosen by the Almighty or one of his angels—

—and the phrase *angel-woman* returned to haunt his thoughts.

He took shelter on the far side of the common house. No boys were playing skittles; they would be helping with the harvest. Ernald sat in the sunshine, his back against the warmed stone, weighing the wooden ball in his hand. He would wait for None to complete and the brothers to return to the cloister. Gregory spoke true. He needed labour to still his whirling mind.

A bell roused him. Ernald saw the ball a handspan from his open fingers, except it stood upright against a wall, not supported by the ground. The crick in his neck and shoulder warned of a mismatch in his perception and he righted himself to see the ball sitting on the ground beside him. His mouth felt gritty and dry. His eyes stung. As he clambered to his feet his head swam. Touching his pate, he found it tender, his cheeks hot against his hand. Sleeping when he should have been at labour and his sin marked for all to witness.

And witnessed it was as he walked to the cloister garth to wash.

You should wear a coif when you cut corn.
Forgot your brimmed hat, did you?

The sniggers and smiles were worse than the comments, but Ernald told himself that he had brought merriment and a lighter heart to their gathering before the meal, and each would mark him well and so not follow his path.

From his table on the dais, Sub-Prior Maugre did not smile but glared, his lips pressed thin, as the reading continued and the bread and wortes pottage was allotted. Ernald kept his gaze to the table, but the smell of the cabbage made his stomach heave. He was glad of the bread to dip into its liquor and chewed well until he could swallow. The small ale did little to ease the throbbing of his head.

When Graces were intoned the second time and the brothers began to leave the frater house for their dusk walk in the cloister, Ernald was called to stand below the dais, his head bowed.

'With heavy heart I confess—'

'Confession is for the Chapter House on the morrow,' Maugre retorted. 'I had thought in you, Brother Questor, I had a man of trust to send on the Lord's mission out in the world. Was my thinking misguided?'

'No, sub-prior.'

Ernald stood in the silence that followed, watching the sub-prior's chest heave with irritation, but when the man spoke again his tone was easier.

'Go to the fermery for a balm and a clear head, Brother

Ernald. In the days to come you will require it.'

The infermarer tutted when Ernald presented himself at its door.

'Not come to replenish rushes this time,' he noted, and called for a bowl to be brought in case Ernald's queasy stomach caused its need.

Ernald was told to remove his cowl and lie on a pallet, though it did not help his spinning head. A lay-brother brought a cloth and cooling water and left him to apply both to all parts above his neck. The bell for Vespers rang, and Ernald laid still as the infermarer intoned the prayers and those who could gave answer.

When the bell rang for Compline the infermarer gave the blessing and, with candle close, came to inspect Ernald's head.

'There is no blistering, brother, give praise for that.'

One of the lay-brethren applied an unguent and supplied a clean coif. When it was done Ernald was urged to stand, and found he could without the chamber spinning. Only the pounding in his head remained. He was given a draught and ordered to his booth in the dorter.

'Tell the circa from me, no Matins or Lauds. If you lose either your bowels or your stomach overnight you are to return here with the dawn bell. If not, return after the reading of the Chapter.'

Ernald thanked the infermarer and the lay-brother for their assistance, and promised to show himself for work in the pestlry on the morrow. He left as the singing from the quire finished, cresset flames lighting the short distance to the dorter.

At first the circa was affronted by the infermarer's request, but as the monks filed in from the quire he acceded and Ernald was allowed to shed his habit and lie on his pallet. He expected his thoughts to writhe as they had every night since his return, but he knew nothing until the circa roused the House on the bell for daybreak.

His stomach felt settled and his legs steady, but the singing of Prime, and moreover the tapping and banging from the masons' yard, showed that his head remained delicate. He broke bread and felt stronger in body for it, and filed into the Chapter House to hear from the teachings of Saint Benedict and to join prayers for the souls of the convent passed into Heaven. As all settled for the reading of notices, Ernald took strengthening breaths ready for Confession that would follow.

'A messenger brings news of our Lord Bishop and the Prior,' Sub-Prior Maugre announced. 'They are within two days' ride and will inspect and bless the harvest in the fields as they near. We will pray that the rivers remain low for their safe crossing, and that the good Lord stays the rains until the blessed fields are cleared.'

There was a murmured response and the sub-prior led the prayer.

'Is there one who stands for Confession before the convent?'

There were three. A brother had shouted at two of the master mason's labourers kicking a ball close to the breached apse protecting Saint Cuthbert's shrine. He was given to read from the life of Saint Benedict for three days. The sub-prior would speak to the master mason about his labourers. A novice had taken a half-loaf destined for the Almonry. For his gluttony he was given to have no bread, to recite the psalms twice daily at the gate, and to wash the feet of the poor who came for alms, all for three days.

As the chastised novice stepped back, Ernald stepped forward. His mind was full of images, of the crying man speaking of *angel-woman*, of the struggling novice unable to plead for God's grace. If it had been God's will that he witness these, how could he confess them? Yet, if he were wrong...

The sub-prior looked down at him, so he started with his least perplexing admission.

'I slept in the fullness of the sun when I should have celebrated the service of None, and I—'

'So it shows, Brother Ernald, so it shows.'

Ernald risked raising his gaze, surprised to hear humour held in the sub-prior's voice, especially after the angry looks he had received the evening before.

'Remove your coif, Brother Ernald.'

He obeyed, the unguent and the skin beneath sticking to the linen in parts and lifting his tonsure in a gluey mass. Pressure between his shoulders reflected smirks at his back. The sub-prior was openly smiling.

'It seems our Gracious Lord did not wait for your Confession to mark you with Penance, Brother Ernald, and in so doing used you as a tool to teach us all. I am informed by the infermarer you also offered penance direct to the fermery.'

'To help restore medicaments ill-used on this sinner.'

'Are you practiced in this field, questor?'

'I will take instruction.'

'Perhaps this may prove the first step to a new calling.'

Ernald tensed. He raised his gaze a little higher. Was Sub-Prior Maugre speaking of the spring-water that had healed the crying man?

'I have a labour for you, too, and you will need boots to protect your feet, Brother Ernald, not just a hat to protect your head. You will await my charge.'

He was being dismissed, yet he had not... Ernald bowed and backed from the chair, making much of replacing his coif so as to hide his unease. Perhaps it was God's will that he should not speak of what he'd seen. Not now, at least.

The day's tasks were allotted, and the brothers filed out into the cloister. Ernald waited on the sub-prior as the man spoke with the cantor and the sacristan below the chair. When they turned to leave, Maugre glanced at Ernald and walked towards the wall ledge to rest. Ernald joined him and the sub-prior indicated that he could rest, too. Considering he was in a state of disgrace, Ernald felt perplexed by this show of accommodation, but did as he was bid, determined to both listen to the sub-prior's words and watch for their intended meaning.

'I am told you have not been at peace these last days, Brother Ernald, that you prowl the cloister in search of spiritual succour.'

Brother Gregory had spoken of him. Even though he did not feel it, Ernald knew he had to be bold.

'I think I have found it.'

'In letting the sun broil your face and addle your brains?'

'Indirectly. In the healing of the fermery.'

'Scraping up soiled rushes and sitting with a learned brother whose wits are wandering?'

Ernald moistened his lips. Was everyone speaking of him to the sub-prior?

'I helped the almoner, too.'

'I heard.'

Ernald hesitated. Should he stop now, or should he speak?

'Hunger at a time of harvest is a warning.' Ernald watched the sub-prior incline his head in agreement. 'If we seek out the spring that cured the serf, we could return a cask of its waters—'

'The Blessed Mary the Virgin and Saint Cuthbert the Bishop guard the sanctity of our House at Durham. You and I, we look to secure the waters – *if* they can cure – for the House. If the waters can cure, it will become a dependency of this House, *not* a usurper. Your charge, Brother Ernald, is to find the water, mark its route so it can be found again, and report to me alone.'

Ernald blinked.

'I am to become a *map-scribe?*'

'Do you not travel the hollow-ways, the packhorse tracks, on your questing with Saint Cuthbert's relics?'

'Yes, but—'

'There is no *but*, questor. What can be achieved close to the House can be achieved at a distance.'

'There was mention of Lastingham.'

'If I recall, questor, it was the blessed saints of Lastingham who were mentioned. And you speak to no one of that meeting.'

There was a pause, and Ernald lowered his gaze in supplication.

'Have you spoken of it?'

'No, sub-prior.'

Again a pause.

'If you are fearing for the sanctity of the quest because it may take you into the wildwoods, be at peace. You will not be travelling alone.'

It would not be the same. In his role as questor Ernald had always known where he was going, that he would be on a path well-trodden, that there would be a welcome at its end. His usual companions were villein's teeming children and their dogs, the grown sons of cottars who played flutes and vied to catch the eye of maids who led his pack animal to their village bounds. He feared his companions this time were to be the silent gaolers in the confinement chamber, their cudgel barely hidden beneath a cloak.

'Will I be escorting the minor relics of Saint Cuthbert?'

There was no pause this time; there was a yawning silence.

'You are not venturing out to the warmth of manor halls, Brother Ernald.'

In truth that had not been in Ernald's thoughts, and in his truth he dared to raise his gaze to meet that of the sub-prior.

'That they may protect the travellers,' he said. He did not lower his gaze. It was Maugre who sat back to consider him.

'I will think on it.' He sat forward again, re-grasping his control.

'The Prior and the Bishop return for the Feast of the Nativity of the Blessed Mary so as to take their places in the processional. On the morrow after the market closes you will take your leave on my call and travel south with returning pilgrims, hence the need, Brother Ernald, for *boots*.'

The sub-prior tapped him playfully on the chest with his knuckles. 'Go speak to the chamberlain. There are few enough days for the making of boots.'

Ernald walked out into the bright light of the cloister and stood a moment trying to ease the tension from his shoulders. It could not be done. The weight he was carrying was increasing. He had boots, and a soft linen undershirt, both hidden beyond the precinct wall and neither confessed. Was that why he was being tested?

Not only had he been chosen by the Lord to bear witness, but by Brother Maugre to keep secrets from the convent, both a sin and against the teachings of Saint Benedict.

He would go to the chamberlain, because doubtless the chamberlain would speak to the sub-prior. But first he would return to the fermery, to have his pate inspected and to ask for another draught against the hammering in his head. He had offered Penance to the infermarer. If he could keep no other, he would keep that vow.

Chapter 11

Winding the torch, Nick set off at a stumbling jog, counting on the exertion to warm him.

The darkness rolled in as if a sentient being. One moment he could see shadowy heather reaching away either side, the next there was nothing beyond the fuzzy beam. He had to keep his gaze on its circle of light for fear of turning an ankle on the path that now seemed scattered with loose stones and riven by channels.

He had no idea where he was, how long he'd been jogging. His wristwatch insisted it was just gone five, but that was ridiculous. He'd had to stop twice for a stitch gnawing at his ribs, his lungs feeling as if on fire. How out of condition was he? The path turned as if a switchback, left and right and up and down, and the torch wouldn't keep its charge, needing to be re-wound every few minutes, slowing him further.

When the slapping white thing erupted in the beam, eyes the size of plates, he cried out as sharply as the owl, throwing himself back in his shock. Only when it left on silent wing-beats, and he re-wound the torch to continue, did he fret about his direction. Had he spun round in his fright? Was he returning to the farm or to the Pool? He needed to think this through and he hadn't the energy to think at all, only to put one foot in front of the other.

He stepped one way, searching the ground for his boot-prints, then behind him to do the same. There were lots of boot-prints as firm as concrete in the dried mud, but nothing that seemed new or his size in the dust.

A sound carried on the still air, a pheasant's call, a grouse perhaps. Nick stood on the track, the torch by his thigh, trying to calm himself. He stared at the sky, trying to think. Which way was north? A gauze of cloud muted the starshine but gave him sight of a million pinpricks of light. And no moon. Alice had come to him without the pull of the moon. No, that wasn't right, either. She was reliant on the pull of the moon, on the moon's pull on the water. At least she had been at York.

The pheasant's call again, off to his left, an odd call for a pheasant. Then he saw the light. Lower than the star-line, though hardly brighter, it was moving, making a cross, making a circle. Relief burst from him, and he matched the movements, rewinding the torch to ensure a brighter beam, covering it three times as a signal. His signal was returned. Phil was on the ridge.

Nick crawled the last few metres of the incline, hearing Phil's encouragement *...just in time for dinner...* and the man's hand was beneath his armpit helping him along. *Got the beasts bedded down and thought I'd check...* They were climbing the stile *...Rosemary has a pork casserole on the go...* crunching over gravel *...be good to get some food down you...* pushing open the front door.

Warmth engulfed him.

'We're back! We're back!' Nick winced at Phil's bellow in his ear.

As they entered the patch of light falling through the open kitchen door, Phil grasped his arm.

'Whoa, there... Sit on the stairs and take them boots off. Rosemary don't like mud on her carpet. Mmm... Better add them jeans and socks. Don't worry, we'll sort them. You go upstairs and wash. Straight down, mind. Dinner's about to go on the table.'

Nick thought he'd said *thank you* as he'd pulled himself up by the banister but wasn't sure if he had, or if Phil had heard. The man had kept up his bright chatter all the way from the ridge, and now it had stopped Nick felt as if he were floating again. Had he floated through the trees? No, that was nonsense.

The reflection which met him over the basin was dishevelled and pale, but he made himself believe it was due to the low lumens of the light bulb. The hot water was wonderfully soothing yet he dared not surrender to it. He'd hindered Phil enough. Combing wet fingers through his hair, he unzipped his sports bag to rummage for spare trousers and a clean jumper. His shivering had long stopped though he still felt chilled.

The door to the kitchen stood ajar. He rapped his knuckles against its wood and pushed it open to step into its moist warmth.

'Sorry to put you to so much trouble,' he began. His boots were standing on the Aga, drying. Rosemary was bringing a tureen of steaming vegetables to the table. The smells coming off the food were mouth-watering and he knew he'd devour everything put before him.

'Nonsense,' Phil said, his grin too wide. 'Good timing. Take a seat, lad, take a seat.'

Nick reached to pull out a chair. 'I didn't think it would get dark so early up here.' He glanced at the clock on the dresser, checked his wristwatch.

'Stopped, has it?' Rosemary asked. He looked at her. 'Thought it might.'

The hot casserole dish followed the vegetables and she pulled out her own chair beside his.

'Rosemary, you let the lad eat. Bet you've hardly had a bite all day, have you? Too far, driving all the way from Portsmouth.'

'Southampton.' He drew breath and sat back; he'd not rung his mother. He looked for his dirty jeans, but saw only his phone and some coins sitting on the worktop.

'Jeans are in the wash,' Rosemary said, 'but they'll be aired by the morning. Here, have some potatoes. There's plenty.'

'And bed soon after,' cautioned Phil. 'We'll have you up early for travelling to Durham, no worry about that. Farmers are always up early.'

There was no other conversation and he was too tired to grasp at the questions he needed to ask. The food was good and he thanked them, but he could see that they didn't want him to linger. He didn't want to linger, either. It had come to him during the meal. *Wait for me*, she'd said.

After the apple pie and strong tea, he collected his phone, thanked them again, and went up to his room. He sent his mother a text saying he'd ring her tomorrow, and he lay on the bed to let his meal digest. And to wait for Alice.

Wait for me, she'd said, and he knew what that meant, even though he couldn't keep his eyes open.

When she came she nuzzled at his ear to wake him, breathing his name, her touch warm, so very warm, her body pliant, her need of him as strong as his need of her.

He woke in the night, gratified to find her snuggled against his chest, an arm and leg snaked over him. She was warm. She was *warm* and she was *with* him. He wanted to wake her to share that joy, to talk as they used to talk, touching and smiling and... but that was so long ago, and part of him feared it was more his fixed dreaming than remembered reality. Yet she was here, and she was whole and she was warm. Perhaps it was enough, enough to hold her and kiss her and tell her that he loved her, even as she murmured in her sleep.

Chapter 12

The sharp knocking jolted him awake. A strip of yellow light round the opening door bore into the gloom and automatically he flung out an arm to protect Alice. His hand found only a pillow and he jolted again.

'You awake, Nicholas?'

Rosemary's voice; she wasn't coming in. He answered in a croak. The smell of grilling bacon wafted round his bed.

'Good. No rush. Phil's minding the animals. You've time for a shower and shave. Breakfast when you're ready.' The door closed leaving a faint corona around its edges.

He looked at the bed, at the flat duvet beside him. There was a devastating moment when he thought their night together had been another figment of his need, but as he reached for the bedside lamp his body told him Alice had been real. The sheet, too, was spread with soiled tissues, and he pulled the duvet over his head to immerse in her lingering flower scents before they faded beneath the pervading smell of bacon.

Hot water flowing over his head and shoulders fired his brain. How had she come into the house, into his room? How had she left? Why didn't she tell him she was leaving? Why hadn't he woken her when he'd had the chance? They could have talked the night away.

He switched off the shower to lean his forehead against the tiles. He'd wanted only to make love to her. Nothing else had mattered.

Heaving a sigh, he reached for the towel. Alice was cold in the Pool and warm in his bed. How could that be?

He had to get her out of the Pool. Sod Durham. Sod the talk. He was going back to the Pool.

No sooner did he step into the kitchen than he was handed a pair of overalls.

'Glad you're here,' Phil said. 'That blasted ram would give me a right run-around, but with two of us we can get it into the trailer.'

They started down the yard. Phil seemed intent on keeping up the one-sided conversation he'd embraced the night before.

'Exchanging it with a pal's across the moor. Y'know, improve the herds.'

There'd been no mention, Nick realised, of the state he'd been found in. Rosemary had left a mug of tea beside his folded jeans and dried boots and was busy in the utility area, giving them no opportunity to speak. He'd been grateful at the time. Now he thought perhaps it was intentional.

'Turn your back on 'im an' 'e'll 'av yer.'

Phil's speech was growing broader, a sure sign of his anxiety. Nick didn't believe it had anything to do with a ram.

He changed his mind on seeing it. The animal was huge; its curl of horns both spectacular and deadly. It eyed them through horizontally slit irises, and snorted as if ready to do battle.

'Got to be prepared. Folks think they're placid. Not when tuppin's due, they're not. Take these.' Phil passed him gloves stiff with dirt.

Pushing his fingers into the course material, Nick mused on his need for gloves at the Pool. And a coat. And waders. And what else? Knowledge. He thought he'd filtered every facet from the archives at Durham University, but he hadn't. Not one had mentioned bone-piercing cold.

Phil passed a heavy board into his hands. 'When I open the gate keep that 'tween you an' 'im. Can kill a man, it can. Be warned.'

The trailer back was dropped, its pen-sides unfolded. Phil gave the nod and Nick made ready with the board. The ram held its ground, refusing to move even when Phil encouraged it with stones thrown at the metal sheet behind it.

They went in. A feint, a turn, a squeeze, the curl of horns

thudding against the board with unbelievable force... For Nick it brought back memories of playing rugby, except his shoulder muscles were screaming with the weight of lifting the board. And then the ram jumped across the ramp. As its hooves skittered on the metal flooring of the trailer trying to turn for a charge, Phil threw across one of the pen-sides trapping it inside. Even though they were both breathing hard, they grinned at the ram and at each other.

'A wash an' breakfast, eh?'

Breakfast was enormous – sausage and bacon and black pudding and eggs – enough to keep him going until evening.

'The talk you're doing in Durham today,' Rosemary said, 'it's good that your friends are so loyal, and you to them.'

He looked across at her, his fork halfway to his mouth.

She smiled at him. '...considering your poor mother on her own in Southampton.'

He'd hardly given his mother a thought. 'It's been three months,' he reminded her.

'There's no statute on grief,' she returned. 'I'm sure you found that, yourself, under the circumstances.'

Alice isn't dead. He clamped the words behind his teeth leaving the gap in their conversation to lengthen. It was Rosemary who became engrossed in her meal.

'Now, let the lad eat. You'll be going via Castleton and Stokesley, right? I can guide you across the moors the farm way, much quicker. No trouble. On my way with the ram, ain't I?'

Nick stared at him. Unlike his wife, Phil didn't flinch.

'We have visitors booked this weekend,' Rosemary added, 'in case you were thinking of returning this way. I wouldn't want you to be disappointed.'

They wanted rid of him. What had they heard last night? Had they seen Alice?

'That's okay,' he heard himself say.

They wanted rid of him. He couldn't leave. He needed to return to the Pool, to Alice. They knew something was odd down there.

Placing his cutlery across his plate, he made a point of checking his watch against the clock. 'It's working now. You knew it would stop.'

Rosemary shrugged. 'A lot of walkers report it. They usually work fine once they're re-set. It's probably something to do with the old mine workings; magnetism below ground or something.'

Nick didn't respond.

They ushered him to his car, ostensibly to wave him off.

He couldn't leave. He needed to return to the Pool, to Alice. He needed gloves, something to protect him from the cold. Her cold. She hadn't been cold in York; she'd been wet in York. It had been the water that had been cold.

Unlocking the car, he slung his bag onto the rear seat so they wouldn't see their damaged sign he'd secreted in the boot. They shook his hand, wished him well with his talk, and then Phil brought up the Land Rover and its trailer and they made their way in convoy down the gravel drive, Rosemary bringing up the rear on foot. He could see her in the mirror.

He was perspiring now, his heart thudding in his chest.

He couldn't leave.

At the road he gazed through the windscreen at the open stile, at the path's pinned route flapping gently in a breeze he couldn't feel. He wanted to be down there, needed to be down there, and he gripped the steering wheel tight feeling his ring bite into his finger.

Wait for me, Alice. Wait for me.

Against his need, he turned the car onto the tarmac.

Chapter 13

It seemed to Ernald that the day of the Feast of the Nativity of the Blessed Mary came upon the House in a tumult. Being out in the world with Saint Cuthbert's lesser relics to urge delivery of the harvest tithes, it had been a goodly number of years since he had witnessed the rite and the much organisation and rehearsal it necessitated.

Ernald had been detailed to carry a thurible and precede the banner and relics of Saint Bede in the processional. It was not a duty he had been pledged on previous occasions, and the master of Saint Bede's relics had imprinted on his soul dire warnings if he allowed the coals to fade by not swinging strongly enough, or he swung with such force that the coals and incense were consumed before the processional's return to the priory. Each contingent – the quire brothers, the dressed statue and banners of the Blessed Mary, Saint Cuthbert's banner and reliquary box, Saint Bede's banner and reliquary box – were rehearsed in separate parts of the grounds, as were the lay-brethren who were to make up the outer honour guard. All such stopped upon the return of the Bishop and the Prior.

The following morning, after the reading in the Chapter House, Sub-Prior Maugre announced a day of contemplation and prayer in readiness for the solemn festivities.

'I would ask you all to think kindly upon the weather so our Lord may continue his boon for the gathering of the harvest and tomorrow's blessed procession.'

'...and the fayre...'

Ernald dropped his head to hide the rush of blood to his cheeks. If he'd heard then he was sure—

'Yes,' said Maugre in a louder voice, 'and for the fayre

following, held in the blessed light and for the greater glory of Our Lady Protector. Be also pleased to hear that the master mason has been given leave of his building work for the duration so our prayers may be lighter, may lift easier, and be heard more readily without the accompanying song of hammers.'

No brother so much as shuffled his feet. The meeting continued.

Upon closure of proceedings, Ernald was signalled to stay. He hoped he wasn't to be questioned on who had spoken, but when he approached the chair he found the sub-prior more affable than his earlier countenance foretold.

'Do you have your boots, Brother Ernald?' he was asked with a wry smile.

Ernald confirmed that he had. 'The chamberlain's man made good work. They will last many a day's walk.'

'They may need to, Brother Ernald. You have writing materials enough? I want a full report, a precise route returning to me.'

Ernald nodded. 'The master of the scriptorium allowed examination of journals and maps from the library.'

'In my experience maps through wildwoods are easy to misinterpret and easier for prying eyes to steal. A daily journal in the Holy tongue will prove more beneficial.'

Deferring, Ernald allowed himself a glow of relief. Journals and quantities he was used to providing.

'At the end of the fayre's day, after the convent gathers for supper, you will walk the cloister until the bell for Vespers. Instead of attending you will collect your satchel and leave by the southern gate where you will be met. Is that understood?'

Again Ernald nodded. The southern gate meant crossing the river by boat, by boat beneath the cover of dusk. As he feared, no one was to see him leave.

'You asked for the protection of Saint Cuthbert for those who travel with you.'

The sub-prior's open hand was offering a blue-dyed pouch.

Ernald took it and slipped free a silver reliquary cross. He gazed upon it, peering through the sliver of transparent crystal mounted at its heart, and felt his emotions welling.

'It holds hairs cut from the head of the Blessed Saint tied with a thread from his vestment. It is not large; it is not gold to draw the attention of avaricious eyes. Guard it well, brother, and may Saint Cuthbert guard you and those who travel with you.'

Ernald spent most of the day on his knees in prayer close to the Blessed Saint, the reliquary cross pressed between his palms. The church was thronged with pilgrims come for the feast fayre, each in turn being taken to kneel beneath the Blessed Shrine. Ernald felt his own entreaties strengthening theirs. Most appeals were for the cleansing or easing of ailments, and Ernald set aside his forebodings at his given quest and concentrated on the advantages for these people should the waters he sought prove as health-giving as the crying man's testament.

That night he could hardly sleep. He was determined to be as Daniel, fearless in the grace bestowed upon him.

The morrow dawned sunlit, and the convent pressed into the quire for the reading of Saint Benedict's chapter and to be blessed by the Bishop dressed in the sacred majesty of his embroidered robes. The banners and relics were carried to the high altar, and finally the Blessed Mary was brought in procession from Her chapel into the quire to bow before the eyes of God and Her Holy Son. Throughout all, lilting prayers from the cantor's quire monks gave gratitude for, and servitude to, the Holy Day.

By degrees the rites within the church were completed and in the nave the procession gathered in true form. At the toll of the bell to alert the town, it began to unwind, first from the church, and then from the precincts of the Bishop's castle, and out into the bailey. Ernald wore the given reliquary cross against his skin, feeling its heart beat in time with his own as he slow-stepped through the shadowed arch of the gate and out into the world.

The steep cobbled street was thronged with townspeople and visitors who offered murmured devotions as the procession passed. People were leaning out of upper-floor windows, Ernald noticed, or sitting precariously on the low thatch, their feet resting on painted saddles and other leather goods hoisted high to display the industry of the dwelling and the street. So many people were standing in doorways and in front of the shuttered shops Ernald didn't think he'd seen the like before: children by their mothers, young boys holding the hands of their fathers, who in turn proudly held aloft the banners of their guild-houses. With the chants of the leading quire monks drifting back up the hill to his ears, Ernald swung his thurible before the canopy and relics of Saint Bede, and, following those of Saint Cuthbert, began the slow descent into the town.

In the market place the canopied statue of the Blessed Mary and retinue of Saints' relics processed a winding route between the brightly painted stalls, their covers bulging with wares packed tightly behind, each stall carrying the ticket asserting payment of its fee to the House.

There was a stoppage in the line while the Bishop took obeisance from the priests of the Church of Saint Nicholas On The Wall. Beyond the shoulders of the carrying monks, Ernald glimpsed the canopy of the Blessed Mary being folded as Her statue was carried inside. The relics of Saint Cuthbert followed, and then of Saint Bede. Ernald remained without the small church, close to the Claypath Gate, gently swinging his thurible as he and other brothers created an honour line beyond the door.

A murmur began to rise from the crowd as people pressed closer between the stalls. Ernald gazed at them – the townsfolk, the visiting merchants and stallholders, those from the manors come within the walls to witness the spectacle and make what purchases they could afford – all eager to gain their first view of the Blessed Mary as Her statue emerged from the shadowed doorway. The lay-brethren moved to create a cordon to keep the people at bay, yet it was having little effect.

The host began to sway on the sloping ground, their murmurs resolving into a low chant that held intonations never heard within the House. It seemed unnatural, so many people so close together. Ernald laid his hand on the cross hidden beneath his habit and sent up prayers to calm their fervour. He gazed into the face of each in the front rank, impressing upon them the peace of Saint Cuthbert – a woman with hair straggling free from her head-cloth, a youth wearing a dirty coif, a thick-set man with a full—

Ernald focused on his full beard, the shape of his face. The man grinned at him. Dark curly hair and broad at the shoulder... it was the gaoler from the confinement chamber. The man tipped his head in a nod, his eyes unblinking as he continued to grin at Ernald over the shoulder of a lay-brother. Ernald caught his breath, uncertain what the gesture meant. And then the man's gaze averted, his expression softening, and the entire host gasped and swayed back a pace.

Ernald turned to the church door to see the Bishop stepping into the sunshine. Behind came the Blessed Mary, the blue of Her cloak glittering where the sun shone on its jewels. As Her statue was brought clear of the low door and Her litter lifted to shoulder height, Her halo of gold sparkled, yellow light radiating strongly enough to block all else from view. Ernald felt his mouth drop open. Around him people were falling to their knees or giving thanks where they stood. And then they were being pushed back by the lay-brethren to make room for the Blessed Mary and the relics of the Saints, and when Ernald looked back the canopy was once again protecting the Holy Mother and Her halo no longer dazzled.

As the Bishop stepped forward to offer succour in his words and to give blessings to the town and its people, Ernald felt himself nudged into position by the brother on his right. He took a tremulous breath. Tears were coursing down his cheeks, glazing his sight. He had no care. Questioning sinner, blind as he was, he knew he had just borne witness to the crying man's *angel-woman*.

Chapter 14

The cramping ache in Nick's chest eased the further he followed Phil's Land Rover and its trailer. Anxiety, he told himself, or anger. He wanted to be with Alice, yet he wasn't dressed for the cold at the Pool. He was too reliant on Phil and Rosemary and they didn't want reminding, did they? He was a link to a death on their farm. Another death. There'd been others before Alice. They'd let that slip during the search for her six years ago.

Six years... *I glimpsed you, and then you'd gone.*

He'd not been fast enough in York, but he knew Alice wasn't meaning York. The glimpses she'd seen had been through his dreams, when he hadn't been looking for her at all.

The flashing hazards on the trailer sharpened Nick's attention, but he'd no idea what it meant. Their route had been over miles and miles of switchback single-track road, more gravel than tarmac, the line of grass at its centre beating the underside of the car. He hadn't a clue where they were and neither had the sat nav so he'd long since turned it off.

The trailer indicated left and started slowing. Phil's arm emerged from the Land Rover waving him on, giving him a thumbs-up, and then the vehicle and its trailer turned onto a stony track. Nick just had time to wave back before Phil was lost to a cloud of dust, leaving him staring through the windscreen at purple moorland without a tree in sight. Where was he?

At the next ridge a valley opened below him, showing the green of trees and fields, a two-lane road and buildings. With a sense of relief, he swept down into civilisation with its hedges and fences and give-way markings, and signs to Castleton and Whitby. He turned west and reconnected the sat nav. An hour to Durham. He could be back with Alice tomorrow. Maybe even tonight.

By the time the sat nav was talking him through Stokesley the town was opening for business. He crossed the river expecting the voice to lead him across country to regain the A1M, but it insisted he take the A19. Stretches were so straight it had to be an old Roman route. He wasn't complaining. There was less traffic and it was still fast for being a dual carriageway. With mild surprise he realised that his restless thoughts of Alice had become a warmth, a contentment in his mind. He wasn't sure when the transition had occurred. He'd make it up to her, would free her from the Pool.

'I promise,' he murmured, knowing he'd promised before. This time he would. Durham would be the place to get what he needed, his talk no more than a distraction.

With an eye on the dashboard clock he didn't hang about. He'd be cutting it fine.

The traffic slowed as Nick neared the city, the great square towers of Durham Cathedral high on its promontory as much a beacon as the White Horse had been on its cliff. He knew the Market Place venue stood almost in its shadow, and he also knew how congested it would be on a Saturday morning. The problem would be getting the car close enough.

During one of the stop-starts outside St Bede's College he pulled out his mobile, surreptitiously keeping it below the window-line as he dropped Simon a text.

On Gilesgate. Aiming for Claypath. Need help unloading NOW!

In truth, he'd need a miracle to find a parking spot there, but if he could be met the road was wide enough to double park for as long as it took to leave the boxes with Simon. He'd leave the car by the river and dash up the steps.

There was no returned text. Maybe the system was overloaded. Maybe Simon's response was queuing. Nick kept checking his phone. All too soon he was on Claypath.

The pavements were thronged with shoppers, and despite the crawl it was difficult to scan both sides looking for Simon. The steeple of St Nicholas' Church was looming in his windscreen, the cluster of pale stone buildings making up the modern Walkergate complex almost upon him. Simon was a prat. Was he never going to answer his fucking phone?

No sooner had Nick vented than his own phone rang. He grabbed it from the passenger seat, hoping there were no police officers close enough to notice.

'Yo! Where are you?'

Nick blinked. Not Simon; a woman's voice.

'Opposite the entrance to Millennium Square.'

'What car are you driving?'

Nick tossed the phone on the seat and slapped on the hazards, pulling in close to a red Vauxhall parked at the kerb. The van behind him hooted in annoyance, but that was expected. He made conciliatory gestures as he climbed out, the van's driver making not such conciliatory gestures as it pulled round him.

'You Nick?'

He turned to the pavement. A black-haired Goth, a mobile pressed against a brilliant blue flash in her hair, waved her smartphone at him as she stepped behind the parked car. He nodded, taking in her orange t-shirt and green camo-pants. Not a Goth, then, despite the kohl-rimmed eyes and heavy lipstick.

A set of bright purple fingernails snaked out on the end of an anorexic arm. 'Izara,' she said. 'Simon sent me to packhorse.'

He took the offered hand which felt too delicate to shake. Apart from the tiny backpack hunched high on her shoulders, Nick wondered what the small figure could possibly carry.

'Where is he?'

'At the hall organising the demo. The uniforms patrol on a Saturday. We'd better get you moved.'

Demo? He unlocked the boot, flinging open its lid. She was in there immediately, pulling out the broken stakes and the sign to the Pool.

'That's staying in the car.'

'Not an illustration for your talk?' She was holding it at arm's length to take in its information.

Nick glared at her. 'No. It's the boxes I'll need.' He drew one out and took its weight, swinging round to find her staring at him, a sardonic rise of her pencilled eyebrows and a weakly sloping shoulder saying more than words. He hadn't time for this.

'Guard the box while I park the car.'

Pushing by her, he bumped through the pedestrians to place it on the pavement in front of a shop's window, returning to take the plaque from her hands and slide it on top of the remaining box. If he needed more books... but that was hardly likely. Slamming down the boot, he made for the driver's door.

'Won't be long.'

'Best of luck!' he heard her call, but there wasn't much enthusiasm in her tone.

Killing the hazards, he nosed into the stream of traffic until a vehicle flashed him a right-of-way. Almost immediately he was on the bridge over the arterial road, the roar of the traffic below bellowing up as if from a cauldron. He needed to be down the ramp by the Prince Bishops' Shopping Centre, but he also wanted to see what was going on in Market Place half-hidden by the church. People on the zebra crossing slowed him enough to gain a view. In front of the striped canvas of market stalls was a milling throng carrying placards, others wearing hi-viz vests.

The pedestrians parted and he started down the ramp. From the queue waiting at the entrance to the centre's indoor car park he gauged there was no chance of gaining a space and so carried on to filter onto the main road. It was a short hop to the Walkergate ramp and its twisting descent to the riverside.

The regeneration project had certainly come on since he'd left the city. The last of the old concrete buildings had been demolished and glass and steel were rising in their place. It seemed lighter, more airy, despite the noise of jack-hammers, and he feared the trees had been felled until their mature branches, still full of dark green leaves, came into view.

There were plenty of car spaces available thanks to the cost of parking there, but he didn't begrudge it this side of the river. Sticking the ticket from the machine inside his windscreen, he crammed his sports bag under the plaque in the boot and sprinted back along the road.

He and Simon had used to train by running up the steps to the bars opposite the theatre. At least that's what they'd called it, but that was nigh on two years ago and he could feel his lungs burning and his chest cramping before he was halfway up. By the time he'd gained the square he knew he'd not be able to utter a word, never mind carry a box of books.

Leaning on a wall opposite the weird statue, he sent his mother a text to say he'd arrived okay and was about to give his talk. Not exactly the truth, but it would give him some leeway before he rang her. In front of him the green-tinged monks shouldering a coffin stared beyond his shoulder from within their shadowed cowls. He'd nearly shit himself when Simon had jumped out from behind it one dusk; he'd never got him back for that. The statue still unsettled him, even in the bright sunlight. It seemed to move when he gazed at it; the monks carrying their dead saint juddering forwards, millimetre by millimetre, on their way to the promontory where their church would be built.

He focused, instead, on the shoppers, on the pale building stone on every side reflecting sunlight bright enough to make him squint. It was all such a cacophony of glass and people and traffic noise.

Pushing himself from the wall, he walked to the Claypath entrance. There was no sign of the would-be Goth across the road. His shoulders slumped. *Wonderful.*

Jogging round slowing vehicles, he slipped between the parked cars to find her against the shop's window on her haunches, engrossed in his book. The box beside her had been slit open and he glanced at her array of purple nails.

'Sold any?'

The blue flash in her hair tipped back as she looked up. She didn't answer, just raised her hand for him to help her to her feet. He did, offering his other hand for the book. She clasped it to her chest.

'Reading, aren't I.'

'Reading is for libraries.' He bent to refold the box flaps and lift its weight into his arms. 'Lead the way.'

Izara trotted ahead faster than he anticipated and they were over the zebra crossing and into the maelstrom of Market Place before he had a chance to ask what was going on. It soon became plain. Stallholders were shaking fists and complaining to the police. A youth was sitting behind the hussar high on his stone horse, thrusting a green and white placard into the air as he shouted. Demonstrators, some with children, were stomping between the church tower steps and the Town Hall's door, their cramped figure-of-eight cordoned in by gaping Saturday shoppers.

Someone started up on a megaphone loud enough to burst everyone's eardrums and was waved and bawled at by all. It wasn't until Izara was pulling him round the protestors that Nick realised it was Simon on the steps with the megaphone. As Nick stared he was jerked back so forcefully he almost lost his grip on the box, the momentum pivoting him to face a grimacing council worker in a hi-viz jacket.

'Where you goin'?'

Nick backed away from the spittle flying into his face to see Izara's head and shoulders jump between them, his paperback held cover out.

'Hey! Hey! He's a children's author come to read to tots. Help me get him out of this mayhem!'

Much to Nick's surprise the man did just that, fighting a way through and ushering them between the guard protecting the Town Hall's glass doors.

'Speaker! Let us through!' Izara was calling as she pulled him between the frowning faces crowding the vestibule. He was shunted into the peace of a large room set out with chairs.

Off-loading the box onto the nearest, he looked up at the banner on the wall behind the dais.

CONSERVATION COSTS!
NO Tree-Felling! NO Fracking! NO Turbines!

'Oh God,' Nick murmured. What the hell had Simon got him involved in?

Izara opened the box and was carrying his paperbacks across to a side table. He glanced at his watch and spread his arms to take in the rows of empty seats.

'Why are you bothering?'

'You're giving a talk.'

'There's no audience. There won't *be* an audience.'

'And what has that to do with anything?'

'Is there any tea? It says there's tea.'

They turned to an elderly woman in a neat coat and hat standing in the open doorway, her handbag over her arm as if attempting an impersonation of the Queen.

'Of course, there is, pet,' Izara said, ushering her towards the dispensers. 'We're not councillors who renege on our promises. Black, white, strong, weak, sugar?'

Nick tried to mask his irritation while the two women discussed the merits of the available biscuits. Eventually the woman made herself comfortable on the back row, her cup and saucer resting on the chair beside her as she scanned through the leaflet Izara had pushed into her hand.

'How do you like yours?' Izara asked.

'Strong,' he said. 'Where are the toilets?'

She pointed.

It was calmer in the vestibule on his return, and more people had come into the room. The woman on the back row had been joined by a friend. He thought about asking if they wanted to move closer to the front, but decided not to push his luck. They were probably only there for the free tea. There were also two men near the side tables, and another talking to Simon. Nick moved round the chairs to the tea dispensers.

'One strong tea,' Izara announced, pushing a mug into his hand. 'Help yourself to milk.'

'I'm going to have to go through with this, aren't I?'

She raised a critical eyebrow. 'Southern softie, are we?'

There was no answer to that he wanted to give, and he sipped his tea to hide his face.

'Besides,' she added, 'I want to hear your talk. I'm interested. Other people will be interested.'

Other people weren't there, but he didn't mention that.

'You're right,' he placated, and he smiled at her as he withdrew to make for the tables.

Simon was keeping an eye on him, he noted, and as Nick drew close he saw Simon side-step the man he was talking to and fling wide his arms.

'Our speaker has arrived!' The call was in a voice loud enough for the entire room to hear, and Simon neatly closed the space between them, grinning like a loon. 'We feared you'd been caught in traffic!'

Nick smiled back as his biceps were gripped. 'Thought you'd be in handcuffs,' he hissed. 'What the fuck's going on?'

'Press. Play along.'

Simon turned to the journalist, dragging Nick with him.

'Tony, this is the renowned author on conservation mythology, Nicholas Blaketon. He's our first speaker of the day and he's travelled all the way up from Southampton to support this cause so critical to our local and regional environment.'

Conservation mythology...? Nick expelled a taut breath and hoped his smile wasn't turning rictus. Simon faced him, looking as perplexed as Nick felt.

'Your book, Nicholas. Where's your book?'

'Er, I've only just—' and up sprang Izara to slot one into his hand and another into the hand of the journalist.

'Excellent!' Simon crowed, and he released Nick to usher the journalist towards the seats. 'I'm sure you'll have lots of questions for Mr Blaketon once you've heard his talk. Ample chance for photographs then, eh?'

Simon clapped his hands, addressing the few in the room loud enough for those in the vestibule to hear. 'Take your seats, ladies and gentlemen, please. I'm about to announce our first speaker of the day!'

Nick shook his head. And he'd thought Phil and Rosemary had been slick.

Pressing back his shoulders and making himself exude more confidence than he felt, he took up his position as Simon started his intro.

'It's good of you all to join us only two days after the re-emergence of disturbing news from the Hamsterley Forest site, which follows on so close to the dire news from the North Yorkshire Castleton site to the south. But I don't want to fill your minds with outrage yet. I want to introduce our first speaker of the day, Mr Nicholas Blaketon, who has given his life to enriching our understanding of the part the environment plays in our national psyche. A round of applause for our speaker, please...'

...national psyche? Gritting his teeth, Nick nodded an acknowledgement of the half-hearted ripple of applause.

'Thank you, ladies and gentlemen, and to Simon for that introduction.' He glanced Simon's way, his cheery smile belying his narrowed eyes. When this was over... He took a breath.

'The land we stand on, the land we cover in concrete, the land we erode and pollute, is not our land. We inhabit it for only a short time, a fact we overlook, a fact our ancestors knew and understood much better than we do.'

He began to relax, his taut shoulder muscles easing.

'There is no better way to illustrate this than to consider the water we drink. It does not magically fall from our kitchen taps, it is harvested from the earth.'

The room began to fade, mauve and purple moorland stretching out towards an arc of beacon trees.

'Even today it bubbles up in springs from deep in the ground. In some of these places people do as they have always done, give thanks to the genii loci, the spirit of the place, by leaving offerings...'

The Pool lay between him and the door, an unfelt breeze gently rippling its pale surface.

'...After all, who here has never cast a coin into water to make a wish?'

He felt her fingers in his hair, her breath on his cheek.

'Who is it we expect to grant that wish?'

His thumb touched the ring on his finger, and he wished with all his heart to make her his again, to make Alice free.

Chapter 15

Nick sat on the back row away from the noisy queue for tea, his own cup cold and empty on the chair beside him. Simon was no longer into counting bats or erecting owl boxes; he'd become an activist, one with the zeal of a fanatic determined to stir up righteous indignation in the masses, or have a seizure trying. And for this he'd left Alice. What had he been thinking?

A hand dropped onto Nick's shoulder from behind him, Izara from the colour of the nails.

'Don't look so glum,' she told him. 'So you didn't sell any books. No one died.'

The feather-weight of her hand lifted and in his peripheral vision he saw her forearms float out to rest on the back of the adjacent chair, making the cup shudder in its saucer. Her head was now almost level with his own. He wished she'd go away and pour tea.

'Your talk was great. I closed my eyes and could see it all. And you got a decent response at the end, didn't you?'

They'd clapped, certainly. There had been more people in the audience by then, but they hadn't been arriving late, they'd been arriving early for the next speaker. The gory slides of golden eagles guillotined by turbine blades had certainly hit the spot.

'You should have used that sign,' she said. 'It would have made a great illustration to the bit about the way water calls to us, soothes biorhythms and such. That was good.'

It wasn't quite what he'd said though, was it? He turned to face her.

'And what, exactly, would I have replied to the question of *where had it come from?*'

He watched her dark lips curve into a puckered smile. She

rested back on one arm and brought up her free hand to prod at his shoulder.

'Not quite the up-standing gent you put across, are you?'

Both dipped beneath a hefty slap to their shoulders and a hug from Simon that brought their faces too close.

'Great talk, Nick. Really got the event off to a good solid start. Izzy, pet, we're running out of cups. Can you—'

Her expression chilled and from the corner of his eye Nick watched as she uncurled from the chair to stand tall. Simon's hands were lifting in apology.

'Sorry, Izara, sorry. It slipped out, pet, won't happen again. Nick will help. Good bloke is Nick, aren't you, mate?'

Nick's shoulder took the shock as Simon's hand crashed back to shake him. He was beginning to understand Izara's annoyance. As she stalked away he pulled himself free to mirror her stance. Not that Simon noticed. He was rolling his eyes.

'Bloody groupies. I could understand if Izara was her name. She was Ana when we had the band. Ana for *Andromeda*, for God's sake. And she gets tetchy over *Izzy*?' He frowned at Nick and then shook his head. 'After your time, mate. Do me a favour and give her a hand, eh? Keep her sweet?'

He didn't wait for a response, but looked past Nick as if he wasn't there and clapped his hands to gain the attention of the room.

'Okay, people! We have to get this march organised before our next speaker. If everyone can take a seat, please!'

Nick picked up his crockery, musing on why Izara needed to be kept sweet. If the two of them had a thing going it looked to him as if it was tottering, and he didn't want to play go-between. He had Alice to consider, Alice to get back to.

He collected more cups as he made his way down the row. When he walked into the kitchenette he was balancing a tower. Izara was running hot water into a bowl.

'Thanks,' she said. 'This side, and I'll make a start.'

She didn't sound miffed, and her body language seemed easy. He placed the crockery where she'd indicated, watching as she unbuttoned a thigh pocket of her combats to bring out a pair of pink rubber gloves. The absurdity made him chuckle.

'Come prepared, eh?'

'That's my motto.'

He left the kitchenette acknowledging that it should have been his, too. Alice had moved beyond his far imaginings. They could talk to each other, touch each other – until the cold got too much. Where did that come from? Why was she so cold in the Pool but warm in his bed? She'd worn the torc at the Pool. He couldn't remember it at the farmhouse, and he would have remembered. The drawings he'd seen in old manuscripts had never shown the woman wearing a torc. There again, they'd been 15th century and couldn't be relied on any more than the fanciful Victorian renditions the publisher had insisted including in his book. According to those, the woman was always standing besides water not in it as Alice had been. They needed to talk. He needed to discover what she could and couldn't do. Or thought she couldn't do. She'd been warm in his bed and she hadn't been wearing the torc. Was that it? Was it the torc that shackled her to the Pool, to the *thing*?

Using a whisper and a smile he prompted drinkers to retrieve cups and glasses from under chairs. Around him people were signing petitions and offering to transport demonstrators out of the city to the turbine site being targeted. When he brought his final stack to the kitchenette two older women were making short work of the drying. He felt unnecessary so sidled out again.

Simon was introducing the next speaker, talking in strident tones about the heritage of the Durham coalfields and the proposed coal gasification.

'...this means we could see 2,000 twin wellheads drilled along the coast from Hartlepool to Alnwick...'

Nick's phone sounded and he fought his pocket to pull it free and silence it. A text from his mother filled the screen.

How did it go?

Oh, damn; not now. His thumbs glided over the keys. *Very*

well. Good event. He needed to ring her at some point and see how— Another text came through.

Great. Have news. Good time to ring?

He stared at the words, his stomach tensing as he sifted through possible problems, and he pushed his way to the door. In the vestibule he slid through the menus to draw up the house number and waited as it rang.

'Hello?'

She sounded guarded.

'It's Nick. What's wrong?'

'Oh hello. Did it go well?' That sounded brighter. 'Were there lots of people in the audience?'

'Er, a reasonable number. The talk had a good reception. What's happened?'

'Nothing's happened; everything's fine.'

He looked through the glass frontage at the shoppers, at the striped canvas of the market stalls gently lifting and falling in a breeze he couldn't feel. He waited, but she wasn't going to fill the gap.

'And your news...?'

Again a pause, then it came in a rush. 'I called Mr Bartlett on Friday and he was ever so understanding and he invited me to go in so I did. He's offered me a job. Not my old one, obviously, but there's a part-time one and I thought....'

Nick could feel his eyes widening. Four weeks ago he'd hardly been able to get her out of the house.

'...well, I know them all, don't I?' she was saying. 'And the girls were ever so nice when I went in, and... well... I thought...'

'That's brilliant news,' he said. 'Congratulations.'

'Oh thanks. I hoped you'd understand.' She was breathless now, he noticed. Was she worrying over how he'd react?

'Well done, you,' he said, and he made himself chuckle so she could hear it. 'When do you start?'

'Monday. That's why I thought I'd better ring, in case you came home and found the house empty. I thought it might be a bit of a shock if I just left a note.'

'Yeah... that would have been somewhat surreal. Er, Mum... sorry to cut it short but I can hear clapping so the speaker's finished.'

'Oh, of course. Will you be back Monday?'

He closed his eyes. 'No, I'm... stopping a few days.' The pink behind his eyelids was flickering through purple and mauve. 'If that's okay..?'

'That's fine. No need to rush back for me. You enjoy time with your friends. Keep safe, Nicholas.' It was she who cut the call.

It took him a few moments to release the phone and slip it back in his pocket. He wasn't sure what the matter was. He lying to his mum, or his mum lying to him. Not lying. His mother didn't lie. Had she waved him off and then made her call? How long had she been thinking about returning to work? Why hadn't she discussed it with him?

'Bad news?'

Izara was behind him, sitting on the corner of the reception desk, making herself look even smaller than she was. He shook his head.

'Mum, she's....' but he didn't want to discuss it.

'Sorry about your Dad.' He looked at her again. 'Simon told me. You know about his gran? About his mum?'

'He mentioned it.'

'Not good,' she said.

Nick thought of Simon in the adjacent room, empowering the audience as if nothing else in the world mattered. The sound of applause drifted through. Izara pushed herself off the desk ready to go back in.

'That seems to have gone down well.' She giggled. 'All four thousand of them. I think it's fracking next.'

'There's no fracking up here, is there?'

'You want to wait until there is? It'll be the Castleton gig.'

He stepped back as people started coming through the vestibule, pushing through the outer doors and into the sunshine. Simon was hard on their heels brandishing a stack of leaflets which he thrust into Izara's hands. His colour was high and he looked pumped.

'Last section. People are making a move and I've got to grab them. See if you can rustle up a few more. No sign of him?'

Izara shook her head. Nick watched as Simon muttered something he didn't catch and fought against the surge of leavers to return to the hall.

'Are we missing another speaker?'

Shrugging, she handed over half the leaflets. 'Probably see him later. Fancy doing a meet 'n' greet? Shouldn't take long to shift these.'

She slipped behind two women, smiling as she took the glass door from their hands. Nick fell into step.

'What am I supposed to say?'

'You'll think of something,' and she peeled away.

Nick gazed at the busy throng intent on the wares displayed on the stalls, then glanced towards Izara. Despite her size, she was easy to pick out between the moving people, and he wondered if that was why she dyed her hair that colour, reinforcing it with such a bright blue streak.

He tried to engage the shoppers, but for the most part it was wasted effort. Like him, they had other things on their minds. Perhaps he could find a bin and just lose the leaflets. The nearest was overflowing with market waste and would leave the eye-catching flyers too visible. He looked for another.

Along the run of mediaeval buildings, the access to the Indoor Market beckoned. He started down its ramp, passing Tudor-styled doorways to enter beneath a pointed arch. The bustle resonated from the stone floor and high roof, and he paused to breathe in scents of coffee and hot food, reminders of forays to buy provisions when he'd lived in the city. The space was a warren of narrow walkways. Modern refrigerated stalls stood against those selling craft items, clothing, musical instruments, all beneath striped awnings as if no roof existed. He stepped to the nearest without customers, a leaflet prominent in his hand.

'Sorry to barge in, but there's a meeting in the Town Hall

about the appalling effects of industrialisation of the local landscape and—'

'Is that those ruddy turbines?' the man said, reaching for Nick's handout. 'I'm all for ecology but those things are gawpin' monsters.'

'Wait until they start drilling along the coast,' Nick said, watching for the man's reaction.

'*What?*'

'We wondered if you'd be kind enough to display a leaflet?'

Within a minute the leaflet was clipped to the edge of the stall at eye-level and Nick left the man reading another. A stall selling bird food took two after Nick mentioned the guillotined raptors. The response from others was mixed but better than he'd hoped, especially after he'd bought a packet of safety pins and offered a couple with each leaflet. As Izara had maintained, it didn't take long.

He walked back up to Market Place in a lighter mood, turning the remaining flyer in his hand. It was the first time he'd looked at it properly. Among the sponsoring advertisers was an outdoor pursuits shop off the square. He thought of Izara with her pink rubber gloves. He needed a warm pair, and a better torch than the one Rosemary had lent him.

Chapter 16

The conversation in the corridor passed beyond the closed door and Tim unglued himself from the wall. Damned labs with glass everywhere; there was no privacy.

He'd had to use the keypad to get in, unsure whether it would show up on a panel in the university's Security Services. He hoped not, hoped that sort of stuff only went live during the night. At least the department's analyzers were positioned at the far end, and he was thankful for that. The mass spec was even noisier than the ancient thing the bottling plant owned, or at least it sounded it in the silence of the empty lab.

He shifted from one foot to the other, waiting for it to complete its sequence. The faculty's equipment was more sensitive, could identify more elements and certainly more pathogens, but it took forever. He'd considered leaving it to do its thing while he grabbed a drink, but what if someone walked in? It would take far less explaining if he were interrupted than if he returned with a carton of coffee to find his professor standing there, foot tapping, the results in her hand.

There was a beep from the chromatograph and Tim jumped forward to check the reading: 1.6. He consulted his tablet, the results the machine at the bottling plant had coughed up. No change in the potassium. There was a second beep and the display altered. Sulphate: 9.9. A third beep. A fourth. So far all were within tolerances, almost identical to the plant's diagnostics. That was good. It meant new data could be relied on.

The rest came in quick succession: calcium, iron, magnesium, all mirroring his original data. He couldn't remember what came next. And then his eyes widened. It couldn't be.

Unidentified – and it was off the scale.

The display started blinking, requesting the data to be downloaded. He reached for his tablet with trembling hands. What the hell could it be? Boranes. Maybe it was one of the boranes. What did he know about those? Not enough. No fret, the mass spec would identify it.

The data was transferred and the chromatograph cleaned and reset. He'd brought a bag for the wipes and packaging to be binned off-site. No one would notice it had been used. The mass spec continued to whirr through its sequences. It was all taking too long. His eyebrow was itching again and he started to scratch at it before pushing both hands into his pockets to stop himself. *Come on, come on...*

A slow walk around the benches did little to calm his rising agitation. He was almost level with the admin section when the phone on the wall began to ring. Sweat erupted across his skin as he stared at it. Who could know he was there? He must have triggered something in Security.

Pulling free his hands, his gaze snapped along the ceiling-line as he searched for cameras. Behind him the spectrometer beeped, and beeped again, and he shot round the benches to view its data screen. Trace. Trace. Nothing significant enough to register. The phone stopped, the spectrometer, too. Tim could hear his own pulse in his ears. And then the machine started again with a low hum. There was an unaccountable fizz and then a gurgle. He scratched at his cheek and returned to his pacing.

His hairline was itching now and he curled his fingers to wait out the need to rub at it. When he drew beside the admin section he reached up to the shelving and pulled down the mirror to study his face. The inner edges of both eyebrows were inflamed. That's all he needed, to look as if he'd done four rounds with a boxer, especially— He checked his watch. Too late anyway. He began to relax. That was good. That would help. He breathed slowly, deeply, forcing down his shoulders, slowing his heart rate. They could say what they liked, he'd made no promise.

Behind him came a beep and then all hell broke loose. Dumping the mirror, he rushed across the lab to try to stop the high-pitched alarm. Which button to press? Amber and red warning lights were flashing and an error code he didn't recognise was showing on the display. How could he turn it off? He reached for the instruction manual to find it wasn't in its designated place. Damnit, how could he turn it *off*?

His gaze strayed to the mains socket, but he changed his mind. Cutting the power might lose him the data. Fumbling with his tablet, he initiated the transfer. As soon as the two connected the noise cut but the lights remained. Tim glanced at the door to the corridor as he waited for the download to complete. It remained closed, but that didn't mean someone wasn't on their way and he needed time to reset the machine.

With the data saved he brought it up on screen, scrolling through the figures until he found the anomaly.

Unidentified.

How could it be unidentified? He wanted to punch the thing. It was exactly the same result as the bottling plant's piddling analyzer had given. And then he realised it wasn't the same.

Pulling up the bar chart, he checked the figures against the plant's analysis from earlier in the week. He checked the readings from the chromatographs. The spikes on the corresponding graphs were nowhere near as high. Whatever the unidentified contaminant was, it was degrading.

Chapter 17

Nick stepped out of the shop into a cascade of people determined to make it down the mediaeval cobbles to the river slower than gravity intended. He'd bought a torch, a ground sheet, a lightweight storm shelter and gloves. He'd picked the thinnest thermals he could find, but despite her numbing cold the thought of touching Alice through them made him squirm. But they'd been added to the bag, just in case.

As he pushed against the flow to climb the hill to Market Place, he wondered if he could make his excuses and drive south that afternoon, wondered where he could leave the car if not at the farm.

The banner was being folded when he returned to the Town Hall's meeting room, chairs were being stacked. He regretted not being there to help, it would have given him a chance to talk to Simon, but they were clearing out now. He crossed to the information table to dismantle the display of his books.

'The wanderer returns!' Simon called across the clatter. 'Getting started on a pint before the rest of us?'

Nick wasn't certain what to make of the sarcasm, and he set down his carrier to lift the book box from beneath the table.

'All your leaflets are pinned to the stalls in the Indoor Market,' he called back.

Simon changed immediately, opening his arms and his expression. 'Heeyyy! Good man!'

Nick turned his back, annoyed. He'd driven all the way up— Had Simon no idea how far Durham was from the south coast?

He slammed a handful of his books into the box, then another, stopping when he realised he was light. Izara had taken one, the journalist had been given one... Izara walked in with a cloth to wipe the cleared tea table.

'Were any books sold?'

'Not that I noticed. A few people looked.'

He slid the rest in the box and folded its flaps. It was his own fault; he should have been guarding them.

'I waited for you,' she said from behind his shoulder.

He glanced round. 'Did a bit of shopping.' She was gazing at the carrier, the name of the shop emblazoned in red on the white plastic.

Simon bellowed across the room. 'Come on, people! If we aren't out by two we have to pay extra. Pints all round at The Bishops' Mill, eh?'

'It's food I want,' murmured Izara, and she left for the kitchenette.

Only the faithful remained. The speakers had gone, and that meant they'd been paid. Nick walked across to Simon.

'Before we hit the pub, you promised me expenses.'

Simon blanked him. Nick held out his palm.

'Of course,' Simon said, smiling now and delving into his pocket for a plastic bag of notes. 'You weren't here. Good job you reminded me.'

He handed over a couple of twenties. Nick stared at it and then at him, but Simon jumped in first.

'The speakers donated half their expenses to the cause and I knew you'd want to do the same.'

Nick felt his shoulders tightening. 'You could have asked.'

'You weren't here.'

'I was distributing your damned leaflets.'

'They're not damned, Nick. They'll help raise awareness and save the *damned* planet.' He grinned. 'Don't be a grump. Besides, it'd only go on beer, and better in the group's coffers than in those of The Bishops' Mill, eh?'

Nick felt himself nudged as Izara slipped her arm through his. 'If you two are ready, we have about five minutes grace.'

Simon made a show of looking at her. 'Thank you, Izara, for keeping an eye on the important stuff. I'd better go sign on the dotted line,' and he left them standing there.

'Don't take it so bad,' she murmured. 'No one died.'

She was all for accompanying Nick to the car park, offering to carry his bag while he carried the box, but he was having none of it. He left her on the square just past the creepy monks. From the way she'd slowed her pace when he'd lengthened his stride he knew she was watching him descend the steps. He didn't look back. He was no one's go-between, no one's agony aunt. If she and Simon wanted a domestic they could have it without his intervention.

Down by the river he wished he hadn't been so abrupt. Simon was acting the arrogant prat to him and he was doing the same, taking out his resentment on Izara. *No one died*. It wasn't a statement of fact, more a trite excuse for the prat's behaviour. She should dump him. Perhaps he should buy her a drink and tell her that. Perhaps he shouldn't get involved.

Opening the boot, he tried to force the box of books into too small a gap and ended up unloading his sports bag and sliding out the sign to the Pool. He laid his palm on its metal facia, cold like Alice's touch. Yet her touch hadn't been cold when she'd joined him in his bed, and that had been real enough.

I waited for you. I knew you would find me.

She'd waited too long.

His fingertips traced the three wavy indentations depicting water, so similar to the design on his ring. He looked from one to the other, removing his hand to grip the ring in the curl of his fingers. The pine tree on the plaque was wrong. Deciduous trees had been planted round the Pool. He'd not asked Phil why he'd done that. In truth, he'd not asked Phil anything, and it was Phil and Rosemary who held the answers he needed, not the university's archives.

He took it easier up to the top, turning down the secondary steps to enter the glass frontage of The Bishops' Mill. Izara waved his book to show where they were sitting, and he nodded an acknowledgement as he walked through to the bar. For a Saturday afternoon the pub was surprisingly quiet and he was soon served. He would have ordered food, but didn't have their table number, so sidled past the brick pillars and mock mediaeval wainscoting to join the group.

Simon wasn't sitting next to Izara, but was deep in conversation with a bearded man in a striped sweater Nick hadn't been introduced to. Izara sat alone, intent on Nick's book. He wondered if the two of them were specifically slighting each other. When she raised her face to give him a warm smile and she patted the seat beside her, Nick decided they were. She hadn't been reading at all.

'This is interesting,' she said, flipping its cover towards him.

He didn't bite but picked up the menu. 'Have we ordered yet?'

She shook her head and looked over his arm. 'Want to share a platter?'

He declined; he didn't want to get that cosy.

Despite his refusal she followed him back to the bar and paid for a platter. He paid for a steak and kidney pudding. He wasn't sure when he'd next eat, and it seemed a long time since Rosemary's cooked breakfast.

'What made you interested in water deities?' Izara asked.

He shrugged. 'Fell into it.'

'Oh very funny.'

Back at the table Nick purposely took her seat to introduce himself to the bearded man, Rob he said his name was, so he wouldn't have to follow up on her conversation. That proved a mistake.

'There'd be hell to pay if you tried getting permission to erect a 30-storey skyscraper,' Rob emphasised, 'but those things...'

Simon leaned over the table. 'The turbines they're building in Germany are 160 metres tall, and that's not including the blades. And where do you think they'll end up if we don't stand against the ones we have now?'

'It's happening all over,' Rob chimed. 'Smaller ones are being replaced with ever-larger structures and there's nothing anyone seems to be able to do about it.'

'Now he arrives! After the event as usual.'

Nick followed the line of Simon's accusing finger to see a sandy-haired man about his age standing in front of the tables. He held his pint as if a shield and was frowning down at them.

'We expected you to speak at the event,' Simon chided.

'I told you I'd get there if I could.'

'So what happened?'

'I was tied up at the university.'

'Ah! So what fracking news is there from those sell-outs in Earth Sciences?'

'I am not your spy!'

'Are you theirs?'

'Simon!' Izara admonished. 'That was beyond a joke.'

'He wasn't joking,' the newcomer rasped 'and you know he wasn't.'

'Of course I wasn't. Ten million gallons of toxic waste but no threat to water courses. *That's* the bloody joke.'

Everyone else had gone quiet, Nick noted. If he hadn't trapped himself next to Rob he would have left them all to it. He could see that the new man was having the same thought.

'Don't go, Tim. I've bought us a platter.' Izara began moving glasses; the food was arriving. 'Come and sit down,' she persisted. 'I want to introduce you to Nick.'

The man glared at everyone round the table, including Nick, but eventually he sat to allow the waitress space to off-load the plates.

'You share an interest in springs,' Izara told him, forestalling a return to the argument. 'Nick has written a book on ancient water lore. Nick, this is my friend, Timothy. He's collecting water sample data for a project.'

Nick nodded in his direction and received a guarded acknowledgement in return.

'Yeah,' stressed Simon. 'The government hands out fracking licences left, right and centre, but there's no national register of the purity of natural springs. Without base-line readings to refer back to, drilling companies can put any spin on a contamination. And Earth Sciences is working with the fracking companies.'

'It is doing independent research,' Tim countered.

Simon guffawed.

Nick cut into his pudding, watching it disembowel its steaming contents, dark and meaty, to flood his chips. Good menu choice, he decided, even if his fellow diners weren't.

'Tim talks about the calming effects of water the way you do,' Izara said in an attempt to turn the conversation.

Nick gave her a glance to show he wasn't ignoring her, and filled his mouth with chips.

She turned to Tim, waving the book under his nose.

'Yeah, yeah. Reasonable enough for a fund-raising exercise, but superstition is hardly scientific data, is it?'

Nick forked a square of steak across his plate, turning it a couple of times before stabbing it. It was easier to eat than to argue. In his peripheral vision he saw Izara glance at him, probably wondering what to say to lighten the mood. Nothing could as far as he was concerned. He was decided now. As soon as he'd finished his meal he was going back to Alice.

Chapter 18

The pittances with the Feast meal were gracious and welcomed, particularly the slices of dried apricots boiled in honey and the salted butter for the bread. Ernald considered keeping back a portion of his loaf, but decided it would be a sin against the Blessed Mary whose Feast Day they celebrated. Sub-Prior Maugre had not mentioned how Ernald's band of travellers were to eat if they were not to journey between the manors. Yet all hollow-ways led from village to hamlet, so that made little sense either.

He contented himself knowing that the Blessed Mary guided both his feet and his thoughts. As had Saint Paul, he was about to embark on a journey. Ernald's moment of revelation had blinded him with tears, and now he would undertake his given task. It was apt that it should be on the Feast of the Nativity of the Blessed Mary, his beginning in the light of Her Blessed beginning.

During his walk of contemplation in the cloisters, Ernald pressed close the reliquary cross while intoning prayers of fortitude and strength. On his third circuit he noticed Brother Gregory watching him. Careful not to impede the other monks, he stepped from his line to approach the older man.

'You are at peace with yourself and with Heaven,' Gregory said, adjusting his weight against his stick. 'I can see God's Love shining from your eyes.'

'It is due to you, brother, for offering the first hand to lead me to my salvation.'

'I was an instrument, as are we all.' The bell sounded for Vespers and Gregory inclined his head. 'Walk with me. Together we will give praise in the quire.'

'My path leads in another direction. I will recall you in my prayers, Brother Gregory. Be at peace.'

The older man pursed his thin lips and nodded. 'Be at peace,' he echoed, and Ernald watched as he turned to tap his way behind the other monks towards the church door.

No one remained in the dorter. Ernald sat on his pallet to pull on his new boots. They felt comfortable. He'd taken time to wear them in the House so they moulded better to his feet. His sandals he pushed into his satchel, arranging them flat alongside his board, close against the pot of ink and the leather roll containing his quills and scrapping knife. It was always good to journey with spare footwear. In the remaining space he nestled his sheaf of trimmed parchment, wrapped against the damp. His prayers were in his head, Saint Cuthbert's cross against his heart. He needed nothing more. As the plainsong drifted up the nave stairs he paused to listen. Offering a prayer for his brothers, he made his way down to the cloisters and out into the garth.

The sun was already setting, its yellow glow as if from a candle to light his way through the shadows in his life. The porter nodded but offered neither word nor look when unbolting the gate to the world. Ernald wondered if those had been the man's instructions. Then the gate swung closed behind him, the bolt driven home with noisy force.

It was darker in the shadow of the precinct wall. He could hear faint sounds of carousing from the saddlers' street, though could recollect seeing no sign for a good-wife's ale-house down the hill. He cast the thought aside. The route to the bridges was not for him this night, and he turned alongside the dimming wall. The rough-cut steps in the cliff would be difficult to gauge without a lantern and he wasn't certain where he'd meet his guide, or the craft to take him to the farther bank. Instead, he praised God for holding back the rains for the harvest. It meant he'd not be crossing the river in spate.

At the tip of the promontory he paused to look about him. The horizon was now no more than a pallid line, the land below a black abyss. No wonder the sub-prior had decided this was the place to cross. Not even the Devil would see him. A few steps further and he could make out the flickering light of torches marking the towered bridge. The new chapel he knew from his journeys stood beyond, lay hidden in the darkness as was he.

'No' tha' way, brother.'

Ernald shuddered to a halt. As he clutched at his breast to feel Saint Cuthbert close, he heard a low chortle.

'D'na be tumblin' to river in yer shock. Yer worth more dry than drippin'.'

Ernald couldn't see the man, though now he was breathing harder it seemed he could smell a tallow lamp.

'Who speaks here?' he demanded.

Almost at his feet a glow reached for his boots through a lantern's membrane as its cover was peeled away. Ernald blinked. Another stride and he would have stood on the crouching man. Or stripling, it seemed, when he rose from his haunches with the fluidity of quicksilver.

'Watch yer step, now, brother. D'na yous be falling on me and takin' us both on a hangman's drop. I cannae fly, even if yous can.'

Taken aback by this impudence, Ernald fought for a response, but his guide was beginning the descent and Ernald had to follow in haste so as to see the steps in the lantern's glow. As he reached out to balance himself his arm was locked in a bracing grip and he leaned back against jutting rocks, scrambling for what roots offered themselves, his satchel banging his thigh as it tried to trip him. The stripling descended at an alarming speed, dragging Ernald behind him. At last Ernald felt his boots sink into the gravelled silt of the shore and he stood, sweating and breathless, waiting for the trembling to ease in his limbs.

'Follow, brother. D'na delay.'

He lifted his gaze to see the lantern-glow alone, it swaying as if a faerie light leading towards the Devil's Pit. Ernald signed himself and murmured a prayer, but when the glow dropped and blinked out he hurried forward in a panic, his left boot sliding away into the chill water. His arm was grabbed again.

'Here, brother. Step within an' we'll away.'

Reaching with his leg, Ernald located the craft. It did not feel substantial enough to be made of wood. Indeed, when his hands found its lip it came to him that it was no more than hide and pitch over a withy frame. Appealing to the Saint to protect him, he stepped inside to crouch in its spill of water, his satchel trapped between thighs and chest so its precious contents remained dry.

The boy was strong, and even with Ernald as lading he pushed the craft free of the silt and into the current. Ernald closed his eyes, reminding himself Saint Brendan had travelled safely in such a vessel. Perhaps one a little larger. The craft rocked when the boy climbed in, his bare heels forcing into Ernald's shins as he settled to his task.

When the rocking changed to an easier swaying Ernald risked gazing about him. The darkness was not as total as his imaginings had portrayed. The river glinted, setting the stripling as a black figure moving the paddle in rhythmic slurping strokes. He glanced skywards to be rewarded by sight of a star in the firmament. It would guide him, Ernald realised, as the Holy Star had guided the kings to the Blessed Mary and his Lord in His manger.

The craft grounded and the boy was out and reaching back for Ernald's arm.

'Lift yer skirts, brother.'

The warning came too late. Ernald stepped into chill water that nearly topped his boots. Two strides and he was on firmer footing, feeling the sodden wool drag the habit at his shoulders as the river water poured from its hem. His guide did not pause but led up a steep track between bushes which stank with the contents of piss-pots. The glow from his lantern showed only the turns in the narrow path, not where Ernald put his feet or placed his hands, and he hugged his satchel to him as best he could to stop it becoming soiled.

They topped the bank to see the light of fires, some mere embers brightening on the breeze, others licking yellow. It took Ernald a moment to realise they were pilgrims' fires clustered for safety outside the town's walls. The stripling had covered his lantern, or extinguished its light, Ernald was not sure. He stood close, grasping again at Ernald's arm.

'Pull yer hood t'hide yer head,' came his whisper. 'Be a blind beggar led, an' mute if we're approached. I'll taal us by.'

The boy hardly waited for Ernald to raise his cowl or wonder at the reason, and then it came to him that perhaps these cloaked and recumbent figures were not pilgrims. Not traders, either, for where were their carts? As they walked between the fires he heard the grumbles of an argument, the chitter of conversation, and music, a sweet refrain that turned into the jolly jig of a bawdy-song. If there were whores with a master there would be cut-purses and worse. Ernald tightened his grip on the boy's arm, glad he stood tall.

They were through and out into darkness with no shout to stop them. The stripling increased their pace. Low bushes gave better the star-shine on ruts and holes in the cart track than the shadows of trees, but the needed concentration made Ernald's eyes sting.

The boy began to hum and then to lilt a tune. A light appeared, and his song ended partway through a phrase. They moved as one off the track, the light guiding their direction but leaving their feet to snag on roots, their clothing on briars. Ernald remembered the stripling walked bare-foot.

In a delve the flames of a small fire swelled about a pot. Around it men stood or sat against packs. Away in the darkness Ernald heard a pony snort.

'Ee'as late,' the stripling announced.

'He's here,' replied the darkness. 'It's enough.'

The boy shook free Ernald's arm and stepped forwards to meet an emerging shadow. The two touched hand to hand, a coin being passed. Without farewell, the stripling walked into the night.

'Now, Ernald,' rumbled the bass voice, and into the glow of the firelight stepped the bulk of the bearded man from the confinement chamber at the House. 'This is how it will be: there will be no holy brother among us, but a pious clerk returning south from his pilgrimage. Hence, let me relieve you of that cowl so it may be stored for your return to the priory.'

Remove his cowl? Was he not on a journey sacred to the House? Ernald saw the man's thick arm reach out to him, his open palm the size of a serving dish.

'I do not understand.'

'Yours is not to understand, friend Ernald. Yours is to ink the route for the sub-prior. Mine is to travel you safely to your destination, and safely back to the priory. Your cowl.'

Again Ernald hesitated, but could think of no response that would be accepted, so he removed his satchel from across his shoulders and the cowl from his head. Without its weight he felt lighter, almost as if he stood in his nightshirt. Another man came to offer first a coif and then a cloak. Ernald saw the rood stitched to the material and began to perceive the man's thinking. A monk might be begged to intercede in prayers, a pilgrim merely smiled upon. A broad-brimmed hat was handed to him, and finally a staff.

'And a goodly pilgrim you make, friend Ernald.'

The dimming firelight reflected bright on the teeth showing through the dark beard, and Ernald was reminded of the man's malevolent stare in the town's market place. He stood taller, determined to regain the dignity of his vocation.

'Am I to know your name?'

'You will call me Master Ore Reeve, for we travel south to seek new groves of lead for the roofs of the Bishop's houses. You travel with us for companionship and safety. Does that sit well with you, friend Ernald?'

He nodded, and then remembered the darkness. 'Yes, Master Ore Reeve, if that is our story for the telling. May I ask after the...' He stuttered over *crying man*, but the reeve was pointing towards the seated group.

'Be comfortable, friend Ernald, and regain your sleep. We rise when I say we rise and it will be with the dawn. The fire dies now, so leak your water and wrap yourself in your new cloak.'

Ernald walked across to those recumbent on the ground. Even in the brighter light from the fire it took him a moment to recognise the crying man. Dressed in better garb, and fuller in the face from good meals, the man smiled and nodded in welcome. The one behind, barely older than the stripling who had borne him across the river, squinted from beneath his lashes in no such companionable welcome. As Ernald lowered himself beside them, he noticed the youth's bristled crown amid a ring of hair and stared at him afresh. Dressed in a serf's tunic, it was the novice he'd seen dragged along the cloister.

'Brother...'

But the youth turned his shoulder to lie on the grass, one arm held oddly behind his back. It was then Ernald realised both men were pinioned by a leash to the ground.

Chapter 19

'You can't leave!'

Izara's plea caught Nick by surprise, and he glanced at her as he stood.

'Good of you to come and help make the event a success,' Simon said as he, too, rose to offer his hand as if they'd been no more than delegates at a conference. All the talk on the phone of them catching a band had been forgotten. Or had the camaraderie been false from the start, a mere enticement to get him up to Durham to fill a gap in the speaker schedule? Ignore it, Nick told himself. Ignore them all.

'But I've not had chance to talk to you about your book,' Izara whined, snatching it up from amid the empty plates to wave it as he pressed by her bony knees. 'I can pay for it. If you'll sign it for me.' She even produced a pen.

His irritation broke with the absurdity of the exchange. He took the book and wrote *To Izara – Belief is more powerful than fact.*

'Treat it as a gift,' he told her, 'but you have to read it all, including the bibliography.'

Radiating gratitude, she hugged it to her chest and beamed at him.

As he climbed the steps into the sunshine, it came to him that what he should have written was *Dump the bastards*. But perhaps not. Perhaps they were the only bastards she had. At the top of the flight he came face to face with the creepy green monks shuffling their way through eternity. He wouldn't be sorry to see the back of them, either.

The traffic was heavier going south than it had been coming north, but moving fast for all that. Stokesley was closing for the night when he passed through, Castleton near enough deserted. An excitement at seeing Alice again was growing in his chest. As the land swelled up to the moors in the windscreen it became a need making his palms perspire. He hoped Rosemary had been lying when she'd said the farm's bedrooms were taken for the night. He didn't want company at the Pool. Even if she'd not, her guests would have to be die-hards to venture down to it so late in the day. There again, she and Phil would have talked any hapless walkers out of the idea. He stopped worrying about it, concentrating on Alice, on what he'd say to her.

A cattle grid flagged the edge of the hedgerows and the beginning of the open sheep moor. The road markings became intermittent at the summit and then, as the road narrowed, disappeared altogether. He was coming in from the north this time, not Phil's complex route out, and he feared he might not find his way. He needn't have worried, and actually smiled when the first of the small signs hammered into the verge warned him he was close. He slowed to take the turning where the large plaque had stood, and wondered if Phil had missed it yet.

The sun shone directly through the windscreen now, too low for the visors to offer protection. Despite his sun specs, Nick was forced to squint against the golden glare. He dropped his speed, not wanting to run off the road, or worse, into a milk wagon. But the glare kept drawing his attention, blistering at his sight. It was turning from yellow to orange ready for the sunset, the same colour, if not the same intensity, as the torc that shone with its own light about Alice's neck. She'd not worn it when she'd joined him in his bed at the farm. How had she escaped it? How had she escaped the Pool? He needed to get her out of it, away from the *thing's* influence. Where they'd go, how they'd live once he'd freed her, was no more than a haze in his mind, but if asylum seekers could melt into the landscape he was sure they could manage it, too.

He followed the dips and curves in the road, noting this time the way its surface was breaking up, more gravel than tarmac in places, grass tufting in its centre. Another couple of winters...

His attention jumped to a stand of trees rising in the corner of the windscreen, and he eased his foot further off the accelerator to scrutinise the copse as he closed on it. The cover of mixed woodland would be an ideal place to stash the car if he could find a way in. A day or so, that's all he'd need, just so it wasn't visible from the road.

Stamping on the brake, the Nissan stopped past a shadow-filled opening. The trees were a dark mass now, the run-in overgrown with tall grass and dead man's oatmeal. He abandoned the vehicle to check out the break. Tractors' ruts scored the hard ground, but if he took it slowly Nick reckoned the car could negotiate them.

He took it more than slowly, wincing at every drop of a wheel and clunk beneath the hatchback's body. He hoped the sump would remain intact. There was an offshoot holding a stack of moss-covered logs, and he bounced the car over more ruts to pull up in its lee. Getting the vehicle back on to the road might be tricky, but he'd sort that when he needed to.

Dumping his spare clothing in the boot, he stuffed the groundsheet and storm shelter into his sports bag with the car rug and his padded jacket. The zip wouldn't fasten, but nothing would fall out. He considered wearing his boots, but decided to stay with his trainers. He could run in his trainers.

Running was soon beyond him, even on the tarmac, never mind with the bag thumping a bruise into his back. He'd definitely let his fitness slide. He settled into a jogging walk. It couldn't be that far to the farm.

When he reached the fencing and its Welcome sign, he slowed, breathing hard. Lights were already shining above the farm's door and across the car park, but there were no vehicles beyond their own. There were no paying guests. He smiled at catching Rosemary's lie. There was no sign of Phil, either. They'd probably be eating dinner. He should have brought food. Too late to think of that now. A couple of steps and he was over the stile and striding between the fenced pastures, leaving the farm and the road behind.

At the ridge he stopped to take in the view. The mauves of the heather were easing into purples with the coming dusk, its scent soporific now the breeze had dropped. Nectar floated in the air as if a transparent cloud demanding to be sucked into his lungs. And he did breathe it in, long and strong, as insects buzzed and fizzed about him drinking in their own fill. A dragonfly hovered close to his face, the sun's rays glinting from its wings as if they were formed from slivers of sapphire. It left as it had come, on wing-beats too quiet for him to hear, and he watched it zigzag along the line of the path until it merged with the colours of the moorland.

Nick gauged the position of the sun. Half an hour and it would spread on the horizon, and he needed to reach the Pool while there was still daylight. Checking his watch against his phone to make sure they tallied, he began the descent. He wasn't going to run along the winding route. He wanted to see how far it was, to see when – if – time began to bend.

Up and down and round, barely looking either side, he followed the yellow gravel as it dissolved into the worn earth of the track. The straps of his bag bit into his shoulders and the scent from the heather was making his eyes itch, but he wasn't going to be deflected from his steady pace.

At the turn beneath the dank pond he checked his watch against his phone. They tallied at twenty-six minutes. He felt almost sad at that, but it meant the route was not two miles.

The trees came into view at thirty-four minutes, the sun a streak of fiery amber smudging along their tops. He reached them at forty-two minutes, the sun lost behind their massed silhouette. Phil's map was wrong. The route was near enough three miles long.

The air was cooling rapidly. Nick switched off his phone. He didn't want disturbing, and if time did bend enough to stop watches he'd rather it not scramble his phone. He might need it when the two of them were leaving.

Pushing through the branches, he shivered as perspiration

caused by the walk began to chill on his skin. The Pool came into view, its water stretching dark across the land, the bubbles at its centre bathed in the last glints of reflected sunset caught in the thin clouds. Beneath his feet the ground felt firmer than he recalled, and he dropped the bag by the trees to step to the water's edge. A fine debris line showed that it had receded at least the length of his trainers. The shrine-log was no longer an island.

The day before, Alice had simply appeared, walking through the shallow water as if from the further bank. The trees across there were turning charcoal as the dusk developed, their branches burnt out by the receding orange glow. It struck him that the curved line of their thin trunks was taking on the form of a Neolithic timber circle, and he wondered whether that had been conceived in the planting or was merely... He smiled as the term *coincidence* slipped through his mind. Alice had never believed in coincidence.

It seemed wrong to call her, as if the sound of his voice might shatter the serenity. Yet from the deepening gloom of the foliage he was sure he could hear the tinkling of bells – the offerings draped in the branches. Hadn't he been calling her when he'd left the silver coin?

Walking along the water's edge, he dug in his pockets. No fifty-pence Britannia lay in his palm; a ten-pence piece would have to do.

His trainers kicked a quiet splash catching his attention. Water was streaming silently round his feet, round the shrine-log. Open-mouthed, he turned to the Pool to see the dull reflections of the sunset playing over the rising bubbles. Raising his gaze he found only a cobalt sky.

Alice.

Her crown broke the surface with no sound at all, and she rose from the Pool as if climbing steps. Then water began to cascade from her hair and her face, her shoulders and her arms. The torc at her neck glowed, but it was in response to the light emanating from her skin, from her hair, from her clothing. He'd been mistaken last night. She was shining with her own light, a yellow nimbus marking her path. He couldn't take his gaze from her, his sight roving over each line and curve as she walked towards him. His chest constricted with emotion. Lifting his arms in welcome, he took a step forwards, the water splashing around his calves. He was ankle-deep in it, his feet already numbing, the cold liquid soaking up his jeans.

'Alice...'

His words faltered. She was powering towards him, her shoulders set, her expression fierce. There was no mist about her legs, but he knew it wasn't Alice. Raising his hands in defence, he tried to back away but his legs wouldn't move, and it was closing on him, the *thing* that looked like Alice, its hands lifting.

Its icy grip shuddered along his jaw, up his cheek-bones, and a searing pain shot through his head. He gasped a breath, choked off as cold lips enveloped his. It drew back, its eyes alight.

'Yes!'

Everything hurt. He couldn't think. It still had hold of his face but he couldn't feel its touch, couldn't move his hands locked around its forearms. Had no strength to fight. And that grin. Triumphant.

If it didn't let go...

But his knees buckled anyway, his vision filling with its glow.

Chapter 20

'Nicholas... Nicholas... Come on, Nick. You're all right. Come on back.'

He thought it day, the light was so bright, but it was Alice holding him – not holding him. His coat was round his shoulders, and something red. Odd. Scratchy.

'Drink, Nicholas, you have to drink.'

It wasn't tea. Liquid ice dribbled over his chin burning a line along his neck as it scored into his skin, seared down his throat. He shuddered and lifted his head. Branches sawed through his hair.

'That's better. You're okay. Look at me, Nick, look at me. That's it, that's better.'

He'd thought his eyes were already open, but it had been her light shining through his lids. He had to squint, she was so close. It was like looking into the sun. That was ridiculous.

Again he shuddered. Something was pummelling at him. She was pummelling his arm.

'Come on, Nick, don't go to sleep.'

A sense of floating and then a hammering at his back, the red itchy thing scratching at his cheek.

'*Move*, Nicholas. You have to get your circulation going. Come on, help me.'

Pain shot down one leg and his foot started burning, a muscle spasm separating his toes. He started to cry out, then remembered the *thing*. It hadn't been Alice walking across the water. It had been the *thing* intent on killing him. It had tried in York.

He looked for the tell-tale mist, but couldn't see beyond its glow. Everything beyond its glow was as black as if it didn't exist. Its face, Alice's face, swung in front of his and he had to squint again.

'Can you see me? Can you hear me? Nod if you can hear me.'

He nodded, then cursed himself for acknowledging it. Closing his eyes against the light, he tried to build enough response in his muscles to fight it off.

'Thank goodness. I really thought... I'm sorry, Nick. I was so determined to lose the shadow people that I forgot. But it worked! They've gone. That's good, isn't it? And it was all down to concentrating on you.'

His eyes sprang open as he flopped over. There was more pummelling, his face being pushed into the scratchy thing. It was the car rug, he realised, and beyond that was the groundsheet he'd bought in Durham, crinkling as she moved him. He was wrapped in the groundsheet like a parcel.

'Enough!'

The pummelling stopped. He used his elbow to ease himself onto his back. The groundsheet gave a bit and he forced it apart close to his throat, his coat apart, the rug.

'Careful, you'll end up in the water. Can you feel your toes?'

He breathed hard despite the meagre effort, squinting at her, at it. At Alice. It had to be Alice, hadn't it? She'd wrapped him for warmth. The *thing* wouldn't have, would it? He shuddered against the memory of York, it pretending to be Alice and covering him with frost as it tried to drag him through the portal; another shudder as a spurt of renewed feeling shot down his leg. The pins and needles in his fingers were growing in intensity and with effort he pulled free his hands to shake them out.

'I'm sorry,' she said. 'I didn't think. I mean, I forgot. It's just so— Do you want to sit up? Will that help?'

She didn't wait for him to answer. With a slurp of water she rose from kneeling beside him to grasp the edges of the groundsheet and drag him to rest against the trunk of the tree.

'How's that?'

'Better,' he managed, but it wasn't. Branches were sticking in his back now, as well as sawing through his hair. They felt like sharpened fingers clawing at him.

'It got rid of the shadow people. Did you hear me tell you that? They disappeared when I focused solely on you. I should have realised.'

He blinked, surprised, and looked at her again.

'You're synced.'

She chuckled. 'What?'

With effort he pulled himself further into a sitting position. His feet wouldn't respond properly, but his ankles moved and he smacked his trainers together inside his bindings to help regain some feeling.

'You're synced,' he said. 'Speak to me.'

'What do you want me to say?'

He was cold, he was shivering, but it felt as if the biggest smile was spreading across his face. 'You're talking and moving in real time. You weren't yesterday.'

'Yesterday?'

He felt his smile fade. 'Don't you remember me coming here?'

'Oh yes, but it doesn't seem like...' she frowned, 'yesterday.'

Time bends.

He struggled to pull free his mobile. At least it wasn't wet. While it cycled through its wake-up he leaned in to her glow to read his wristwatch: four-thirty. In the morning? He stared at the black void beyond Alice's shoulder. Not a void. There were trees there, water, he knew there were.

'What are you doing?'

The screen of his mobile lit. 23:13.

'Time distorts,' he whispered, not quite believing it.

'Oh, I know,' she said. 'It can be very disorientating.'

He looked at her. 'You *know*?'

'Yes, I'm sure it's something to do with the shadow people. Or they're to do with it. I've not worked it out.'

'Shadow people?'

He checked his watch again – its second hand wasn't moving – but the digital figures on his mobile were flicking through at speed, the same as it had yesterday. He hit its Off button and hoped for the best. Rosemary's explanation had been guff.

'It was lovely to see you... yesterday.'

He locked on to Alice's wistful tone, drawing his gaze across the smooth lines of her eyes, her cheeks. Did she know it was three years since York? Could she remember York?

'What shadow people?' Again he tried to penetrate the black beyond her shoulder. 'Are they here? Are they chasing you? Are you in danger?'

'Danger?'

She seemed to wrap the word around her tongue as if it was an alien concept. He squinted into her face. She seemed... Was she trying to *sense* them?

'I'm not sure,' she said, 'but they've gone now I've concentrated on you.'

He sat straighter. 'I've come to free you, to take you away from here.'

It sounded such a hollow intent, him shivering for his life wrapped in a car rug and a ground sheet. He rubbed his hands together, seeing her smile, seeing her gaze slide away from him again.

'It can be done. I've researched it. All the folklore tales insist it's possible.'

Possible, yes, but they'd been vague on the practicalities of *how*. He couldn't dwell on that now.

'You can live outside the Pool,' he persisted. 'We can be together again. You can be free.'

He made himself believe it so she would believe him. And she did, he could see it in her growing smile, the way her hand—

He flinched back, couldn't stop himself, and with a sinking heart watched her hand retract. His held breath released in a shuddered gasp.

'Still cold.' He rubbed at his arms, wishing he'd said nothing. For long moments he daren't look at her, and berated himself for that, too. He needed to be positive, to act.

'We need to go now,' he said, 'before these shadow people

return.'

He started to pull at the groundsheet that bound him, trying to find its edge, and wondered if he could stand unaided. His legs felt like jelly.

When she didn't respond, he dared a glance and saw that her attention was fixed on the ground. He leaned over to discover what she was looking at and understood why she'd bound him so tightly. The Pool had extended to the trees. Water flattened the grass, carrying her reflection as if a mirror. The knees of her trousers kissed, the glow from her t-shirt accentuating the torc at her neck, the auburn of her hair.

She was moving deliberately, he realised, her hand from the water reaching for her hand from the air. He wanted to say something, but words wouldn't come. There was a mesmerising moment when he was unsure which was real and which reflection, and then he saw it, as silver as the shrine-coins, rising above the black band of the trees near their shoulders. Never had the mottled greys of the moon looked so much like a human face.

They were reaching for it, the hands of Alice and her reflection, their fingers melding as they slid through its surface. And then the moon juddered, the water vibrating with tight ripples that broke its reflection into shards. They were arching their backs, the Alice of the water and the Alice of the air, their faces turning to the sky, the nimbus about their heads—

Nick dragged his gaze from the water to stare at the Alice of the air. The bright nimbus about her head had grown as her hair rose in individual locks to sway in a flaming mantle. There was a tinkling in the trees around him, a pressure in his eardrums. Her up-raised face eased down.

'I can warm you now,' he heard. Her lips hadn't moved.

A power swelled in him as he looked at her. He didn't want to be warmed, he wanted, needed, to make love to her, to throw off the pinning rug and the groundsheet and rake his fingers through her hair, feel her lips pressing against his own, her teeth, her tongue. He wanted to feed from her flesh, carry them into raptures that filled their single being with fire. But he couldn't move beyond the trembling threatening to shake him apart, the high-pitched whistling piercing his brain. Her glow was growing in intensity so he could hardly see her features, but he could feel her arm scooping beneath the groundsheet. She was pulling him towards her fiery mass, cradling him to her.

'Be warm,' he heard. 'Be warm.'

Not me, you.

Alice had been warm in his bed at the farm.

Chapter 21

Ernald slept poorly. He was used to the snoring of his fellow brothers, not the calls of night creatures fighting in the darkness, nor the cold earth beneath shoulder and hip. He had become used to the rhythm of the House, too, and woke on unheard bells for Matins and Lauds. Pressing Saint Cuthbert's cross to his chest, he listened to the soft breathing of those around him while the rise and fall of the plainsong drifted through his head.

When roused by a tap to his shin, the light of day was no more than milky-grey and the grass and his cloak wet with dew. As did others, he used it to wash the sleep from his face and to coat his tongue. There would be no breaking his night's fast for many an hour, and he knew better than to mention it. Instead, he took himself a little way distant, brought out his chaplet and undertook the office of Prime as he did when out in the world as the priory's questor carrying the Saint's minor relics.

A man in a leather jerkin and a bright-eyed youth made up Master Ore Reeve's group, and as Ernald watched he could see they needed no instruction as to their duties. He wondered if the man had been the guard on the door to the confinement chamber, the owner of the hidden cudgel, but his mind would not bring the memory clear enough for recognition. Certainly no cudgels were in view as the rough-coated ponies were loaded, only mattocks and hammers and different lengths of iron rods – tools for many labours and none to snag a questioning eye.

In turn, the crying man and the novice were allowed to empty their bowels and bladders, and were tethered either side of the larger animal. At a gentle tap from a switch the group set on their journey, crossing the common land to join the rutted trackway.

Why were they tethered? The novice was a dispirited youth, all sloping shoulders and mouldering frowns. The crying man, the *smiling* man, was a man reborn, eager to watch for a signal to move, to gather his leash and hold his arm for inspection. Why tie a willing man?

Ernald walked some while before matching his step to that of their leader.

'Good morrow, Master Ore Reeve. The weather looks set fair.'

'There's a maiden's blush in the horizon clouds.'

Ernald looked east. The sun was rising through a tinted haze, but nothing he considered bearing rain. He inclined his head and smiled. 'A very young maid,' he conceded.

His attempt at levity was met by a grunt.

'The man I saw in the confinement chamber looks in better repair.'

'Food, clothing, a cleanse. To you, friend Ernald, these the priory provides. Even a fermery waiting to treat to your wounds. Not you shivering in line for a dole of thinned pottage with barely cloth to cover your beaten back.'

'If a man gives his life to God...' He paused on seeing the reeve's dark eyes turn his way.

'Fatted goose and warm fires in manor halls?'

'Only occasionally Master Ore Reeve. Mostly it is bread and small ale. And pottage. And labour. And learning. And service to our Lord and to Saint Cuthbert and the Blessed Mary.'

'And will you be interrupting our journey to give service to our Lord, and Saint Cuthbert, and the Blessed Mary, seven times a day?'

Ernald felt the hackles rise on his neck at the man's questioning of the Faith, but he kept his gaze on the uneven track as he formed his response.

'Out in the world a brother keeps Prime and Vespers, and offers blessings for hospitality provided and on behalf of those who provide it. I have no wish to usurp your authority, Master Ore Reeve.'

'You'll not do that.'

'Then can we not be plain-spoken companions on a shared quest that is blessed by our Lord God?'

'Blessed by our Lord God, is it?' The man turned to gaze into Ernald's face. 'My mistake, friend Ernald. I believed it was blessed by our Lord Sub-Prior. I take comfort in your greater knowledge.'

The mummers' smile that eased a show of teeth from the thick beard was plain-spoken enough: their exchange had ended. Ernald stepped two more paces with the reeve then inclined his head in deference and tempered his stride to fall behind the man's shoulder. He had not found his answer, had not even proffered his question, but the day was young, as was the journey. Patience would be his virtue.

The group met the old stone road a little further on, and joined merchants' ox carts and pedlars' handcarts, and a throng of pilgrims returning to manors south of the priory's town. In his given garb of cloak and brimmed rush hat, Ernald brought no attention, not even when his dark habit was in open view. It was, he realised, accepted that he had undertaken a pilgrimage with restraints.

'...on behalf of others,' he told a man who asked, which was not even a bending of the truth.

Perhaps it was why no one questioned the need for two men to be tethered to a pack-pony. Pilgrimages were made for penitents and reforming wolf's-heads as well as for a man's soul and the greater glory of God and his Saints. And who could cast aspersions for the need of profit at the fayre? Neither pedlar nor merchant had done poorly, it seemed, contributing to a jocular atmosphere among the travellers. Ernald was pleased to note that there was as much conversation about the priory's processional as there was of bawdy houses and quaffing ale.

'Were you witness to the moment Mother Mary shone in all her majesty?' asked a man. 'Her light filled my eyes brighter than the sun. I am truly blessed.'

Ernald smiled and nodded, agreeing that many had been so

truly blessed, not least himself. He watched the man press along the line eager with his question, and smiled again at the animated reactions it brought. The man was sure to be voluble all the way to his home manor where he would imbue the wonder of the day on family and neighbours, in turn lifting every heart.

The sun was halfway to noon when Master Ore Reeve spoke of breaking bread. Ernald could not say that he was sorry to rest. His boots were pinching and he would do well to check his feet. When he saw the wayside cross rising above the heads of the travellers, he knew where he was and what lay in the dell below the road. Our Blessed Lady's spring. It would be a marker on their quest, the first to be penned into his report.

In the shadow of the painted stone, boards had been set on trestles to carry baskets of fresh loaves and pungent cheeses, their scents designed to whet an appetite. Women were busy at fires a little way off, baking more bread by the smell that wafted on the breeze. There were flagons aplenty, too, of both small ale and spring water. As were many, Ernald was set on visiting the spring itself and said so to the reeve.

'Carrying coin, are you, for the benefits of the water?'

Ernald frowned, his gaze drifting down to the man's chest as he considered his predicament.

'You're a pilgrim now, friend Ernald. Unlike holy men, pilgrims pay their way in the world. You, being the priory's questor, should know this.'

Ernald did know this. He simply hadn't taken it to include himself, nor in truth, their quest. Perturbed, he raised his gaze to find amusement in the reeve's expression.

'It is well that the sub-prior thinks on these things,' the reeve said, and he dug into his jerkin to bring out four quarter-pennies which he offered to Ernald. 'Don't be wasting them on whores down there. Your dole will be awaiting your return.'

Ernald thanked the reeve and clasped the coin pieces in his palm, trying to recall when he had last done such a thing on his own mark. Coins aplenty passed through his hands into the priory's coffers, each accounted for in his reports. But, as the Reeve had said, his every need was provided. Even the linen undershirt and good leather boots waiting for him beyond the priory's walls had been gifted, each for bringing comfort to the dying. He felt repentant, now, for accepting them, for hiding them, for persuading himself they eased his mission in the world. Fatted goose and warmed mead, and not one quarter-coin offered in their exchange.

Steps to the dell were marked by a withy arch woven in God's greenery and interspersed with bright flower-heads. A fresh flower was available from a rosy-cheeked maid for a coin. Watching others, it seemed a kiss came too, some less chaste than others, and Ernald marked the reeve's warning of whores. Surely not defiling Our Blessed Lady's spring? He deferred to the maid's outstretched hand but passed beneath the arch without her flower.

At once the ground fell away into earthen steps barely kept in place by stakes and board, and he was pleased he held a pilgrim's staff for support. A platform of the same, large enough to hold five people, had been carved from the hillside halfway down so those coming up might pass. Even so, there was such a press of devotees that boys top and bottom regulated the flow.

The hillside had long been cut of its wood, yet a stand of coppiced ash had been left to both mark and screen the spring. Talk around him dropped to a whisper as they entered the walkway of leafy stems, and Ernald shuffled along in an echo of the processional. The tight woodland opened in an apse around the spring, itself covered in arches of garlanded withies forming an open arbour. A small but intricately carved wooden rood balanced at its apex. Ernald reached up to press Saint Cuthbert's reliquary cross into his chest as he made obeisance to it. The only whispering now were snatches of prayer and invocations.

Upon his turn, he bent his head into the bower and nodded to the old woman seated low on her stool. She acknowledged him in return. Beside her, coated in the gold of unseen sunlight, a line of water chortled across a retaining stone to fall into a narrow trough the length of a man's forearm.

'D'ye commen t'drink o'Our Laddee?' Her voice was clear but her speech thick and Ernald had to listen close.

'I do,' he said.

Her gnarled hand reached out. He wondered how many quarter coins to place in her palm, and rebuked himself for not paying closer attention to those who had gone before. One quarter seemed enough, and the woman took up a wooden cup and dipped it into the brimming trough. She nodded as it passed from her hand to Ernald's, and she ushered him beyond the bower opening to where others were sipping from their cups.

The water was fiery cold and left a sharp taste of metal on his tongue. He could understand why none was taking it as a full-throated draught. Men and women both were standing with eyes closed, their hands encircling their wooden cups as if supporting a Holy vessel. Some murmured invocations, some touching the head of a child at their sides. It was not God's Sacred Word given in the Holy tongue, nor was it God's Holy Church in which they stood, but it was Saint Mary's waters freely given for the people as She had freely given the world Her Son. Ernald could envisage finding such as this far into the greenwood and marking it with a stone-wrought arbour, a place to kneel in prayer, a place for the sick to be bathed, perhaps a hospital in which to rest after their arduous journeys.

As he sipped, he thought of the crying man, the *smiling* man, and the novice tethered to the pack-pony on the road, with neither coin nor choice to visit the Blessed Mary's spring.

When he had emptied his cup he did not give it to the waiting boy, but stepped back into the line to request more water.

'...for sore companions on the road,' he told the old woman. She frowned at him, and when she proffered her palm it stayed proffered until he'd paid both for the water and for the cup.

Up on the road he was again met with a frown, from Master Ore Reeve.

'Bartered for a pilgrimage token from the crone? You surprise me, friend Ernald.'

'I have brought water for our tethered companions,' Ernald told him, 'to inspire them in our quest and show that their souls are not forgotten, neither by their fellow travellers nor by our Blessed Saint Mary.'

He felt a spurt of pleasure on seeing the reeve's eyes widen, but immediately chastened himself for his sin of pride. Stepping by the man, he approached the novice sat on the ground by the pony's legs.

'I have brought you water from Our Lady's spring so it may ease your troubled thoughts and return the bright light of our Lord to your countenance.'

The novice glanced at the cup but, as Ernald expected, he turned aside.

'What is your name?' There was no response. 'I am known on this quest as friend Ernald,' he told the novice, 'and I offer my arm as a staff to lighten your load. You only need to reach for it.'

The youth's head bowed further, giving Ernald sight of a pale mark half-hidden in the line of his out-growing tonsure, the fading remnant of the blow witnessed in the cloister. Ernald tipped water into his palm. Murmuring the Rite of Blessing, he spread the contents across the youth's crown. The novice tried to shrug Ernald aside, but the Rite had been completed to Ernald's satisfaction.

In contrast, the smiling man was on his feet, eager for the cup. Ernald passed it into his hands and watched him gulp down the contents before the Rite of Blessing had been completed. He did not take the cup from the man's offering hand, but gripped the hand itself, the cup held between them.

'My name is Ernald,' he said, touching Saint Cuthbert's reliquary cross beneath his habit. 'Ernald,' he repeated. He pointed to the chest of the still smiling man and nodded encouragement.

The man blinked, slowly raising his tethered hand to touch his own chest. 'Wulfrith.'

Ernald grinned at him, and the man's smile grew wide in return. 'Well met, Wulfrith. We will walk together and do God's Holy work.'

Ernald dried the cup on his cloak and was setting it in his satchel when the reeve approached with a serving of bread and cheese.

'Your choice of place to rest was guided, I think, Master Ore Reeve.'

'Perhaps. But it has proved no rest for you. We leave now. You can eat as you walk.'

Ernald fell into step with Wulfrith and the two shared the bread and cheese.

Chapter 22

Nick woke to the light of day shining through his eyelids and an insistent sound in his head, a curlew calling as it circled the Pool. Strands of Alice's hair were draped across his face, sunlight firing russet tones along their lengths, and his thumb sought the ring carrying three of those strands. He smiled, more content than ever he had been, as he breathed in the scents carried in her hair. Bracken and wildflowers, and a faint tang of wood smoke.

She lay half on top of him in a form remembered from their night at the farmhouse, one leg hooked over his, her arm draped across his body. Here they were separated by his padded coat, the car rug and a groundsheet that crinkled when he moved. He was warm, though, cocooned in the groundsheet and the rug. His jeans were stuck to his shins, and when he flexed his toes his feet felt wet in his trainers. He didn't care. He was warm and it was daylight, Alice was with him, and he could touch her again.

Locks of her hair slid through his combing fingers, clearing a path to her cheek. His fingertips hovered, then stroked her skin, not shining now that he could see, and only as chill as the water pooling about her. There had to be a way to free her from it. Perhaps all he had to do was take her hand and lead her out through the trees.

The inane thought unnerved him. It couldn't be that simple, could it? None of the mediaeval manuscript fragments, none of the folklore tales he'd pored over, had explained how the woman left the water. Perhaps they'd not explained because it was obvious: the man simply led her away because she wanted to go with him.

But what about the cold? Not one manuscript fragment had mentioned the cold. Or a fiery brightness in the darkness. His building enthusiasm faded. Few mentioned the moon. None the *thing* that had taken her.

Alice began to stir. He raised himself on one elbow to reach his arm across her back to capture her, tucking his hand into the edge of his sleeve for insulation. It meant he could hold her close as she lifted her head, could brush a kiss across her cheek – not as cold as he expected – a second kiss, a third, until he could feel her smiling beneath his lips. When her eyelids fluttered he gazed down into those pale green-grey irises.

'Good morning,' he whispered, and he brushed her lips with his own.

She angled her head and purred. He smiled at her response, brushing her lips again, lips no more chill than if she'd walked in from a snowy day.

'You sound satisfied.'

She stretched against the groundsheet making it crackle, and slid her arms either side of his face. His heart gave a thud as the terror of the night tried to reclaim him and he forced himself not to flinch, but her touch was delicate, featherlike. Her lashes closed over her eyes and her lips sought his again. His need overrode his sense of unreality, his body craving a warm being it knew existed. Yet her searching tongue felt odd and he drew free to stifle the urge to chuckle.

'What's funny?' She reached up to chafe at his jaw-line with her teeth.

Closing his eyes, he surrendered to the sensation, arching so she could follow down his neck. He felt her fingernails rasping at his hairline. His blood pounded in his ears... *need you, need you*. He frowned, drawing a tremulous breath as he pulled away. Why was he doing this to himself?

'Come back to bed.'

Her murmured words stilled him, and he opened his eyes to study her. It wasn't just him. She was floating in the after-glow of making love. Except... except she hadn't been wearing a torc when they'd made love.

He reached up to draw her hand from his hair, a hand that wasn't truly cold, merely chill. He kissed her fingertips, wondering what was happening, what to say. Had she been warm last night, or had she only warmed him?

'Alice,' he breathed. 'Alice, we're not in bed. We're at the Pool.'

Her eyes snapped open, her head jerking as she looked about her.

Time bends.

'It's all right,' he whispered, reaching to kiss her cheek. 'It's all right. I'm here. We're together.'

Confusion radiated from her small movements, but she wasn't cold, not truly cold.

'You're okay, Alice. Were we in bed? In sheets? At the farm? It's okay. I'm here. I'm with you.'

She tried to snatch her hand away, to wriggle free, but he clasped her tight.

'I'll freeze you.'

'You won't.'

Was this why she didn't feel as cold as he'd expected? Because she'd been at the house?

'We did make love,' he told her. 'It was fantastic, mind-blowing, and you stayed with me all night; I held you in my arms. But it wasn't last night. It was the night before.'

Momentarily he doubted whether it had been the night before. *Time bends. It's disorientating.* Too right; he was even questioning it himself.

Her hand slid free of his. He needed to maintain their physical contact, and reached out to brush strands of hair from her eyebrows.

'Do you feel warm, Alice?'

'I always feel warm.' She turned her face away, a catch in her voice. 'That's the problem, isn't it? I'm not, am I?' Her head snapped round, her expression fierce as she pushed herself to her knees. 'I'm dead, aren't I?'

'*No.*' The word exploded in a punch of breath.

'No,' he said again. Her eyebrow raised and torc lifted, solid on her collarbones as she set her shoulders. She didn't believe him.

'I thought you were, I thought I'd lost you, but I'm here and I'm talking to you and you're talking to me, so you aren't, can't be—' Relief swept through him as he saw her shoulders ease.

'Something happened,' she said. 'Something had to have happened but I can't remember.'

Tears were brimming, and he reached out to stroke her cheek. He didn't understand it himself. What good would it do to try to explain?

'Alice, if I knew I'd tell you, but I don't. I only know that at the farmhouse you were a woman on fire.' He pulled her back to him. 'You're *hot* now.' He was pleased to see her smile, and he dropped a kiss onto the end of her nose.

'You don't feel cold, either. Not the way you were before. I'm tempted...' He grinned. 'I'm so very tempted to drag you in here and lick every square centi—'

Her lips enveloped his, the groundsheet crackling as she launched herself on top of him, her weight pressing him down into the slurping water. She pulled back to smile, her eyes alive with mischief.

'You should be careful what you wish for.'

He couldn't laugh with her. He had to make her understand, make her believe he was sincere.

'I wish for you, Alice. I wish to take you away from here, to set you free. I've come to take you home.'

His feet were growing colder, but he was more concerned to see her smile fading.

'We can do it, Alice, if we believe, if we work together. You're not in the Pool now; you're on top of me.'

She moved against him and he heard a splash. 'That's a fish, then, is it?'

'There was no water when we were in bed at the farmhouse.'

Her smile left altogether, her gaze drifting to her hands, flat across his chest. 'That might not have been... entirely me.'

The *thing*. No, he wouldn't accept that. And there'd been no torc round her neck, had there? Not like now. He stared at the open circles of the terminals lifting from her collarbone as she angled her head.

'It was you,' he said. 'I know it was. Believe me, I know the difference.'

He licked his lips. Should he ask her about it? He didn't want to break their spell and she was shaking her head, her gazed unfocused.

'Sometimes I seem to be in two places at once. It's difficult to explain.'

The cold was creeping along his legs. The bottom of his jeans were wet.

'I'm listening.'

She took a breath and eased down to rest her chin on her hands. He strained forwards to peck at her lips and she reached to meet his. It felt gloriously serene, as if they were truly still in the afterglow of making love. He could ignore his cold legs, he told himself. Would ignore them.

'Sometimes I look and the trees aren't like this. They're taller, darker, their trunks are in the water. Sometimes there's only a grassy bank, and sometimes there are animals – deer, birds.' Her eyes widened. 'I saw a wild boar once. Its tusks were enormous. We frightened each other and it ran away.' Her smile faded.

'People?'

'Sometimes. There was a man. It was a bit like the boar, we frightened each other, I think.'

'One of the shadow people?'

She shook her head, adamant.

'No, no. They're...' she shrugged. '...shadows. He was real. I think he was ill. I just wanted to help him.' She shook her head making her hair dance. 'Memories are hazy. They don't seem like mine. Sometimes it seems I can hear people but can't see them. Other times I can see them, can see that they're talking but I can't hear anything.'

'Can they see you?'

'I'm not sure. Sometimes I think so, but often they're indistinct. Some talk to me, though, I'm sure they do. Especially the women. At least I think they're talking to me. I— Sometimes I hear the sounds but can't make out the words. They wash their children in the water. Lovers come, too. They drink the water, pour it over each other... almost as if they're enacting a ritual.'

Nick rasped in a breath. *Time bends*. Was it bending around Alice. Was she travelling through time? Was time travelling through her? He hadn't been wrong. The Roman at York, he'd been real.

A thought gripped him, a horrendous memory from their days in Hull. He reached out needing to protect her. 'Do you see —?' But how could he ask about men with bloodied swords? About a massacre?

She looked at him expectantly.

'Fire,' he said, 'the smell of smoke?'

He watched her mentally trawl through memories and willed her to stop, wishing he'd said nothing. 'It doesn't matter. Maybe it was just a dream.'

She smiled again, her fingers reaching out to trace an arc down his cheek. 'That's what I thought when I first saw you, that I had to be dreaming. I think it must have been when I felt I couldn't cope anymore.' She looked at him directly, snuggling herself into his arms.

'I missed you so much I began to see you, glimpses of you like the glimpses of the shadow people. It was so unexpected I thought I was dreaming. And then I saw you again and I knew you were searching for me, that you would come.'

He gripped her tightly, desperate to keep his voice steady as emotion threatened to choke him.

'I'm here, Alice. I'm not leaving. We're going to get you out of here.'

He blinked as if coming from a stupor. Why was he just saying it? He needed to do it.

Pushing against his coverings, he said, 'Now, Alice. Come with me now.'

She slid off the groundsheet and he was able to wriggle free of the cocoon she'd created to clamber to his feet and flex feeling into his ankles. His feet felt numb, his trainers squelching as he stepped forwards. She looked up at his offered hand and slapped the wet ground beside her.

'I can't leave the water.'

'Alice, you left the water to come to the farm. We made love. You were warm. You were *very* warm, Alice.'

She looked away and he crouched beside her to take her hand. It wasn't wet. Was it cooler? He wasn't sure.

'Think warm,' he told her.

She gave a snorting chuckle. 'It's not that simple. And I can't leave the water. Don't you think I've tried? I've tried many times. I get onto the bank and then... and then I'm not on the bank.'

'You're on the bank now.'

She slapped the wet ground again, the spray hitting his already wet jeans.

'Plan B then.'

He was pleased to hear her laugh this time, even though he couldn't match it. His gaze kept sliding to her throat, to the twisted rope of fine gold wires glinting in the sunlight. It had to be the torc that shackled her to the Pool. He knew where it came from, or thought he did, and he wanted to ask her, to hear it from Alice – she hadn't been wearing it at the farm – but then what?

'What's wrong?' she asked.

He mentally side-stepped. 'These shadow people, are they following you?'

Her demeanour became guarded. 'Don't talk about them. You'll draw them close.'

He grabbed her hand. 'Are they threatening you?'

'No, no. It's not like that. It's hard to explain. They're just there, like shadows at the edge of my vision. But they disappeared. When I concentrated solely on you, they disappeared.'

'Then let's go,' and he pulled her to her feet.

'Nick...'

'No, Alice, we're going. You have to believe that you can. You came to me at the farm and that's miles away. All you need to do is walk through the trees.' He hoped that was all she needed to do. 'I'm with you. You can do this. You just have to believe you can.'

He set off, gripping tight her hand. She was cooling. He could feel the change in her temperature and his alarm grew. His fingers hurt and he couldn't feel his palm. He needed to let go of her. Where was his bag? He should have worn the gloves. Two steps, just two more steps and they'd be parting the branches.

She was pulling against him.

'Believe it, Alice.'

'Nick... the shadow people.' Her whisper became shrill. 'Nick, they're in the *trees!*'

He stared ahead, seeing nothing but leafy branch fronds swaying in a breeze he couldn't feel. She was dragging on his arm. He looked back to find her expression full of fear. She was cooling rapidly. He couldn't feel his hand. He tried to grasp her tighter but his fingers refused to respond.

'Alice, calm down.'

Beyond her shoulder small puddles stood in the grass, footprints full of water. One set, too small to be his. A rivulet was defying gravity, reaching from the Pool to connect them, a finger of water creeping up the gradient towards him and Alice.

Nick gasped, his breath clouding. He couldn't feel his forearm; his hand felt like stone.

'Alice, you're turning everything cold. Calm down. There's no one here.'

She was shivering as he was, her hair dark with damp, perspiration glistening on her face.

'They're shadows in the corner of your eye. I've brought them, Nick, I'm sorry. I didn't mean to, I'm sorry. It's that man.

Everything changed after I helped that man.'

'What man? Alice—'

She was crying, tears streaming down her cheeks. They dripped from her nose. Not tears. Water was running from his hand, from her hand in his. It was running from her hair.

'Alice, *no!*'

He stepped close to wrap his free arm around her shoulders, to keep her with him. He felt the torc dig into his chest. Then there was no pressure and he was bathed in water so icy he cried out with the shock of it.

Chapter 23

Nick shuddered beneath the gnawing cold. Around his trainers, on his trainers, water bubbled and broke, each silvered dome carrying an image of Alice. He daren't move his feet, wasn't sure he *could* move his feet, and watched, stricken, as miniatures of her foamed and melded, her images refracting through rainbow colours until the final three locked to ripple through the grass towards the spear of water reaching from the Pool. The Pool was taking her back.

'*Alice!*'

He followed on unsteady legs, wincing as pressure built in his head, in his ears. Something thudded into his back jolting him forwards, and he ducked his head into his shoulders as debris flew by him – leaves and twigs and grass – and the groundsheet he'd been wrapped in stood like a sail at his side to collapse as his coat rolled in its wake towards the frothing water. He turned to the trees, expecting to see shadow people, expecting to see monsters. There was nothing except flailing branches easing back to their natural stance.

The Pool was receding, ripples building out of the froth to peak in concentric circles as they tightened towards its sucking centre. Horrified, he watched water pouring back into the ground from where he'd seen it erupt six years before.

Fear for Alice overtook all else as he chased its edge. Sodden grass gave way to a mat of stranded vegetation which separated beneath his weight to reveal slime-covered rocks and oozing mud thick enough to swallow his trainers. Each time he pulled free the fibrous stalks clung to his feet, impeding his momentum. If the water disappeared completely would it return? Would Alice return? Would she be able to?

The water's suction eased, its ripples flattening to leave a pond near enough three metres wide. Nick slowed, too, breathing hard with effort expended, his coated trainers sinking into its glutinous margins between the rocks. There was no sign of Alice now. There was no sign of the feeder spring.

The centre bounced in slow motion, seeming to be sucked down and pushed up in an egg-shaped bubble that didn't burst. He hoped Alice would rise from it, renewed, but the water flattened to a surface as still and glassy as if it had never moved.

Nick stared, hairs rising on his skin as memory brought sight of Alice lying face-down in it; of a second eruption that had almost claimed him. He took a slurping step backwards, nearly losing a shoe. Behind him the sticky morass stretched towards the trees, small in the distance.

He freed his other foot. A mist wafted across his face and his heart beat wildly in his need for escape, but it was his own breath he was seeing. His skin started to prickle and pucker beneath his wet clothing, and a shiver shot through him as his body tried to adjust. The temperature was plummeting again. He had to gain the trees. Alice had opened the portal and the *thing* was coming through.

Slithering across frosting rocks, he fought his way forward on numbed feet as slurried ice crept around his mud-encrusted trainers, crept ahead of him, causing every footfall to splinter its whitening surface. His arms flailing for balance, his chest heaving with exertion and fear, he picked his route, on and on, refusing to glance behind, refusing to recall the memory of *her*, of *its*, chill touch. He could save himself; he'd done it in York.

Keep moving. Focus on the trees. On one tree. One trunk.

Feathered branches scored lines across his cheeks, tried to rip out his eyes as he fought his arms around its trunk and tried to grip hand to forearm to lock himself in place. His ears popped. There was a sound of tinkling bells and above his head branches sawed and shook.

Warmth caressed his hair. He prayed for it to be Alice's touch, but it was the air which was warm. He turned to stare at the Pool. It had returned to half its normal size. There was no ice, no frosting, only faint swirls of mist retreating across its surface.

Dropping his head onto his bicep, Nick let tension slip from his muscles. The ground smelled of bracken and forest flowers where only matted grass grew. Fatigue flooded through him.

Gripping his shirt-front he pulled its sodden material from his chest, shivering as the sunshine changed his temperature as surely as Alice's fear.

Shadow people in the trees. He'd seen nothing. But what had caused that blast? The *thing?* Shadow people? *Glimpses in the corner of your eye.* He stared across the now calm water, paying attention to his peripheral vision. There was nothing odd, no shadows, not even of the trees.

He focused on himself. His feet were cold, his trousers streaked with mud, his trainers lost in thick casts of it. How he had dragged that weight so far he'd no idea. Banging his trainers together dislodged little and he knew he'd have to scrape it off before it set concrete-hard. His eyelids were heavy. He needed to sleep. Yet he didn't trust that to be his own exhaustion, either. Forcing himself to crawl across the ground, he grasped the nearest stick and set to scraping free the worst of the mud.

The Pool was creeping wider, slowly regaining former ground. If Alice had opened a portal that the *thing* had slipped through, what else might slip through? There'd been a Roman in York. A madman. Or a man tumbled into a mad world with no hope of understanding or return. Shadow people? Nick studied the circle of trees. Their branches waved gently in a breeze he couldn't feel, couldn't see. Who was Alice seeing on the banks when the trees she saw weren't these trees? How could grass smell of bracken and forest flowers? How could time bend? It was all too much to comprehend. He didn't have enough information, not enough of the right information.

Banging his trainers together he stood to collect his coat. His feet still didn't feel right, though that could just be his sodden socks. His wet jeans felt like sandpaper as they chafed his knees, his thighs, his shirt a dead clinging thing sucking him of warmth.

He was a coward, he told himself as he folded the groundsheet. He should stay. Yet he stuffed it and the car rug into his bag. The storm shelter would remain unopened, at least for tonight. The sun was already dropping down the sky and he couldn't face his intended stay, not when he'd jump at every sound. Or maybe... maybe not jump fast enough.

Despite his decision, when he stored the bag under tree and turned to gaze over the Pool's glassy surface, the need to step to its creeping edge was felt as an ache in his chest.

'I'll come back.'

It sounded a weak excuse. Though he wasn't intending to, he took a step into the water.

'I'll come back,' he said more forcefully. 'Are you hearing me, Alice? I'm coming back for you. And when I do we're leaving. Do you hear me? We're leaving together.'

His muscles were ready to take another step. He refused them. Shrugging on his coat he turned for the trees to force a way through their grasping branches.

His muscles ached, but the going grew easier, despite the gradual incline of the land. Remnants of the Pool's mud crumbled with each footfall, dropping in his wake as the leather of his trainers regained their flexibility. Insects buzzed over the resplendent heather, harvesting the swell of nectar that fed Nick's senses each time he took a breath. Not until he was within sight of the dank pond cut from its rocky outcrop, and his shadow stretched before him twice his own height, did he remember to check his watch. It had stopped at ten past two. The weight of his phone in his pocket beckoned but he hadn't the energy to switch it on. Time bent, he knew that.

He kept walking, following the path as it rose and snaked and dropped, noticing dragonflies zip and hover, hearing bees drone close, and birds he couldn't name call across the moor.

The steep rise to the fenced sheep pasture caught him by

surprise, and he looked at it a moment before dragging himself up its partly gravelled path. At the stile he gazed across the narrow tarmac to the fencing with its *World Famous* signage, to the cattle grid and the fold yard. There was only one car parked there, Rosemary's, and he wondered what she'd say when he rang the doorbell. He didn't need a mirror to realise what state he was in.

As he crunched towards the house he raked his fingers through his hair to tidy himself and caught his cheek with his knuckle. Slowing his pace, he scraped his fingernails across his chin and down his throat. It didn't feel like a single day's growth. He licked his dry lips, and realised why he felt so thirsty.

Chapter 24

Damned Izzy. How the hell was he going to shake her off?

The song finished. In the pause Tim heard the mass spectrometer shifting through its cycle, the sounds abruptly crushed by a full-throated scream and the first notes of a guitar riff. He adjusted the volume on his iPod as he glanced along the bench to the machine. He was fine. It would be ages before it completed its routine.

Lifting another sample pot, he noted the code on the last and wrote the next in sequence on its label. This was going to be one of his better ideas. Izzy, on the other hand, was going to be a pain, he could tell. She had been the last time, but he never learned, did he? Far too needy to sleep with just occasionally. She was going to want to be forever in his space and never take *No* for an answer.

It had been a shock to have his phone ringing at that hour. A bird had launched into the air close by, shrieking as it flew low around the water. If it had had half a brain it would have lifted above the trees and been away.

He picked up the next pot to write on its label.

In reality it had been a good job the bird had given its alarm. He would probably have stepped onto that wino wrapped in his groundsheet. He'd never backed out of anywhere so fast in his life. Thankfully, he'd put the phone on vibrate after he'd killed her call because he'd hardly got ten paces and she was ringing again. What the hell did she want to keep ringing for? Hadn't he told her he was leaving early to collect samples?

His phone was still switched off. He'd sent her a text saying he'd ring when he could, and he'd shut it down. He'd get sorted here and switch it back on or she'd be filling his voicemail for the rest of the day. Christ! Did she have the firm's—

The stab into his shoulder blade made him yell at the same pitch as the guitar riff, his arm jolting and the lid of the pot spinning free to shower his face and hair with water. Wheeling round, he found John standing there, his eyes narrowed, his lips a compressed line.

Dragging free his earbuds, Tim tried to both wipe his face and switch off his iPod, but instead increased its volume. Eventually only the sound of the mass spectrometer could be heard in the lab.

'Brilliant,' John spat. 'The alarms are off and the site's wide open. Copper thieves could have entered and stripped the place and you wouldn't have heard a thing.'

'I'm sorry.'

'Of course you are.'

John turned to the row of sample pots aligned on the bench and Tim jumped forward, surreptitiously brushing aside the water he could feel furrowing from his hair to his eyebrow.

'I've already done the plant's samples. The results are—'

'I'm only interested in the results for sample TG15-29.' John swung back to face him. 'You know the one. It has a contaminant off the scale. You can't have missed it. The analyzers didn't, and you're a fucking idiot if you believe they download their data to you and then automatically wipe their memories.'

'It's not the plant,' Tim said in a rush. 'The plant's samples are fine.'

John glanced at the analyzer. 'It's in there, is it? TG15-29 was the reason for you going to up the university, wasn't it? And the result from *its* machines...?'

'Not identified.'

'Brilliant.'

Except it wasn't, Tim knew that. He'd not marked John as aggressive, had never even heard him raise his voice as his older brother did, but his shoulders were rounded, his head angled down. All that was missing was the rugby shirt and the growl before the charge. And he was blocking Tim's way to the door.

'Where's the source?'

'It's not the plant's. It's miles away.'

To Tim's surprise John straightened and eased his shoulders.

'So... it's not our sample, it's the project's sample.'

'Yes.'

'And the project's water source area is the North York Moors National Park.'

'I have the central section.'

'The central section. And that makes it okay, does it? Nothing to do with this plant?'

John's eyes widened with incredulity and Tim braced himself.

'We don't pump our water from some underground tank, not even an underground lake. It's from an aquifer. We don't know the exact size of the aquifer, or how far it extends; it's all a best guesstimate. The water's trapped between rock formations, trapped *in* rock formations. That's why what we bottle is called *mineral* water. The *minerals* in the rock formations give our water its signature.'

A stabbing finger rose to point at Tim's chest. He tried hard not to hold his breath yet could feel the hairs beginning to rise on his skin.

'To the south of us there's a gas extraction plant wanting to pump enough polluted water back into the ground to raise the entire table. To the north of us, fifteen square miles of prime water catchment moorland has been licensed to a fracking company, and God alone knows what they're doing up there. To the east of us they're mining potash on such a scale that they're building an underground conveyor system to take the ore from Scarborough to Hartlepool, and *you* think we shouldn't be interested in a contaminant registering off the *fucking scale?*'

Tim could feel his heart battering his chest wall, but he couldn't think of anything constructive to say.

'And stop blinking at me like a bloody owl! You can walk away from here, you tosspot, but if so much as a whiff of a water contaminant gets out to the press, five families and an entire business go belly up!'

The spectrometer beeped its completion. To Tim it sounded a God-sent time-out and he drew a breath. John looked at the machine, then back at him. He seemed to have deflated.

'This is going to be good,' he muttered. 'Get that tablet of yours hooked up and let's take a look.'

Tim inserted the leads, conscious that his fingers were trembling. He wondered why John didn't want to read it direct from the machine. Too small, perhaps, too monochrome. *Going to be good?* Tim sensed that the result was going to be appalling and in desperation he cast around for a qualifier.

'It'll be a high reading,' he said. 'It's a fresh sample.'

John tucked in close behind him, making him wish he'd said nothing at all.

When the bar chart opened Tim couldn't accept what he was seeing. The spike was so high that it made the other readings look like a bobbled flat line. All he could hear from John was a murmured *Shit, shit, shit.*

'No, it's okay. This is what I was expecting. Well, almost this. I took the sample direct from the bubble stream and stored it in a vacuum vessel. It's had practically no air to it. In the air the contaminant degrades. I realised this in the uni's lab, look...'

Tim tapped the screen, found the file and opened up another graph, then did the same again.

'I haven't had time to amalgamate the data yet, but this shows the original sample I tested here last week. And here it is again from the uni's analysis.'

John hunched over to look.

'And if you think that's a marked drop, look at this one.' Tim stood back almost triumphant as the new graph showed the spike to have dropped to less than a quarter. 'I didn't have much of the original sample left but decided to pour it into a saucer to stand.'

John reached across to slide between the graphs. 'For how long?'

'Just over twenty-four hours. But it wasn't from a vacuumed

sample. It had been reacting to the air in its container for days. That's why I set up this,' he gestured to the line of sample pots on the bench, 'so we can undertake some sort of controlled experiment. I thought perhaps we should open one a day and take a reading, then pour half the remainder in an open dish and trap air in the pot with the rest, analysing the water in each as we go.'

'*We?*'

'Well, it would be good for the project, certainly, but as you say, monitoring it could prove beneficial to the plant.'

He wasn't sure if he was reaching too far with that one, but John didn't mock him.

'Where is this source?'

'Off the Wheeldale Moor road in the middle of nowhere. It's called The Pool. The farmer there is trying to make some sort of tourist attraction.'

John stared at him. 'With a contaminant like this in the water? Are you kidding me?' He reached up to the shelf to pull down an Ordnance Survey map. 'Show me.'

'I can do better than that,' said Tim. 'I've got a GPS location.' He plunged into his pocket for his phone, switching it on as he drew it free. A cloud of voicemail and text notifications pinged in, followed by the staccato buzz of arriving emails. *Izzy*.

John eyed him. 'Girlfriend trouble by any chance?'

'Sort of.'

His finger stabbed hard into Tim's chest. 'She's to be told nothing, you understand? You tell *no one*. Got that?'

'Yes.'

'Have you told her?'

'No.'

'This is between me and you, Timothy. We're not even telling the others here until we have some hard data, okay? There's to be no interim reports sent to your project manager, nothing printed out, nothing on social media. Got that?'

'You want it kept under wraps. I've got that.'

Tim couldn't believe the exchange. It was as bad as dealing

with Simon and his activists.

'We need to keep the samples somewhere secure.' John walked to the chemical cupboard pulling open its door. 'Empty a shelf and put those pots in here with the vacuum container.'

'It might not fit. It's five litres. It weighed a ton.'

'Make it fit, and keep it locked.'

'What about the dishes? They'll need to be in the open air.'

'Use your initiative, Timothy. Clear the shelf above the bench and mark it up as a project experiment not to be touched. We're the only ones who come in here in any case.'

Usually, Tim thought, usually.

It took a while to get the cupboard sorted, but at least John wasn't at his shoulder to chivvy him. It looked as if the shelves hadn't been cleaned for years, but by bringing one down a notch the vacuum container fitted in the space, leaving plenty of room for the sample pots. He replaced the one he'd spilled, ensuring the lid fitted properly this time, and added the cupboard's spare key to his ring before raiding the kitchen for saucers.

His phone rang while he was walking back through the plant. It had to be Izzy. He thought about letting the call go to voicemail, but that was only putting off the inevitable. He needed to take control of this.

'What the hell's the matter with you, Izara? I said I'd ring when I had the time. I've had a very, *very*, bad morning.'

'Huh! Welcome to my world, Timothy. This is important. You said one of your project samples was showing something odd.'

He suppressed a groan. Why couldn't he keep his mouth shut?

'I've read Nicholas' book—'

'Book?'

'Yes. Book. Nicholas. Keep up, Tim. You met him at The Bishops' Mill on Saturday. He's written a book about water deities, the old pagan religions.'

Tim rolled his eyes. 'For God's sake—'

'*Listen*, will you. I looked him up on the internet. A colleague died excavating one of those springs where you are. There was an explosion or something and she was killed. It seems to be called the Pool now. There's a nature trail and—'

'What's it called?' But he knew he'd heard the first time.

'*The Pool.* It's miles from a decent road. I've got the coordinates and I wondered if it was the same—'

'It is.'

'And?'

He licked his lips. 'Coincidence.'

'Don't be ridiculous,' she snapped. 'There's no such thing.'

Chapter 25

Accompanying pilgrims thinned as the day wore on, the pedlars with them, drawn to occasional clusters of mean homes by the roadside. On a stool or a bench they took ale and bread in exchange for a coin and tales of the wonders of the processional, the fine coats of the merchants, the goods from far lands...

'...the like o'which has nivver been seen – ev'n in York!'

As Ernald watched, packs were unlaced. Doubtless trade would be two-way. Master Ore Reeve, though, was not to be drawn, despite the heat of the day, and kept the pace with a look to the group that brooked no argument.

It was not a slow pace and it was not a fast pace, but it was constant and Ernald was not used to such constancy. His bones ached and his boots were pinching. He had thought himself used to walking, but it was from one manor to the next where in each there would be rest and sustenance, and an eagerness in his hosts to be in the presence of the relics of Saint Cuthbert. Through the thick weave of his habit he touched the reliquary cross to his chest, feeling the hard metal against his breastbone. He increased his step until he was level with their leader.

'Master Ore Reeve.' He nodded in deference to ease his words. 'Are we resting this past noon?'

'If your belly grumbles, friend Ernald, you should not have shared your cheese with one who had already eaten.'

Ernald smiled. 'A gift to smooth the way, Master Ore Reeve. I know I cannot speak with him but Wulfrith—'

'—if that's his name.'

Ernald felt as if he'd misstepped. 'Why should it not be his name?'

Dark eyes turned to range across his face. 'You would give

your birthed name if dragged to the church court for questioning over an act you should not have undertaken?'

It was as if Ernald were standing in the Chapter House trying to untangle the words of the sub-prior. 'What act? Was he not healed at a spring?'

'I don't know, friend Ernald. We've been tasked with this journey to discover the truth of it. Are you growing lame, friend Ernald? You're hobbling like an old nag. We'll stop at the next bridge and you can bathe your feet.'

The reeve turned aside, and Ernald knew he'd been dismissed. Never did he seem able to voice the questions he needed.

He waited for the others grouped about the ponies to draw alongside. The novice gazed a little ahead of his sandaled feet, a stubbornness about his shoulders that the walk had not shaken free. Wulfrith grinned at him, and nodded, saying something in a dialect Ernald did not understand. He wished to understand it, and chided himself for the lack. Even on so short a journey he should make the effort to learn this new tongue. But what did they have in common except bread and cheese, and he now knew the words for those.

When they came to it, he found the bridge a rude affair, unlike the graceful arches and rising gatehouse of the crossing below the priory. Thick slabs of stone perched on water-smoothed blocks on either shore met above another centre-stream. Grooves worn into its surface told of its age and the many carts it had carried, yet it exuded strength and would be serviceable during a flood. Beside it ran a ford with a wide-cut pool to slow the waters and offer a safe place for beasts to drink. There was little water coursing through now, and in the afternoon heat clouds of flies hovered over churned hoof-marks.

The leashes holding Wulfrith and the novice were released from the pack saddle and the bright-eyed youth took both ponies down for water, or it looked to Ernald that they took him. The men sought their own refreshment, and Ernald removed his boots to walk a little way upstream before dipping his hand. Releasing his rush hat, he wet his linen coif, too, bringing a welcome coolness to his head and neck.

A call drew his attention, and he turned to find the reeve's man waving to him. Wriggling his blistered toes in the water, he made his way back until the mud grew too thick when he sought the sturdy bank. Sharp stalks of dead grasses needled at his soles with every footfall.

There was more bread, and this time slices of what looked like pottage boiled to a sticky mass. It was welcome, despite its lack of seasoning, and this time he was sharing it with no one.

'Do you carry a salve for your feet, friend Ernald?'

Whatever the reeve said to him seemed to carry a chiding sarcasm, and Ernald did not raise his eyes.

'I have my sandals.'

Without response the reeve moved on. It was Wulfrith who came close, offering a piece of his doled bread scraped with pottage. Ernald looked at him, remembering his first sight of the man, so ragged and forlorn in the darkness of the priory's confinement chamber. His broken-toothed smile was sincere, and Ernald accepted the offered food, as heart-warmed in its giving and receiving as he knew Wulfrith to be. Perhaps speech was a lesser thing to a mutual understanding.

The reeve did not let the group rest long, but it was time enough for Ernald to cut a thin strip from his roll of parchment and tie his boots about the strap of his satchel.

'Move, friend Ernald, move!'

Ernald did as he was bid, nimbly crossing with a rush of pedlars before a train of ox carts from the south blocked the bridge. He need not have hurried as the lead animals threw their heads and bellowed in consternation at the narrow causeway. Rugged men, thick of arm and neck, came to goad and haul them forwards. So many men, so many laden carts.

'What are they carrying?' Ernald asked the reeve's man as he re-tied Wulfrith and the novice to the pony's saddle.

The man shrugged. 'Anything. 'tis safety in numbers when travelling the waste.'

Ernald looked along their forward route. He had been but once to the ministry church in York. Many had travelled in the line, those from the priory and merchants from the town, each with their baggage carts. The Bishop had given men-at-arms to accompany them. Perhaps the mattocks and rods protruding from the pony-pack were not carried solely to aid a man's industry.

The stone road rose from the valley. At the ridge they left it for a rutted drovers' track devoid of sustenance for any beast. Ernald was pleased for the dry days of harvesting; wet mud would have sapped any man's strength. Yet as he looked about him it seemed thistles alone grew tall, bloomed purple; the only food being shrivelled berries on briar tangles. As the way dipped and wound about the shallow hills he could see no cooking smoke, no moss-covered roofs, only the dark bulk of the greenwood creeping ever closer. He glanced at the height of the sun behind its thin cloud cover and hoped they would not be spending the night in this place.

'Friend Ernald!'

The reeve's call caught his attention. He obeyed the gesturing hand to hurry forward, aware the ponies at his back were slowing.

'Quietly, friend Ernald. Smile with piety and trust.'

Ernald did not understand what was being asked of him, and then an animal's thin leg kicked out amid the weeds, and he saw a dog-cart on its side; a small face, its chin poisoned blue.

'Be not afeared, mistress,' the reeve called out. ''tis but returning pilgrims and the Bishop's ore-men for the ferry at Yarum. We do no harm.'

For long moments nothing happened. As the reeve trod slowly forwards, Ernald stayed at his side.

When he saw her fully he removed his rush hat and dipped a bow. 'Mistress.'

Her chest was heaving, her face so pale it might never have seen the sun. Her eyes were wider than the children's at her shoulder. One hand clutched at the dog's reins keeping it flat, the other the smallest of the three youngsters he could see.

'Are you hurt, mistress?'

'She's not hurt,' the reeve murmured. Louder he said, 'Pilgrim Ernald will help collect your wares; I'll see to your dog-cart.' He reached for the reins, and she allowed them to slide through her purpled fingers.

Ernald placed his hat back on his head and knelt in the dried grass to right a basket part filled with dark briar berries. Immediately the older boy, no more than six or seven, grasped at its handle to take possession. Ernald smiled at him. The smile was not returned, but when he reached for the fallen fruit the boy did the same. A younger girl retrieved rolled apples, stumbling across hardened hoof-prints to place them with care in the righted cart. Some looked bright-skinned and juicy, others Ernald saw were small and would be bitter. At least it seemed a better crop than the berries, no matter how they'd gorged themselves.

The woman was on her feet, though she seemed to be holding herself against the world. Or was it against the reeve? His height and countenance were enough to cow many a man.

'You should not be here alone,' he was telling her. She nodded an acknowledgement but offered not a word or a look to his face. Ernald was reminded of the novice's stance. They were coming past now, the ponies and the men, and Ernald noted how her head raised enough for her eyes to follow them with suspicion.

'You're not far from the stone road,' the reeve told her. 'Go with care,' and from one of the passing saddlebags he offered a half loaf. The children stepped forward immediately, their fingers more eager than Ernald had ever seen at the almoner's dole table, and he understood why they'd gorged on berries.

The reeve was following the ponies. The woman walked in the opposite direction, ushering her children about her without a word. Ernald watched her go, watched her stop a few paces on to break the bread and distribute it. Even the thin-ribbed dog received a portion. He remembered, and darted after her.

'Mistress! Mistress!'

Her pale face, those large eyes, turned to fix him as he held out his last quarter coin. 'For your family, mistress. Go with God.' He remembered more, and recognised the need.

Pulling the silver cross from beneath his habit, he pointed to the crystal at its centre. 'Saint Cuthbert,' he whispered.

A blink of understanding, a gasp, and she closed her eyes, holding her hands in supplication. As the power of the Holy Saint heated his hand, Ernald pressed the reliquary cross to her forehead and uttered words he was not ordained to speak.

The reeve was waiting for him further up the track.

'And what was that you pulled free of your habit, friend Ernald?' The sarcastic tone had returned. Ernald did not meet his gaze.

'Saint Cuthbert keeps our party safe.'

'I'm sure he does, friend Ernald, but they'll still be dead by the first frosts.'

Ernald looked then, but it was the reeve who would not hold his gaze.

Chapter 26

The sense of intrusion hung heavy as Nick walked along the flagged passage in the farmhouse. As ever, the kitchen door stood partially open. He took a breath to fortify himself and tapped on its wood.

'Come in if you're coming.'

There was no lilt to her voice; Rosemary knew she wasn't talking to Phil. Pushing the door wider, Nick saw her leaning on the counter beside the Aga, a two-way radio in her hand.

'He's here,' she spoke into it. There was a short response lost in static.

'Sit down before you fall down,' she told him, and she placed the radio on the counter. 'Tea?'

'Yes, please.'

He draped his coat over the chair's back, grateful to lower himself into it. His thighs were trembling. He didn't think he'd ever felt so tired.

'I'm sorry,' he said, 'I didn't mean to startle you. I should have rung the bell.'

'You didn't startle me. I heard you on the gravel and looked through the window.'

The kettle began to sing on its hotplate. The teapot was waiting and the boiling water went straight in.

'Dinner will be about an hour. Do you want a scone to tide you over?'

Scones again, as if he'd never left, as if time was repeating. 'Yes, please. That would be good.'

She was all stiff angles and curtly spoken words, a mother figure full of censure barely held in check. He knew he looked a mess. He wondered what day it was. As she buttered a scone he searched the walls for a calendar. Its days hadn't been crossed off. Unlike the one at home, it didn't carry lunar icons.

There was no china crockery this time. Alongside the scone she set an earthenware mug and he was grateful for the full half-pint. He'd hardly tested its temperature when the outside door thudded against the passage wall and the kitchen door followed.

'An' just 'ow are you expecting to get y'car out o'there?'

Nick winced at Phil's bellow.

'Boots!' snapped Rosemary.

'To hell wi'me boots!'

Careful not to spill tea, Nick placed his mug on the table and turned to face the coming wrath. But the pair seemed a spent force, neither looking at the other or at him, despite Phil's heaving shoulders.

'I'm sorry,' Nick said again. 'I didn't want to intrude.'

Phil glowered at him. 'You were supposed to be goin' t'Durham t'give a talk.'

'I did. It wasn't quite what I expected.'

'Oh, let him be,' said Rosemary. 'Dinner's in an hour. We can discuss this after we've eaten. Go finish up, Phil. Nicholas will want a shower as soon as he's drunk his tea.'

Phil continued to huff until she offered to fill him a mug, when he decided to return down the yard. While she pulled out a broom to collect the debris left by her husband, Nick drew out his phone, switching it on as soon as she moved into the passage. As he waited for its wake-up to complete he checked his watch. 2.35; so it was working again. The digital readout on his mobile was static, showing Sunday: 09:12. And then the figures began to roll.

Rosemary walked back in and replaced the broom and dustpan in the cupboard.

'The clock behind you is correct, and it's Monday.' She took a handful of potatoes to the sink and started scrubbing them under the running tap, stopping to look back at him. 'What day did you think it was?'

He shrugged, then flicked his fingernails across his stubble.

'I'll get a razor with the towels.' She returned to preparing the vegetables.

The readout on his mobile had stabilised. He checked it against the clock on the crowded dresser and reset his wristwatch.

'Thank you for the tea,' he said, 'and the scone.'

Switching off the water, she leaned both hands on the edge of the sink, her shoulders almost up to her ears. 'What is it that you think you've found down there?'

There was a moment's pause, and she turned to look at him again. Beneath the intensity of her pained expression his tongue formed Alice's name, but he couldn't face her response.

'I'm not sure,' he said, and felt the stab of his own betrayal. 'I need information and you and Phil have lived here years. You know about this.'

He watched her lips compress.

'We know more than any person would ever want to.'

For a moment his tired mind refused to accept what she'd said, and then the implication sat him forward on his chair. 'Tell me.'

She shook her head, turning away. 'Later.'

He wanted to press her but caught himself. He'd seen his mother close to tears enough to recognise the signs. And she'd want Phil with her, of course she would.

When she left the kitchen he washed his crockery and carried on scrubbing the vegetables. It seemed a long time since he'd shouldered the responsibility of cooking and he wondered how his mother was faring. He needed to ring her.

Pausing, he weighed a carrot in his hand. How did Alice sustain herself? Did she eat? Drink? Would she be able to once... Once what? He'd brought her here? He spluttered at the impossibility of it. Yet Rosemary and Phil held secrets, she'd just confessed as much. That among them might be the key to releasing Alice felt a long shot now he was back in their company, but it was the best he had.

Rosemary returned with a pile of linen, her shoulders squared, looking more in control. She hesitated in the doorway, surprised, he thought, to find him at the sink.

'Thank you,' she murmured.

He dried his hands and took the towels. There were clothes in the stack, disposable razors balanced on top.

'You know the drill.'

He nodded. 'Clothes in the washer.' She gave him a weak smile.

The bedroom felt stuffy and Nick opened wide the window. Across the garden and through shrubs bordering the road, patches of the moor could be glimpsed turning blue-purple in the setting sun. Would Alice visit him tonight? Her skin warm, her limbs lithe, her need of him—

How had she got to the farm? How had she known where he was?

He touched the ring, its sweeping decoration mirroring the open terminals of the torc about her neck. She'd not worn that when she'd come to him.

Throwing back his head, he sighed. A year in Durham attending lectures, burying himself in its mediaeval archives, discussing water-lore with tutors until they'd started to question his motives... What time he'd wasted. And what had all the effort delivered him? A crappy book not worth the paper it was written on. Deities rising from the water to become lovers to mortal men, to become wives and mothers. *Just* like that. No mention of shadow people or water disappearing into the earth. Or frost. Or... or the *thing*. What was that? Where was it now?

Whatever was going on down there on the moor had started long before he and Alice had arrived. Rosemary and Phil knew all about it. He wasn't leaving until he did, too.

He felt calmer after a shave and shower. The jeans were a bit loose, the shirt a bit short, and certainly not a style that would have appealed to Phil. Whose were they? He thought of his own spare clothing dumped in the boot of the Nissan, his clothes at home in his wardrobe. It had been his mother's first day back at work.

She picked up immediately, almost as if she'd been waiting for his call.

'It went really well,' she said. 'Everyone was so kind. It didn't take me long to get back into the swing, I was amazed. A bit slow, of course, but I'll quicken up. How did your weekend go? You sound tired.'

He forced a chuckle for her benefit. 'Late nights; out of practice.'

'Thick head?' He heard her laugh. 'Self-inflicted. You can't match them pint for pint, Nick; you're not used to it.'

'I know,' he said, and he wondered if the exchange counted as lying. 'I'm staying over a few more days.'

'That's fine. Have you eaten yet?'

'We're about to, that's why I called now.'

'Me, too,' she said. 'The pinger has just gone off on the oven.'

'You enjoy it. Er, Mum... We'll be going out on the moors. Conservation work. Signals might be a bit rough. I'll call in a few days. Okay?'

She understood, she said, and he wondered how much she'd understand when he brought Alice home. He would do it; he would set her free.

As soon as he opened the door to the landing his mouth began to water. The aroma creeping up the stairs made him realise how hungry he was, his stomach rumbling before he was halfway down. In the kitchen the smells were stronger still, bursting with piquant herbs. A dish of apple sauce sat on the table already set for three.

Rosemary pointed him to the utility room and he set the washer on a cycle, re-entering the kitchen as Phil emerged from the passage. They eyed each other and exchanged a nod. Phil took a seat at the table. Nick followed his lead.

'Come morning we'll 'ave your car outta there. Too dark now.'

Rosemary set a serving dish between them. 'Discussions

later. We eat first.'

Phil shuffled in his chair and reached to take hot plates from her hands. They'd had a talk while he'd been in the shower, he could tell. It was going to be an awkward meal.

It was a delicious meal, the pork succulent, its crackling crisp, the vegetables tasting so different to Nick's usual supermarket fare, but conversation was nil. They ate their way through blackcurrant and apple crumble, the portions so large Nick wondered whether Rosemary was purposely feeding him up.

With the dishwasher humming, three mugs of tea were placed on the table, anchors to hold them all steady. When Rosemary lifted hers to sip, Nick caught the steady look she gave her husband, and he jumped in to steer the conversation.

'I need to know about the Pool, about that area, why you planted the trees.'

They tensed in unison, their gazes locking across the table. Neither was going to speak, Nick could tell. He'd been too blunt. The earlier anger spurted afresh and he reached out open hands to them.

'You have to explain to me. I am trying to make sense of—' He stared at the cuffs of the shirt, straining about his wrists. 'Whose clothes am I wearing?' A memory stirred. 'You had a son.'

'We *have* a son,' Rosemary retorted. She blinked as if shocked by her own vehemence, and clutched at her mug. 'Jason is working in Qatar.'

Jason. Nick ran the name across his tongue. Had Jason been there when he and Alice...?

'I remember seeing pictures from a webcam.' He looked at Phil, rough-edged, ponderous Phil, at ease with machinery and animals, not electronics. 'It was your son who set up the webcam.'

'Aye.' Phil sat back, fatigue etched in his face. 'A few trees, he said, an' a seat. A bit of a memorial, like, and who were goin' to argue wi' that? But that's not what were goin' on.' He shook his head. 'It were like history repeating.'

Nick jolted at the phrase, but Phil didn't notice.

'We should o'known; should o'seen it comin'. He'd plastered it all o'er the internet, hadn't he? They'd turn up at the door, an' he'd lead 'em down there to plant trees, or scrape flat that ground. They'd come back all bright-eyed to sleep in the barn, an' talk an' talk an' talk. They never seemed t'sleep. It was like they were on summat.'

'We tackled him,' said Rosemary. '*Nature is the wonder*, he told us, *not man-made drugs.*'

'He'd got the look,' Phil added, 'same as my uncle.'

Nick bit at his lip to stop himself from prompting. He just wanted them to tell it, tell it all so that he had something to work with.

Phil sighed. 'Family said he were touched, but he weren't. Not the way they meant. Sheep drowned in that water long afore he did.'

Nick frowned. 'What water? The Pool wasn't—'

'No, no. The—' He glanced at his wife. 'That stone-cut hollow on the rise.'

The dead reeds; the dank water. Nick knew where he meant.

'It were allas fenced. The sheep—' Phil sighed again with the effort of dragging free the words. 'And then he were found face-down in it.'

Nick shuddered. Just like Alice. Except not there; he'd not found Alice there.

'I was only a young 'un, o'course. Family didn't talk of it. Accident, that's all. Allas happening on farms in those days. Gone to save a sheep, I were told, 'cept even a ten year old knows when a lie's being spun.' He paused, his gaze glassy as he locked on to the memory. 'We had 'ands back then. I asked one o'them. T'was him that explained about suicide, about it being a sin, a stain on the family no one wants to talk of.'

'Except it wasn't, was it?'

Phil's gaze shot across to pierce him. 'I've no idea, Nicholas. The certificate said Accidental Death. Why would anyone argue?'

Just like Alice, and that had been no accident. He'd seen the Other, his own oblique reflection, with a sword at her throat. Saw him minced by the water, by the *thing*.

Nick clamped down on the escaping image to focus on the present, on the conversation around the table.

'Had... Had your uncle been the first?'

'In modern times.'

What did that mean? Then he realised. 'There's stories? Hearsay? *Folklore?*'

Lifting his mug, Phil shrugged. It was Rosemary who set hers down.

'You have to realise that the countryside around here wasn't always this green. Iron and lead was mined for centuries, much of it open-cast. The water table was higher. Men drank. They fell down holes in the dark. They fell into the mires. Stories told as warnings became fable, became fact.'

In his surprise Nick looked from one to the other. 'You researched it?'

'Think we can't read up here?' snapped Phil. His shoulders were heaving again, his face flushed. Nick turned to Rosemary.

'How many deaths?'

'A few.'

'Over what period?'

'Centuries. At least to the seventeeth.' Her chin came up and she took a determined breath. 'You get your eye in after a while, start to read behind the legalese, behind the copperplate handwriting in parish records.' Her gaze flicked across to him. 'You'd be surprised how many notes are written in their margins. People knew something was wrong.'

Nick felt his chest tightening in anticipation. 'Did you make copies? Can I read them?'

'Aye, there were copies,' Phil said. 'No, you can't read 'em. They're gone.' His eyes glittered as he sat forward. 'Burned 'em. Burned everything.'

'Phil, please...' Rosemary murmured. 'This isn't helping.'

Nick pushed aside a spurt of dismay. He had to keep on.

There had to be some information he could use.

'Your uncle, tell me about your uncle.'

'He died.'

Nick's fists clenched in his frustration and he forced himself to relax, to not let anger have its head. If the exchange descended into a shouting match he'd lose everything.

'That's not what you're saying. You're telling me your uncle had a look, that he was drawn to that moor like it was—' He glanced from one to the other. 'Are we talking about some sort of magnetic pull? About being— What? In tune with the iron in the ground somehow? That doesn't make sense.'

'Makes more sense than being mesmerized by hobs and boggarts!'

'Phil!' Rosemary's rebuke broke the rise in tension, camouflaging Nick's intake of breath.

Phil leaned across the table again. 'Got them in that book o'yours, have you, eh?'

He was spoiling for a fight and Nick didn't know why. Rosemary was a safer bet.

'Your son, Jason, did he say he'd seen a hob, a boggart, in that stone-cut hollow?'

Phil's cold chuckle forestalled any response from her. 'Something was drawing him there. He started disappearing an' we'd find him 'cross the road, or halfway down the bank. When he were seven I caught him trying to climb through the fencing.'

Seven? Nick thought he'd meant recently.

'Why didn't you fill it in?'

Phil glared. 'You think I didn't try? Bottomless, that thing. Water always rises to the top. Stinking dead water.'

'It's not fenced now.'

'Doesn't need to be, does it? They all goes to the Pool now.'

'How can you sit there and be so surly about it? You're the one who put up all the signs. Or did your son do that, too?'

'He said we'd need 'em. He were right about that.'

Rosemary intervened. 'Jason believed it would add income to the farm, and it has helped us.'

'For a while,' returned Phil. 'Not been worth it, though, has it? None of it.'

'And now he's in Qatar?'

'Aye. In Qatar. Got offered a job.'

In a desert country. Nick wondered if that was relevant but decided not to ask. He needed information about the Pool, not their son.

'What about time altering? Watches stopping?'

Again they looked at each other.

'You know what I mean. You've made no attempt to hide it. What's happening? *Why* is it happening?'

Phil's mouth dropped open. 'You think we *know?* It just *does.*'

'Not to everyone,' Rosemary added quietly. 'The dislocation doesn't happen all the time. It doesn't happen to everyone.'

He looked at her, read her body language. Emotion was rising to the surface. He'd need to tread carefully.

'But it happened to Jason?'

She nodded. 'And those he took down there, those who helped with the path. Like we said, it was as if they were on something.'

'I'm sure some of 'em were,' Phil muttered.

'Have either of you felt this dislocation, this magnetic pull?'

'O'course not,' Phil spat. 'Still here, ain't we? Shoulda sold up years ago. All this trouble.'

'No,' said Rosemary. 'We couldn't sell and just leave.' She gave Nick a tight smile. 'It's not that easy when you're in a National Park. There's a lot of red tape.'

'Any'ow,' said Phil, 'it were all beginning to calm down an' then you turn up. An' you've got the look, Nicholas. An' I don't want to be pulling any more dead bodies out o'any more water.'

He pushed back his chair to lean over the table, his finger pointing. 'We want you to go home. Think o'your mother an' go home. She don't need another death in the family, and we don't need another death on our land.'

Chapter 27

Nick twisted the ring on his finger, its decoration catching the pale light from the bedside lamp. He'd always believed it gave an illusion of rippling water, but now all he could see were the terminals mounted on the torc Alice wore. She'd never believed in coincidence, and there were far too many here.

Drawing the ring from his finger, he peered at the rock crystal lining its inner surface, but even held under the lamp's glass shade the light wasn't bright enough to give him sight of Alice's hair. The jeweller had told him the crystal would be polished by his skin, but that hadn't happened. It had absorbed his sweat, creating a haze that hid the contents it was meant to reveal.

He felt ashamed for breaking his word – again – and leaving. It was disturbing enough to see her merge with the water, but to see that water plunging back into the earth... He wanted her to come to him as she had the other night, warm and lithe, so that he knew she remained whole, remained Alice. What he feared might appear was the *thing*.

Hobs and boggarts.

Is that what the *thing* was? A version of Jenny Greenteeth, Peg Powler? A Grindylow? He'd mentioned them and others in his book, those still carrying a name, but Phil's sneer was deserved. He'd followed the accepted norm, hadn't he, distancing himself by intimating such creatures were a ploy, a personification of a real danger. In truth, wasn't he as in denial as those who buried their dead and left notes in the margins of church ledgers? *Stories told as warnings become fable, become fact.* Alice was real. The *thing* had been real, pretending to be Alice. What had appeared to entice Rosemary and Phil's son at such a young age? What had led Phil's uncle into the dank pond to drown?

He could recall dreams where he'd walked into clear water with Alice. But water black with peat? Of thick particles filling his nostrils and clogging his airways? Nick's shudder made the bed creak.

Glancing about the dimly-lit room, he re-set himself in the present. Patterns from the glass lampshade scored curves of faint yellow light across the dark oak wardrobe, across its speckled mirror, across the carved chest of drawers carrying the obligatory refreshment tray. The flowery design of its china was echoed in the pattern of the curtains and the duvet cover, the room dressed to lure bed and breakfasters into a feel-good past that had never existed. Certainly not on this property. He wondered how old the farm was, how many incarnations it had been through. How many deaths it had truly seen.

Pushing the ring back on his finger he placed his hand on his chest. 'Think good thoughts,' he murmured, but not a single one came to mind as weariness overtook him and his eyelids began to droop.

A tapping had him sitting upright, blinking into shadowed corners. When it came again he stared at the door, his heart pounding. Alice hadn't—

The latch clicked and began to lift. He was off the bed and on to his feet, breathing hard. The door's swing stopped, a distant glow creating a halo around an odd-shaped silhouette. Light burst in from the landing and Rosemary stood there, his laundry in her hands.

'I'm sorry,' she said. 'You looked so tired I thought you might be asleep already and I didn't want to disturb you.'

'Just dozing,' he managed, and he breathed slow and deep to calm his pounding heart.

To his surprise she stepped fully into the room, easing the door behind her. For privacy from Phil? He looked at her afresh, wondering what was coming.

'You'll be going to the Pool.'

He nodded.

'Wait until the morning. Don't go tonight, Nicholas. Please don't go tonight.'

'I won't, I promise.'

She glanced down, her relief visible. He felt a fraud.

'Don't mind, Phil,' she said. 'He's on edge. He's not as young as he was and won't accept that he can't do as much.'

'He must miss Jason's help. You both must miss him.'

She gave him a tight smile.

'Phil wants to get your car out of the copse before breakfast. Rain's on the way and he doesn't want it getting bogged down in there.'

He thought of Alice's belief in good weather. 'Is it going to rain?'

'We don't know. It's hard to read the land anymore. They tell us it's global warming.'

Nick raised an eyebrow at that and her gaze slid away again.

'I'll pack a few provisions for after breakfast in case... in case you're down there longer than you intend.'

'That's good of you.' He reached to take the offered laundry.

'It's not ironed,' she said. 'I didn't see the point. It'll be going back in the washer soon, won't it?' She gave a low chuckle and he smiled to share a joke barely made.

When she turned to leave he stepped forward to forestall her.

'I'm sorry Jason is in Qatar,' he said. 'I would have liked to speak with him.'

'Perhaps you will when you visit again. It's only a short-term contract. That's the way the world works now, isn't it? It's not like being tied to the land for generations.' She backed a pace, feeling behind her for the edge of the door.

'Better get on. Early start. Phil will give you a knock, so don't worry about missing him.'

He shot out his arm, halting the opening door.

'Why do you stay, Rosemary? Why didn't you sell up and leave?'

She stood tall, lifting her chin, he thought in defiance until he saw the glisten in her eyes.

'We sold. Of course we sold, but it was through a land agent. When the buyers came to look round they brought their twin sons.' A tear streamed down her cheek. 'How could we? *Twin sons*. How could we ever have lived with that?'

'What about your son?'

'Jason went to live with my sister in Durham.'

Nick blinked at the city's name.

'Small world, isn't it?' she said, and jerked the door to break his pressure, shutting it behind her as she left.

Coincidences. There were far too many here. The knowledge banished sleep, at least for a while.

He lay on top of the bed cover considering the couple he'd thought he sort of knew but didn't know at all. What decisions they'd had to make. No wonder they'd researched the moor. But why had Phil burned their findings? To stop his son from acting on the information? Nick had engaged in enough arguments with his own father when he'd been a teen. How much more bitter had been Jason and Phil's with his son's life at stake? A son who thought he'd been sent away to an aunt because his parents didn't care. Nick didn't know them at all, did he? He wondered if Jason did.

He shed their son's too tight clothing and pulled on his own. They smelled of meadow flowers. The fragrance was from the detergent, but he still thought of Alice, thought of her smiling. Happy. With him.

Easing back into the pillows, he allowed his eyelids to droop, his breathing to lengthen. He needed to sleep, he told himself. Think good thoughts and just let go.

He awoke with a start. Someone had touched his shoulder. No one was there. He was disappointed; oddly grateful.

'I'm coming back,' he said aloud. 'I'm not leaving you, Alice. I'll be with you in the daylight.'

He rested against the pillows. Perhaps the touch had been conjured by his own mind.

I saw you and knew you were searching for me.

But he hadn't been, had he? That's not what he'd been doing

at all, and he felt sick with disgust.

Twisting the ring around his finger, he murmured, 'I'm sorry. I should have come sooner. I'm sorry.'

Increasing his grip, he swallowed down his rising emotion, felt the indentations of its design press into his thumb and fingertip. The pattern no longer had the fluidity of ripples, and he turned onto his side to splay his fingers beneath the lamp's glass shade. He'd been right. The design was more a succession of roundels mimicking the terminals of the torc Alice wore. Open roundels. As if a string of sightless eyes.

He was being paranoid, he told himself.

But was he? Where was the *thing* that had taken her? Why hadn't it put in an appearance? In York it had seemed to dog his every move. Who were these shadow people she feared? He thought of the way Alice differentiated between them and the people she saw at the edge of the Pool. Was the torc shackling her to the Pool, to the *thing*... or was it a means of monitoring her attempts to leave it? Of seeing what she saw. The shadow people... were they being sent to...?

He laid back on the pillows to stare at the light patterns on the ceiling. He didn't know. The bottom line was he didn't know and he was letting his fears run away with him because he was tired. He was extrapolating horrors that might not exist, the reverse of Rosemary's rationalising away hobs and boggarts as metaphors for dangers in the landscape.

Except there *were* dangers in the landscape. He wasn't being paranoid about that. Tomorrow. He would sort it all tomorrow.

Altering his breathing, he forced himself to relax, to surrender to his fatigue. Eventually, he began to nod.

Eyes wide, he shot upright. It had happened again. Another touch; his hair this time. But had he seen something? A glow retreating between the wall and the wardrobe? Or had it been a reflection in its speckled mirror? Static from the bedcover as he'd moved? He told himself it had and checked his watch. 2.40.

At 3.10 he was awake again. No touch this time, but something was there, something glimpsed from the corner of his eye. Not his movement in the wardrobe mirror. Not the pattern from the glass lampshade.

I'm sorry, Nick. I've brought them, I'm sorry.

He sat up, this time determined not to give in to fear. The temperature in the room was normal. Not the *thing*. Yet he still peered over the edge of the bed before swinging his bare feet onto the rug and reaching out to snap down the light switch. The ceiling lamp glowed a dull yellow and then flooded the room with bright white light, scorching away the shadows and the pattern from the bedside lampshade.

Chapter 28

Tim stepped from the shower cubicle towelling himself and dripped his way into the bedroom. At least in the bedroom there was enough space to flip the towel behind him and drag it diagonally across his back without fear of cracking his elbows on the partition walls. Living in a caravan hadn't been quite what he'd envisaged when *accommodation included* had been flagged, but it was attached to the mains and roomy enough, if out of the Ark.

The tingling across his shoulder blades made him want to scratch, and he hoped he'd been too abrasive with the towel, prayed it wasn't the start of an eruption of psoriasis there, too. He was so careful with the shower gels he used. He needed to calm down, to restart the meditation techniques Izara had taught him. Anxiety was a fuel, and he shouldn't be anxious now, not when his research data was finally showing something worth investigating. He wanted to be in the plant early because it was going to take forever to get all the samples through its ancient analyzers. Doubtless he'd be beset with interruptions, too.

Relaxing the muscles in his back, he took a couple of deep, slow breaths. Yes, that was better.

No, it wasn't. He could feel the weirdness starting again, like insects crawling across his skin making him want to twitch. *Bastard.* He could do without this. He walked back into the shower room to cover himself in medicated talc.

A soft t-shirt, a coffee, toast once he'd removed the mould from the bread, and he was back in the shower room. As he was brushing his teeth he peered into the mirror above the basin and noticed that only his left eyebrow showed signs of inflammation. Grateful for small mercies, he applied ointment to both and headed out to the Freelander, the crowning asset of his placement.

He was in first again. Fantastic; no one to crowd his shoulder. The company's daily water analysis needed to be out of the way so he could concentrate on his true research. And it looked good, despite it being no more than labelled saucers on a shelf above the work-bench. It was his. And the light falling through the high windows was just right. He pulled out his phone to take a couple of images. If this became something, if he ended up writing a paper on it, he'd need early-days images, and the sheer ordinariness of a shelf of saucers couldn't be bettered.

With the internal pipe's sample in the machines, he donned his outdoor wellingtons, plugged his iPod buds into his ears, and left by the rear door to follow the intake pipe down the leafy slope to the well-head.

It was during his return that he saw the first car, or at least its dust-cloud as it thundered along the potholed driveway. Remembering the bawling he'd received for leaving the place insecure, he broke into a run, closing down his music and dragging the buds from his ears. Breathless, he entered the lab. Raised voices from the corridor sent him into a sweat – Douglas was definitely one of them; he recognised his reverberating bass – but the men by-passed the lab to clang up the metal stairs to the offices.

Placing the samples on the workbench, Tim changed his footwear and went to the sink to run water onto a paper towel to cool his face and neck. He didn't want anything to betray his lapse. The outer door's buzzer sounded and he made a grab for a ring-binder, laying it wide on the bench. Paperwork always looked good. The door remained closed as again footsteps hurried by to resonate up the staircase. Tim checked his wristwatch. He'd expected to have the place to himself for at least another hour. What was going on?

The chromatograph had completed its cycle. At least he would have something to occupy him if someone came in. There was nothing worse than standing around like a dummy. He'd never worked out why the company had offered a full-time placement. There wasn't enough lab work to occupy John as far as he could see, and the bottling line was just about fully automated. Not that he was going to mention it. The slow pace of work gave him time to study, which most jobs wouldn't.

The outer door buzzed again and a few seconds later the lab door opened. Tim knew who this would be and turned with a smile to underline how conscientious he was being.

'Morning.'

John nodded as he crossed the floor to his locker. 'Started on the experimental samples yet?'

'No, just finished the internal pipe. Setting up the well-head sample next.'

He watched John nod again, looking distracted, he thought, as he buttoned his coat. John never buttoned his lab coat.

'Everyone's in early today,' Tim tried, and to his surprise John stopped mid-step to squint at him.

'Bit of a flap,' he said. 'How's the reading?'

Mentally, Tim crossed his fingers. 'Dead on.'

'Good.' With that John opened the door and walked into the corridor.

As he listened to the stairway resounding to John's rapid footfalls, Tim checked the readout. Dead on, as he'd predicted. Thankfully.

With the well-head sample in both analyzers and the analytics filed on the first sample, Tim made himself a coffee and patrolled the saucers. In turn, he lifted down each one, trying to note by eye how much water had evaporated overnight and chiding himself for not using a set of marked vessels. He visualised the shelves of the equipment cupboard in the university's lab, but borrowing equipment might not be a good idea; there'd be too many questions to answer. He wondered if John would sanction purchasing a set. While the analyzers moved through their cycles, he trawled the internet for suitable dishes, leaving his coffee to grow cold.

He was inputting the well-head's analytics when footsteps sounded on the stairs, the rumble of voices echoing off the breezeblock walls. There didn't seem to be the urgency of earlier, and when John entered the lab he looked more relaxed.

'How are we doing? You okay to be left for a while?'

'Sure. Plant samples are fine. I'll be engrossed in the, er, experimental samples for most of the day. It's going to be slow with only these machines. I don't suppose there's a chance of hiring in—?' From John's tight smile he could tell it was out of the question so he shrugged off the rest of his request.

'Just don't cut corners,' John warned, and he left.

Tim huffed his annoyance that anyone could think he'd sink to cutting corners. And he hadn't asked for the purchase of marked vessels, had he? He eyed the saucers, his mood sullen. If that wasn't cutting corners, what was? They weren't even porcelain. An image of a line of saucers to illustrate a paper? He'd never be taken seriously again if he tried to publish that.

He set about the samples from the TG15-29 spring source, the *experimental* samples – there was a euphemism if ever he'd heard one – his irritation easing as he slipped into a rhythm: sample from saucer, mark and re-date, replace on shelf, input results; sample from corresponding lidded container, mark and re-date, new saucer sample, mark and date, input results from container... on and on until his knees hurt from not walking enough and his stomach craved food.

Yet with each new result he was gripped with a need to know, a need to see it confirmed without deviation. The saucer results all showed comparable levels of heavy degradation in the unidentified contaminant but none in the other constituents, whereas the containers which had been full to their lids showed barely any degradation in the contaminant. What was left of the original sample from days ago now registered a *trace* reading.

It had to be the air. Air neutralised the contaminant, whatever the contaminant was. He kept telling himself that one day's testing didn't create a chart, reliable or otherwise, but it was a good start. He was pleased he'd followed his hunch.

He was taking a break in the kitchen, eating a cereal bar and letting another coffee grow cold while he checked the university's databases, when the phone in his hand beeped an incoming text. It was Izzy. *Good time to ring?*

He stared at the words, small on the screen. He'd not contacted her, hoping she'd take the hint, but she wasn't going to, was she? And then the phone vibrated in his hand and he knew who it would be before the name slid on-screen. His thumb hovered, but it was better to get this over with than having her ringing him all afternoon.

'Hello, Izara. I've not got long; just finishing my break. How's it going?'

'How's it going with the Pool's water samples?'

He felt a spurt of perspiration. Thank God John hadn't been in the lab to overhear that. He turned down the volume, just in case.

'Found the anomaly?' she said into his silence.

'I'm working on it. It's nothing to worry about, I know that. Probably a misreading, a miscalculation.'

He heard her snort. 'It won't be. I've been making enquiries, asking around.'

'What!' It came out as a croak, his mind filling with the memory of John's anger, the jutting finger aimed at his chest. 'Just stop it, Izzy. Just back off.'

He closed his eyes, knowing he'd been too forceful, and cast round for words to soothe her.

'Have you any idea what it'll do to my career prospects if you put it about that my data can't be trusted? I've made a mistake, that's all.'

'That's not all, Tim. People have died down there. Nicholas Blaketon's colleague was just the most recent. Before the war—'

'*War?* What war? For God's sake, Izzy...'

'I've found three in the nineteenth century, and I've hardly looked. And stop calling me that.'

Nineteenth century? He couldn't believe what he was hearing. She was loopy. No wonder Simon had off-loaded her.

'Enough, Izara. I have to get back to work and I can't be doing with you interrupting me all the time. Goodbye.' He cut her off and set the phone to silent. He'd hardly left the kitchen when it logged a missed call and then a voicemail.

'For God's sake,' he muttered, and he slid the phone into his pocket.

His shoulders were rising towards his ears, the irritation in his mind starting to be mirrored again in his back. Why was there always this hassle?

Throwing the remaining contents of his mug into the sink, he dumped the cereal wrapper in the bin and went through to the toilet to empty his bladder. Staring at his reflection in the mirror above the basin, he washed his hands, making a conscious effort not to rub at his inflamed eyebrow. At least only the one was inflamed now. Be grateful, he told himself, be calm. He switched off the light and returned to the lab.

But his mind kept repeating Izzy's information, John's fear of rumours of the contaminant being made public. He even envisaged Doug's roar in his face when it was, and Tim knew the volatile CEO wouldn't restrain himself to prodding a finger at his chest. It got so that Tim made himself check and double-check each inputted result, constantly reviewing the growing charts.

His head was buzzing by the time he reached the last double samples, and when it came to removing the lid from the container he was all fingers and thumbs. He set the pot on the workbench with trembling hands, grateful he hadn't repeated slopping the contents over himself as he had yesterday. Tearing off a piece of tissue, he wiped at the droplets on his knuckles, hoping that the deficit wouldn't wreck tomorrow's reading.

He stopped. And stared at his now dry knuckles, at the open pot on the workbench. The air would degrade the sample, his calm internal voice was telling him; complete the routine, close the container.

He performed the task as if in a dream, all the tasks: the new saucer, the marking up, the inputting of data, until everything was up to date and he had only to wait for the long-winded analyzers to finish their cycles. He didn't; he returned to the toilet to switch on the light and study his face in the mirror.

One eyebrow was puffy, showing pink inflammation, loose skin peeling between hairs. The other looked smooth, normal. His fingers sought his hairline. There was flaking skin above the inflamed eyebrow; nothing on the other side. He raked at his scalp with his fingernails, parted his hair again and again in lines back to his crown. A scattering of yellowing flakes; nothing above his right eyebrow.

Yesterday the water from the exploding pot had caught him on that side of his face, dribbling down his forehead and over his eyebrow. He'd wiped it away with his hand, spreading it across to his temple where... where what? He couldn't recall. It must have evaporated; he was sure he hadn't wiped it dry.

He stared at his reflection, trying to think it through, trying to find holes in his deduction. Then he slipped his phone free of his pocket and began taking images.

Back in the lab, he pulled the five litre vacuum container from the chemical cupboard and filled three sample pots to the brim. They'd be marked when he returned to the caravan, and he'd be leaving the plant as soon as the final result was in. He was planning his own experiment, and he didn't want anyone crowding him.

Chapter 29

Despite pleasant birdsong and the chittering of thrushes, the drovers' track wound through a land ill at ease. No lowing of cattle drifted on the warm breeze, and the briar tangles were devoid of pinched fleece. A pair of kites came to study the travellers, gliding away and returning to match their progress. Ernald hoped they'd leave. He wished them to leave. Circling high above, they were a marker to any watching wolf's-head that prey strayed beneath.

When next he looked and met their sharp eyes and beaks, he pressed the reliquary cross to his breastbone and beseeched Saint Cuthbert to distract their hunting with more suitable forage. His entreaty completed, he found the reeve's man watching him, leaving Ernald to wonder whether a wolf's-head might be closer than he feared. To his inner eye came a reflection of the confinement chamber, the cloak on the table hiding a cudgel. Yet were not all present engaged in God's bidding? In the sub-prior's surreptitious bidding?

Refusing to think on what was not his to think on, Ernald instead filled his mind with the blessed strains of the priory's plainsong and cast his gaze skywards. The kites, he saw, had taken Saint Cuthbert's direction.

At a drovers' hollow the group rested. The cleared brook had been widened into a pond, and stacked hurdles were in good repair showing men's industry. There were no dwellings. It was a place for a night-camp, and he checked the fall of the sun behind cloud beginning to bruise purple.

'We'll be safer within sight of Yarum's pools,' the reeve told him. 'You'll have time enough to ink your report before dark.'

Ernald was thinking not so much of quill and parchment, but

of his feet. The change to his sandals was not helping.

The land eased into a decline showing less briar and more rough pasture. Ernald took comfort from that, despite the lack of ruminants. When the track dropped again, a vista extended better than any map-scribe could fashion. A river carrying merchants' craft wound in great glistening loops across a wide vale. The sight of smoke trails rising above roofs swept him with relief. He breathed deeply, hoping for the scents of the settlement to reach his nostrils, but the breeze had fallen away with the closing of the day.

They passed a mill built half into the hillside, its brook a weed-choked trickle, its charred wheel and solitary wall testament to its misadventure. Only a cluster of crowding birch kept it standing. Ernald considered it a good position for a mill, especially with the untended brook still running in late summer. He wondered why it hadn't been rebuilt. Perhaps it had been replaced by one closer to Yarum.

Their group bunched as the drovers' track joined a much-travelled cart route which soon forked east and south around a loop in the river. The scents of the settlement grew evident now, especially the acrid stench from the tannery pools that the drift of cooking smoke did little to mask. Ernald could hear lowing from the cattle in the water meadows, and the occasional honking of unseen geese. Close to the fish weirs and the many catch pools, the ferry was doing a prosperous trade despite the lateness of the day.

'We cross on the morrow,' the reeve announced. 'I'll not have us fleeced for the price of a loaf or a pallet of fleas. We'll walk the river and find ourselves a placing.'

Master Ore Reeve was not alone in his thinking. They came upon an encampment of carters with their oxen and loads, mostly firewood it looked to Ernald. While the reeve spoke with them, Ernald set himself apart with his board-rest, parchment and quill, much to the curiosity of Wulfrith. Ernald urged him closer, allowing the man to watch the sparse lettering journey across the skin, and showing how he scratched out the quill's splatters. To Wulfrith it was a wondrous display, and the reeve's man and the youth came to stand at Ernald's shoulder while he worked. The novice looked on with a disapproving gaze.

As the sun left the land and the first stars glowed in the firmament, Ernald withdrew the silver cross of Saint Cuthbert and for the benefit of their small party recited the Vespers prayers he spoke when journeying between the manors. At their close he bade each man step forward and he touched the cross to their brows. The novice sat as stiff as a niche statue. When Ernald stepped towards him he hissed low in his throat, the phrase catching Ernald as if a blow to his cheek. Ernald stared at him until the reeve came to his shoulder to claim his attention.

'And might I be blessed by the good Saint?' He bowed slightly and Ernald touched the cross to his forehead, finishing with the appropriate blessing of guidance.

As they parted, the reeve's hand came out to lock about the cross. Caught by the thong round his neck, Ernald stared as the reeve opened his fingers to peer at the crystal sitting at its centre. As his calloused hand let the cross slip free, his gaze rose to Ernald's face.

'You will do well, friend Ernald, to leave that hidden beneath your habit. Otherwise I will be shamed standing before the sub-prior attempting to explain why it was lost and you left with your neck severed.'

Ernald blinked at him and the reeve shook his head. 'For the priory's questor, you are naive in the ways of the world.'

'I choose to believe in the good of every man.'

The reeve pursed his lips. 'That is pleasing to know, friend Ernald. What did our good *errant* man say that stung so sharply?'

Ernald paused, still unsure of its meaning, but he knew he hadn't misheard. 'That I was a sinner.'

The reeve raised one eyebrow and looked from Ernald to the novice and back again. He walked away, saying not a word.

Was he a sinner? The question gnawed at Ernald half the

night. His dreams were full of the sub-prior's dark looks and chiding words. He thought of his soft undershirt and his comfortable boots placed for safety beyond the priory's walls. He recalled standing for Confession, and not confessing.

The morning came both too soon and not soon enough. Ernald's head felt as if he'd taken too much ale, and despite wearing his coif and rush-woven hat he was reminded of his discomfort at the priory. There were also blisters burst on his feet that he carried no salve for. He hoped the two were not well-met.

With the ponies loaded, the tethered men were tied close to the pack. To the sound of a bell pealing across the water the group retraced their steps. Despite the grey gloom of dawn, men and animals were gathering for the ferry. The reeve's man distributed doles of bread, but it was now so trencher-dry that not even a spoonful of the sticky pottage could make it edible, though as Ernald glanced between his companions it seemed only he who could not masticate it. He looked to the river for a draught, but the current was laced with floating midden debris from the settlement, and he decided to stay dry.

The immoderate toll demanded for the crossing startled Ernald, but he held his tongue as the reeve handed over coins. The eyes of the skittish ponies were covered and the animals cajoled across a dung-covered board into the wide-beamed vessel. Ernald understood their apprehension. He felt no safer clinging to the shaky rail than he'd felt kneeling in the skin craft below the priory's wall, but the standing oarsmen were skilled and the coin collector kept up a haranguing exchange with other barge and boat masters manoeuvring across their route.

Rope-boys were soon throwing lines to waiting hands on the further bank, and the ponies were led onto firm ground. Liveried men-at-arms stood ready, and another toll was paid for their party to pass through the gate into Yarum's street.

Immediately waiting bakers' apprentices and inn-keepers' pot-boys jostled to press their wares, their clamouring worse than gulls from the coast. Trapped by his leash, Wulfrith cowered into the pony's withers, despite the animal's high-stepped prancing. Ernald saw its eyes roll and for a drawn breath thought it would spring forwards, dragging its two men by their arms, but the reeve's man was there with a shout and a snarl, a knotted rope swirling before him to create a passage. The young traders parted as if the waters before Moses, to seek easier buyers behind.

Ernald staggered a pace, his sandals slipping on the fouled cobbles and causing him pain. He steadied himself against his pilgrim's staff. Reaching out, he patted Wulfrith's curled shoulder, understanding how the man felt. He was breathing heavily himself.

'Still wearing that holy cross about your neck, friend Ernald?'

A spurt of terror gripped him and he clutched at his breast, grateful to feel the solidity of it strike his ribs.

'Aye, now you know why you should keep it hidden.' One of the reeve's dark eyebrows raised and his bearded chin jutted forwards. 'And where, friend Ernald, are your boots?'

Ernald clutched at his satchel, swinging it from his hip to his belly. No boots hung from its shoulder strap. He felt air rush from his lungs, and he looked into the reeve's placid face.

'I— I never felt the loss.'

From behind his broad back the reeve produced the boots.

'Still believe in the good of every man?' he derided. 'And us not into the wolf-lands yet. Can you use that staff, friend Ernald, for more than merely leaning on?'

Chapter 30

With the panniers restocked with fragrant bread and an arm-cask of small ale, Ernald approached the reeve.

'I have asked directions of the inn-keep to the home of a poultice-maker, for I fear my feet will slow our progress.'

'And now you ask for coin.'

Ernald nodded, watching the reeve's expression darken to the shade of his beard.

'You've had four quarters, friend Ernald, and kept none. Am I to give you four more quarters? And four more after?'

Ernald felt himself floundering as he tried to read the man's animosity.

'When the quarter coins are gone,' the reeve continued, 'what are we to eat? Your poultice in a broth? Or should we boil those boots you cannot wear?'

On his journeys between the manors, Ernald had heard stories of cottagers boiling leather for broth to eke out meagre supplies. People feared a late spring more than a hard winter. He thought of the woman with her dog-cart, her children hungry during harvest-time. He should never have given her his last quarter-coin. He should have given her his boots to sell.

'If it were not that you would slow our stride, to which I would need to answer to the sub-prior, I'd make you walk, friend Ernald, on your blisters.'

Ernald let his gaze and his demeanour drop as he did in the Chapter House when faced with the ire of the sub-prior.

'A goodly penance for my sin of pride, Master Reeve. In my heart I knew they should not be worn.' He looked up. 'This settlement is a living market, Master Reeve. I do not have the skill, but you could barter the boots for coin, for food for our companions.'

He began to untie them from his satchel. The reeve stayed his hand.

'Better you carry them as a reminder of your pride, friend Ernald, at least for today.'

It seemed to Ernald that he was held long in a gaze, and then the reeve returned to the inn's entrance where the man's broad shoulders disappeared into the dark of its open door. The reeve was, indeed, a mystery to him, and he didn't even know his name.

Save for Wulfrith, he knew not the name of any of his companions, where they called home, what families they had left behind. He looked over them, wondering who to ask, and found himself pierced by the accusing stare of the novice. Ernald could not hold his gaze. It was as if the novice knew of his boots and soft undershirt hidden beyond the priory's walls. Yes, he was a sinner, the novice had not been wrong. Ernald touched the cross of Saint Cuthbert to his breast and asked for forgiveness, and for mercy.

The reeve returned to confirm the group could wait in the yard. Ernald followed at the man's heel, back into the swell and din of people and carts coming from the water-gate. He wrapped his arms around his satchel and boots alike, adamant he would lose neither to a jostling cut-purse determined to make good the ferry fare.

Beyond the water-gate the maelstrom eased. Here the buildings were packed tight into the loop of the river, signs of each industry hanging so low from a pole above open doorways that the two men had to duck and weave around them. Dwellings wide enough for shutters had them down as boards to display their work-a-day goods. Sounds of hammering and the rhythmic chipping of adze blades became loud and then soft as doorways were approached and passed, the smell of hoof-glue stronger than the smoke drifting in the air. Alleys ran from the narrowing cart-route as if dark veins on a man's gnarled hand. Boys carried loads, girls water-crocks. Ernald wondered where they sourced the water. He hoped not the river but dared not trust the thought.

'Ee be seekin' sum'un.' A thin boy joined them, his face full of smiles, his accent thicker than trencher-bread. He kept pace with a limping gait on a turned-in foot and Ernald felt Saint Cuthbert's admonition for having cares for mere blisters.

'I can tek ee,' the boy said. 'G'me 'is nafn.'

The reeve slowed but did not look down. 'I don't know his name.'

''is purpose. I'll ken him by 'is purpose.'

The reeve seemed more intent on the surrounding buildings than replying so Ernald made to respond, his words choked off as the reeve's hand shot out to grab the boy's cap and a handful of his hair. The boy cried out, then stilled.

'We seek the poultice-maker, the pepperer, the draiman—'

'I ken 'im, mestre, I do, mestre. I tek ee. Short way. Safe way.'

The reeve bent so that the tip of his beard was level with the boy's eyes. 'Truly it will be a safe way, for you already know what will happen if it's not.'

'My oath, mestre.'

'Aye,' murmured the reeve, standing to tower over him. 'I would nae g'ee oath too loud, limper. The Devil may hark an' come collect. Which way?'

They were led beyond a fish-seller and down an adjacent alley, its churned mud stinking of putrid wash and humming with fat flies. Yet doors led off this shadowy place. Voices raised in argument came to Ernald's hearing, a babe's whimper, a man's hawking cough. He looked again at the narrow-way between the buildings, wondering why these people did not lay faggots, or better, cobbles. His sandals gave his feet no protection. Another penance. And a lesson in humility, perhaps. Hitching the hem of his habit, he followed the reeve and the boy.

The poultice-maker had his narrow shutter down. Strings of mildewed hedge-herbs hung from the frame. On a narrow ledge stood rawhide containers of differing sizes; unguents, Ernald realised, but their encrusted dirt made him wish he'd never approached the reeve for coin. This place was no infermarer's pestlry.

The boy called something Ernald did not catch, and the reeve followed by announcing his presence. There was an answering phrase and they all passed through the open door into a hovel as fetid as expected, the air skeined in smoke trails from the only source of light. Another step and the vapour from bubbling tallow caught at Ernald's throat.

As the reeve pushed the boy to the beaten floor, a stool was brought from the gloom and Ernald bade to sit and untie the lacings of his sandals. The reeve was speaking to the poultice-maker in the dialect he used with Wulfrith. Ernald realised if he had come alone, even if he had found the place, he would never have made himself understood.

A rough tunic, a discoloured coif, a greying beard... as his feet were inspected it was as much of the man as Ernald could discern. Yet his eyes were growing accustomed to the gloom now, and above the glowing embers in the hearth Ernald could pick out pottery vessels standing on a shelf, pouches of leather and bunches of drying herbs hanging beneath, all in a crude imitation of that at the priory.

He looked again, squinting at marks partly obscured on the wall behind. Was that a... *pentangle?* He touched Saint Cuthbert's cross and silently mouthed prayers. Fortified against Devilry, he looked again. Not a pentangle; more elaborate. He leaned forward. An astrologer's chart? *Say not...*

When a bowl was handed from the gloom, he caught sight of another figure. A woman, he thought. Was she stitching? How could she see? Water was poured from a leather pail. Had he been within the priory's walls, his cleaned feet would have been bathed in cider vinegar, and an unguent of comfrey administered. Here it was salted river water that stung so ferociously he gritted his teeth, and a salve smelling of rank cabbage. Dark leaves were cut and warmed on a pot's lid. There was an exchange of phrases and Ernald was offered a pair of shears.

'If you want your feet binding, you should cut it from your undershirt,' the reeve told him.

Ernald looked at the poultice-maker's garment and took the shears. As he watched the warmed leaves bound about his feet, his only thought was that the man's good offices, if good they were, would be undone during the short walk along the alley.

As he re-laced his sandals, coin passed between the two men. Ernald received a mix of leaves pouched in a square of old leather, and a lidded rawhide container which looked clean and felt new. After storing both in his satchel, he tested his standing against his staff to find it no worse than before. Thanking the man, he stepped out into what seemed bright light and clear air.

They did not return the way they had come. The boy, still held by the reeve, led to the riverside packed with jetties and barges. Men were lading and unlading, more it seemed than toiled under the masons at the priory. The calls of masters announcing their wares interspersed with those on the water demanding space for their oarsmen, thuds on planking, and the squealing of windlasses. There the reeve freed the boy, giving him coin that changed the youngster's glower into a grin. Altering his weight against his staff, Ernald watched the boy limp back into the alley.

'You are contrary, Master Reeve.'

'And you are too trusting, friend Ernald. He was no mother's child. A whistle in that maze and you would have lost more than your boots, and I the sub-prior's purse.'

Ernald's arm was taken in a grip such as the boy had felt and the reeve's voice took on a cooler tone. 'Turn about, friend Ernald. Methinks we will away.'

Ernald looked round the reeve's pressing shoulder but could see nothing beyond men's labour. They walked on, skirting barrels and baskets, Ernald's memory studying the wall of the hovel in the alley.

'What was that place, Master Reeve? How could a poultice-maker be so hidden when such administrations are sought so often?'

'A pepperer does not make only poultices, especially if he's a draiman.'

Ernald caught his breath. He'd not been wrong. The design scratched on the wall beneath the drying herbs... '*Devilry?*'

'That depends on how you like your poisons, friend Ernald.'

'*Poisons?*' He glanced at his sandaled feet.

There was cry behind them and Ernald turned. That grip again, the forceful push he felt all the way to his cabbage-bound blisters.

'Do not look back. We and our companions need to be away.'

The pair rejoined the thoroughfare close to the water-gate, and through a gap in the buildings opposite Ernald noticed a stone church. How had he not seen this? He had need of its sanctity, need to give thanks and especially to receive blessing to cleanse the unguents he carried.

'No.'

The reeve's response brooked no opposition but Ernald, too, was adamant. 'Master Reeve—'

'Your habit and tonsure would bring questions you would answer too openly, and there are too many armed men in the precincts to have them come questioning me. Or worse, our held companions.'

'They are our Lord Bishop's men.'

'Use your eyes. They do not wear the Bishop's colours.'

Again the man's numbing grip possessed Ernald's arm, and he was pushed into a throng leaving the water-gate. Yet it was not as it had been close to dawn. Stall-holders were clearing their wares. Where were the shouts of tray-sellers? Of pot-boys? The people, too, seemed unnaturally subdued.

Their company was waiting outside the inn. The reeve's man approached, relief clear in his expression, though their muted conversation was in the unknown dialect. Ernald's attention drifted to the discomfort of his feet, and then he noticed that the novice and Wulfrith had already been tied to the saddle. Behind the animal the inn's gates were closed. He looked further. The dwellings either side had their shutters pegged high.

The reeve motioned they should slip behind a laden ox cart, and they headed south between the river's loops. As the dwellings gave way first to quays and merchants' warehouses, and then to tofts, it seemed that men-at-arms congregated at every turn.

'Don't look at them,' warned the reeve, 'or they'll be by our side for coin faster than hungry wolf's-heads.'

'I don't understand,' Ernald murmured.

'They are demanding tolls.'

Ernald felt wrong-footed, yet as they neared the rough palisade he saw that Wulfrith had buried his cheek into the pony's withers, his free hand stroking the animal's neck to soothe it. The novice walked at its other shoulder, his head higher than of late, his tethered hand gripping the pack as if aiding the pony's direction.

'For protection against the Scots?'

He heard the reeve rattle phlegm in his throat as if he were about to hawk.

'That's what we're told when they take the coin. Those heathens and the Danes.'

And yet what few colours the men carried were not of the Bishop. Whose men were these?

The land opened to fields in harvest and the route diverged. On a ridge at the confluence of the river and its tributary Ernald saw where the men-at-arms were from. It was not a castle with a bailey as stood beside the priory, but an enclosure of earthen ramparts topped by a palisade of forest timber. It was enormous, and not a single fluttering banner bore the Bishop's standard.

Chapter 31

Tim left the Freelander with the other cars and jumped out, sliding on the uneven gravel in his rush to reach the main door. He powered across the tiled reception area and keyed in his entry to the corridor beyond. Despite the parked vehicles he could hear no voices. Someone had to be in. Pushing into the lab, he grinned as John turned to him.

'You're late. Car break down?'

Tim shook his head. 'The car's fine.' He stood facing John, knowing his grin was widening but unable to temper his excitement.

'Well, don't just stand there. The plant's samples need to be analysed and a monthly report sending off to DEFRA. And I'm going to need you in the bottling section later, so no dawdling over your own samples this morning. It's going to be a busy day.'

With that John brushed by him, leaving Tim to listen to the clang of the stair treads as the man went up to the offices.

How could he not notice?

With a twinge of disappointment, Tim removed his white coat from his locker, his sense of elation kicking back in almost immediately. Draping his coat over the locker door he walked through to the toilet to peer into the mirror above the basin.

It was nothing short of miraculous, and he still couldn't get his head round it. Neither eyebrow showed any inflammation or flaking skin. Drawing a paper towel from the dispenser, he opened it across the basin and started rubbing at his scalp. As had occurred in the caravan, there were no skin particles to be collected.

It was the water; had to be. The unidentified constituent in the TG15-29 sample wasn't a contaminant, it was some sort of curative. If it could be isolated, identified...

The thought left his heart pumping. He drew out his phone and took a couple of photographs to add to the many he'd taken at the caravan. And then, just to be sure, he took some more and timed and dated the sequence. Tonight he'd need to check they'd automatically uploaded and delete the non-essentials; the phone's memory would be close to capacity.

John was back in the lab, and he stared, wide-eyed.

'I thought you were down at the well-head, but you haven't even got the internal pipe sample organised yet, have you?'

'My psoriasis has gone.'

'Hurrah for medical science. Get the samples sorted.'

'It wasn't anything I was prescribed. It was the water sample from the spring that keeps flagging an unidentified constituent.'

John blinked at him, and Tim felt a spurt of anticipation in sharing his discovery.

'You mean, this whatever-it-is spring—'

'—TG15-29—'

'—is issuing something akin to chalybeate waters?'

'Sort of, but it isn't impregnated with iron salts. Well, it is because they registered in the analysis, but not in such quantities to—'

'This *is* a mineral water bottling facility. You are not talking to a twelve year old, Timothy, despite sounding as if you are one. Are you implying that the water has healed your skin condition?'

Tim grinned. 'Yes.'

'Fuck's sake... There is no such thing as *healing* waters, only *healthy* waters. Read the company's literature, but not before you've been to collect a well-head sample. I'll do the internal.'

John turned his back and Tim felt like the twelve year old he was being labelled dismissed from a teacher's presence. It was his own fault; he should have kept his mouth shut.

Pulling on his white coat and his outdoor wellingtons, he collected his sampling equipment and was grateful to escape.

When he returned he found the lab empty, and he was grateful for that, too. Both analyzers were humming and a Post-It with a scrawled *DEFRA* reminder had been pressed to the mass spectrometer. Perhaps that meant John would be missing for a while and he wouldn't have to look him in the eye. Tim changed his boots, washed his hands, and set to work.

It was after the prescribed break for lunch, which no one seemed to take, that John returned to the lab. Tim was partway through the extended samples of the spring-water.

'And the results?'

'In keeping with the originals,' Tim told him. 'The rate of degradation in the air seems more or less a constant, but I haven't got to the end of the sample line yet, and to be certain I'd need—'

'Never mind that. I need you with me in the bottling section.'

'I'll have to close off the current sample or—'

'As soon as.'

John was out of the door again, leaving Tim peeved. He might have stumbled across something significant here and he wasn't being allowed to finish even one sentence.

With the individual sample halved, marked and re-dated, he left the analyzers plodding through their routines and took the corridor to where the bottling section opened into the storage and loading bay. Even as he approached its door he realised something was wrong – there was no sound of machinery – and once inside he was confronted by pallets of bottled water higher than his head. Hearing John's call, he walked over.

'Are we due a deep clean?' Tim asked, looking at the empty stainless steel line.

'Not for another week, but it might be an idea to bring it forward.'

Tim glanced at the transparent section in the feed pipe. It was empty. The pump had been switched off. 'Is there a problem?'

'Merely a hiccup with one of our distributors. Transport. It can't collect and we've been asked to store on-site for a few days. We need to shift product about to ensure the pallet dates remain consecutive.'

In practice it meant the pallets were numbered and pushed closer together, starting with the storage area nearest to the bay door. Even with the motorised jack it took some strength to manoeuvre the loads, and Tim began to appreciate the skills of warehousemen. Then he made a misjudgement guiding one through the narrow gap between the bottling and storage sections, trapping two fingers against the door jamb. His cry was automatic, and as he jumped about shaking out his hand he caught sight of John smiling at him.

'You'll live. Go run water over it.' His smile eased into a grin as he raised his eyebrows. 'Perhaps you should dip it in a pot of your healing water.' And he chortled.

Tim bared his teeth and walked out, holding his throbbing hand until he reached the kitchen and could turn on the tap. The force of the water caused a different type of hurt, but it didn't take long before he could flex his numbed fingers. After patting dry his hand, he returned to the bottling sector. John was manoeuvring the last of the pallets, leaving enough free space for another eight or so.

'How is it?'

'Grazed knuckles seems to be the worst.' He shook out his thrumming hand.

'We'll start the deep-clean tomorrow. Tell me about your psoriasis. What made you treat it with the spring water?'

'You surprised me on Monday, remember? The lid wasn't secure on the pot and when I jolted its water went across one eyebrow. By yesterday morning that eyebrow was clear, but I didn't make the connection until I was working on the samples later in the day.'

He looked down at his hand and flexed his fingers again. Manipulating those pots was going to be problematic if he couldn't grip the lids properly.

'So you decided to experiment on your other eyebrow?'

'It wasn't so much an experiment as giving it a try. I filled a couple of pots from the vacuum flask and bathed it last night.'

John looked sceptical. 'One wipe with damp cotton wool and it was clear?'

'Of course not...' and he explained how he'd timed the bathing every thirty minutes over four hours, and had then lain with a dampened cloth over his upper face and head and drip-fed the cloth until he'd used all the water.

'So it's documented?'

'Sort of. Not to the last millilitre, obviously. It wasn't a test under laboratory conditions.'

'But you've got before and after images?'

Tim pulled free his phone to bring up the photos, mollified now John was taking an interest.

'There's quite a visible change,' John murmured as he scrolled through. 'No uploading these onto the Net, eh? We still don't know what the unidentified constituent is, and I don't want anything being traced back to this plant.' He returned the phone.

'No, of course not. You made that clear.' At least John was calling it a *constituent* now and not a *contaminant*. Tim felt he was getting somewhere at last, bringing his colleague round to share his thinking.

'So how much water is left in that vacuum vessel?'

Tim shrugged. 'Not much. Enough for five or six more pots probably. Certainly not enough to keep the experiment going beyond this week.'

John stepped to the window and gestured for Tim to follow. 'Let's have a look at that hand of yours in better light.'

Tim walked over, extending his fingers, wondering if they'd swell or the nails would bruise. John grabbed his wrist, turned it and before he could resist was scrubbing his knuckles over the rough surface of the breezeblock wall.

The pain was excruciating and he yelled, trying to pull free, but John's grip was fierce. Then he was released and Tim fell onto the concrete floor, banging his elbow. He had the wit to roll and scramble away. His knuckles and finger joints were ripped open, there was blood on the wall, on the floor, and he was breathing harder than he'd ever breathed in his life. As he looked up to John standing by the window he felt himself start to tremble with an adrenalin surge.

'What the *fucking hell*—'

'Oh be quiet, Timothy. I knew you'd be a baby that's why I did yours first.' Without blinking, John scrubbed the back of his own hand across the wall leaving another smear of blood.

'What the fuck—?' but Tim's words left him hardly stronger than a whimper.

John was shaking the pain from his own hand. 'An experiment, Timothy. Scientists have always experimented on themselves. I'm surprised you didn't know that.'

He stepped away from the wall and Tim scrambled to his feet to back away.

'Don't be a pillock,' John told him. 'Get out that phone of yours. We need before and after shots.'

'Are you *nuts?*'

'Stop complaining and just do it. Then we'll rinse them off, apply a clean dressing from the First Aid box and nothing more. You can siphon off two pots of water from the flask and we'll leave the dressing on until 9pm. You can work out a schedule of bathing and we'll see the results, if there are any, tomorrow morning. What do you say?'

The photos taken, John watched his assistant back away to the door, what little colour he usually had still not returned to his face. Too soft by half.

'And make yourself a coffee. You look as though you need a stimulant.'

He let Tim get well ahead and then followed him into the corridor. Instead of making for the kitchen, he took the stairs to the offices. Doug was on the phone and frowned at the interruption. When the call was finished, John gestured for silence and approached his brother to display his hand.

'You say nothing. You don't tell the others. I just want a witness. Take a good look.'

Chapter 32

The group plodded on while the sun rose behind gathering cloud, the tended fields slipping to pasture, the pasture to thorn tangles and thistles flowering purple. Ernald leaned heavily on his staff, altering the length of his stride to ease the pressure on his feet. It seemed the group were moving faster than of late. On several occasions he caught the reeve eyeing him but decided it not prudent to voice his appeal. The cabbage leaves bound beside his skin were turning slippery, mottling their bindings. He thought of unlacing his sandals to rid himself of them, but he could no more face the reeve's castigation than he could the novice's reproachful stare.

In truth he feared being left to follow, and pilgrim he may look, questor he truly be, he feared to travel alone. The fortified enclosure outside of Yarum had not shown the Lord Bishop's colours but the colours of many men. Mercenaries for the Empress? For the King? He knew the two were locked in battle, had been for many seasons, but so far north? Or were they, as he now considered it, in the service of a man of might whose aim was to carve himself a hock of the Lord Bishop's lands while more noble families were engaged elsewhere? He set his mind; he'd add mention to the penned route for the sub-prior.

As the undulating country began a steady rise and running brooks crossed their path, they passed woodmen with pony-panniers, open-ended carts carrying sawn timber, oxen dragging tree trunks. On one occasion they pushed their ponies from the track while a mailed rider leading a column of men-at-arms took the route. Ernald followed the reeve's lead, removing his brimmed hat and bowing from the shoulders. No order was given and the troop did not slow.

'Don't look so fretful, friend Ernald,' the reeve murmured as he watched their kicked dust. 'A half-day and we'll see no more of them.'

A half-day and they saw no more of anyone. Woodland crowded the thinning track and Ernald thought he caught the scented traces of charcoal-burners, but they saw those, neither. Twice they came across the scattered stones of buildings covered in nibbled turf, and Ernald was reminded of the fired mill they'd encountered on their way to the ferry. It had been on the north side of the river, and they'd passed no other dwelling.

At the last they rested to allow the ponies to crop where they could. Ernald took the weight from his feet and gave thanks to Saint Cuthbert for the respite. He expected bread for themselves, but the reeve's man produced pasties from the panniers and their distribution lifted everyone's spirits.

The edges of the hardened crusts were collected by the reeve's youth, and while he crushed them between stones, Ernald uncorked his ink-pot to add what little he could of their route to his report. In truth, the discomfort in his feet had misguided his attention and he had not been counting the streams crossed nor the direction of their flow. The reeve would know, but Ernald felt too sore to counter the cold raising of the man's eyebrows.

Wulfrith, alone, had regained his cheery countenance since the trees encroached, and he came to squat at Ernald's shoulder to watch him work. They exchanged words for quill and ink and grass and trees, and Ernald cut a band of parchment to ink the words as his ears conveyed them.

The reeve gave notice that they were to walk again and told them to empty bowels and bladders away from the track so they'd be less noticed by any prowling wolf's-head. That was when the body was found.

It lay twelve good paces from the track by Ernald's reckoning, and had been covered in cut briars, now leafless and brittle, since moved by the beasts of the woodland so they could take their fill. There was not much maggot-work, and little smell from what was left of skin shrunken over bone. A spring corpse, perhaps, perhaps a winter, but it was no calling of God's grace. From the lack of clothing the corpse had been stripped naked.

Ernald remembered himself and brought free Saint Cuthbert's cross to hold it above the remains and begin a quiet litany on its behalf. All present bowed their heads, genuflecting when Ernald completed the rote.

'You'll not ink this to your report,' the reeve told him.

Ernald looked at him. 'It is a dangerous path, and that should be noted for the sub-prior.'

'The sub-prior already knows.'

'Then we must give him a Christian burial.'

'His soul has long fled. There will be no marker and no fresh grave. If you wish to alert a wolf's-head to a band of men travelling with tools to complete such a task, then we will all meet our Lord Jesus Christ in the same manner.'

'*Peccatum.*'

The Holy tongue's word for man's sin hissed across the encircled group, missed by no one. All turned to the novice, his limbs rigid, his countenance glaring. For a heart's beat everyone just looked, then the reeve's shoulders came up like a bull's and he made a move. Forgetting his feet and his staff, Ernald jumped across the man's intended line, still clutching Saint Cuthbert's cross.

'His eyes are misted and his mind unthinking. It is no sin, Master Ore Reeve, to consider the safety of the company above the eternal rest of a man long dead. Be at peace. Please, Master Ore Reeve. It aids no one but the Devil for us to fall about one another in this wasteland.'

'*Peccatum.*'

Ernald swung round. The young novice's ire was aimed directly at him.

At his side now, the reeve pointed. 'One more and your next meal will be your teeth. Get him to the ponies.'

As the novice was bundled back to the track, Ernald's memory returned to the priory's cloister, seeing the youth manhandled through the door to the confinement chamber, his tongue stilled by a wad of cloth. Was this the reason? Why was he travelling with them?

Once again they became a subdued group, the hooves of the ponies making more noise than men's tongues. The novice had been tied close to the pony's shoulder, Wulfrith on the other flank allowed the length of his leash which he used to put distance between them. This was not how a group in the service of the sub-prior, ultimately in the service of the Bishop, should be conducting themselves, and Ernald felt himself at fault for allowing it to fester. He called the reeve, and hobbled to meet with him.

'Might I lead our company in the singing of psalms, just for a while, so as to lift everyone's heads and dispel this lassitude?'

'We stay quiet.'

'Against who, Master Reeve? Wolf's-heads?'

'Perhaps.'

'Men-at-arms?'

The reeve lifted his eyebrow. 'Perhaps. How are your feet?'

'They will carry me, Master Reeve. I will not slow the pace.'

'I'm pleased to hear it. We need to be beyond Stocheslage before the curfew bell. There's ramparts there, too.'

That meant more men-at-arms. 'As large as the last?'

The reeve looked at the group ahead and then back at Ernald. 'The sub-prior did not say, and it is not my place to question.'

The group bore on, Ernald now leaning so heavily on his staff that his hands were chaffing against its wood, his knees against the rough wool of his habit where no undershirt intervened. The clouds thickened, making it impossible to know how high hung the sun. Birds did not sing; insects did not hum. Ernald prayed to Saint Cuthbert to stay the rain, then chastised himself for his selfishness and prayed for forgiveness.

When the trees broke it was as if the companions had been recalled to the Garden of Eden. There were briars and weeds certainly, but standing tall were the trees of an orchard, God's beneficence hanging low from every limb. The men's spirits lightened. Ernald found tears in his eyes. Giving grateful thanks for the mercy and protection of the Saint, he took the weight from his feet and the pressure from his hands to sit at the edge of the overgrown path. He considered unbinding his feet, but there was no water close to bathe them, nor to renew the poultice. He had no notion of how far they still had to journey, so he eased his muscles and listened to the men's banter rising like a lark's call as bags were filled. An undershirt tied at neck and wrists became a bulging sack, and once fastened to a pack, the two ponies shared in the bounty. Ernald was helped to his feet by the reeve's man. Each with a rosy apple to chew, the company continued along the path.

Their good humour faded as they came upon a field of heavy-headed corn choked with flowering weeds. When they spied the charred walls of a dwelling, juice was cuffed from chins and fruit held in stilled hands.

'Might this holding belong to the dead man?' Ernald ventured.

The reeve shrugged.

'He lies long dead,' Ernald pressed. 'Why would his neighbours not tend his land, not harvest its crops for themselves or their lord?'

'I do not know, friend Ernald. I do not know.'

They continued with a heavier step.

No marker showed where one holding met another, but corn had been reaped and the earthen strips gleaned. Weeds had grown tall here, too. They'd been cut with the corn and set in a pile to shrivel, their elongated stalks reminding Ernald too much of the dead man's skeleton in the wood.

There was another dwelling. This one stood unmarked by flame, its thatch intact, its door latched, but there was no pig in the sty, no scratting of fowl. Where the orchard had seemed part of God's garden, this seemed a desolate place.

'Pestilence?'

No one replied to Ernald's question. No one ventured to look. As they followed the curve of the path a shroud of solitude wrapped about each man. When the view opened to the valley floor and the smoke trails of Stocheslage appeared, the group released a collective sigh.

Chapter 33

A rap on the door heralded Phil's drawn face and wild hair. Nick saw him blink at the brightness of the overhead light.

'Oh... You're up. Well, kettle's on. Come down for a cuppa as soon as you're ready.' He didn't wait for a response.

Nick followed him on to the landing to visit the bathroom, and then down into the kitchen. A mug of steaming tea was waiting on the table.

'You look shattered, lad.'

'You don't look so brilliant yourself.'

Phil snorted. 'Drink that and we'll be off.'

Nick took a draught, wincing against the heat as it blossomed in his chest. Phil seemed calmer, or perhaps just tired. Maybe Nick wasn't the only one to have had a rough night.

'I'm sorry to put you to all this trouble.'

'We all makes mistakes. Soon have your car out o'there and be back for breakfast. Got its ignition key, 'ave you? Don't want to get down there an' find you've left it in your room.' A chuckle was added for show.

Phil knocked back his remaining tea, slapping the mug on the counter before turning for the door. Nick glanced at his own mug, barely any of the too-hot tea drained from its rim. He set it down to follow Phil into the passage and outside.

The clear sky of previous days had been replaced by cloud. Nick raised his face, trying to judge how high the sun was behind it.

'It'll burn off later,' Phil told him. 'Get in. It's open.'

With the engine's noise reverberating through the old Land Rover, talk was minimal. Nick was pleased for that as much as Phil seemed to be. Inane conversation felt misplaced considering last night's belligerent exchange.

Encouraged by the motion, Nick wanted to surrender to his need for sleep. Perhaps it was relief at being out of the confines of the house. Or just out in the daylight. He tried not think of the hours jolting from slumped dozes, but concentrated on the road ahead, on the grass breaking through the tarmac at its centre.

He sat forward. The grass was tall enough to move in the breeze. Had there been any when he'd left the car?

'Damned stuff,' he heard Phil say. 'Going to 'ave to take a scythe to it soon. Wish the council would come an' re-chip the road. Been on to them about it, but y'know what it's like.'

They drove by one of the signs hammered into the verge, its back obscured by wilting stalks and fading flower-heads. Nick visualised the bright flowers by the Pool, half hidden among the tree-roots.

'Did you sow the wildflowers around the signs?'

Phil looked at him as if he were mad. 'I've no time for stuff like that.' He gave an off-hand shrug. 'Jason might have. Or his followers.'

The copse emerged from a bend and Phil slowed to pull the vehicle onto the verge. Nick opened his door and jumped into thick vegetation he didn't recall when he'd bumped the Nissan into the woodland. He stared at it a moment then walked on. Three steps and his shins were registering the chill as heavy dew soaked his jeans. Phil was more organised, wearing wellingtons. The wood, too, was not as Nick remembered, its canopy seemed to be thicker, though he told himself it was an illusion caused by the cloud cover.

'Pick your footing,' Phil warned, and Nick focused on the ground. The ruts were full of water.

'Did it rain last night?'

'Not at the farm.'

Phil started in, Nick following. It wasn't just the puddles which were different. The stack of cut wood he'd thought would hide the car seemed further in, the trees crowding closer. Twice he slipped, rocks hidden beneath sphagnum moss popping free to lie on the surface, a hazard to his car.

Rounding the log stack, he caught his step. Grass and bracken reached higher than the Nissan's axles.

'Better try the engine,' Phil murmured.

Nick drew the fob from his pocket and hit the central locking button, relieved to see the indicators flash and hear the soft click of the locks. Once inside, the engine turned but refused to fire. His sense of unease grew.

'Quit that,' Phil told him, 'you'll drain the battery. I'll get the Land Rover an' pull you out. You release the towing point.'

Nick stepped out of the car, his blood roaring in his ears as he watched Phil walk away towards the patch of light. *Get a grip*, he told himself. But a grip of what? The hatchback looked as if it had been hidden away for two weeks, not two days. Is this what Alice meant when she'd said the Pool didn't always look the same to her? But the Pool was three miles away; the farm was closer. That thought widened his eyes.

Urging himself to move, to free the towing cover, he walked round the vehicle stamping down the vegetation and checking the tyres. They were inflated, but the back wheels had sunk past their treads into the wet earth. The ground had been drier than a bone when he'd parked, as solid as concrete.

His fingers came away sticky from the bodywork, and he pushed his hand down his thigh, snapping his head to the left as something caught his eye. Variegated greenery filled the space.

'Alice?' he breathed.

No, Alice couldn't leave the Pool. Except she had when she'd visited him at the farm, warm and—

Could the shadow people? He studied the vegetation, taller, thicker than he remembered. If Alice could be warm, could the shadow people manifest—?

Get a grip. It had been a small animal, a stoat or something, parting the leaves. He glanced at the dark canopy, barely chinked with what passed for daylight. There was no birdsong, he realised, not even the buzz of insects. It was as if the copse was pausing; waiting.

Tapping his toes to hear the squelch, he looked again at the sodden ground, remembering when he'd first pushed through the trees around the Pool. His heart beat harder. Phil was right. It hadn't rained last night, not at the farm and not here. The water was seeping up from the ground, not soaking into it. Was the Pool trying to claim his car? Did the *thing* know he'd hidden it here?

A deep-throated roar cut the silence and the Land Rover filled the opening, its headlights slicing through the gloom. Nick watched it rock across hidden ruts, its tyres spraying water, making the vegetation dip and sway. The Land Rover wasn't going to get bogged down. Nick's relief burst from him in a smile. They'd get the hatchback out onto the road.

Phil was all business, giving instructions in curt, condensed sentences. A cable was connected to the Nissan. Handbrake off, neutral engaged, Nick readied for the inevitable wrestle with the steering wheel. The winch screamed, and for long seconds it was not the hatchback that juddered and slid, but the Land Rover. Nick's eyes widened as its battered hulk crept towards him, its headlights turning in an arc to whiten the grimy windscreen so he could see nothing at all. He tried to call out a warning, but with no power the electric windows wouldn't open.

The windscreen dulled, leaving an after-glow imprinted on Nick's retinas. He was reaching for the door release when a vibration started through the steering wheel. The metallic groan that followed sounded like a living thing in pain, and the car jerked over stones at an oblique angle, the wheel wrenched from his grip. Clamping his palms back onto it, he leaned forward to stare through the coated windscreen trying to decipher Phil's hand-signals.

Once out from behind the log stack, Phil shut off the winch. They met between the vehicles.

'The motor's overheating. I don't use it much an' it's old. I'll lock it down an' try towing you out. Shift a few o'these rocks. We don't want 'em taking out your exhaust.'

Or the sump, Nick thought. Or the radiator. What had he been thinking, parking the car in here?

While Phil adjusted the cable, Nick searched out the stones which had threatened to turn his ankle, kicking at likely lumps of moss to reveal others. Digging them free with his fingers, he dragged them from the sucking earth to throw them out of the car's path. Some were jagged lumps, scratching at his skin, others smooth with rounded edges as if tumbled through water. All were of a double-hand size as though they'd been selected. Had there been a building here, a byre? By the time Phil was ready Nick was muddied to the elbows, his boots caked.

He returned to the car to grasp the door's handle. It wouldn't release. Again he pulled. Through the murky window a light winked red from the dashboard. The Nissan had self-locked. Slapping his pockets, he was relieved to feel the key. He slotted it into the lock, not wanting to draw Phil's attention to his lapse by activating the central locking. Seated inside, he leaned forward to wipe at the misting windscreen, leaving a trail of leaf-slurry to run down towards the inert air vents.

The Land Rover's engine roared to life and Phil began to reverse it. The cable lifted, dripping water and clinging grass and fronds of bracken. The car shuddered and slid, its tyres finding no grip. Nick fought the wheel as the rear fish-tailed, and he winced at the bumps and clunks from underneath the bodywork. The off-side of the car dropped and rose as he dragged on the steering wheel trying to keep the wheels out of ruts he could barely see. And then the tyres bit and daylight haloed round the Land Rover. Next moment he was squinting against the glare of the clouded sky as the hatchback bumped over the verge and onto tarmac. Tension released, Nick flopped back against the seat.

Phil brought the Land Rover to a halt and Nick stamped on the brake to stop the car rolling into it, engaging the handbrake to make it secure. They both stepped onto the road to grin at each other.

'There y'go,' Phil said. 'Had me worried for a minute, though, don't mind admittin' it.'

Nick raised his eyebrows – *only* a minute? He turned to survey the car. In full daylight the sticky film covering it was plainly visible. How he'd managed to see out of the windscreen was beyond him. Grass stalks and seed heads speckled the bodywork as high as the windows.

'It wasn't like that when I left the car.'

'It weren't like that when I found it.'

Nick frowned at him. How could he remain so calm? Was this how he coped, by denying the unexplainable? Anger spurted.

'You told me nothing happened to you.'

'It doesn't,' Phil said. 'It happened to you, Nicholas, not to me. You still intending to go down there again? Or are you gonna be sensible an' return home?'

Nick felt a moment's quiver of indecision and slapped it down. 'I'm going to the Pool.'

Phil sighed, then nodded and glanced away. 'We'd better get you back for some breakfast, then. Try the car.'

The Nissan hadn't self-locked this time. He sat in the driver's seat to push the key into the ignition. The engine coughed once, twice, then fired.

Phil leaned on the still open door. 'Bit o'damp, that's all.'

Chapter 34

He wasn't first in again; he could see cars parked in front of the plant's main door.

Tim slapped the steering wheel in irritation, immediately glancing at the back of the hand which fourteen hours before had been a mass of bloody scraped skin. Now it looked as if the entire experience had been a figment of his imagination.

Clearing his psoriasis was one thing. This was just weird. Sinister. Stuff like this didn't happen. It was against the laws of physics.

Indicating into the drive, he cut his speed further so as not to kick up dust that might catch the attention of anyone close to the upper storey windows. After John's psycho episode he'd been in two minds whether to turn up at all, but half his project papers were in the lab, weren't they? And what would he tell his supervisor at the uni about losing his placement? And if he did just walk away, where was he supposed to live?

He groaned as he realised it was John's SUV beside the boss's Jaguar. There would be no easing into this.

The lab was empty, the analyzers quiet, and that was unexpected. He gazed at the saucers, their contents evaporating into the air. What was he breathing? It had been emphasised in his fresher year: *To accept an unknown chemical compound as inherently benign is to court disaster*. Scheele's Green had been trotted out as an example, its arsenic vaporising from wallpaper and clothing to kill hundreds during the nineteenth century. He'd no idea what this unidentified contaminant was, and the lab didn't have any windows to open, not even an extractor fan. He made a fist of his injured hand. Not even a twinge. In truth, that didn't mean anything either, did it?

Slipping on his white coat, he wondered if he should escape down to the well-head to give himself some breathing space, his choice of phrase prompting an ironic chuckle. But as he closed the locker door the steel staircase in the corridor began to ring with rapid footfalls. Pushing his hands into the pockets of his coat, he turned his back on the saucers to rest against the bench with an affected nonchalance.

John bounced through the doorway, surprised, Tim thought, to see him. Then John grinned and walked slowly across the space, both hands raised so Tim could see the difference. There wasn't any.

'Don't keep me in suspense. Show yours.'

Tim complied and John's intake of breath was audible. In silent consent they laid their palms on the bench. Even downy hairs had returned. Tim could feel his own hair rising at the nape of his neck.

'Did you see it happen? I couldn't stay awake.'

Tim shook his head. He'd not been able to sleep, only dozing in snatches, a part of him not wanting to apply the water to the gauze, another fascinated by what might transpire. He rocked as John slapped him on the biceps.

'What's the matter? You should be celebrating.'

When he didn't respond, John's expression grew questioning.

'You're not still sore at me for yesterday, are you? Hey, I'm sorry, okay? It was a bit OTT, I agree, but I... I didn't believe you, Tim. I truly thought you were winding me up.'

'So you raked my hand across a *wall*? You raked your *own* hand across a *wall*?'

John altered his weight, tilting his head in embarrassment.

'What can I say? I figured it would shut you up, show you how...' he shrugged. '...*stupid* you were.' He smiled again. 'Except you weren't, were you? You were dead on. You've actually discovered something, something *sensational!*'

He opened his arms wide. 'Hell's teeth, Timothy. Don't you understand what this means? The university will bend over backwards to fund forward research. It's name-in-lights time!'

He became earnest, which Tim found even more disconcerting.

'I'll be more than happy to sign a statement of fact that you can take to your supervisor to get the ball rolling. Of course, the company will want its name in there somewhere as an originating sponsor, but Douglas will sort all that.'

'You've *told* him?'

'Not yet, no.'

Tim stared at the door leading to the stairs. 'But you've just seen him.'

'Of course I have. We've a distribution problem to sort, haven't we? What did you think I would say to him? *I cut this hand yesterday and this morning it's cured*? I was waiting for you to arrive so we could go up together to break the news.'

'No!'

'What?'

Tim could feel himself mouthing like a goldfish and fought for a coherent reason that would make an impact. 'We don't know what this unidentified contaminant is.'

'Constituent, Tim, *con-stit-u-ent*.'

'We don't know what the side effects are, whether it's a poison, whether in a week our hands are going to start to shrivel or gangrene set in.'

'*Whoa!* Calm down. Sheesh… and you thought my reactions were over the top? It's early days, I know it is.' He gestured to the shelf of saucers. 'And I agree, all this is hardly rigorous scientific testing.'

Tim guffawed and John's exuberance faded. Tim watched him turn to the saucers on the shelf.

'In fact, it's piss-poor scientific testing, isn't it?'

'Yes it is. And we don't know what the unidentified marker is, and until we can verify otherwise it has to remain a *contaminant*. For safety's sake.'

John didn't seem to be listening. 'The whole thing needs to be undertaken at the uni, doesn't it? It has the facilities.'

'I can't commandeer its facilities. It doesn't work like that. I'd have to speak to—'

'I know, I know, to your supervisor, who'd have to speak to the head of department, who'd have to take it to a committee, and then there'd be funding issues—' John turned back, narrowing his eyes. 'That would mean tapping up the pharmaceuticals. And they'd love it, wouldn't they? A naturally occurring therapy that would put them out of business. Their accountants would be overjoyed.'

Tim ignored his sarcasm. 'We don't know if it is natural. You said it yourself, if the media get wind of a possible contaminant in the water table—'

John tensed. 'Not in our water.'

'It wouldn't have to be in the plant's water, that's what you said.'

John looked at the floor. 'I wasn't wrong. The adverse publicity would kill the company in days.'

They stood in a silence Tim felt pressured to fill.

'So what do we do?'

'It's your discovery, Timothy, your call. My suggestion, for what it's worth, is that we keep this under our hat and...' he glanced at the shelf of saucers, '...and keep doing what we're doing. Data collection is the priority, don't you think? It gave you one breakthrough; it could give you a second.'

'There might be another problem. The contaminant is degrading as the water evaporates into the air. This air. What if the contaminant isn't degrading but changing its structure? What if we're breathing it in right now?'

John stared at him, his eyes widening.

'Good point.' He licked his lips. 'However, let's not jump to negative conclusions. This water is from a naturally occurring spring in the middle of a tourist attraction, right? A lake?'

Tim nodded, following his thinking.

'Evaporation from such a surface, if toxic, surely would be noticeable, don't you think? Especially at a tourist attraction. People would be overcome by fumes, or be sick or something.'

Tim nodded again, feeling a little easier.

'But it's a good point,' John said, 'shows you're considering all the angles. I'm sure we can set up a small experiment to analyse the evaporation. You list the necessary equipment and if we can't cobble something together we'll see about purchasing it. Not top of the range, mind, we're not made of money, just something to show a yes—no—maybe result so we know whether or not to take it further. Is that okay?'

Tim's shoulders were relaxing. He even managed a smile. 'Sounds good.'

'We need more water, don't we? This time I'll tag along. I could do to see this place.'

'Sure, good idea. That five litre vacuum flask is heavy.'

They turned as rapid footfalls sounded on the stairs.

'And in the meantime,' John said, lifting his hand, 'we say nothing to anybody about this. Okay?'

The door sprang back with such force that it hit the locker behind. The CEO strode in, his face like thunder.

'Are today's results in yet?'

'Not yet,' John said. 'Tim's about to go down to the well-head.'

'Then get on with it. There's been an earthquake south of here. I want samples taking every four hours.'

'Where and what magnitude?'

John's tone was unconcerned and Tim saw Douglas bridle. If the brothers were going to have a row he wanted to be out of there, and he moved to the bin to retrieve his wellingtons.

'Does it matter what magnitude? It's those damned contractors and their test drilling. That's if they're not doing a test *frack*.'

'Their licence doesn't allow—'

'Don't give me that shit,' Douglas spat. 'They only call it hydraulic fracturing when they're using a full spectrum of chemicals.'

'Give me the coordinates.'

Tim had his wellingtons but he also needed a clean-room container, and the box was near the lockers. He hesitated, then decided to slink outside and wait until the brothers were done.

'Timothy.' He stopped dead. 'Make yourself useful and find out where this is exactly.'

He took the paper from John's outstretched hand and pulled out the maps.

'Samples every four hours,' Douglas reiterated as he dragged open the door.

Tim glanced along the bench as the man's footfalls sounded on the stairway.

'Don't fret about him,' John said. 'He's under a bit of pressure right now with this distribution problem. When you're done you can go collect the well-head sample. I'll do the internal pipe. When we get those out of the way you can make a start on your primary samples.'

Tim liked the sound of *primary samples*, though it still didn't make the saucers any more legitimate. Spreading the map on the bench, he checked the hand-written figures against the map: 54.40— He stared at the coloured terrain, feeling his fingertip tremble against the paper, then scrambled in his pocket for his mobile, pulling up the app, sliding through the notes he'd made.

John was at his shoulder. 'What?'

'It's the spring,' he said. 'The earthquake is centred on the Pool.'

Chapter 35

They returned to the farm in a convoy of two, the noise of earth and stones dropping from the wheels of the Nissan reminding Nick of his walk back from the Pool, of his trainers and trousers shedding drying mud from its uncovered bed. He thought of the litter of stones down there, covered in a web of stringy vegetation. They'd also been rounded, about double-hand sized, and he was certain no building had ever stood down there.

The Land Rover turned into the drive and Nick followed, its gravel clattering at the wheel arches, freeing the last of the debris. He caught Phil's hand signal so didn't park at the top of the yard, but drove past the picnic tables and round the corner by the sign for toilets. In front of an outbuilding was a stone trough, a tap and a reeled hosepipe, and he knew why he'd been taken down there. Phil came to his window.

'I'll power-wash the car later. You clean yourself up a bit or Rosemary will have a fit. Got spare clothes in the boot?'

Rubbing dried mud from his hands, Nick walked round to the rear of the car and popped the hatch, too late remembering the broken sign he'd secreted there. Phil didn't say a word, just reached in to lift it out of his way and grasp the roll of clothing jammed in beside the boxes.

'Just a swift scrub off, mind. You ain't goin' to a dance. I'll put your shirt and jeans in the wash later when Rosemary's busy.'

Nick smiled at the man's attempt at conspiracy. Rosemary would notice. Of course she'd notice.

Stripping off by the tap he scraped his arms and legs free of the clinging grime, rubbing himself dry with a scratchy towel Phil produced.

'It ain't clean but neither are you,' he said.

They walked round the outside of the house like a pair of schoolboys expecting censure.

The smell of grilling bacon was a thread of normality to draw him from an unnatural morning. Nick breathed it in as if the smell alone would feed him.

'Got it out,' Phil called as he pushed open the kitchen door. 'Took longer than expected. He'd got it wedged, hadn't he?' Nick caught Phil's eye-roll, the unvoiced *townie* clear. 'Easier to use the winch. Tea freshly mashed, is it?'

'Waiting on the table.' Rosemary gave Nick the same suspicious flick of her eyes he knew from his mother.

'Hello, Rosemary.'

'Good morning, Nicholas. Did you sleep well?'

There didn't seem much point in lying, and she nodded her understanding.

'Eggs in one minute.'

'We'd better wash up then,' Phil said, steering him towards the utility room. 'I'll just put Nick's boots in the Aga to dry. We washed them off down the yard.'

'Did it rain down there last night?'

'Oh aye,' Phil said. 'Puddles all o'er road. Must 'ave been an isolated shower. Grass were sodden.'

Nick was pleased to escape their company to scrub his hands, this time with soap. On the counter above the washing machine sat a bulging day-sack. For him, he realised, the provisions Rosemary had promised. Phil came in as Nick was drying his hands. They didn't make eye contact.

Breakfast was huge, served on platters. Even Phil blinked. Bacon and sausage and black pudding crumbling with oatmeal, fried bread, eggs, potato patties, beans… To Nick's surprise he found he could eat it all.

He sat back. 'That was fabulous. I feel I could sleep for a week after that lot,' and he wished he'd said nothing.

Rosemary merely smiled, entering the utility room to return with the day-sack. 'Food,' she said. 'It'll keep you going a couple of days.'

'Don't rush the lad,' Phil mumbled, but Rosemary ignored him.

Nick stood to accept the pack. Just as on Friday they wanted him gone.

'Thanks.' He attempted a smile. 'Any scones in there?'

'They don't keep,' she said, and the lightness faded from her face.

He took his boots from the Aga's warming oven and tied his trainers to the pack. Rosemary still stood; Phil still sat. The atmosphere could be cut with a knife.

'I'll be back for dinner,' Nick said, and he grinned at her to make the joke. 'I just don't know which one.'

She bit her lip. Worse, she reached out to hug him, the tremor in her breathing all too evident.

'I'm coming back,' he murmured.

She pulled away to pat his shoulders. 'And your room will be waiting.'

'I'll walk you down,' Phil said, and Nick knew that was his cue. He picked up his coat.

'She gets fretful,' Phil told him as they walked along the drive. You're about the same age as Jason.'

'I know.'

The fencing with the stile and its map post became visible ahead. The point of no return. They crossed the tarmac. No grass grew through it here, Nick noted. He wondered why it did elsewhere. Slinging the pack over one shoulder, he readied to mount the stile. Phil blocked his way.

'You'll be wondering 'ow it is our son's one minute so obsessed that he's plantin' trees an' cuttin' a path, an' next he's away to work in Qatar.'

Nick wasn't sure what to say. It hadn't even crossed his mind. He watched as Phil became uncertain, looking down, chewing at his lip.

'Rosemary, she found the job on the internet. She completed the form, got 'im the interview. It were me drove 'im to Manchester Airport. Bought meself a cheap ticket to Dublin so I could walk 'im through Security.' His chest heaved as his gaze slid away. Nick felt his own breath leave him in a thin stream.

'We don't hear from 'im much,' Phil added. 'Rosemary's sister, she's good, sends on 'is emails. Got a new life now. He's happy. That's all that matters.' He made to speak again, stopped.

'I understand,' Nick whispered.

'I'm only telling you 'cos I don't want *your* mother...' Phil stopped again. 'I'll not be searching for you, Nicholas, not this time. There'll be no light to guide you back.'

'I know.'

There was a moment of immobility and then Phil's mouth tightened. His chest heaved, and when he looked up Nick faced the flaring temper and staring eyes of the previous evening.

'You know *nothing*.'

Bunching his own shoulders, Nick glowered back. 'Then stop farting around and fucking well *tell me*.'

A fist shot by his face, the punch connecting with the map with such force that the board twisted on its post.

'I helped Jason mark out the path!' Phil bellowed. 'It were two miles then and it were *straight*.'

Chapter 36

Stocheslage seemed more fortified than Yarum to Ernald's untrained eye, even though he could see only a small hall standing on a rise. Sight of its church, so lofty against the village's scattering of roofs, made Ernald glow. Here the lord held the spiritual sustenance of his people close to his heart. Maybe there was even a pestlry where his feet could be treated properly and with prayers.

A web of becks flowed towards the river that cradled the settlement in its loop, just as Yarum had been cradled and, as he thought on it, the priory and dwellings at Durham. He was both surprised and gratified to find that most of the becks were bridged, the fords left to cattle and draught animals. From the quagmire on the banks and the churned earth beyond, it seemed a great number of animals passed through the settlement.

Their group joined a cart-way that led to the palisade gatehouse. Men-at-arms stood firm, their colours of a hue that matched the single standard. This was no minor manor lord's holding, Ernald realised. It was his duty as questor to travel between the manors closest to the priory. Most offered some protection from incursion by the Scots, but none with such a spiked ditch and formidable palisade.

Despite the defences, people were being allowed unquestioned entry, some nodding to the guards, others offering a quiet salutation. Their company followed, but as the reeve led the first pony into the narrowing entrance men-at-arms stepped close on every side.

'Strange faces at a strange time o'day.'

The accent was fierce, flatter than the reeve's, but

understandable to Ernald.

'We travel on the instruction of the Lord Bishop,' the reeve told their interrogator. 'We seek new veins of lead for my lord's roofs.' He indicated the mattocks and hammers strapped to the pony. 'With us travel two penitents and a pilgrim.'

'No penitent, I!' the novice roared. Ernald turned to stare. 'A true Disciple cast from—'

A fist above the ear from the reeve's man cut short his exclamations as his head rocked on his shoulders. The leader of the men-at-arms did not falter, but turned his scowl on Ernald's satchel and marked cloak.

'Pilgrim, be it?'

Ernald removed his rush hat to bow from the shoulders.

'An' a sore-footed pilgrim, eh, despite yer boots. Or maybe because ov'em, eh? Pilgrim where?'

'The priory at Durham,' Ernald answered. 'We left after the Feast of—.'

'Durham?' He swung back to the reeve. 'Aye, the voice betrays the Scot in ye.'

'I be no accursed Scot,' the reeve bridled.

'Why would the Bishop o'Durham be sending ye to the lands o'the Bishop o'York if not for mischief? To steal his lead, eh? What else y'stealing?'

Ernald's gasp of surprise escaped before he could suppress it. Had he heard true? ...*lands of the Bishop of York?* The men-at-arms took no notice, intent on riffling the pony-packs.

'We steal nothing,' the reeve countered. 'We travel east on the Lord Bishop's instructions. If this is where we pay the toll—'

'Apples, be it?' said the man at the pony-pack. 'Think to offer y'apples at yon market cross an' steal from the purse o'Lord de Baliol?'

'Never. I swear my oath true. The apples come from a deserted toft on the path, picked for our bellies only. Take them. They are sweet and may our labour be our toll.'

Heads turned. The man who had been handling the apples through the cloth of the undershirt stepped back with widened eyes and began scrubbing his palms down his tunic. Their interrogator pointed an accusing finger towards the reeve.

'Ye try to pass the Devil's temptation—?'

The question turned into a snarl and then an order. Pole-arms were brandished and Ernald felt a pain in his side as the group were forced through the gate and pressed against the stockade wall.

'What's happening?' he asked the reeve.

'Keep your wits an' your tongue, friend Ernald.'

The men-at-arms began arguing among themselves. Ernald caught a second mention of the Devil, but they were speaking so fast now the context was lost to him. He thought of the deserted toft, its fired dwelling, the unreaped field. Wulfrith, he saw, was trying to hide behind the pony's shoulder. Ernald touched the cross of Saint Cuthbert to his breastbone and silently called a blessing of peace upon them all.

The argument halted and one of the guards strode away with purpose. The group was gathering a crowd, now, the men-at-arms keeping the inquisitive from coming too close. Whispered words were exchanged, and with shocked expressions the people backed away, signing themselves in the Holy Cross as they ushered their children before them.

Ernald looked to the novice. He had called out so clearly, whereas on their journey he had refused to speak, except to denounce in the sacred tongue. His head was held low, his shoulders hunched in his known demeanour. Why speak now?

A jab in the ribs from an elbow switched his attention to the reeve, a nod diverting it to the returning man-at-arms. Behind him hurried a priest in the sun-bleached cloth of vestments. Ernald was relieved to see him, and tried to take a step forwards, his momentum blocked by the reeve's jutting elbow.

Their ring of guards parted and the priest stepped through to stand and stare, hard-eyed, upon the company. Immediately the reeve bowed, followed by his men. Ernald clutched his rush hat to his chin and did the same. Not until the sacred tongue flowed to his ears, as sweet as the priory's plainsong, did Ernald dare to lift his gaze. Held aloft was an altar cross in shining silver. He let his eyelids fall, bathing in the goodness of the liturgy and the blessings of the Trinity. Then Saint Michael the Archangel was invoked to drive out *serpents* and *demons* and *shadows that ride the night*, and with a trembling breath Ernald realised the priest was calling for Saint Michael's aid against him and his fellow travellers.

When the priest concluded, the company gave the murmured response and genuflected before the held rood. Ernald licked his lips, wondering if he should speak, but the priest nodded to the waiting guard and turned away. Within a moment Ernald's staff had been wrenched from his grasp and he was pushed in the back to hobble after the reeve and his men. A cry made him glance behind. Cut free of the pony, Wulfrith and the novice were being beaten as they hurried to catch up. The pony, so mild of temper on their travels, was kicking and coughing, its eyes rolling, as pole-arms were used to push it against the wall of timber and cut the undershirt of apples from its pack. No guard, Ernald saw, was venturing close.

The group was herded to the church. It was a dim building in comparison to the church at the priory, its windows tiny, but as Ernald's vision grew accustomed he made out The Suffering On The Cross filling one lime-washed wall, Saint Peter Before The Gates filling the other. At the candle-lit altar the priest placed the silver rood in its stand, finishing with a prayer to the Almighty. When he turned, the guards stood back. The companions fell to their knees, Ernald slightly after.

'You are from the priory at Durham.'

Ernald's head shot up at the accusatory tone, yet the priest was not pointing to him, but to the novice.

'Sed peccatores,' the novice spat.

They be sinners. Ernald drew breath at the youth's condemnation of his convent. He had to speak or the exchange would lead to misunderstanding and ill-will.

'Holy Father, he is but a lowly novice under a penitent's constraint. He knows not what he says.'

'Sed quid?'

Ernald moulded the sacred tongue to respond, but uttered none. Yes, he did know, and he realised he was undone. Reaching for his coif, he drew the linen from his head to show his tonsure.

'Not a pilgrim, then,' the priest said. 'You travel under service of the Lord Bishop with these protectors?'

Ernald blinked. His satchel felt heavy on his shoulder, but it carried no seal from the Lord Bishop. The truth of it would out. Slowing its way to the light would not aid their cause.

'In the directed service of Sub-Prior Maugre, Holy Father.'

He expected to be questioned closer, but the priest merely clasped his hands and straightened his back.

'The Devil set a demon among us and Saint Michael turned its foul trap to the good Lord's work. Your satchel, Master Pilgrim.'

Ernald lowered his gaze, unsure how to unravel what he'd heard. A man-at-arms stepped close, hand out-stretched, and Ernald lost no time in divesting himself of his satchel.

'The penitents.'

The priest turned to leave. Wulfrith and the novice were grasped by the ears and hauled after. Ernald rose higher on his knees at Wulfrith's cry, but could only watch as they were enveloped by the searing daylight from beyond the opened side door. He turned to the reeve.

'What is—?'

The world tilted and the earthen floor came up to meet him before Ernald reasoned the pain at his temple. Breathing hard, he shuffled back to his knees. An insect was crawling down his cheek. He brushed it away, covering his knuckles in blood. He looked at the reeve in his shock, but the man's downcast gaze never strayed to him. Unable to stop himself from trembling, Ernald clutched at his fallen coif and pressed the linen to his wound.

The light dimmed slowly, the cold rising from the beaten floor entering Ernald's knees to creep up his thighs. His feet throbbed worse than his head, but he dared not change his stance to offer them respite. The reeve and his men remained around him, mere shadows carved from stone. Only their guards altered their weight, foot to foot. None spoke.

Ernald heard a latch, felt a draught of air pass his ears. A boy on silent feet glided by with a lamp and proceeded to light the cresset wicks. Their flickering flames did little to lift the gloom, but one illuminated the pained expression of Our Lord Jesus Christ, another the fierce countenance of Saint Peter holding open his scroll. Ernald closed his eyes. Making his spirit return to the cloister at Durham, he began a litany of murmured prayers begging for succour on behalf of his fellow travellers and himself.

Partway through the third rote the side door opened. No bright daylight slanted in, just a grey pall through which passed a man-at-arms. Ernald's name was called, and a gesture given for him to rise. The pain in his feet made him wince. A strong hand did not wait, but grasped his upper arm and he was hauled outside, across a cobbled yard, and into a dwelling.

The heat from a central hearth embraced him, its smoke catching at his throat and tearing his eyes. Wiping them, he found himself facing wall paintings of The Trials of Our Lord Jesus in the Desert.

'Brother Ernald...' The priest rose from a high-backed chair at the edge of a trestle board to indicate the bench on its longer side. Ernald's gaze strayed across the contents of his satchel displayed beside a jug and platter.

'Divest yourself of your cloak, Brother Ernald; take the weight from your injured feet. A little sustenance?'

As Ernald eased himself onto the edge of the bench, the priest poured water from the jug, placing the leather cup beside the cut bread and milky cheese. Ernald drank the water but did not touch the food. The priest lifted Ernald's parchment as if to read, then gestured with it.

'The tainted waters of everlasting youth are found, it seems.'

'*Youth?*'

The priest sat back to open his hands in surprise. 'You do not believe its waters are the lair of a demon cheating Heaven of men's souls by offering everlasting youth?'

Ernald pressed the cross of Saint Cuthbert to his chest. 'My lord, no. It is the Blessed Lady Mary who—' He hesitated. 'At least... at least it is my service to seek the truth in the healing gifts of Her waters.'

'Then it is true. I have heard tell of this from the Bishop at the Abbey of Saint Mary. The spilled tears of the Blessed Mother sprinkled far in her grief during Our Lord's Passion. I know of those falling in Normandie, as will you, I can hear the lilt in your voice. In which House did you reside before travelling to the House at Durham?'

'Notre-Dame du Bec.' Ernald saw the priest's eyebrows rise, and he added, 'It is long years since I saw that holy place.'

The priest nodded. 'It is ours to do God's bidding, and that of our lords. In the house at Durham you are chosen for...?'

'Questor.'

The priest sat forward and again Ernald hurried to settle any misunderstanding. 'For the lesser manors close to the House, you understand.'

'But you have touched the relics of the Blessed Saint Cuthbert?'

'The minor relics.' Beneath the priest's attentive gaze Ernald felt himself reaching for the Saint's reliquary cross, pulling it free from his habit. 'It was passed to my hand for the protection of—'

'—on your quest. I understand.' The priest took it in his palm, pulling at its thong, and at Ernald, to bring its crystal close to the rush-light at the end of the table.

'It holds hairs from the head of the Blessed Saint,' Ernald told him, 'bound with a thread from His vestment.' He looked into the priest's face. 'The Gracious Saint has given His aid.'

'Then your heart is seen to be true. This humble church, and the people of the Lord de Baliol, will also give what meagre aid they can in support of your Holy Quest. Men for protection.

Unguents for your feet. A horse for your comfort until you can walk well again. Food!' He caught his rising tone to smile at Ernald.

'Your journey through the settlement of the Lord de Baliol blesses us all, as it blesses his lands and his people.'

Without taking his gaze from Ernald he laid his hand on the parchment listing markers on the route.

'On your return we will sit as men of religious worth and discuss the wonders of your quest. It will allow time for the clerk to the Lord de Baliol to take a fair hand of your writings so as to be set before the eyes of the Bishop of York. But now, now we will treat your feet.'

The priest clapped his hands and the door opened behind Ernald, sending a chill draught around his ankles.

The man who set down his scrip could not have been more different from the poultice-maker of Yarum. He wore a velvet hat, not a dirty coif, and it was trimmed with fur as was his padded coat. His shoes were of incised leather, Ernald noticed, his hose bright yellow. He did not give his name and Ernald dare not ask.

Deft hands divested Ernald's feet of their undershirt bindings and the mulched cabbage leaves. They, the herb-pouch and the poultice-maker's salve, were dropped into the bright flames to sizzle and burn, tainting the air with their stench. A bowl of water was set to warm, a potion mixed, his feet washed. Gripping the edge of the bench, Ernald set his teeth against the stinging. An unguent was applied with a horn spatha and clean bindings secured. The man nodded to the priest and withdrew.

'There will be a little discomfort,' the priest advised, 'but it will ease. Be mindful to your chaplet and to the good Saint Cuthbert's relics, and you will be delivered.'

A man-at-arms escorted him to a byre close by, where he was grateful to ease into sweet-smelling hay. He could hear no animals, though he could smell them. In the little light given from the single cresset his companions seemed to be in a huddle, all except the known shape of the novice who sat alone.

The reeve stepped to Ernald's side to peer down at him. A tap to his foot made Ernald catch his breath.

'Warm fire, was it, while your feet were rebound? Spiced wine? Good eating?'

Ernald looked up at the shadowed bulk above him, not understanding the man's hostility. 'Water, Master Reeve. Only water.' He drew his memory from the platter of cut bread and milky cheese, grateful he hadn't touched it.

'More than we've had. Do you still carry Saint Cuthbert's cross?'

'Of course.'

'Then come and administer its blessings. There's nought we can do.'

Ernald sat upright, his throbbing feet ignored. 'What is it?'

'Wulfrith. They broke his hand.'

The reeve turned aside, his scowl at the novice plain in the flickering cresset light. 'I'd like to break someone's neck.'

Chapter 37

The 4x4 juddered across the cattle grid at too high a speed. Tim grabbed the door handle to steady himself and glanced in the wing mirror to confirm the trailer was still attached.

When he'd explained about walking the path from the farm to the Pool each carrying a five litre vacuum flask, John had guffawed. *Leave it to me* had translated into a two-seater quad bike carrying a polyethylene tank of a size that had made Tim's jaw drop.

'We can't fill this.'

'It's not going to be *filled*. It's the only sterile container I could get at short notice.'

But as Tim had helped tie on a camouflage sheet to cover its stark white body, his gaze had locked onto the empty roll-cage mountings and he knew that was exactly what John intended. This wasn't sampling; this was stealing.

'Don't look so grim,' John had mollified as he'd driven from the plant. 'A couple of five litre flasks will go nowhere. And trailing backwards and forwards across farmland is a sure way to draw attention we don't want. Besides, if the earthquake has been caused by those gas-shalers doing a test frack, we'll want plenty of original water on hand so when you return for another sample we can compare the two. And if there *is* a difference it'll be data which can get that damned operation closed down. Isn't that what your survey is all about?'

True, it was. Tim hadn't expected to be in the front line, that's all. He'd never had the stomach for Simon's grandstanding.

Except it wasn't all, was it? This *jaunt*, as John was calling it, had had to wait until after-hours when the brothers had left for the night so no questions were asked by them, either. The delay meant they were now entering the moorland as the sun was drifting close to the horizon. By the time they reached the Pool it would be twilight. The coincidence seemed too convenient.

'Jesus, Timothy... Buck up. It's like taking a maiden aunt on a date to a strip club. We're not going to rustle sheep, for God's sake. Grab the map and make sure we don't miss the turning. I wouldn't trust my life to a sat nav up here.'

The lab's Ordnance Survey was pushed across and it didn't take Tim long to orientate himself. They were heading for a point on a side road that John had marked in red. From it led a track through shooting butts, which probably meant it was used by Land Rovers, so it shouldn't cause a problem for the quad bike.

He opened the map further, searching for the farm so isolated on its own, and back across pale brown contour lines marked solely by heath and icons signifying rough grassland. The track would pass close enough to the unmarked Pool. He didn't think it had rained since he'd been there; the land shouldn't be boggy. Perhaps they could get in and out before it grew truly dark.

'Have we brought torches?' he asked.

'Of course.' John turned to look at him. 'But we won't be using them, will we?'

No, mused Tim. Lights shining across a dark moor would draw attention, wouldn't it? Especially when they were crossing someone's land to steal their water. How had he allowed himself to be drawn into this?

The sat nav was switched off and Tim navigated round groups of dozing sheep taking the last of the day's warmth from the broken tarmac. Not until they'd crossed a culvert did Tim call a halt.

'We've missed it.'

John didn't believe him, even when he pointed to the thin blue line beyond the red mark on the map. Annoyed that even his map-reading was being dismissed, Tim disconnected his seatbelt and slid out to walk back, scanning the shadowy terrain for signs of shooting butts. He picked out a lumped peaty pile, and a few strides further recognised the indentations of an overgrown track. He waved to the vehicle and waited for it to reverse, its brake lights bright as it pulled to a halt beside him. John stepped out to look.

'If you'd given me the position earlier I would have checked the map against Google Earth. This hasn't been used for years.' Tim felt smug in stating the obvious, especially when it elicited no response.

With the 4x4 backed into the mouth of the disused track, a ramp was secured to the trailer and the quad bike driven off. Leaving the car locked was one thing, but to Tim the unsecured trailer was a gift to thieves.

'And who's going to come round here at this hour?' John snapped as he tied a bag to the quad's front rack.

'Sheep rustlers?'

John curled his lip. 'Get on or walk.'

It wasn't long before Tim wished he'd elected to walk. The quad bounced and jolted across terrain hidden beneath clumps of tall heather that whipped at his jeans and scratched at his hands as he clung on, very aware of no roll-cage. How it would handle with a hundred litres of water strapped to the back he didn't want to consider.

As the sky dimmed the heather grew woolly, the course of the track beneath indistinct. Sometimes there was no smell to notice; others the scent was so thick it clawed at the back of his throat and made his eyes water. A rounded hillock of nibbled grass and toppled stones erupted to their left, an incongruous island in the purple-hued swell flowing by them. If a sheep broke cover in front of their wheels they'd have no chance.

With a snatched breath of realisation the sheep was forgotten, Tim turning back to the knoll, but it had been swallowed by the deepening gloom. An Iron Age burial mound. He'd seen them marked on the map. The area was littered with them.

Once his mind had registered their existence, their eroded stones glowed in the dying light to catch his attention, their grassy backs arching out of the heather with increasing frequency. Tim felt sweat ooze across his upper lip, turning cold in the breeze their momentum created. He focused, instead, on the front of the quad, on the solid blocks of heather that bent and disappeared beneath their bucking wheels.

'Slow down.'

John ignored him.

Tim released his grip to slap his knuckles against John's arm. 'Slow down! We won't know where to turn off.'

John grinned, or grimaced, it was hard to tell they were being thrown about so much, but there was a nod of his head and Tim followed his gaze. Rising from the darkening moor was a solid line of black, the ring of shrubby trees.

They slowed, John eventually bringing the quad to a halt, the engine rasping as it ticked over. He leaned across the bonnet to unzip the lumpy bag and extract a thick-handled torch.

'Here. Find a route across there. I'll follow.'

It sounded easy enough. It proved anything but. He needed a walking pole, something to test the depth of terrain beneath the undulating heather. As he cracked his ankles on unseen stones he became painfully aware that his workplace trainers and jeans provided little protection. The cut path from the farm had been effortless in comparison, and he'd been wearing boots. He should never have allowed himself to be herded into this *jaunt* without full knowledge and adequate preparation.

His foot sank into a boggy patch, and cold moss and God knew what was pushing up his ankle inside the leg of his jeans. There was a glooping suck as he pulled free, holding his breath against the rank smell that followed. Skip-leaping over the bushy heather to escape, he hoped it had been a natural mire and not the entrails of a dead sheep. By the time he was within touching distance of the trees, his thighs were aching, his feet tingling, and he was breathing hard.

He turned to wave the torch, to find the quad bike's lights illuminating the heather purple behind him. The engine cut, the lights followed, plunging him into a rippling darkness that took a moment to clear. John's silhouette was moving towards him, and Tim lifted the heavy torch to guide his way.

'Well you were a lot of use, zig-zagging about like a bluebottle. Where's the entrance?'

Tim's spurt of irritation was supplanted by embarrassment. 'There isn't one; I should have thought. We can't get the bike through.'

'Bollocks. Let's have a look.' John pushed by him, flashing his own torch at the supple leafy branches and thin trunks. 'How far is it to the water?'

'Just beyond the trees.' A memory jolted, and he strode forward to catch at the whipping branches as John forced his way through. 'There was a man, a tramp sleeping rough. I nearly stood on him.'

'Yeah, well, if he gets in my way I will. Where's this water?'

The grasping branches released his jacket and Tim caught his balance as he was propelled into a ring of darkness which seemed to reach far above the height of the trees. He brought up his torch to be sure they were just bushy shrubs and not a solid wall. In the deepening indigo overhead the first stars winked.

'Yeah, this is just beyond the trees all right. You're such a pillock, Timothy. The hose won't be long enough.'

Tim turned his own beam on the ground, swinging it across a debris line onto a dry mud bed strewn with stones and a mesh of collapsed vegetation.

'But—' His beam found the water-line at the edge of its reach. 'Christ! What's happened here?'

Immediately he closed his eyes against John's blinding light, raising a hand to deflect it.

'What?' he heard John demand.

'It was here, where I'm standing. The earthquake must have shifted something in the rock strata.'

'Fucking frackers is what it'll have been, the bastards.'

It mattered little what or who had caused it. The sheer power of the change stunned Tim. He crept forward behind his torch beam, picking his way to the edge of the water. Moving the light slowly, he watched the planes of its surface glint and shift as he searched for the bubbles he'd seen, the spring-source that would prove the Pool was still being fed and wasn't slowly draining.

He straightened; listened; turned. He could hear sawing. There was sawing, a light flashing on the trees, and he was slipping and sliding over the matted surface desperate to reach John.

'You can't do that!'

'Done.' John pushed at the narrow trunk which emitted a straining cry beyond its size as it leaned and fell. Tim stared open-mouthed, then caught himself.

'You fucking vandal!'

'It's a sapling, for God's sake. You can return and plant another one. Let's get the quad in here before it's too dark to see.'

Tim stepped across to inspect the tree. It had been all but sawn through and lay twisted on its lick bark. When the lights erupted on the quad, he grasped at its branch fronds to drag it further aside, and found himself holding a stiff white parcel hardly bigger than his thumbnail. It slid from his opening hand, dragging its cord behind it, to fall into the flattened branches. Horrified, Tim swung the beam but couldn't pick it out from the mass of twigs and shower of sawdust. Headlights engulfed him and he pressed into the next tree as John bounced the quad over the mutilated trunk.

'Come on!'

There were times when he understood Simon's rampant activism, bolt-croppers, placards and the rest.

Trudging after the quad, he watched its lights bounce and jump then arc as John turned the vehicle round. The sheet was off the tank when he reached it, a hose being loosened from its reel.

'Grab hold and don't disturb the water.'

John was already disturbing the water. He'd backed the quad into it as far as its rear axle and was splashing in its shallows to release the hose. Not until the nozzle was placed in his hands did Tim realise what was being asked of him.

'I can't walk in there. I'll cut myself to ribbons on the rocks. I need waders.'

'Well we haven't got any so just get on with it. You'll dry off. And how deep can it be? Come on, I don't want it sucking air. And I don't want it sucking sediment, either.'

Tim shone his torch over the Pool, jolting forwards as he was shoved from behind. Water seeped cold into his trainers and wrapped his feet in a chill that made him gasp.

'You're such a wuss, Timothy. Think of the science. Get on with it and we can get out of here.'

Grimacing each time he placed his foot, Tim stepped and stepped again, feeling his way across slippery rocks that looked closer to the surface than they were, trying not to get his ankles entangled in the submerged vegetation. He played the beam across the surface seeking the bubbles sat above the spring-source, and caught them in the beam just as John called a halt. He wasn't within reach, but knee-deep he was close enough, cold enough.

The water was glass clear in the torchlight, the double hand-sized rocks oddly uniform, and his mind jumped back to the eroded burial mounds sprouting from the heather. No sediment. He was shivering already and knew he'd never keep the hose stable just by holding it.

No air. No sediment. It was going to be cold, he knew it was going to be cold, but he gripped the hose in one armpit and reached down to break the surface, sucking in breath as the chill enveloped his hands like a pair of tight-fitting gloves and reached up the arms of his jacket. Grasping a smooth rock, he placed it on top of another and trapped the hose in place with his foot.

'Okay!' he yelled. The quad's engine started, and the hose bucked as it drew water.

Tim shook out his tingling fingers and straightened his back, breathing hard through his teeth against the cold reaching up his legs further than just the wet of his jeans. How long would this take? Too long, no matter how short a time.

For warmth he pressed one hand into his armpit and flashed the beam along the tree-line ahead, pausing as the light caught among the branches. What was there to reflect? He thought of the white parcel. People left offerings here. It had been a prayer or something. He'd seen them in Jerusalem, folded tight and pressed into the cracks of the Wailing Wall. Here they were bound with cord and hung for the elements to shred.

Pulling the beam away, he changed hands and let the torchlight flicker across the water seeking the source-spring bubbles. Despite the contraction in the Pool it was still being fed. That was a good sign. Were the bubbles smaller? Coming to the surface more slowly? Perhaps. He should have taken more notice, should have videoed it, the first time he was here in his warm coat and his waterproof boots. Not that they would have stopped this cold. He wondered if fish were swimming round his legs, and mentally slapped himself at the idiocy of his thoughts. He was shivering and it was growing worse. He couldn't stop. How long was this taking? Too long. Too cold. Focus on something else. The bubbles.

The beam juddered in his hand as he tried to realign it, found them, watched each bulge the surface tension so close that if he leaned over he thought he might be able to touch them. It meant there was gas rising with the water, just air perhaps, except air was never just air. They needed to get the experiment started, discover what was evaporating. He considered his train of thought and began to shallow breathe. What was coming up from the earth with the water? What was he breathing in?

There was a flash at the corner of his eye. He looked, swung the torch. Not something hanging in the branches. Too low. Eyes, perhaps. An animal come to drink. What animals were wild on the moor? He caught a giggle as a movie about a werewolf came to mind. Not wolves; foxes maybe. Maybe a pheasant, a grouse. Yes, there were plenty of those on the moor; the broken shooting butts were testimony to that. People with guns.

Again. To his right, this time. Something among the trees. The beam showed nothing except branches gently swaying. Was there a breeze? He could feel no breeze. A chill against his cheeks, against his forehead. He couldn't feel much of anything below his knees. Why was it so cold? How could it be so icy cold? The water had had all summer to warm. It wasn't the depths of winter, yet he was shivering now, shivering uncontrollably. And he knew if he moved he would stagger and fall, fall full length into it. The knowledge panicked him and he tried to look back to John, to the lights from the quad bike, but he couldn't turn enough. And it was there again, at the corner of his eye. Something in the trees, watching. They shouldn't be here. They were trespassing, stealing water that wasn't theirs, destroying trees that had been planted for a reason. They shouldn't be here. Shouldn't be here. Shouldn't be here.

Chapter 38

'*Jesus!*'

John said something else but Tim didn't catch it, grateful he hadn't fallen in the freezing water, grateful John had caught him, that John was warm, that he could burrow into him for body-heat.

His head rocked and his eyes sprang open. His cheek smarted. He was walking alongside John, his arm caught around John's shoulder, his hand, milky white in the backwash from the torch-beam, looking as if severed and hanging in the darkness, hanging from one of the trees.

'Walk, damnit! Come on, Timothy, *walk!*'

He was walking. No, he was being dragged. And he saw the black wall of the trees and realised where he was. He moved his legs; took his weight. John stopped but didn't let him go.

'You okay now? You with me? Nod if you understand.'

'I understand.' John's expelled breath hit him in the face. It felt wonderfully warm. 'What happened?'

'You collapsed on me like a big—' There were a couple of rasping breaths. When John spoke again his tone was less abrasive. 'Can you stand on your own? Good. Now flap your arms. You need to get your circulation moving.'

Tim knew that. He was shivering, still so very cold. He tried a half-hearted attempt. Remembered.

'We need to leave. There's people watching. We're being watched.'

John grasped him by the shoulders until they were facing. 'Listen to me, Timothy. There is no one watching. No one is here but us. *Enough*, okay? You were out on your feet. Your mind was playing tricks. Got that?'

Tim blinked at him and John nodded. 'Yes, you told me. Blubbed it all down my front. Now, if you've got it together we'll get back to the plant and get some hot coffee down us, okay?'

It was more than okay, and Tim stumbled after John's pool of light. Where was his own torch? His sleeves were wet, his trousers soaked almost to the crotch. He couldn't keep up. *Slow down*, but his words weren't strong enough to be heard.

The roar from the quad made him wince, its lights filling the gap in the trees, bouncing as its wheels bumped over the felled trunk. John was *leaving him!* He struggled to follow the receding red lights, couldn't see his footing, tripped and sprawled, was enveloped by the cushioning fronds of the downed tree, the prayer tree, the watchers' tree. Had to find the parcel, the white prayer-parcel, had to find it and set it back up.

'What the hell are you doing?'

His coat choked his throat as he was hauled upright.

'Tree. Watchers—'

His mouth formed a circle as a hot hand grasped his lower face. 'There's no one here, do you hear me? Look at me, you dickhead.' White light blinded him; nails dug into his cheeks. 'You're okay, do you hear? There's no one here but us. Believe it, Timothy. *Believe it!*'

His head rocked on his shoulders as John's hand let go, and he was dragged over the broken tree. He couldn't see properly. White flashes against black, against red. So much like the watchers.

The white receded with the red; greyscale returned as dark as — It was night now, fully night.

'Here. Are you happy now? I've propped it up. Let's go.'

The tree was leaning on its neighbour, not quite upright but upright enough. It blocked the gap. The watchers couldn't get out. Couldn't get him.

His arm was grasped, he was swung round, hauled to the quad and pushed onto its seat.

'Hold tight,' John told him, and Tim grasped the edge of the front rack to stare into the black unknown beyond the track of headlights, the black where burial mounds arched from the broken earth in a sea swell of heather. He closed his eyes against it all and hung on as the quad laboured up the rise, the weight of the slurping water trying to drag them back.

'Lean forwards!' John shouted. 'Put your weight over the front wheels.'

Tim did, though he would rather have cut loose the tank. Lose the water and they'd be free.

The quad changed its growling tone as its front wheels found the old track and Tim released his tension to open his eyes.

It was as if the quad sat inside a sphere. There were no stars, no clouds visible in what should have been the sky, no left, no right, nothing beyond a hedge of heather disappearing below the headlights, being replaced by more of the same. As the wheels rose and fell, the water behind his head gurgled and slurped, setting up a whispering, a laughing, a coaxing, as his body slid and leapt from the hard shiny seat. He kept hitting John fighting with the steering, wanted to vomit. Only a dribble came up that ran down his chin. His trainers lost their grip in the tight footwell, sending him sliding out the doorless gap, the reaching heather slicing at elbow, knee and thigh as he tried to brace himself, tried to protect jarred muscles and torn skin. And not fall out. If he fell out the land would swallow him, and God only knew what would greet him below the heather. *Please, God...*

'Tim, we're here. Look.'

He opened his eyes, saw the grey steel and red reflectors of the trailer, the back of the 4x4 growing to meet them.

'Come on, give me a hand.'

But it was his own hands he saw being prised off the quad's front rack. His bones grated; his muscles wouldn't function. He was pushed into the vehicle, its leather seat cushioning his aching body, its interior so bright he closed his eyes again.

'Touch nothing,' he heard John say. 'The engine will push warm air through in a minute.'

The door shut; the light faded. He could see the narrow road through the windscreen, man-made tarmac breaking up to grass in its centre. He smiled even though he knew it was stupid.

Light filled the vehicle from behind, shone into his eyes from the mirror as the 4x4 adjusted to the weight of the quad on the trailer. The lights cut. Tim could hear only the hum of warm air coming through the grilles, and he reached out for it, glad he couldn't see the state of his hands. They felt as though spongy balloons.

During the journey back John kept glancing at him, but didn't speak. Only the sat nav spoke, its female voice eerie in their silence as hedgerows grew and buildings shone beneath streetlights. He recognised his own route, and sat straighter, breathed deeper. They'd be at the plant soon and he had to get his shit together before facing John.

'Feel better?'

The question held no punch and Tim licked his lips, surprised to find them dry, the skin brittle. 'Yeah. Thanks.'

'Hot coffee down you and you'll be fine. I'd have dropped you at the caravan but you'll need the Freelander for the morning.'

The vehicle pulled into the plant's entrance, thumping over its loose stones, jarring across its potholes. Tim eased his shoulders.

'What are we doing with the water?'

'Later. We need a hot drink inside us.'

John drew up across the empty car spaces and jumped out to unlock the main door and shut off the alarm. Tim eased himself out of the vehicle as light flooded the vestibule. Blisters on his feet made it painful to walk, and he paused to lean on the doorframe and realign his spine.

It was gone 1am. Tim stared at his wristwatch not believing the time, and then focused on his scratched and cut hands. He looked down at his squelching trainers, up his jeans, across his jacket. He was filthy.

They propped themselves on stools in the lab, each wrapping their hands round a steaming mug, coffee laced with whisky.

'Feel better?'

That question again.

'You gave me a scare out there, y'know.' John grinned at him, but it held no humour. 'Howling at the moon, you were. What did you see that spooked you so much?'

Tim sipped at his coffee. 'Not sure.'

'I was there and I never saw a thing, Tim. You didn't either. It was the cold.' John sipped from his mug. 'Or perhaps, perhaps you're right. Perhaps there are gases coming off the water. They'd stay closer to the surface with the cloud cover, the air pressure. But you're okay now, aren't you? Just tired.'

Tim sank his face into his mug so he didn't have to respond.

'Listen. It's Plan B, okay? You get back to the caravan, have a shower and get some sleep. I'll store the water and clear up. Come in late tomorrow – today. 10am earliest. Doug's got a meeting off-site so won't be in until midday; he'll never know. I'll get in when I can. After lunch probably. But one of us has to do the plant's tests, and get the DEFRA figures off. Okay? Can I count on you to come in and do that?'

'Yes, I'll do that.' He took a big mouthful of coffee, even though it tasted foul and was too hot. He wanted to leave, be on his own. 'I'm just tired,' he said. 'Still cold. I'll be okay tomorrow.'

'Finish your coffee. It'll help warm you through. I'll bring the Freelander round to the front for you.'

It seemed to take an age. Tim finished his coffee, checked his watch. It still read 1.10. Then he heard the car and went out to meet it. John held open the driver's door for him to climb inside. On the passenger seat, secured with the seat belt, sat a two litre vacuum flask. He didn't need to ask what was inside.

'No falling asleep at the wheel, okay? Have a shower, something to eat, and then do the business. Got that? When you wake up you'll feel like a new man.'

Tim nodded and started the engine. His feet felt swollen, his toes rubbing against dislodged pieces of inner sole as he pressed the pedals. He slipped the vehicle into gear and John shut the door on him. The heater was already turned to full.

As Tim slowed for the junction he looked in the mirror. John still stood in the light spilling from the plant's vestibule. He hoped no police passed by or they'd call in to ask about the lights. The flask sat upright beside him, and he hoped no police stopped him, either, to ask where he'd been, to see the state of him. He watched his speed after that.

It was only a short ride; he wasn't going to sleep at the wheel. But as he passed hedges crowding the bends, reflected light from the headlamps glinted off the metal flask. He didn't want to look, wanted to keep his eyes on the road, on the bends, but the glints kept catching the corner of his eye, mirroring the glints from the trees around the Pool. He gripped the wheel tighter to control the trembling in his arms, in his stomach. John might not have seen anything, but he had. And it hadn't been gases off the water; it hadn't been the penetrating cold. Someone had been there, some *thing*. Watching. Angry. And now it was sitting next to him, upright as if a metal dwarf, its ribbing marking a head in the solidity of the cylinder.

He swallowed hard, checked his speed... *too fast, slow down*... eased his foot on the accelerator. Why was it taking so long? He didn't live far. Ten minutes, fifteen at most and there was no traffic, not at this hour. Whatever hour it was.

Swinging round the last corner, he heard the tyres screech, felt the seat belt cramp his chest. He daren't look at the cylinder. Raindrops on the windscreen obscuring his view. Wouldn't look at the cylinder. The turning... *too fast*... under the trees, the hawthorn scratching at the doors, and in the headlights the caravan, bright as if it glowed from within.

He hit the brake and the Freelander fishtailed on the loose gravel before drawing to a halt. His fingers felt for the ignition but he didn't turn the key. Beneath the open porch a black bin bag was uncurling. He hit the wipers, telling himself it was moving in the breeze.

A hood. A head. A shoulder.

He heard his indrawn breath whistle past his teeth, felt it expanding in his chest. The figure stepped from the shiny bag and raised its face. A flash of blue – *Izzy*.

One hand found the door release as the other clicked the seat belt mechanism. He almost fell out of the car in his haste.

'Don't be angry. You wouldn't answer my calls and— *Tim*... What the hell have you been doing?'

He fell on her, wrapping his arms around her until she took his weight.

Chapter 39

In the grey of dawn they were taken from the byre to relieve themselves, Ernald hobbling with every step. Their doles were hunks of stale bread soaked in pottage so thin that it ran as if water from a loose-weave cloth. Ernald followed the reeve's lead, cupping his hands to catch what he could and licking each finger after. He remembered those who queued before the almoner's table at the priory's gate, their eyes wide with expectation. To them he'd given bowl and spoon. This would not sustain a man a day.

Chiding himself for his ill-feeling, he intoned a short blessing for sustenance given and asked forgiveness for his ingratitude. The tenderness of his feet had robbed him of sleep, but perhaps that had been visited upon him for a reason. While others snuffled in the hay, Wulfrith had mewled like a disconsolate child. Ernald had shuffled across to the man to share his pilgrim's cloak and press the reliquary cross to his arm while murmuring prayers to the Saint. They'd awoken together with the dragging open of the byre door, one man spooned against the other in compassion and warmth.

Wulfrith was hunched into himself, holding his injured hand by the wrist. The fingers Ernald could see poking from his sleeve were swollen, and remorse welled within him. Had Wulfrith managed to save the pottage liquor one-handed? Had he eaten at all? Leaning on his heels against the byre wall, Ernald pushed himself upright, but the pressure in his toes made him draw a wincing breath. If he'd had his staff to lean on...

The clatter of hooves on cobbles drew attention to the yard's entrance. Their ponies were being brought in. The reeve's muttered oaths were clearly heard as he and his men stepped forward to remove their packs and rub down the animals. Had they been fed? From their eagerness for the hay the reeve's youth brought, it seemed not. What hospitality was this? The priest knew of their quest to find the healing waters of Saint Mary. Try as he might, Ernald could not balance the one with the other.

Men-at-arms arrived, one leading an ass and carrying Ernald's staff alongside his pole-arm. The reeve and his men stared at the animal, stared at its pad-saddle.

'For the pilgrim,' came the announcement.

And the reeve and his men stared at Ernald.

They left Stocheslage by the postern gate, the novice tied by a short leash to the second pack-pony, the reeve leading the first with Wulfrith at his side. Astride the ass, Ernald brought up the rear. No one looked behind. The six men-at-arms murmured only among themselves, if at all.

Ernald felt as a man cast out, and all because of his sin of pride in a pair of leather boots. Clutching his satchel to his chest, the new boots tied to its strap for all to see, he focused his gaze on his mount's twitching ears and his thoughts on the saints in their adversities.

They took a cart-way east, passing occasional dwellings, more shelters for the spread of ridged fields than homes. There was no one to be seen. Crops had been harvested and the strips gleaned so finely not even birds pecked at the dry soil. Ahead the land rose, packed tight in the mottled green of trees making it difficult to distinguish needle-pine from oak or beech or alder. Ernald hoped their escort's show of arms would deter roaming wolf's-heads.

Progress was slow, too slow for the soldiers' ease. As the breeze veered he began to hear snippets of their mutterings. Not the English tongue this, not Wulfrith's; one from his youth, perhaps. Were these men Flems? Then the ass caught a thump from the end of a pole-arm to hurry it along, setting off a fearful braying and a kicked hind-leg that almost unseated Ernald.

From their laughter, the men-at-arms thought this fine sport, and before Ernald could plead for pity it occurred again. The ass jumped between the pack-ponies, trapping Ernald's right leg, and he cried out with the pain in his jarred foot. Pitching forward, he lay along the animal's neck as it bucked and jostled the pack-ponies, and was still clutching at its rough coat when the reeve and his men parted the animals. Urged to sit upright, through his pain Ernald saw Wulfrith kneeling on the ground holding his forearm to his chest, his engorged hand swallowing its stiff fingers. Shamed, Ernald scorned his own anguish as unworthy.

'Are you injured?' demanded the reeve.

'Wulfrith,' he said. 'Do we have meadowsweet? Willow's bark?'

'I've given him willow to chew. Not that it seems to be helping.'

The reeve turned away and Ernald took deep breaths to help drive the devils from his feet. The reeve was berating the men-at-arms, he realised, and he wondered whether that was wise.

They walked until the sun was past its zenith. It was the reeve who called a halt to eat, and an argument ensued with the leader of their escort. Ernald winced against the raised voices, but could not find it within himself to intercede. His bones ached. He needed sleep.

'Get off that animal and mark the route,' the reeve snarled as he passed. 'Don't look at me; do it.'

Ernald knew he'd been too preoccupied with his own discomfort to watch for the turns in the track or the way the waters ran. But it was only noon. They hadn't come far. He could mark his report.

Lowering himself from the ass brought on a sweating that made his undershirt cling to his back. The reeve's boy frowned, but Ernald waved him away to water the animal at the brook. Leaning heavily on his staff, he put his weight on the outer edges of his sandals and lurched off the track to sit. Gathering himself, he opened his satchel's flap to pull free quills and inkpot, pausing to gaze at the gap where the poultice-maker's pouch had nestled. Without the herbs or unguent, unbinding his feet to check them would gain him no respite. Vespers would be soon enough for that.

He brought out the wooden cup from the holy spring and held it a moment in his hand, its outer surface smoothed by so many giving praise. How long ago that seemed; how few the days. Time was shifting in his mind. He needed to keep better account, for himself, for Sub-Prior Maugre.

He was penning against his board when the reeve crouched beside him carrying a hedge-fruit pasty and a little bread.

'I am failing you, Master Reeve.'

'Not at all, friend Ernald. Point to a line with your quill.'

The reeve's chubby finger came across his hand to point also, and he nodded.

'Yes, I understand,' he said in a louder voice, and he nodded again. Taking a bite of pasty, in a lower voice he added, 'If they think I can read your script they will believe me higher born and will be wary.'

'Wary?'

'Where is their food, friend Ernald? Also, the sub-prior's coin was taken from me. On whose orders, I do not know, but these men have been sent on a task that is not to protect us from wolf's-heads.'

Ernald caught his escaping gasp, and felt the reeve's hand on his shoulder. 'Fear not, friend Ernald, I will protect you. But you must protect us also. We need a route we can read in case yours is taken for delivery to the priest at Stocheslage. Or his lord.'

While they were eating the reeve took his youth to forage for pottage herbs. Ernald noted that none of the men-at-arms followed. They were eating from belt pouches, the new season's nuts perhaps, Ernald did not want to be noticed watching. Wulfrith was curled in an exhausted sleep, his hand held out in the dewy shadows of a bush. The novice was talking to himself in tones too low to hear above the grazing of the pack-ponies. From the rhythm Ernald thought it might be prayers. Hand on

Saint Cuthbert's cross, he spoke one himself, asking that the youth find comfort in his diligence. At least the soldiers sought no sport with him, but Ernald could see they were growing restless.

Moving aside his chaplet, he drew another parchment sheet from his satchel to gaze at its blank face. How best to pen a route the reeve could interpret? He saw again the parchments in the Scriptorium penned by map-scribes years before, all small houses, and land routes, and waving rivers in colours he did not carry. Where to start?

The Holy Land lay to the East, so he marked the top of the sheet J. The priory at Durham he marked to the left with a house topped by a cross. A circle was added to its centre to show the reliquary. He touched the true reliquary, knowing the Saint's hand would guide him.

They had journeyed south on the old stone road, and southeast on a drovers' route. The river had looped at Yarum where they'd crossed on a ferry; there had been a stockade-castle carrying many banners and many men. Then south-east again to Stocheslage, and this day – he checked the position of the sun – east. Licking his lips, he dipped the quill. Yet even so close to the parchment it hovered in his hand. The sub-prior's warning echoed in head: *maps through wildwoods are easy for prying eyes to steal*. What could be read by the reeve, could be read by the men-at-arms.

The ink was forming a heavy globe on the quill. Moving it aside, he let it splatter into the grass, and he touched the reliquary cross beneath his habit to thank the Saint for his caution.

It seemed only a breath later that their escort took to their feet, their pole-arms close. A nod. A whisper. The reeve's man was leaking his water; the novice intoning his prayers. Wulfrith did not stir. Ernald felt the cross against his breastbone resonating with the thudding of his heart.

'Do you bring us to journey, masters?' he called in a bright voice that seemed not his. The soldiers caught their step to turn their gaze on him. 'I shall plug my ink and take my place. The Bishop's report can wait.'

He made a show of plugging the ink pot, his own gaze rising to the reeve's man who had turned to frown. 'Wake Wulfrith. Gently, mark, his arm is sore. And call the Master Reeve, he'll not be— Master Reeve!'

Ernald's chest swelled at the sight of the reeve and his youth, their arms laden with the fruits of their foraging. The Saint had, indeed, delivered them.

Shouldering his packed satchel, he grasped his staff to lever himself upright. The pain in his feet was cruel, as if scalded by bubbling waters, yet Ernald vowed not to let it deter him as he hobbled to the ass. It was the reeve who helped him mount the pad-saddle.

'You're as pale as the moon,' he said. 'I'll see those feet when we stop for sleep. I've brought you a fist of water-pepper to chew, but you'd better have willow's bark, too.'

'Wulfrith has more need, Master Reeve.'

'That and others we have collected. Chew your willow and open your ears. I will trust you to tell all at day's rest.'

'I believe them to be Flems, Master Reeve.'

'Aye. Bought to help fight the Scots. So why are they here with us?'

It was many hours until day's rest. The track grew narrower, the underbrush more thick, the insects sharper with their biting. They passed through a hamlet, or the roots of one long dead, the stumps of its burned timbers reaching through the over-growth like black teeth from a shrunken jaw. Only the oak tree stood proud on what Ernald recognised had been its green, the tree's leaves still bright and leathery despite the season.

And then he noticed those ahead marking themselves with the Holy Rood and mumbling prayers of protection. He looked again. Mossy ropes were suspended among those bright leaves, and below, amid the verdant green, he saw the white of bones. A man-at-arms came to stand at the ass' shoulder. He rattled an oath in the Flemish tongue and spat. Ernald tapped his mount to walk on, leaving the soldiers to hawk and spit on those who'd not had God's words spoken over them.

The land rose steeply and kept on rising, through trees thick with the smell of charcoal-burners' fires, up onto heathland where only startled deer ran, and into a vast hollow of moor-mires, dry-crusted and stinking beneath the summer's sun. It was a Devil's place of buzzing insects with scarcely a white-barked birch standing taller than the dying grass.

It felt to Ernald that he'd swallowed half the midges swarming beneath the brim of his hat. His back ached and his haunches jarred with each step of the ass. Even so, his eyelids drooped and, like Wulfrith at noon, he knew he could sleep anywhere.

Forcing open his eyes, he shook himself of his lethargy. This was no route for a man who'd sworn service to God and His Son, who journeyed under the protection of Saint Cuthbert. His fingers found the cross beneath his habit, and he raised his head to see the reeve's arm about Wulfrith, part carrying him as if Reprobus on his trial across the river to become Christopher. Mean of eye, harsh of temper, strong of shoulder... Man and name were surely well-fit.

Out of the moor-mires and into a glade carrying a clear brook, the reeve called a halt. The men-at-arms refused, even to brandishing their pole-arms in his face and those of his unarmed men who stood at his shoulder.

'Our guide is beyond walking,' the reeve told them again.

Ernald stretched his back. 'Let him ride with me.'

'The ass is tired and cannot carry two men,' argued the reeve.

'It will not need to carry them far,' a soldier told them.

The decision was made. Ernald shuffled back beyond the pad-saddle, grateful his feet were no longer paining him so much, and Wulfrith was hoisted over the animal's neck. It brayed in complaint, but with the reeve's youth at its halter it walked when urged. Wulfrith's head lolled back with the motion, his eyes rolling into his head. Ernald caught him to his chest and pulled free Saint Cuthbert's cross. Laying it on the man's sweating brow, he began the Saint's sacred litany.

The cluster of dwellings was a most welcome sight. Two old women with distaff and spindle sat on a bench spinning thread; boys herded swine across their path into a hurdled enclosure for the night; a girl tended flames licking beneath a pottager. Such plain tasks Ernald knew from his travels between the manors and his heart swelled at the sight. He was used to bright smiles, though, more people, but this was probably a forester's tun, the manor house and its village dwellings a distance yet.

From a dark doorway a sturdy man emerged, followed by three others in breeches and undershirt. They had a look about them that caused Ernald to caution, and then there were smiles and calls to the men-at-arms. The Flemish tongue again. These, too, were fighting men. At a forester's tun?

The reeve was speaking with the old women. His man and the youth came to lift Wulfrith from the saddle and carry him to the bench. Ernald eased his cramped muscles and leaned over the ass's neck to slip from its back. His feet flared as hot as the fires of Hell, and he shrieked with the pain as he fell. Hands turned him over, but he could utter no words as he tried to keep even his heels from the ground. He saw the reeve staring at him, and then his youth was holding down his shoulders and his man grasping his legs. A blade was in the reeve's fist, and Ernald knew his sandals were being removed.

'The cross! The cross!'

The youth moved, helping to pull the thong at his neck and free the warm silver to the light. Ernald grasped it, forcing the words of the Saint's litany between his teeth until Saint Cuthbert's balm reached out from the reliquary to embrace him.

He saw a fleeting cloud, and the frown of a man-at-arms. And the bearded face of the reeve, his mouth open as he stared, wide-eyed, from the sky.

Ernald lifted his face at the change in the dim light of the forester's dwelling. The reeve sank to his haunches beside the pallet.

'There is nothing to be done for your feet,' he stated.

'The women— Their touch was as if Mother Mary's.' He heard the reeve snort.

'Aye, it was not by their hand that we had to hold you down.'

Ernald could recall little except the pain, and the smell of the honey spread on his soles, its sweetness forced between his teeth as cloths were applied to his feet.

'I did not soil myself.'

'You did not, friend Ernald. Saint Cuthbert stood strong by your side.' The reeve leaned over him to feel his brow. 'Your face sheens, friend Ernald, but there is no heat. Give praise for that.'

'Perhaps it is the potion. My head swims. Henbane?'

'And nightshades, and more I'll wager. I did not ask.'

Ernald glanced beyond the reeve's thick shoulder. 'Wulfrith seems easier.'

'We poured it down his throat, but unlike you he's not eaten. It does not augur well for him. But that... that I think was the reason for his injury. Yours, too, friend Ernald. Say naught to others, but to my reckoning either this curing spring will cure or you and he are dead. Maybe all of us by the hands of these Flems. It seems they've been bedded here many a day seeking the spring or those who know of its existence.'

'Then we are close?'

'Perhaps.'

'There is a priest, Wulfrith's confessor. The sub-prior showed me his missive.' Ernald thought back to the barely decipherable Latin he'd read when he'd first set eyes on Wulfrith. 'Not a learned man. Of a lesser manor perhaps.'

'Speak not of him, either. No one else will. I think he's another who rots in a wayside grave.'

The dead man they found before the apple-picking; the deserted hamlet, the bones beneath the roped oak. Ernald's fist tightened on Saint Cuthbert's cross as he closed his eyes to shut out the horror. This land was supposed to be God's Eden. It seemed to have slid into a Hell of man's own making.

'Fear not, friend Ernald. As long as Wulfrith is not taken by dance-devils I give my oath that I will get you to the spring. But what after? You may see York. I doubt you'll see the sub-prior at Durham. You may see no further than Stocheslage and the priest who believes more in demons ravaging men's souls than in God's beneficence. Think of my man and the boy. We need a map we can read.'

Ernald looked at the dark beard and into the bright eyes. 'Keep the soldiers at bay, bring me God's good light, and I will swear on Saint Cuthbert's reliquary that I will ink you a map.'

Chapter 40

Nick stood alone on the ridge surveying the moor. No jewelled dragonflies kept him company. Beneath the cloud cover, the heather showed as a sullen purple swathe lost of its magnificence and holding tight its scents. The darker line of the path led to the horizon in exaggerated loops, riding the ridges, disappearing in the dips. Phil had finally got to the nub of it, to the reason for his outbursts. The land was remaking itself and it was unnerving him. It unnerved Nick, too.

And it wasn't just the moor, was it? What was happening at the copse? Was the water from the Pool resurfacing there? Would Alice resurface there as she'd managed to resurface in the river at York?

He looked back to the narrow opening between the pasture fencing, undecided where to go. But no, Alice had joined him at the farm; she knew where to find him. Besides, what need did she have to claim the hatchback? That was another's hand, doubtless the *thing*. Though if such an entity was causing the land to remake itself, he had seriously underestimated what he was up against.

Shutting off his phone, he shouldered the pack and made his way down the slope, gravity and the incline dragging at his calves. Once on more level ground he strode with purpose. There was no sense that the track was twisting back on itself, merely meandering round natural hollows and rises. Maybe if the sun was visible to cast his shadow it would be more apparent, not that he'd noticed on previous occasions.

He didn't time himself. Too much depended on the length of his stride, his line on the bends, and there didn't seem any point after Phil's revelation. Instead he focused on the crumbling earth of the track and that beneath the browning tufts of thin grass and the brittle-looking heather at its margins. If the copse was now oozing water, was the moor being sucked dry?

A clump of bulrushes standing tall looked familiar and he stopped to check the moisture at its roots. There wasn't much, but there hadn't seemed much before. Beetles scurried from the shaft of light he created and he let the stalks spring back to protect their domain. Worlds within worlds. When it came down to it, he knew so little about anything.

He thought he felt a raindrop but wasn't sure, and he glanced at the clouds. They didn't look rain-bearing, just thick. But since when had he been an authority? Clouds passed overhead each and every day. He couldn't name a single formation, never mind read their intent.

A few more strides and a rash of fine droplets peppered the track in front of him to be swallowed by its broken surface. Three or four touched his face, his hand, but no more followed. A lone butterfly crossed his path, a tortoiseshell, he thought, perhaps a red admiral. He castigated himself for not knowing, not knowing the type of beetles he'd seen, how they lived. It wasn't just Alice; he'd no idea how anything worked. The years spent pratting with folklore would have been better spent studying ecology.

When the path turned below the pond he climbed the rise to its stone-cut basin so he could use its height to gain a better view of the route. Its smell reached out to him when he was halfway up, making him hesitate as he wrinkled his nose against it. Dank water brimmed its edge, a layer of feathered peat reaching to its black centre in a semblance of earth firm enough to bear weight. No matter what Phil said, it needed to be refenced, for the sheep's protection as much as people's. He'd tell Phil when he returned, would help him erect one.

He gazed at it afresh. This was what Rosemary had alluded to, what the landscape would have looked like in centuries past, each the haunt of a Peg Powler or a Grindylow. Reaching down he lifted a piece of the outcrop's crumbling edge and tossed it in. It broke the peaty surface without a sound and he reeled back to hold his breath against the escaping stink. Something was decomposing in there, and it wasn't just vegetation. Letting his weight run him back to the track, he didn't look behind him.

The arc of shrubby trees began as a line in the landscape, growing thicker and darker as he neared it. One moment it seemed to waver in the air currents, the next it had the solidity of a wall.

He made the flattened camping ground, disappointed to find no sheep there to welcome him. The grass was lush and reached around his boot welts. It hadn't been so high before, had it? Why did the sheep ignore such easy fodder? Were they wary because they sensed a threat?

His gaze rose to the interlocking branches screening the Pool. Their leaves were the bright green of midsummer.

He'd vacillated enough. Bracing himself, he pushed through.

There was an awful lot of shore-line. The shrine-log stood marooned a good three metres from the water. Lowering the pack, he stepped to what had been the Pool's extent. The grass he'd seen beneath the encroaching water now lay limp, the bed beyond a skeletal grey-white littered with rounded stones; double hand-sized, he noted. He picked his way through them. The plants which had formed a slippery net to trap his feet were now little more than shrivelled stems crumbling beneath his boots.

It seemed a desolate place. Yet there was water. The Pool had reformed to half its size and reflected the dour colour of the sky. Bubbles still rose at its centre; it remained live.

'Alice! Can you hear me, Alice? I've returned and I'm not leaving without you.'

The water didn't tremble. No waves appeared.

'Come talk to me, Alice. I've brought food we can share.'

His gaze crossed its surface, fixing on the rising bubbles that broke in the air. Kneeling by the water's edge, he smacked its surface with his palm, changing arms to use his ringed hand. The vibrations would carry, even if she couldn't hear his words.

'I'll be here,' he called. 'Alice, come join me.'

He smacked at it, and smacked at it, creating ripples as she'd created them, until his hand was numb and the cold of the water reached halfway to his elbow. Dropping back to his haunches, he pulled his arm free of his wet coat to shake feeling back into his hand, making his fingers smart.

A raindrop plopped beside him. Another. He gazed skywards, no longer certain of the clouds. When he looked back at the Pool it was flat, carrying no sign of his exertions, the air no echo of his call.

Raindrops fell about him, slow and heavy. One hit the back of his head with such force he nodded at its impact and slapped his palm to it to stop the chill rivulet crawling inside his collar. Gaining his feet he shook himself, another hitting his cheek. There was no wind by the Pool yet overhead clouds were scudding, the rain falling at a slant. He headed back to the trees, to his pack and his possessions.

Something caught his eye and he scrutinised the trees. No, it had been closer: the shrine log. He focused on it as a piece fell away, tumbling coins into the darkening earth. Running across, he stood over it. The once green moss had retracted for lack of moisture, its tiny fronds browned and brittle. Heavy raindrops fell as missiles to puncture the fragile wood. One fell directly onto a ten pence piece, spinning it to the ground. With a sense of dismay he reached out, before drawing back his probing fingers for fear of accelerating the damage. It had been a day, just a day since he'd been here.

Again he looked at the white-grey shore, at the desiccated plant stalks. This was no single day's decay. He checked his watch. It was working, showing just over an hour since he'd left the farm. His heart thudded as he pulled out his phone, jabbing at the start button to initiate its wake-up. Its screen brightened. The logo blossomed. He could feel his fingers tightening round its casing as he waited for the time to show. The numbers didn't roll.

His breath left him in a gasp and he stared at the water, at the trees, at the corpse-like shore.

'Alice!'

It was wasted breath. Alice wasn't here.

He stood in the increasing rain, decrying his betrayal as the shrine log slowly disintegrated and he incapable of stopping it. If he'd stayed the night – but he knew the age-old fear of the dark had reached out to claim him.

Retrieving the backpack, he plodded to the trees to deposit it with his sports bag in the bole of roots.

He couldn't sit, couldn't think. He walked the outer debris line, the extent of the Pool when he'd held Alice in his arms to kiss her chill lips and talk with her. He recalled each phrase, each look, each ribald rise of her pale eyebrows, each smile. There had to be a way to reconnect. Had to be.

He turned to walk the tree-line, not caring how wet he grew, how cold. There had to be a way to reach her.

The branches at his shoulder dipped and lifted beneath the pummelling rain. Except for one. Its branches dipped but didn't bounce. It stood at an angle, leaning against its neighbour.

As he neared he saw that its leaves weren't glossy; they were as dull and curling as the moss on the shrine log. He veered towards it, slowing as across his path tyre tracks were being washed out by the rain. He stepped over them, unbelieving, to follow their line. The tree wasn't leaning. Its thin trunk had been sawn almost through. At Nick's touch it fell aside to leave a gap. Tracks of flattened heather led out to a ridge on the moor.

Anger welled up at the desecration, then fear for Alice. He swung back to jump over the felled tree and race along the tracks as they softened into the wet earth, seeing them splay and bounce over rounded stones as they made an arrow-sharp line for the bubbles rising in the Pool.

He didn't stop even at the water's edge, but followed them in until they dispersed in the silt. Who had been here? What had they been doing? Had a vehicle gone in and *sunk?* No, tracks in, tracks out. Someone had forced a route through the trees big enough for a vehicle. To take something? What was here but water? *Alice.* No. Who knew but him? *That man. That man*, she'd said. *What* man? Had he misunderstood? She'd not meant a shadow person, but a real man. Had she meant a real 21st century man?

Branches rippled along the trees at the other side of the Pool. He stared, looking for shadow people among their flowing limbs, caught movement in his peripheral vision and snapped left. She stood there, frowning at him.

'Alice.' He felt himself sag with relief. 'You're okay. Are you okay?'

Splashing across the shallows he wrapped his arms around her. She felt very cold, very still in his embrace. He pulled away to smile at her, to stroke her hair untouched by the rain. Already he could hardly feel his feet. The cold was reaching up his legs.

'You're not safe here, Alice. Something's happened. There's been a vehicle. The tree.' He should be wearing the gloves; shouldn't be in the water. Why wasn't she pleased to see him?

'What's wrong?' He grasped her arm. 'Come onto the land. It's freezing in here.'

'Not to me.'

'That's because...' He eased his tone. 'That's because you're trapped here, Alice. I've come to free you. I nearly had you in York. I will free you this time, I promise, but I can't do it alone.'

He took a step on to the shore, the water running from his jeans, and turned back to offer his hand. She didn't take it.

'Don't you remember York?'

'It's a haze, Nicholas, everything's a disjointed haze. I can't separate what I remember from what I dream. I no longer know what's real.'

'I'm here, Alice, I'm real. We made love at the farm. That was real. You were warm.' She didn't respond. 'You recall that, don't you?' He daren't give her time to her deny it. 'Do you remember coming here six years ago?'

'I've always been here.'

'No, you haven't. It just seems like it. You came searching for a shrine to a water deity. You were excavating.' He wasn't going to mention the Other, wasn't going to put her through that. He wouldn't explain the horrors of York three years ago unless he had to.

'A geyser erupted. You were caught in its force.' He was willing her to understand. He wasn't going to say it. She was standing in front of him. He could see her breathing; he could touch her. They'd made love, for God's sake. She wasn't *dead*.

'You've been calling me to free you.'

Alice tensed. '*I've* been calling *you*? I'm here because *you* called *me*. They all call me. I can't shut them out. I thought it would be different with you here but it's not.'

'Different? Alice, I'm here to *save* you.'

She spread her arms and looked around her. 'From what?'

He pointed. 'From the *thing* that put that torc round your neck.'

She looked surprised, her hand rising to the twisted gold. Nick saw it move at her touch, then gasped as its wires faded, her spreading fingers stroking her throat.

'What—? How did you *do* that?'

She turned away.

'Alice!' He jumped forwards, splashing back into the Pool. 'Don't go, Alice. Don't shed yourself into the water and leave me here. Talk to me.'

Tension cramped his chest as they stared at each other. He eased his tone.

'Where do you go to in the water? What do you do?'

Her lips opened as if she was about to speak, but confusion made her frown and she offered no response.

'Don't you want to ride in a car? Fly in a plane? Do you remember those things?'

She nodded so imperceptibly her hair hardly moved.

'Don't you want to make love to me?' He took a step closer, his fingers reaching for her cheek. 'For me to make love to you?'

His fingers slid into her hair and he leaned forward to brush his cheek against hers, so cold, so very cold. Why wouldn't she respond to him?

'You were warm, Alice, you were warm in my bed at the farm. Come back with me. Come back with me now.'

A cold tear imprinted on his cheek, tracking a line to his jaw. 'I can't. I don't know how.'

'With me, Alice.' He fed his arm round her waist and eased her into him, her chill sucking at his shoulder and his ribs.

'We can do this if you believe in it. If we both believe in it.'

He took a step and she stumbled after. 'Think warm,' he told her, and they took a step together onto the shore. He tried another but she dragged against him.

'I can't. I'm too tired.'

And so cold. He was shivering now. He had to get her to the trees, to his bag, had to wrap her in the car rug so he could hold her. He needed to hold her, wasn't going to let her go this time.

'I'll carry you.' He tried to flex his fingers as he bent to lift her. They hardly moved. His arm was numb, his chest lancing with pain.

'I'm not strong enough, Nick.' She was shaking her head. 'I've stayed too long. And people keep calling me, and I can't not hear them. It never stops, now. It never stops.'

'Who keeps calling you, Alice?'

'You. The shadow people. Everyone.'

What could he say? How could he persuade her?

He glanced up, seeing nothing but clouds, thick clouds and pittering rain that fell to warm his face. He was soaked, every movement a shiver, every breath snatched. The cold was slowing his brain. He couldn't think.

'I'm freezing you, Nick. Let me go. I need to go.'

His open hand was wet, wet from her.

'No, Alice, *no!* Stay with me.'

In a concerted effort he lifted her from the ground and ran knee-deep into the Pool to set her down, holding her so she wouldn't collapse.

'Stay with me, Alice. Concentrate. Talk to me. We can do this. We have to do this.'

The cold was worse than before, reaching up his legs, seizing his joints. He braced himself so he wouldn't fall.

'Tell me where you go.'

She angled her head. The torc was returning in faint outline round her neck.

'Talk to me, Alice. Tell me about the shadow people, about the man. You were telling me about the man. You helped him, you said. That was good, wasn't it? Tell me about this man.'

Her hand came up to rest against his chest, and he shuddered as her cold raced along his ribs.

'He was ill, horribly ill. He fell into my arms... almost fell. The water...' She shook her head. 'Something happened. His face... the boils, the bruising, everything... I think I helped him. I hope I helped him.'

Her expression clouded. 'The voices started after that, and now I can't shut them out. They keep calling and I can't not hear. I can't stop them pulling at me, and I'm so tired, Nick, so very tired. I just want it all to stop.'

'I'll look after you, Alice. I will if you'll just stay with me.'

Her frown eased, her pale gaze roving across his face. 'I saw you among them, Nick. I knew you'd find me.' Her hand came up, thin fingers reaching for his cheek but not quite touching. 'Thank you for finding me.'

'I did find you, Alice, and I'll—'

He was standing alone, drenched to the skin, gasping against the cold.

Chapter 41

The sun shouldn't be setting, but it was. He shouldn't have stubble, but he did.

No emotional outburst met him this time. Phil stared as Nick dragged himself over the stile, and he dropped his tools to cross the road. Nick refused his offered arm, fearing if he were to accept he would collapse, body and mind alike.

'You didn't eat the food, did you?' was whispered as they walked the gravel to the farmhouse.

Rosemary pulled out a chair and placed a mug of tea in front of him. A scone followed. Nick smiled at that.

'You can't go on like this,' she said.

'I know.'

'You look ill.'

He wished they'd not crowd him. His gaze sought the wall calendar, but it carried no lunar symbols. 'What day is it?'

'Thursday. You've been gone nearly two days.'

That meant tomorrow was the third quarter, then Alice wouldn't return at all. ...*so tired*... He'd realised the significance on the trudge back, tried to count how many days it had been since she and her reflection had warmed him, cocooned in the groundsheet. He'd been wrong to think she was free of the moon's pull. He should have stayed by the Pool, wrapped himself in the car rug and slept in the storm shelter he'd bought.

'Nicholas, you look as if you've been gone a week.'

He ignored that, too.

'Do you want a shower before dinner?' A change of tone, the censure gone. Rosemary was going to be conciliatory.

He shook his head.

'A sleep?'

He felt he could sleep for a week, but shook his head, determined to rouse himself.

'Is it over?' Phil this time, Rosemary waving to shush him. 'The lad's got to see sense and return home. This ain't no place for him.'

'Like it was no place for *Jason?*'

Nick looked up at the sharpness of her tone. Phil was staring in astonishment, Rosemary thrumming with emotion behind her pointing finger.

'Can't you see what he's going through? We have to do more than just deny anything's wrong.'

Phil began to bluster but she cut him off.

'What's down there, Nicholas? What did you see?'

He closed his eyes, letting his head loll into his hands. Not now. Please, not now.

'He saw nothin',' Phil retorted. 'There's nothin' down there but wind an' a few trees.'

'What did *you* see, Philip? And don't tell me again there's nothing down there to see, because I know you're lying. You've been *lying* for years.'

Nick sat back to stare at them. Phil's shoulders were bunching, his hands curling into fists. 'I ain't 'aving—'

He started for the door but Rosemary was too quick, slamming her back into it to cut off his escape.

'This isn't just for Nicholas. It's not just for us. It's for *our* son. For Jason. For God's sake... what did you *see?*'

Tears were rolling down her cheeks. Nick glanced from one to the other. Their emotions would soon break and ebb, and they'd return to the safety of denial. He took a breath.

'Alice. I saw Alice.'

Rosemary flopped against the door; Phil spun round.

'There ain't no such things as ghosts!'

'Alice is no ghost. I spoke to her. She spoke to me. I touched her.' And more, he thought, and more.

Their dual gasps filled the kitchen and Phil reached to steady himself against the back of a dining chair. They stared at each other and then the colour returned to Phil's cheeks.

'Alice is *dead*.'

Nick looked at him. 'I know.' He waited a moment for that to sink in. 'So what did you see, Phil?'

The man's lips trembled. He sat heavily on the chair, shaking his head. 'Too long ago. I can't remember.'

'You remember in your sleep,' Rosemary prompted. 'Your nightmares might not wake you, but they wake me.'

'A hob?' Nick pressed. 'A boggart?' A *Grindylow?*

Phil's hand rose to cover his mouth, his eyes squeezing shut against brimming tears.

'I were *ten*,' he spat. 'I knew they were lying. Went down, didn't I? To look. A hand reached out, all brown an' covered in peat an' slime an' God knows what, an' it dragged itsen out, its head an' its shoulders an'—' He heaved in a breath. 'An' I ran. I ran an' I never looked back.'

Nick shuddered. It was the description Alice had given, of her clawing out of the Pool only to find herself back in it. She wasn't Alice any more than...

'Your uncle. The suicide in the pond.'

'It were no suicide. That place *killed* him. Dragged 'im in like a sheep.'

Phil was openly crying now, wracking sobs of release. Rosemary folded her arms round his shoulders and hugged him to her. Nick left them in the kitchen to climb the stairs hoping someone, even Alice, might come to hug him.

Chapter 42

A mug of tea, a tin of soup to warm him, and Tim was beginning to rationalise his experience on the moor as a vivid invention of his own mind due to standing so long in the icy water. That, or his instinct had been correct. Noxious gases were escaping with its feeder spring, gases that were filling the lab at the plant even as he sat on his bed swaddled in a duvet.

And now he'd another problem.

He glanced at Izzy, at the mass of her dark dyed hair leaching the colour from her face. She looked like the wraith he'd first taken her for in the car's headlights. If it hadn't been for that stupid blue flash in her hair...

'How did you get here?'

'I caught a bus then hitched.'

He'd no idea Izzy even knew where he was based. The bed creaked as she raised herself onto one elbow to gaze at him.

'You were hardly being helpful, not returning my calls. And it was meant, wasn't it? Me being here to nurse you when you arrived in that state.'

'I wasn't in a state.'

'Oh yeah, right. Not much. You're as bad as Simon. All over me while I'm of some use to you and then it's *push off*.'

'I'm not telling you to push off, Izzy.'

'It's all in the manner, *Timothy*. And don't call me that.'

'I wouldn't dream of it, *Izara*.'

Jeez... He was stuck with her for the night now, wasn't he? Hopefully only the one.

'So are you finally going to tell me?'

'Tell you what?'

'About the Pool. What you saw there; what you felt; what

happened.'

Tim groaned as he sank back into the pillow trying to remember what he'd babbled as they'd staggered into the caravan.

Izzy flounced, making the bed rock.

'Everyone acts as if I'm some airhead. Nick is the only person to show me any consideration and I can't get hold of him. Simon says he hasn't got his phone number, which I don't believe at all.'

'Nick? Nick who?'

'Nick *Blaketon*. Keep up. You met him at The Bishops' Mill. He was one of Simon's speakers. He gave me his book.'

Her shoulders disappeared over the edge of the bed, and she clambered back up to wave a thin paperback that Tim remembered being waved under his nose in the pub. He rolled his eyes.

'You stole it.'

'Nick *signed* it. To *me*.'

'Hu...rrah.'

'He told me to read it all, including the bibliography. He emphasised that.'

'And you have, have you? Including the entire bibliography?' Tim watched to see if she'd pick up on his sarcasm, but again it soared over her head.

'He's not writing about supernatural beings, Tim, he's writing about his *girlfriend*. She died six years ago – at the spring where you said eyes were watching you.'

He felt his skin prickle, the scratches from the heather crawling across his legs and forearms. 'I said no such thing.'

'I tried to tell you days ago but you wouldn't listen.'

He closed his eyes, determined not to listen now.

'I want you to take me there.'

His eyes sprang open. 'I'm not taking you. I'm not going near the place.'

'Then there *is* something odd down there. Tell me. Something to do with the water.'

'It's not just the water, it's the whole damned area. There are cairns and tumuli—'

'Oh, I know. I've looked at a map. There's a massive hill-fort not far from the White Horse. It was probably a sacred place. People *believed*.'

'Believed what? That the water wouldn't kill them? It probably will now.'

He closed his eyes and sank back onto the pillow. Then he frowned and stared at the ceiling.

'Oh shit.' He sat up. 'I'm such a stupid sod.'

'What? Tell me, Timothy!'

He blinked at her, thinking of the flask in the car, wondering how he could get rid of it, what he could safely say, what to leave out. Sod John.

'Look at me, Izara. Look at me carefully, at my face.'

He watched her concentrate, her gaze roving over him. She wasn't going to notice. Bloody airhead. How could she not notice?

'My *psoriasis*.'

'I don't see—' She looked again, reaching out with her painted nails. 'The water? The water's cured it?'

'Izzy, I've just trespassed on someone's land to help steal nearly a hundred litres of the stuff. John said it was for a lab control.'

'A hundred litres?'

'Exactly. He and his damned brothers are going to sell it as some sort of elixir. It could poison people.'

'*Really?*'

His heart was thudding as the ramifications of what they intended continued to mount, and she was smiling at him as if she was on something. 'Don't you understand?'

'Yes. It has curing properties.' She shrugged. 'Like the waters of Walsingham, of Lourdes.'

'Are you mad? I'm not talking about some placebo effect. The water from that pool carries a contaminant reading off the scale. We've no idea what it is and John doesn't give a shit.'

'But it cured your psoriasis.'

'*Looks* as though it has.'

'Then it might not be a contaminant. It could be an anomaly that science hasn't discovered yet.'

'*What?*' He couldn't believe her crass stupidity. He thought of his hand ripped open against the breezeblock wall but decided not to mention that.

'Don't you understand? If it's powerful enough to cure my psoriasis in a *day* then what else is it doing... to cell structure, to blood vessels, to the nervous system? What would happen if it was ingested? *Drank?*'

Instead of being shocked she became animated.

'Nick knows, that's why he gave me his book, why he told me to read every word, including the bibliography.

'It's fucking *fiction*. A fairy story.'

'No, he was telling me, Timothy, telling me something's down there, that there's something in the Pool. *Belief is more powerful than fact*. That's what he wrote in it. For me. He was telling *me*.'

Tim rolled his eyes and sank back onto the pillow.

Chapter 43

The pain in his feet crept by fiery tendrils beyond Ernald's ankles to his legs. He focused on the trials of the saints, how their belief in God's Grace overcame all adversity. Despite his life at the priory he remained an ungrateful sinner, and was being shown the torments awaiting him in Purgatory. The hidden boots and soft undershirt, the Burgundy wine and spiced foods of the manor lords' tables, returned to scourge him each time the Blessed Mary took pity and bathed his brow in sleep. He confessed openly with tears, and kept vigil with Saint Cuthbert's reliquary for Wulfrith and for himself.

As the daylight grew milky, the reeve rose from his place across the open doorway and brought a bowl for Ernald to fill. His water smelled foul, whether from the feeding of devils or from the old women's potion he did not know, but his thinking remained clear and he gave praise for that mercy.

'Wulfrith?'

'He's pissed himself. Pray we find this spring today.'

The bread and pottage given to Ernald refused to be swallowed. The draught the old woman brought made him cough. Wulfrith's went down by the reeve's hand and he took it all with barely a murmur.

A board was brought and slid under Ernald's thighs, a thick stick beneath his knees. He prayed hard to the Saint, to the Sacred Mother of God's Son, but the pain was fierce and the sweating more, and to his own ears he sounded an infant whimpering in its swaddling as he was carried outside.

Once astride the ass the throbbing of his feet began to ease and with it his breathing. Wiping the sweat from his eyes, he glanced about him. To a man their escort stood mute, watching so dolefully Ernald felt ill at ease beneath their collective gaze. Wulfrith was carried from the dwelling in the reeve's arms, the weight of his own held in a sling, his hand hidden in a poultice pouch. A high-backed frame had been fashioned from withies and a seat prepared on a pack-saddle. The chosen pony stamped its hoof at the difference in its load, but the reeve's youth stroked it quiet and it stood while Wulfrith was strapped in place. He was awake, Ernald saw, nodding at the reeve's murmured words. It was the novice tied to the pack-pony who spoke in a voice clear enough for all to hear.

'*Peccatoribus.*'

To Ernald's consternation the condemnation of their sins was echoed by their escort and he saw the men mark themselves. The reeve turned with a fierce eye and the novice bowed his head, but when the group began to walk Ernald noticed hand-gestures among the Flems, matched by those who watched them leave. No one smiled. No one bade farewell.

The cloud thickened as the group followed deer-track and boar-run, only for Wulfrith to shake his head and they turn back whence they'd come. The first time their escort looked at one another. The second time there was muttering. In shrill tones the novice began to recite a prayer of deliverance from serpents, to which the Flems intoned a ragged, unnerving, response. As the reeve drew Wulfrith's pony by him, Ernald caught sight of the worry etched into his face. There had to be something he could do. He recalled offering to lead their group in the singing of psalms, but now only a single one would fill his head, and the thought of putting tongue to it frightened him even more.

Pressing Saint Cuthbert's cross tight to his breastbone, he closed his eyes and took himself away from this place of pain and fear, back to the priory and the peace of its church. The plainsong drifted into his mind, and then onto his lips. It seemed to calm man and beast alike, and for that Ernald gave thanks to Saint Cuthbert.

The clouds lowered, rain falling in sudden windless squalls. The greenwood scattered into a sodden heath.

Wulfrith sat straighter on his mount. He pointed. The reeve looked and questioned. Wulfrith nodded, circling his good arm. Ernald felt hope rise within and slapped at the ass' rump, wincing at each jab of pain that came with the animal's jolting steps.

'Yes?'

'Maybe,' the reeve murmured. He nodded to Wulfrith. 'And maybe it is too late.'

Ernald stared at the man's blotched face, at his water-glazed eyes. He had no knowledge of the words that trickled from Wulfrith's lips along with his spittle, yet, as it had in the priory's confinement chamber, *angel-woman* wormed itself into his mind.

'The dance-devils gather.'

'It is the Blessed Holy Mother he speaks of,' Ernald countered.

The reeve squinted at him with water-glazed eyes of his own. 'If he speaks it aloud that is not what the Flems will hear and they will fall on us all as rabid dogs on lambs.'

With a heave of his chest the reeve recovered his composure and looked behind to those waiting. 'The line of trees,' he called.

His gaze returned. 'You, friend Ernald, you hold the Holy Cross aloft for all to see, and put your tongue to the song to muffle their ears.'

The pony moved forwards. Ernald watched Wulfrith loll against the withy seat, the reeve's broad shoulders and measured step betraying none of the turmoil Ernald had heard in his voice. He pulled free Saint Cuthbert's cross, removing its thong from his neck to hold the symbol of the Holy Passion high, its crystal protecting the Saint's relics clear for all to see. Embracing the throbbing in his feet, he sat tall on the pad saddle and twisted to face those on foot.

'Saint Cuthbert leads us to the Holy Mother's sacred waters. Give praise to God in His Heaven and to the Holy Saints at His feet!'

To a man the Flems gave quiet praise and marked themselves. Only the novice stood unmoved, his expression a glower of discontent. Ernald thanked Saint Cuthbert for holding tight the youth's tongue, and set his own to draw out the plainsong for all to hear.

It began to rain, the heavy drops arcing down as if watery arrows. The ass twitched its ears, shook its head, and then itself. Without stirrups to support him, Ernald's plainsong cut short in panic, his hand holding Saint Cuthbert's cross dropping to the saddle to hold against being unseated. Pain swept up through his legs with the sudden jolting. The ground lurched beneath him. Sucking in short breaths, he dared to pat the animal's neck and spoke warmly until it eased its gait.

The raindrops continued to thump down, not a true deluge but an assault on his shoulders and his legs, and most grievously on his feet. Fearing to lose the reliquary, he tightened his thighs against the pad saddle, closing his eyes and his mind against the pain as he removed his hat to slide the thong over his head. Releasing a gasp, he retrieved the reins. In front, the reeve trudged beside the pony, Wulfrith lolling in his seat, his good arm swinging limp. It looked to Ernald that he had lost his senses. Neither reacted to the rain.

The trees which had been but a line on the horizon were taking on the bulk of hardwoods. To keep his thoughts from his feet, Ernald concentrated on them as they neared, their leafy canopy shadowed so dark beneath the louring clouds that it seemed a scab crouching on a hairy skin of heathland. What reason could be offered for so many good hardwoods growing in a place of low thickets and spindly birch? Neither were there stragglers at the fringes. Was his gaze deceived, or was the woodland bowing its shoulders left and right? Could it be growing in a circle?

Ernald's drawn breaths became shallower, faster, his fingertips rising to the reliquary as he dared to hope they had found the spring.

Without warning a tumult of ravens rose from within the canopy, cawing and whirling and clawing one another. To Ernald's consternation they turned in the air, diving in a flight towards the travellers' heads. He ducked across the ass' neck. Shouts came from the Flems. The ass brayed as Ernald hung on, the ponies whinnying in alarm. Men-at-arms, heads hunched into shoulders, jabbed at the descending birds with their pole-arms. Only the novice stood tall, railing at the sky with a clenched fist. The flock veered in an untidy black ribbon, the novice maintaining his tirade in the Holy tongue even as the castigating Flems fell to silence. Ernald stared at the youth, saw the Visitation leave his shaking shoulders, watched the crouching Flems mark themselves in piety as they watched it, too.

Ernald swallowed, collecting his wits to seek the reeve's face. They exchanged a look Ernald could not read.

Wulfrith was awake. Seeing the trees so close he became animated, urging on the reeve, but no entrance could be found, at least to pass a pony. After false starts the reeve called on his men to draw implements from the pack-pony's load and cut a route.

It was a painful passage with branches snagging at Ernald's legs. He tried to keep his feet close in to the animal's belly but the touching there sent brands of torment shooting to his knees. Then they were out of the shadowed greenwood and into a realm of toppled trees and pale reed-beds, of leafless crooked limbs covered in bird lime reaching to the roiling clouds.

This was where the ravens roosted. There was no cawing now, no flap of feathered wing. All Ernald could hear was the crushing of stalks beneath hooves, and rain pebbling the lying water.

A gesture from the reeve and Ernald marked his pointing finger. Half hidden amid dying stalks was the ribcage of an animal, picked white. Ernald did not stay the ass but held himself quiet as he passed it, waiting for the muttering he knew would come from the men behind. It arrived as a wave dispersing on shingle, and then it was gone. The novice walked with the Flems, Ernald remembered, tied to the pack-pony.

The trials of their route increased with the rain, the reeve's man and the boy having to lead the mounts over obstacles in a ground more bog than firm land. Wulfrith was unperturbed by the jostling, his free arm giving emphasis to the stream of jumbled utterances escaping his lips. Even the reeve no longer sought clarification; merely set one foot splashing after the other as ahead his men tested their coming path.

A call went up from their escort. Leeches were attaching themselves to the legs of the pack-pony, to the flesh of men. There was spiteful discussion, but nothing to be done until they reached dry ground and could light a fire.

They passed another carcass, a deer half-submerged, half-eaten, its eyes gone below its stumps of antler. How had animals come to die here? Had they been hunted and lost? Wounded and sought shelter among the trees?

How had Wulfrith come to be here? Why had the Blessed Mary chosen this place to rise on Wings of Piety and offer the Balm of Salvation? This place of dead animals and dark ravens. How could this festering basin bring forth healing waters?

Emotion glazed Ernald's sight and he reached for the comfort of Saint Cuthbert's reliquary. He was still clutching it tight when the rain was cut by a piercing cry from Wulfrith. His head was cocked, his good arm held up as if to offer a blessing. The reeve had turned to him, the way-cutters, too.

'What is it?' breathed Ernald.

The reeve listened as Wulfrith listened, as Ernald listened. Then Wulfrith spoke, kicking at the pony and pointing ahead.

'Well?' Ernald urged.

The reeve dropped his shoulders and looked back. 'He says we are close. He says she is calling him.'

Ernald stared ahead to listen again. All he could hear was the distant croaking of what sounded to be frogs.

Chapter 44

Nick hid beneath the duvet listening to the movements in the house. He had to face them, he knew that, but he felt so very tired now the whirlwind in his mind was subsiding.

Alice was dead. She'd been dead when he'd dragged her from the water six years ago. She'd not been real in York, a mere projection of the *thing* that had captured her, captured her soul, or her life-force, or whatever equated to it. All these years he'd been chasing shadows.

He'd cried when he'd thought of his dad, thought of him alive, of them quietly holding hands near the end. Cried as he remembered the dream, his dad stepping out from behind a joyful Alice to stare at him in astonishment and disbelief. Had that been his own subconscious telling him he was contorting a truth he wouldn't face? Was he any different to Phil?

Yet she was down there. Something was down there, something that looked like Alice, spoke like Alice; had some sort of weird existence. In one form or another it had been there for centuries; millennia. Worse, he'd read the narratives and labelled them Folklore.

But she remembered him, remembered their life together. If he left, if he created a life for himself down south, how long would it be before those memories faded, before she became a true Peg Powler? A Grindylow?

He closed his eyes, but it didn't stop the heave of tears.

The shower was refreshing, invigorating even, but as soon as Nick cut off the flow and stepped from the stall the debilitation set in again. His mum had forced a way through. He could do no less. He really needed to call her but feared he'd break down, and he didn't want to worry her over the phone. He needed to go back, sort himself a proper job, a proper life. Start afresh.

The smell of grilling bacon was climbing the stairs to entice him down. He breathed in its aroma, luxuriating in its normality. If scones were served alongside, he wouldn't bat an eye. It was part of the fabric of the house, of Rosemary and Phil, the glue that kept them together, kept them functioning. He needed to find something similar.

He tapped at the kitchen door, wondering how they'd be. Phil was eating toast, his eyes fixed on a television standing on the dresser: a map; a weather report. Rosemary turned from the Aga to smile reassurance.

'Good morning, Nicholas. Tea's in the pot. Would you like a full breakfast?'

'If it's small; thanks.'

She didn't ask if he'd slept well. He wondered if they had.

'Gonna rain,' Phil said, his tone bright as if they were already partway through a conversation, as if last night's exchange had never occurred.

Nick poured a mug, holding it for warmth, and sank his concentration into the regional headlines. This was why the set was on, a reason not to talk.

A plate was set in front of him, sausage, egg and beans. He forced himself to make a start.

'Have you decided what you're going to do?' Rosemary asked.

'I'm not sure.'

'If you need another day...'

'He's going back south to his mother, is what he's gonna do,' Phil stated. 'No place for him here.'

'Let him eat,' Rosemary told her husband.

Nick felt her hand on his shoulder and took a steadying breath. He would have to go. Phil would calm when he left. Their life would return to normal, whatever that was.

'That's Castleton,' Phil said, and he reached for the remote to turn up the volume.

Nick cut into the bacon, his neck prickling as a familiar forceful voice filled the kitchen.

'...shale exploration companies never admit to a test frack because their licences don't allow for it...'

Simon's face was filling the screen, a placard emblazoned *Frack Free Yorkshire* jumping behind his shoulders.

'...earthquake has been picked up by the British Geological Society centred on an area of moorland south-east of here...'

'South-east?' Phil turned to Rosemary. 'Have we had an email?'

'I haven't switched on the computer this morning.'

Nick looked from one to the other. 'Is he talking about...?'

Phil snorted. 'Dratted people. Best check the water.' He rose from his chair.

'Water?' echoed Nick.

'Aye, *water*.' Phil nodded to the taps at the sink. 'Where do you think it comes from? Think we got mains out here, do you? We pump our own from a borehole.'

Nick sat back, stunned. Of course. The farm's water was coming from the same source that fed the Pool.

Simon's voice rose in emphasis. '...already know of anomalies in certain artesian wells. The Department of Earth Sciences at Durham University is working with the fracking companies and are *burying* the results...'

'Look at that idiot,' Phil spat. 'Look at his eyes. Just like Jason's lot. Worse than Jason's lot.'

Simon was brushing off the interviewer's questions. 'As ordinary people we have to make a stand before water courses are poisoned, before our *drinking* water is poisoned. We're travelling south now to take our own samples, and we'll be showing *our* results to the world!'

Nick drew breath as realisation hit. The argument in The Bishops' Mill. Castleton – he'd driven through it on his way. He dropped his cutlery as he stood, slopping tea across the table.

'They're coming here.'

'What? Oh no, not another bunch o'nutters tramping all ov'r

the place.'

Nick stared at Phil, the implication for Alice biting deep.

They keep calling and I can't not hear them. I can't stop them.

'What do you mean you didn't tell him anything? You must have done!'

'I didn't.' Izara shook her head as she wrenched open the Freelander's door and scrambled into the passenger seat. Tim slammed his, making the vehicle rock.

'You must have done. *Jesus!* Where the hell is this going to leave me with the project? With the university?'

'I might have said something,' Izara wailed. 'I don't remember. Neither of you take a blind bit of notice of me.'

'Well, *he* did, didn't he? All over the fucking news!'

Izara thumped her fist onto her thigh. 'Oh stop it, Timothy. I'm sorry, okay? It's done. Just drive me there.'

The car pulled out onto the main road and she was thrust back into the seat as Tim hit the accelerator.

'You mention *one word* of what we discussed last night...' His finger was pointing, his face almost puce.

'I won't,' she said, 'I promise. Just get me there.'

'And don't you even think about coming back.'

Chapter 45

Vaulting over the stile, Nick took the path between the sheep pastures at a run, Phil's bellow echoing in his head. 'What are you *doing?*'

What was he doing? It wasn't Alice at the Pool, he knew that. Yet it was her sentience, her perception of what she'd been.

...I'm here because you called me, Nick...

He couldn't just leave her, had to warn her.

...They keep calling, and I can't not hear them...

He'd seen it in the kitchen, seen it all unfold in front of him, Simon and his mob of activists breaking through the trees, splashing in the shallows to get their samples. They'd wade to the feeder spring, kicking up sediment and muddying the water. How could she not hear? How could she not respond? They'd be calling her and wouldn't even realise.

He didn't slow for the severity of the ridge slope but pounded down, dislodging stones and gravel that followed in his wake.

...I'm tired, Nick, so tired...

A day, that's all they'd needed, one more day and the moon's pull would diminish enough so she wouldn't respond at all.

Jumping the bulrush dip, he severed a loop from the path but landed awkwardly, his ankle stinging. A couple of hops and he regained his pace.

How would she react to the maelstrom confronting her? How would they react to *her?* That she would see them and understand enough to disperse in a heartbeat he'd dismissed even as he'd run up the stairs to reclaim his phone and car keys. He'd need those if he had to hide her, if he had to call Phil for help.

If Phil would help. If he wouldn't deny.

No, he'd help. One glimpse of Alice and the Pool would turn into a regular Nessie hunt, with vigils and motion cameras and God knew what. Phil would help, if for no other reason than to keep the news crews from his door.

A raindrop, fat and cold, hit him between the eyes jolting him from his stride. Nick wiped at it. Another followed, and another. The forecasted rain began to gather momentum, pounding tiny craters into the ground, flattening against his shirt and overwhelming its absorbency. His adrenalin was fading, a pain clawing at his ribs. It was three miles and he'd hardly started.

The path was turning as dark as the clouds lowering to meet it. His view of the mound holding high the chiselled pond was obscured by sheets of rain marching across the trembling heather. He eased his pace to conserve energy, trusting the weather to slow Simon and his group. City people, every one. None would want to be out in this.

The mound appeared, its sheep-track a cascade of peat-laden water gouging a route across the path at its base. Nick jumped it and ran on. He turned into another loop, the rain thumping at his back now, giving him some respite as it streamed from his hair and down his shoulders, gluing his clothes to his body. Each drop felt as hard as a pellet numbing his skin, as cold as the water from the Pool. He told himself not to dwell on it and focused on the haven the trees would offer. He thought of his sports bag containing the unused storm shelter and almost laughed at the irony.

And then the car rug rose in his mind, the thick woollen car rug he'd intended using as insulation against Alice's cold. She'd been warm in his bed; it was the Pool which was cold, not Alice. She needed the water from the Pool to sustain her. If he wrapped her in the soaked rug... If he used his bag as a leaky bucket...

Raw lungs dragged in air but he ignored the pain, forcing his legs, forcing his pace.

His relief when the trees came into view almost overwhelmed him, but he kept on, splashing across the morass that had been the camping ground to push his way through the branches.

'Alice!'

His shout held no power, and he stumbled over tree roots desperate to find his hidden sports bag, dropping to his knees to pull it from the wilting wildflowers and drag free the rug.

'Alice!'

The keys to his car bit into one thigh, the flat bulk of his phone into the other. Half standing, his head pushed into the sheltering branch fronds, he freed them from his pockets and pushed them into the bag, zipping them safe.

'Alice!'

Running for the water's edge, he held the rug by a corner and threw it in. Instead of sinking it floated on the dinting surface. He stared in disbelief, then stepped in, the cold grasping at his feet and hands as he gathered the rug to force it under. Bubbles rose and broke. Scanning the Pool, he searched for the bubbles from its feeder spring, but they were lost in the multitude of ripples and indentations as individual raindrops broke its surface.

'Alice!'

He shook the cold from his hands, conscious of the ring carrying strands of her hair bright on his finger. Splaying his hand he beat it into the water's surface. Had he been wrong? Would the pounding rain interfere with his call? Might she be safe and not respond when Simon arrived with his activists?

Turning his face to the sky he closed his eyes and let the rain wash over him. He couldn't take that risk. Calling again, he waded deeper, to where he thought the bubbles trickled free. He looked at the ring, its silver almost white against the dark water, against the dark trees that closed around him. Clamping the wet rug to his side, he dragged the ring from his numbed finger, held it a moment, and threw. The rain swallowed it. He never saw it break the surface and the pain of its loss erupting in his chest made him groan.

A flicker at the corner of his eye: *Alice*. He spun in its direction. Pale wraiths were gliding out of the trees, out of the rain, the nearest growing in solidity, kicking water as it walked. Nick's mouth fell open in his shock.

'Don't look at them!' shrieked Alice. 'Look at me, look at *me!*'

He snapped round to her voice. She was standing not three paces from him, her hand reaching, her expression stark with fear.

'They'll see you! Look at me, look at *me!*'

Nick took a splashing step towards her as a spear plunged into the water between them. Instinctively he turned back. A gaunt man was pulling free a glove, falling to his knees and holding out his arm. Nick stared in disbelief. A bearded man was resolving from the rain, carrying another on his back. Figures crowded behind, emerging as if through mist, some as fine as curling smoke. Their clothes... Soldiers. One was pulling back to—

He turned for Alice, desperate to warn her, but his movements were slowing, breath refusing to be drawn to shout the warning. She was lifting her hand to point, her lips parting.

'It's that man!'

One moment the man was reaching out, the next he jerked, a spurt of blood following a spear-head emerging from his belly.

Alice's cry transformed into a scream, into a high-pitched howl. Nick made a grab to pull her away, but she was dropping loose from the waist in a faint. His arm slid across her hips to catch her, felt limp muscles turn rigid as her arms sank into the water, her hair following as her head bowed.

Memory ignited. York—Mist—Water—Ice. He glanced at the figures materialising from the trees. The speared man was toppling, the two behind wide-eyed and open-mouthed. Nick could do nothing... nothing...

Angling aside his head, he closed his eyes as the water around his legs began to churn.

It was a man's voice Ernald heard, a man's voice in an unknown tongue.

Wulfrith was off his mount, calling out, splashing through the water as he threw aside his sling. The pony bolted, the ass shied, and Ernald was tipped into the cold mire, sucking in turgid water as he wrestled against the burning in his feet. Then he was fighting for breath, for life, his heart pounding in his ears and in his throat, being raised up to be borne on the reeve's broad back. Cringing against the pain of his thighs being grasped, he glimpsed Wulfrith striding through the water, pulling the poultice bag from his swollen hand. The reeve began to wade after him.

A man's voice. How could that be?

Ernald held his shivering to scour the tangle of leafless trees. Shrill tones from the novice cut through cries from the Flems, but Ernald could hear no other voice.

Wulfrith faltered, sinking to his knees in the debris-strewn water. Ernald felt his chest tightening in anticipation, and he stared as Wulfrith stared.

Rush-light faint, a golden glow was swelling as if God's Lantern in the darkness. Ernald gripped at the reeve's shoulder to alert him where words refused to pass his lips. The light grew bright, brighter, and Ernald trembled as he gazed upon the Blessed Mary radiating in her Holiness. Lifting Saint Cuthbert's reliquary so it might touch Her light, his eyes ran with tears, his heart with praise and adoration.

The jolt, the gasp, came from the reeve, Ernald's eye catching movement, seeing the spear-thrust, the contorted face of the novice, the youth's severed leash a waving pennant as he threw up his arms and in the Holy tongue screeched Damnation To Devils.

Wulfrith was falling, Ernald was falling, the reeve releasing him. Ernald looked to the Holy Mother, a beseeching plea on his lips. *Two* heads stood upon Her shoulders. One. She shimmered, transparent, naked... Pregnant?

The cold engulfed him, pulling him down. Flailing on his back, water flowing over his open eyes, he saw his feet kicking, could not feel their pain for the pain of the cold pressing into his chest, into his head. It seemed the world of the air turned white as a thousand glistening arrows shot overhead. The surface boiled, and greyed, and lay flat.

His habit was full of water, he full of woe, a beetle on its back unable to regain its feet, unable to breathe. His energy was spent. The cold pressed in. He called upon Saint Cuthbert to lend his guiding hand...

There was the coldness of air and blinding light. The world rocked, and Ernald felt his back pummelled by a hammering fist. He coughed, and he spewed, and he dragged in breath through a reed so thin that he heard the creaking of life as it returned to him. His sodden habit ran with water as the glistening trees ran with it, as the reeve's frosted tunic ran with it. The air was full of white mist, and it took much coughing and choking to realise it was their breaths he could see in the icy air. Wulfrith lay on his side amid water icing red with his blood. Behind him, the novice floated face-down.

A rough hand caught at his cheek to turn his head. The reeve's staring eyes were so close he felt the man's beard scuff his chin.

'I saw nothing,' the reeve growled.

Ernald was released and he staggered back. Blood was weeping from the reeve's clothed arm; from his side, too, and his thigh. There were cuts to his forehead, to his cheek.

'Master Reeve... You are injured.'

'Give me your arm, friend Ernald, for I can no longer carry you. The Flems have fled. We must leave this mere or die in its cold waters.'

Ernald looked back. The Holy Light had winked out.

Two heads on one body.

'Did...Did you see—?'

'I saw a good man murdered by a dretch whose dark mutterings had Wulfrith's hand broken, *that's* what I saw.'

What had Ernald seen? He'd been so certain, yet...

'You saw nothing, friend Ernald. Come now or come never.'

Holding tight Saint Cuthbert's reliquary, together they

stumbled two paces, three. Not all the Flems had fled. One floated on his back, his eyes gone, his face a bloody pulp.

'Master Reeve...'

'I see nothing. You see nothing. We are not here.'

A realisation crept through Ernald. His shoulders dropped as he spluttered, and he pulled away.

'We *do* see, Master Reeve. We *are* here. The Holy Light of God touched us, as did His Wrath.'

He stared at the reeve, then down at his feet hidden in the cold, cold water. He was standing, standing on his own.

When he looked up, the reeve was marking himself with the Holy Cross.

'*Nick!* Nick, I'm sorry, I'm *sorry*.'

He couldn't move, dare not try. The frost along his sleeve sparkled as Alice turned in his arms, arms he couldn't feel. He could hear voices. Not the shadow people. The shadow people had gone, merged into the water, into the rain, like the frost sparkling on his sleeve.

'I couldn't stop myself.'

She was crying. He didn't want her to cry.

'It's okay.'

'It's not, you'll freeze.'

She reached for him, pushing his face into her hair. He could feel no pressure, could feel no cold. He could smell, though, could see. He breathed deep the scents of forest fruits trapped in her hair, marvelled at its autumn colours, more gold than copper, the rain not flattening its waves.

'If I can get you to the shore...' Her words hitched with emotion. For him. His Alice.

'Nick, I'm not strong enough. The moon... I can't warm you.'

'It's okay.'

He wanted to sleep. Knew if his eyes closed they'd never reopen.

'Kiss me,' he murmured.

'Nick! I can hear voices. There are people coming. If I can get you to the shore—'

'*No!*'

He wasn't certain he was stopping her, but she looked at him, her pale eyes more translucent than ever he remembered.

'No,' he breathed. 'Just you and me. I miss you, Alice. I love you. Take me with you. Take me now.'

Her anxiety softened. Her fingers lifted to stroke his cheek though he couldn't feel her touch, their lips meeting in a burst of summer sunlight.

It wasn't as he'd dreamed. She didn't take his hand. He wasn't walking with her that he could tell. But she was with him, his Alice, and he was with her. At last. What else was there to matter?

As the water lapped his chin she shimmered through myriad colours in the rain. Tendrils of her auburn hair began to sway around her head as it had the first time he'd seen her. In a shaft of sunlight; in a lecture hall.

The water stung his eyes, glazing his vision, filling his ears and dulling his hearing.

Look at me, Nick. Look only at me.

His gaze ranged over her eyebrows, her cheeks, her chin. Moonlight seen through water. And he was filled with peace... contentment... love.

They kissed again, her heavy breasts pushing against his chest, her swollen stomach against his hips. He broke away to gaze at the bloom of her, of his Alice, and to let the Pool bubble down his throat and into his lungs, water hissing over red hot stone.

Chapter 46

A figure had been far ahead on the path and soon lost to the rain, so Izara knew she wouldn't be the only person at the Pool. Yet she wanted to see it as nature intended, if only for a few minutes. Behind her she could hear Simon calling encouragement to the group. Without looking back, she forced her way through the grasping branches.

Catching her breath at the sight, she pushed back the too-big hood of Tim's waterproof, not believing the dazzling array that met her. Every tree stood frosted white, the crystals beside her head hanging as if diamond pendants, twinkling to grey as they liquefied in the rain.

A drip hit her head and she ducked beneath its weight and its chill, taking a step onto squelching grass to move out of range as she shrugged the hood back on.

There was a lot of bleak shore. A swirl of mist rising at its centre, The *World Famous Pool* was a disappointment after the frosted trees, hardly seeming of a size to sustain its name.

As she stepped from the wet grass to the muddy shoreline she shivered with an unexpected echo of the icy raindrop, her gaze focusing on the mist now streaming across the ground towards her. In the moment it took to draw a breath, it had covered half the distance. Peeping beneath it, a solid bore of water was eating up the ground. Izara turned and leapt for the trees as the first of the group emerged.

'What the *hell*...?'

'What *is* that?'

She dared to look as they passed her shoulder. Water was lapping the grass in small waves, the mist retreating at a pace.

'Was that a geyser? Who saw that? What was it?'

She turned from Simon's voice, grateful for the bulky waterproof and oversized hood. As others pushed through the trees, Izara ducked into their wet and drooping branches, making herself small as she curled into a root bole.

What had happened? What had she just witnessed?

'Hey, there's some sort of marker covered in coins here.'

'Looks like an altar to me.'

'Anyone touches it and I'll have their hands off!' Simon bawled.

By the sound of his voice he was moving away. Izara dared to lift her head. In the bole of roots beneath the adjacent tree sat a sports bag. She gazed at it, not understanding why it was there.

Concealing the bag with her waterproof, she unzipped it to see something orange packed in clear plastic. Beneath was a tightly rolled groundsheet, and as she pulled it free she heard keys ring against metal. There were car keys, a phone. She lifted it out, so cold in her hand, hit a button, watched it cycle through its wake-up. Whose was this? Where was the figure she'd seen ahead on the path?

Her skin began to prickle. Nick's book was in her backpack. Simon had told her he'd returned south.

The screen shone. A couple of taps and she was gulping air, rocking on her knees.

'There's a body in the water!'

Her eyes clenched tight as she clasped the phone to her chest, praying, willing... It couldn't be, *couldn't* be.

'Jesus, this water's freezing! Give me a—'

The silence rang in her head, on and on.

'False alarm! It's a rug. Christ, this water's cold.'

Izara exhaled in a burst of joy, wiping at her eyes, pushing the phone and the car keys back in the bag. She couldn't leave it there, someone would find it. She'd found it.

She was *meant* to find it.

'There's a tree down and tyre tracks. Someone's been here and forced a way in!'

Pulling the bag free of the roots, she backed out from beneath the spread of branches to heft it onto her back, it pushing her own pack nestling beneath the waterproof into her spine. Lots of people had arrived, so many she had to step through them to see the water. Too many. They were milling about in the rain, their boots twisting the grass and the tiny-leaved plants into the mud, compressing their roots into the sodden earth.

'Who's got the containers?' Simon was striding back along the shore. 'Have we got the water samples? Yes or no?'

She looked at him, his back straight, his shoulders squared, ignoring the rain flowing down his face and from his hair. She cut across his path to grab his arm. He looked at her and turned away.

'Not now, Izzy.'

'Simon!' She clung on as he tried to shake her off. 'Simon, they're trampling the *evidence*.'

He turned back, his eyes narrowing. 'Evidence?'

'The plants. It's the flora that'll show it, not figures on a graph. If the water's contaminated we'll need before and after pictures – *videos* – to show the damage to the plants.'

She'd hardly finished when he was clapping his hands and shouting for attention.

'Everybody stand still. Those without a phone, into the trees. The rest in a line from the shore to the treeline. We're doing a slow sweep of the ground around the water. We need close-up video as evidence. Has everyone got that? Shoulder-to-shoulder and *slowly*.'

As his activists began to marshal, phones being pulled free of pockets, Izara took a last look at the water, marvelling at what she'd seen, at what she hadn't seen, and pushed through the branches onto the moor. Ignoring the few seeking shelter against the trees, she splashed across the flat ground, waterlogged now and creating its own pool, and onto the path leading up to the road.

It had been Nick running ahead of her, running to meet his Alice lost to him six years before and waiting to be reunited.

Read every word, including the bibliography.

It was all in his book. Other springs were listed, but not this spring. Not this spring for a reason.

The rain began to ease as she climbed the ridge, her legs aching but her blood racing with empowerment. She knew what she had to do, why he'd given her his book, why he'd impressed upon her its significance. She should have realised, asked more questions, taken more notice. It was too late for regrets. It was up to her and her alone.

The track between fenced pastures was a morass. She slid and slipped her way to the stile, her fist tight around the car keys, Nick's phone safe in her jacket. The road was crammed with vehicles abandoned on the narrow verges, on the gravel drive to the farm's car park. She was looking for a Nissan from the logo, and hoped his car was not blocked in. Hitting the fob, she scanned the cars. Lights flashed, and she heaved a sigh of relief.

Shrugging free the bag, she threw it on the rear seat, stripping off the waterproof and bundling it into the foot-well. Slamming the door, she reached for the driver's.

'Oi! Get away from that car!'

An irate man in a floppy hat and caked overalls was running towards her, his fists bunched. 'That ain't your car!'

She swallowed; looked at him.

'It's Nick's.'

His knees buckled and he leaned on the vehicle for support, his face creasing.

'Oh God... he's in the Pool, ain't he? He's dead. Oh God, his poor mother...'

'No.' She reached towards him before he collapsed entirely. '*No*, no. He gave me the keys.'

She straightened. *Belief is more powerful than fact.* She could do this. He'd asked her.

'The police will be coming. All this—' she gestured to the vehicles surrounding them. 'He asked me to move it so there won't be any questions, so they won't ask you about it.'

She drew his phone from her pocket. 'I've to take it to his mum, to explain.'

The man frowned. 'Explain?'

'He's having to go away. But he'll be back. It's a long story, but he will be back. He said she'd understand. I'm to make sure she's okay.'

She slotted Nick's phone back into her pocket and smiled at the man.

'You're the farmer, aren't you? He talked about you. I'm to tell you that you're not to worry, that he'll be coming back.'

She smiled into his questioning face and shrugged.

'I'd better go before the police arrive. I was never here,' she said. 'We never talked.'

He didn't try to stop her as she climbed into the driver's seat and fired the engine. He walked behind her as she left the car park. She could see him in the mirror as she started down the gravel drive. She waved, and saw him very slowly raise his hand.

Epilogue

The two bishops sat in silence while the platters of milky cheese and pandemayne bread were placed on the board alongside cups and a flagon of small ale. It was not their normal fare, but this was no normal meeting between the Sees of Durham and York.

The door closed and the Prince-Bishop returned to the discussion, keeping to the Holy tongue so prying ears were deaf.

'We have heard Brother Ernald; we have seen his feet. He has sworn on sacred texts, and on the sacred relics of Saint Cuthbert.'

'And all the time clutching so fervently to the good Saint's cross as to seem close to madness.' The Bishop of York gestured beyond their waiting repast to the scrolls on the board.

'While I bring testaments from Lord Baliol's men, set down by his own priest at Stocheslage, again sworn on relics and sacred texts, that the wolf's-head serf led them to a stinking mire where he conjured a demon, a fearsome two-headed beast of horns and Hell-red eyes, which in its displeasure speared him with a tongue of flame and put out the eyes of an accompanying bondsman. Only the bravery of a true believer saved that soul from also being dragged into the hissing abyss. And for that he gave his life and his soul into the hands of God and took his rightful place in Heaven.'

The Prince-Bishop lifted a spoon to push at a square of cheese. His colleague eased his tone before continuing.

'If... *Our Lady*... had appeared to you, even as an unlearned man of the pasture and the stream, would you not be so full of Her light as to be a beacon to all? Yet Brother Ernald stands a man a-quiver. Are you returning him to the priory's convent?'

'As we speak he travels to Saint Cuthbert's Isle in gladness. It is closed by the tides. It is the Saint's own House of work and prayer.' His gaze lifted. 'And of silence.'

There was a nod of approval. 'The demon's lair? I seek your advice on this. The fewer who know of it... Yet to do nothing...'

'The Cistercians—'

The Bishop of York groaned as if injured.

'Complainers, every one. You know as well as I they forever castigate we mere Benedictine brothers for not following our Saint's *true word*.

'I ask, did Saint Benedict have to keep the Scots from despoiling the King's lands? Did Saint Benedict have to keep such a town as York on the chosen path? Half the people speak more Norse than even English! Mark me, our Cistercians brothers desire to infiltrate our lands. *That* is their aim. They seek the ear of the King... whoever *that*, God willing, shall turn out to be.'

The Prince-Bishop lifted a calming hand.

'Our duty is not to the King, nor to the Empress or her son, but to Rome. And to ourselves. We are all disciples of the Blessed Saint Benedict. Our brothers seek the harsher lands, and it is agreed they are devout. Therefore, we should aid our Cistercian brothers, ensure they do build their Houses of learning and prayer – in a ring about the Devil's Pit so as to keep it from leaking into the land of mortal men. No one but you or I need to know the reason. Then you, Bishop, can minister to the souls of York while I marshal forces to keep the Scots from biting at the borders of the King's lands, and the Danes from harrying his shores. Might this be agreed between us?'

The spring sunshine felt warm on her bowed head, and she paused the video camera's recording to straighten the ache from her neck and comb fingers through her hair. She liked its shortened style, and its original mousey colour wasn't as mousey as she remembered, which was a bonus.

The Pool remained calm and glassy, the encircling trees creating the micro climate she was studying as part of her degree at Durham. Prompting Simon to video the margins had proved the most influential decision she'd ever made. Except it hadn't been her prompting, had it? Not truly hers.

A scuffing made her quarter-turn on feet that remained motionless, and the farmer emerged from the trees. On seeing her he stopped to raise his hand in a half-wave she remembered. He still wore the same floppy hat.

'Is it okay to walk across?'

She adjusted her stance to face him. 'Yes, I've covered that stretch. Just mind where you're putting your feet.' She laughed. 'It is your property, after all.'

'Aye, well, turned out a good job I decided to remove the signs.'

'Oh, I don't know. I reckon you'll be able to reinstate them once the extent of the flora growth is determined. The Park doesn't want to stop its custodians from earning a living.'

She could see him eyeing the North York Moors logo on her green fleece, trying to work out whether she was a Ranger.

'You're Philip, aren't you? I'm Aislin.' She offered her hand and they shook.

'Have we met afore?'

That was unexpected. She'd filled out over the months and with the new hair even Simon had passed her during a crowded evening in The Bishops' Mill. There again, he never truly looked at anyone.

'I don't think so,' she said, 'but you may have seen me here with others.'

'Aye, that'll be it. With this up for Special Scientific Interest status we've had a fair few bed an' breakfastin' over winter.' He looked around his feet. 'Anything out o'the norm?'

'You mean, apart from the ophrys?'

His grin made him look younger, certainly more relaxed than the last time she'd seen him.

'Flowers is more Rosemary's thing.'

'I must thank you for replacing the dead tree.'

He nodded. 'Vandals. We get 'em even here.'

'It was good of you. It was good of you for planting the circle in the first place.'

He began to shuffle his feet and then stopped himself. 'Aye, well, it were our Jason's doing mostly.'

'Very forward thinking. We'll have to talk about it sometime.'

'Mmm. You'll be able to talk to him soon enough if you're gonna be around. He's in Qatar at present but his contract's finishing.'

'I'd like to, thanks. Do mention me.'

He looked her up and down. 'You'd probably get on. Like minds, an' all that. Did, er... Did you ever meet Nick, Nicholas Blaketon?'

'I heard one of his talks; very inspirational.'

Phil sniffed. 'Seems he disappeared.'

'Oh, I'm sure he'll resurface.'

'Aye, he's got previous for that.' He chuckled. 'Maybe in another six years.'

She looked across the calm, glassy water.

Read it all. Including the bibliography.

Not six. Two and a half years by her reckoning. Three by three by three. And if he brought Alice with him...

'Well,' said Phil, 'best leave you to get on. What did you say your name was?'

Letting the camera dangle, she pulled free a pen.

'Aislin. I'll write my number on a card. You'll doubtless get a letter from the National Park confirming me as your liaison.' She handed it over and smiled as he read it.

'I'm your new Keeper of the Pool.'

Author's Note

This ends the final book in the *Torc of Moonlight* trilogy. However, a novel is rarely just a story opened, conveyed and closed. Each of the books in this trilogy explores a theme: in *Torc of Moonlight* it is obsession and denial; in *The Bull At The Gate*, it is perceptions of reality; in *Pilgrims Of The Pool*, crises of faith.

The idea for the trilogy came during a period of writing weekend walks for a Yorkshire newspaper. Boot-clad and Ordnance Survey map in hand, my husband and I would enjoy the countryside with me noting historical tidbits to share with readers. Often, surprisingly often, we came upon a natural spring or stone-clad well-head referred to on the map as *Lady Well*. These I took to be springs dedicated to Saint Mary, mother of Jesus. Research showed most to be named for a female deity far older than Christianity.

In Yorkshire there are more ancient springs referred to as *Lady Well* than anywhere else in England. Perhaps they've been lucky in not being subsumed into a later religious ethos, as were the springs beside which churches were built dedicated to All Saints and All Souls. Their feast days of 1st and 2nd November give us Halloween, the dates too neatly coinciding with the celebrations of the Celtic year-end, Samhain, and its accompanying water-based divination rites. And who believes in coincidence?

The Pool with its farm, and the water bottling plant, depicted in the novel, do not exist. Alas, the wind turbines mentioned and the area of the North York Moors National Park licensed to a hydraulic fracturing company do, as does just about everything else mentioned in the contemporary threads.

The historical content is as close to reality as fiction allows. Pilgrimages in the mediaeval period were a source of cleansing one's sins and increasing the revenues of religious houses. In modern parlance, protecting and promoting saints' relics, and curing springs, was a sure way to 'print money', most of which went towards the glorification of God in the building of huge and ornate churches. Of those no longer in everyday use, many remain visible in the British landscape as picturesque ruins, including the Cistercian houses of Byland, Rievaulx, and Rosedale amid the heather-clad landscape of the North York Moors.

Mediaeval Bishops often spent as much time empire-building as tending to the spiritual needs of their flocks. Those of Durham and York, both of whose diocese covered vast areas, maintained an uneasy alliance down the centuries. York was, and still is, an archbishopric, while Durham was the sole prince-bishopric in the country and charged with raising and leading an army against invaders, whoever they were. Although this was particularly important during the period conveyed in this novel, when supporters of the Empress Matilda and of King Stephen fought for the English crown, the military charge of the prince-bishop was not relinquished in name until 1836. His castle, standing opposite the church now a cathedral, is part of the campus of the University of Durham, which is apt when the modern houses of learning chosen for all three novels were the universities of Hull, York and Durham.

The city of Durham and the towns of Stokesley (Stocheslage), and Yarm (Yarum), are all worth visiting. The Cathedral Church of the Blessed Mary the Virgin and Saint Cuthbert the Bishop, now officially known as The Cathedral Church of Christ, Blessed Mary the Virgin and Saint Cuthbert of Durham, but referred to loosely by all as Durham Cathedral, was planned to rival, and be on the same scale, as Saint Peter's in Rome. Despite the ravages of the English Reformation, it retains the shrine and relics of Saint Cuthbert, as well as others. It is still possible to walk its cloister in the steps of the fictional Brother Ernald, and to process down Sadler Street to Market Place and visit Saint Nicholas' Church on the Wall.

History, in all its guises, is mere inches beneath our feet. Springs, many of which were ancient when straight Roman roads were angled to pass them, still filter mineral-rich waters with curative properties from deep within the earth. Not all were embraced by the Christian Church, or have been harnessed by modern bottling plants. Some take a bit of finding even with an Ordnance Survey map, but invariably these carry offerings tied in neighbouring shrubs, or lie bright with silver coins gifted direct to the water. Or its female deity.

After all, who has never dropped a coin into water for 'good luck'? Who are you expecting to grant your wish?

About The Author

Linda Acaster is an award-winning writer of novels and short fiction in a variety of genres, a wealth of magazine articles on writing fiction, and a writer's guide. She lives in northern England, a stone's throw from an ancient spring.

Titles Include:

Torc of Moonlight trilogy

Book 1: *Torc of Moonlight* – set in Hull: Celtic
Book 2: *The Bull At The Gate* – set in York: Roman
Book 3: *Pilgrims Of The Pool* – set in Durham: Mediaeval
How many believers does it take to resurrect a Celtic water goddess? Just one. You, throwing coins into a "wishing well".

Chillers

Contribution to Mankind and other stories of the Dark
Six stories of Dark Speculative fiction

Scent of the Böggel-Mann
Why is a trunk bought at an auction full of foreign bibles?

The Paintings
An art assessor needs more than warm clothing in an artist's derelict studio.

Historical Romances

Beneath The Shining Mountains
1830s Native American drama of horse raids and buffalo hunts

Hostage of the Heart
Mediaeval conflict on the English-Welsh borderlands in 1066

Writers' Resource

Reading A Writer's Mind: Exploring Short Fiction-First Thought to Finished Story
Ten short stories from idea to execution examining decisions taken along the way

Westerns
pseudonym - Tyler Brentmore

Dead Men's Fingers
A wagon train journey in the Classic style

Vigilante Man
Robbing a train becomes a race against a bullet

For information & links
or to sign up for a newsletter:

www.lindaacaster.com

Made in the USA
Columbia, SC
10 August 2017